One Way to Eldorado

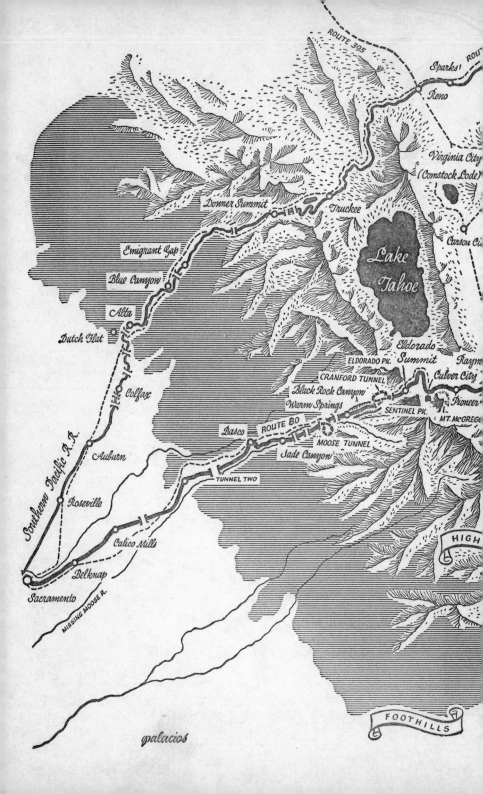

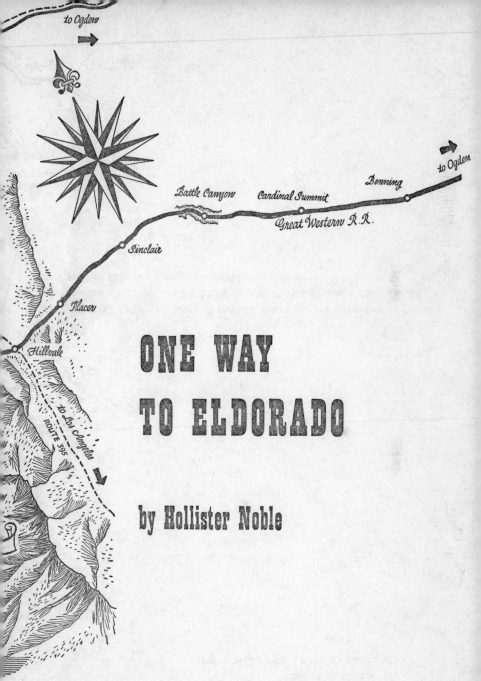

ONE WAY
TO ELDORADO

by Hollister Noble

DOUBLEDAY & COMPANY, INC., GARDEN CITY, NEW YORK

I wish to express my profound thanks to officials of several Western railroads who enabled me to observe winter operations on the "Hill," and to Mr. I. A. Weihe, Southern Pacific Road Foreman of Engines at Bakersfield, California, whose suggestions and reading of this story in manuscript form were immensely helpful.

H. N.

1

My wife and I were almost alone in the lounge car of the Sierra Limited. Two hours out of San Francisco, headed East, we were gliding through the yards of Belknap, an operating stop where the Great Western's heroic ascent of the Sierras begins. Belknap was our home—but for the first time in two years we weren't getting off. We were the proud sovereigns of Drawing Room E in a hermetically sealed stainless steel Pullman tube called the "Azure Palace," bound for a six-week odyssey to New York and Boston that had already created a minor crisis in our lives. As brake shoes bit into whirling wheels Betty rose to go forward to our room. She looked at me with humorous sympathy.

"Darling, why don't you get out and get a breath of air? You look like hell."

She was charitable. I knew what I looked like. A greenish-white bloodless insect of indefinite but repulsive structure sitting motionless under a damp dark board. Incredibly, I managed to talk.

"I'll do better than that. I'll ride the helper to Summit. Do you mind?"

Betty nodded encouragement. "I should have thought of that myself. When you're back, we'll talk."

Betty meant Betty would talk. I'd have to listen. I manufactured a wan smile as she laughed and swung confidently down the aisle, the sky-blue toque on her dark hair bobbing jauntily. The train ground to a stop. I reflected that Betty had her skirmish lines ready, her forces concentrated, the battle to be joined as soon as I'd replenished the oxygen in my sodden smoke-filled lungs by riding the helper to Eldorado Summit, seventy miles closer to New York.

A bit shakily I walked nine car lengths to the head of the train. Hedley, the yardmaster, and Connolly, our veteran white-thatched conductor, were chatting with a signal engineer and two of the train crew. Johnson and his fireman, a young Mexican, leaned from the cab of the big Mallet, grinning down at me. Twenty yards away one of the 3500 Mountain helpers was backing down on us, to help the Mallet boost nineteen Pullman and express cars over the mountains.

I got quite a reception. Hedley had a batch of San Francisco papers under his arm. He tried to hand them to me but I shook my head.

"I read 'em all, Frank. Snatched 'em wet and dripping from the presses this morning—with my tongue hanging out."

He looked at me critically and laughed. "Some night. How's it feel to be famous, Mr. Bierce?" He cocked his head. "Giving up railroading?"

"Not on your life," I snapped with hearty conviction. "I'm riding the helper to Summit right now. Who's on?"

"Billings and McCready."

Hedley glanced up at the Mallet cab.

"You passing up Johnson's drawing room for that boneshaker of Billings?"

The boneshaker, an efficient GS-T-3 Mountain-type engine twenty-five years old, with a conventional open cab and a bounce that reminded me of a Wyoming bronco, was gently coupling on to the Mallet. The latter's front-end cab was fully enclosed, big enough to house a poker party, which it never did, and rode with remarkable smoothness. I grinned at Hedley.

"I need a little shaking up and a hell of a lot of fresh air after that shindig last night." I glanced up at Johnson, smiling down at me from the Mallet's cab. "No hard feelings, Johnson? Next time."

Jennings, Belknap's day operator, strolled over and shook hands. Barton, the assistant trainmaster, a switchman, and the crew of a yard goat joined our group. It was quite a reception committee. Hedley pretended to appear puzzled and began to tease me.

"How come you're headed East on 20? I thought you and Mrs. Bierce would go out in style on the streamliner tonight?"

Hedley knew I was an unreconstructed member of the Ancient and Honorable Order of Old Fashioned Train Devotees and regarded streamliners with aesthetic and patronizing distaste. The Sierra Limited was six hours slower but in my opinion a lot more comfortable and congenial than our vaunted 502, "Spirit of the West," two million dollars' worth and 1,756 feet of sinuous steel tubing, known locally in yard lingo, possibly because of its high speed, as the Burp.

Unless you could afford a couple of adjoining rooms, it was my unshakable belief that riding a roomette or compartment to Chicago confined in a stainless steel, functionally designed, linoleum-lined, gadget-strewn hygienic cubicle, with your sole companion a science-fiction toilet disguised as a rudimentary garden seat, was about on a par with locking yourself up in the family bathroom for two days with a couple of old magazines. Give me the spacious and venerable mahogany-trimmed platform observation lounge cars of yesteryear, the sociable high-ceilinged Pullmans with warm décor and shaded lamps, whose riding comfort on heavy six-wheel trucks has never been surpassed.

So adamant was my position on this question that at a company party, just after I had joined the road, I backed a distinguished old gentleman into a corner and with alcoholic vision conjured up a modern mid-Victorian masterpiece—a high-ceilinged train with red plush drapes, overstuffed chairs, brocaded hassocks, oak-paneled dining cars, and luxurious rooms full of early Americana, a nostalgic train recalling the luxury and relaxation of a vanished past.

Then the old boy introduced himself. He was only George Esmond Fontaine, president of the pike that had just hired me. He eyed me sharply.

"You interest me, Mr. Bierce. Drop into my office at ten tomorrow."

I did so and we had a long talk about my dream train. Fontaine made many notes, but never hearing more of the matter, I judged it had been filed and forgotten.

Meanwhile, standing on the Belknap platform and headed East, I wisecracked to Hedley. Then Jennings asked:

"You got the medal with you, Mr. Bierce? We'd appreciate a look at it."

With no reluctance at all I pulled out the leather case and snapped open the cover. The medal was solid gold and plenty of it, a miniature plaque. It gleamed resplendently in the sunshine. I was damn proud of it. The boys turned it over reverently and passed it around. Hedley read the inscription aloud:

"To Howard Bierce, Road Foreman of Engines, Mountain Division, Great Western Railway, this Medal of Honor and Special Merit for his collection of sketches and paintings, 'High Iron in the Sierras.' 1953."

On the reverse side Hedley read: *"Commonwealth Club of California—Founded 1903,* with the Club's seal."

He handed me the medal and grinned. "I hear you put the Old Man and Reynolds to bed last night. Congratulations."

The Old Man was John Ramsay MacIntosh, our formidable Division Superintendent known as the Brass Collar. Reynolds was his fast-talking young assistant. My wife had informed me that morning, with unaccustomed awe and respect, that I had outtalked MacIntosh, outdrunk Reynolds, and escorted them both to divans in the private lounge of the Commonwealth Club, returning to stand four more rounds of first-rate firewater before she had whisked me off to bed. This double achievement, observed by a considerable portion of the Great Western's personnel, as guests of the Club, had impressed them, I gathered, considerably more than the medal now back in my pocket.

There was a whoosh of released air from the reservoir under the Mallet's tender. Connolly walked back along the platform looking at his watch and caught the brakeman's highball from the rear end. The air whistle in the cab above me gave a measured *beep-beep*. It was time to go. I walked forward, reached for a grab iron, and swung myself up into 3512's cab, leaning out the gangway as we shoved off. The boys waved and shouted good-bys and wisecracks, most of them lost in the first crashing exhausts of the straining engines. I yelled down to Hedley:

"Say good-by to Reynolds for me."

Hedley walked fast close to the trailer truck.

"He's ahead of you. Rode Second 48 to Pioneer Gap this morning."

Nine hours ago I'd left Reynolds dead to the world at the St. Francis. How he'd caught a mail train that early was beyond me.

Hedley was dropping behind me as we gathered speed. He looked up at me, a glint in his eye, and shouted:

"You're sure coming back, Mr. Bierce?"

The intimation of doubt in his voice mildly irritated me.

"You're damn right I'm coming back. By the first of the year. And tell Wharton to keep my shoes polished."

That was a crack. Wharton wanted my job and had jumped at the chance to fill in for me while I was East. I crossed the cab, pulled down the jump seat behind Billings, the engineer, hopped into it, and leaned out the cab window pulling all the fresh air I could into my tired lungs. We were just passing the Yard Limit board and pounding up the first easy grade to Calico Mills, where the Big Hill really began. Behind us the Mallet's double exhaust resolved into a steady roar. We were beginning to roll as Billings opened the throttle another notch and yelled over his shoulder:

"How you going to handle two careers now, Mr. Bierce?"

"It's a cinch, Billings," I retorted cockily. "I'm going to put an easel in every cab and do my painting on company time."

Billings looked speculatively around his cab.

"Might brighten things up at that," he shouted over his shoulder, as if I'd made the most sensible suggestion in the world.

But I was silent. I'd been asking myself the same question for some time now. Hedley sensed my conflict. So did Billings. Maybe most of the boys did. For a road official to gain recognition as an artist was a new and puzzling phenomenon on the Great Western,

10

as it might be on any pike. In my early railroading days in the Southwest, exiled in isolated desert towns with time on my hands, I'd amused myself by turning out simple pencil sketches of scenes and people that struck my fancy—a dilapidated water tank at a desert summit near Kingman, a Mexican gandy-dancer pounding spikes under a brutal sun at El Centro, a poker game in a caboose on a siding at Yuma, waiting for some varnish to streak by—in short, bits of railroad life around me that were as familiar as the furniture in my living room.

But in all honesty I didn't know where I was going until I found myself in a new dinner coat trying to talk to fifteen hundred guests in the St. Francis banquet room. I had spoken briefly, almost facetiously, explaining my modest collection of canvases as the outgrowth of a casual hobby.

But I was lying, and most of all to myself. Whatever random impulse first led me to indulge this seductive hobby of mine had now developed into a major drive that made imperative some decision as to the future of the Bierce ménage. The hobby threatened to become a career, and the career a hobby. Betty knew it and was badly worried.

My brain began to clear. The fresh air, the roar and racket of the engines, stimulated my thinking. The Central Valley behind us glowed in the golden light of an Indian summer day. It was early in December. We were rolling at over fifty, the two engines roaring with thrust and power. McCready whistled for the crossing at Calico Mills. We crashed through Petticoat Cut, a deep gash dug eighty years ago by women and children from the mills, aiding Chinese track crews, in a feverish race to get the Great Western's rails to Basco before the snow fell.

A crossing bell flashed by, its tones descending in a cascade of diminishing sound, like a series of Oriental bells struck lightly. Yellow station, white mill, lumberyard, the blur of two boxcars on a passing track—*whoop-whoop*—and we plunged into another cut, then raced by Armstrong's farm. Low rolling hills, dust-brown, sun-baked, flecked here and there with hardy green trees, rose before us like gentle ground swells. In the distance shimmered a higher darker bank of ragged fir-covered foothills. Far beyond them, like occasional wisps of cotton poking up on the horizon, were glimpses of snow-covered Sierra peaks, sixty miles away.

We swung around our first curve and headed into a two per cent grade. Old 3512 began to rock and pound. The roar of the laboring exhausts of Mallet and helper became deep-throated, urgent. We were heading up the Big Hill. I glanced back at the long line of swaying orange cars. Eight cars behind the Mallet was the Azure Palace, and I pictured Betty sitting there, thinking, and gazing out at

Armstrong's farm, where we often visited. As soon as I went back to her I was in for it. For Betty had taken her last-ditch stand against an art career proposed by my friends. Restless, I got off the jump seat, sanded the flues, and then stood in the gangway between engine and tender looking back at the golden hazy Central Valley as we began the steep sixty-five-mile rise to the backbone of the Sierras. Like most domestic storms the crisis confronting the Bierce ménage was upon us without warning. Or so I thought. Now endowed by the usual hindsight created by pressure I noted a number of warning signs, completely ignored, that had flashed by me in the past.

What the hell was I going to do—stick to railroading or leap from a secure and fascinating job into that whirlpool of intangibles, that misty limitless world of uncertainties called Art? I didn't know. I went back to the jump seat, decided to enjoy the ride and make my decision when I went back to Betty at Eldorado Summit.

My first encounter with the Great Western's Mountain Division two years ago had been a jaunt identical with this one. I never forgot it. I've racked up a great deal of mileage on rails all over the country, but for magnificence of vista and changing scene, for a visible symbol of man's mastery and triumph over nature, for sheer daring of engineering technic in conquering the highest railroad pass in the Sierras, the Great Western's stretch of high iron over Eldorado Pass remains to me without a peer.

There are other great stretches of conquering rail, notably the incredible Colorado passes, standard and narrow-gauge. Loftiest of all, though abandoned in World War II, was the Rio Grande's staggering standard-gauge climb to Ibex, at 11,522 feet. As to gradients, curiously enough the steepest stretches of rail in the nation are both far east of the Mississippi—Saluda Hill with a 4.7 per cent grade on the Southern Railway near Blue Ridge, North Carolina, and a Pennsy branch-line hill at Madison, Indiana, near the Ohio River, with an eye opener of 5.89 per cent. But it wasn't the grades, it was the high places in the West and how to get over them that intrigued me. That Colorado railroad genius, David H. Moffat, had an eye for the sky. Many times, as a youngster, I'd ridden Moffat's Denver and Salt Lake's impractical but spectacular route over Corona Pass, above ten thousand feet, before the Moffat Tunnel was born.

There were also South Pass, Marshall Pass, Tennessee Pass, all triumphs of Colorado rails. And the Canadian Pacific's circular tunnels and Big Hill around Glacier and Field, the Southern Pacific from Roseville to Truckee, the Great Northern's Cascade Tunnel, all exponents of mountain drama and engineering triumph. But the Great Western's final approach to Eldorado Summit, in terms of scenic grandeur concentrated in a last dozen miles, surpassed them all.

A thirty-mile stretch between Jade Canyon and Warm Springs resembled a motion picture montage in its climactic changes, punctuated by eleven tunnels. One left palm trees, orchards, green pastures, and grazing cattle in the Central Valley, battled up ragged fir-clad hills, encountered first snow, and rounded Cape Fear affording a marvelous panorama of the valley, spread like some vast Constable landscape far below and swathed in hazy gold.

Viewed from the head end or the cab of the helper, where I was now, the effect was superb. Before me, like a tortured steel serpent, the shining rails writhed and twisted up Missing Moose River, assailing the flanks of an increasingly steep and narrowing canyon. The nine thousand horses of Mallet and helper were roaring with heavy explosive exhausts as the straining engines worked all the way to the "company corner" of the quadrants, giving valves full travel and admitting all the superheated steam the hungry cylinders could take.

Above me rose pillars of steam and smoke piling high in the sky, splitting into magnificent plumes shot through with sunlight and all the colors of the spectrum.

Even our fleet streamliners crawled up this tortuous climb, the grade varying between 2.2 and 3 per cent just above Warm Springs. Day and night the echoing cliffs of Jade Canyon thundered to the battle of heavy drags pushing up, up, up, through the picturesque remnants of pioneer settlements that had left their colorful names to the railroad from the days of stagecoach, gold rush, and wagon train—Chinese Flat, Tunnel 2, Basco, Jade Canyon, Warm Springs, Sentinel Peak, and at last Eldorado Summit, 8,700 feet above sea level in a Wagnerian world of storm clouds, jagged peaks, and deep snow eight months of the year.

No matter how many years of service he has rolled behind him, every veteran on the Hill experiences time and again the triumph of that ascent. The Hill was the Great Western's lodestone of loyalty that drew and held in fanatical faith the ablest body of operating personnel the road could muster from the rosters of half a dozen first-class systems.

In view of certain onrushing and fantastic events that threw no shadows before them, perhaps a bit of my personal background and some items concerning the Great Western are in order. In an ironic manner I was about to play an unconscious role as a participant in certain extraordinary happenings whose outward aspects the general public well remembers. As to the more obscure elements in the bizarre drama I encountered so unexpectedly, I am certainly recording them for the first time and as accurately and honestly as I can.

I had been Road Foreman of Engines on the Mountain Division for two years. It was an exacting job. The Division extended 158 miles from Belknap, 107 miles east of Oakland, to Placer, Nevada, a Division point on a desolate stretch of salt desert.

I was young for my job, an almost juvenile forty. I was tall, lean, redheaded, blue-eyed, and contrary to redheaded stereotypes, I had an even disposition and a marked ability to get along with people. I suspect this latter attribute really landed me my job with the Great Western. The road had encountered an unexpected problem in personnel relations on the Mountain Division. I'd never been near the Sierras or the G.W. when I got the call. I was a graduate of M.I.T. and had spent a year as an engineer with the B. and B. boys (Building and Bridges) on the Rio Grande. On a sudden impulse I chucked the job and started firing out of Colorado Springs. My engineering friends thought I was crazy. But I climbed the Rio Grande's ladder quite rapidly. Four years of firing, five at the throttle, and five more specializing in Diesels under Oscar Brand, General Motors' great expert who knew more about Diesels than any man decently should.

As a roving technician for GM's Electro-Motive Division at La Grange, Illinois, I racked up a lot of experience delivering Diesels to midwestern roads, and later to the Santa Fe at San Bernardino and the S.P.'s Taylor Roundhouse in L.A. The U.P. and the Santa Fe were the first big western roads to join the landslide to Diesels which began in the mid-thirties. The S.P. soon followed, and the S.P. was the Great Western's big rival. When the Great Western woke up and got a look at the S.P.'s cost sheets—the G.W. was still ordering some of the most powerful Mallets ever built as late as 1946—the road rushed a purchase of ten used Diesels from a shaky mid-western pike at a suspiciously low price, in my opinion, and placed them on its Mountain Division, a mistake from every point of view.

The Great Western's attitude toward the Mountain Division ranged from fanatical pride to savage despair. Operation costs on the Hill exceeded those of any other two divisions between Belknap and Chicago. The herculean daily task of boosting heavy freight and streamlined limiteds 8,700 feet over the Sierras in a seventy-mile stretch east of Belknap was both obvious and audible to the most disinterested traveler. The Southern Pacific had long ago pre-empted one of two low passes through the Sierras, the famous route over Donner Pass at 7,100 feet altitude. The other pass, farther north, at a modest five-thousand-foot elevation between Portola and Chilcoot, and westward down the Feather River Canyon, though discovered in the sixties by Arthur Keddie, a pioneer surveyor, remained unused until early in the present century when the last transcontinental, the Western Pacific, pushed through to Oakland.

So the Great Western, foolishly ignoring the Feather River route back in '71, accepted the last crumb then available from the Sierras' sparse table of practicable mountain passes. It had hurriedly flung its steel over Eldorado Summit, known in the old days as Redbox Pass. And 8,700 feet was plenty of altitude in any railroader's language. For the next twenty years the G.W. tried to unwind the worst portions of this railroad pretzel, modifying impossible kinks, straightening corkscrew curves, and blasting away crumbling cliffs, capes, and promontories high above Missing Moose River, key to the G.W.'s final leap over the Sierras.

All in all, the Division remained a hair-raising stretch of high iron thrust through some of the most difficult and magnificent country in the West. Everyone, from section hands to dispatchers and top brass, felt the challenge of that Division. The challenge never let up and it had broken many men.

The Great Western controlled with fairly efficient ease the rest of its 11,500 miles of rail. But there were times when the Mountain Division not only controlled the G.W. but left it gasping for breath. Twenty or twenty-two feet of snow covered the snowsheds at Eldorado Summit for weeks at a time during the dreaded winter months.

I first saw Eldorado Summit after a heavy fall of spring snow. I wondered at once why any intrepid idiot of the seventies had had the audacity to push rails over that forbidding pass. Heading up the Sierra slope from the west, the road's final ascent of Missing Moose Canyon came to a towering wall of rock at the end of a gloomy narrow gorge far below the pass.

The rails pierced this great wall in a daring circular tunnel on a stiff grade that emerged on a narrow shelf of rock hanging two thousand feet over another gorge called Black Rock Canyon. Climbing dizzily through another semi-circular bore, Cranford Tunnel, the rails then doubled Cape Fear in a hair-raising loop that crept up the last mile of three per cent grade on a ledge blasted out of sheer cliff. And at last the rails pushed across Eldorado Summit in a broad shallow cut covered with snowsheds under which, in eternal dusk, dwelt an entire community. More of Eldorado Summit later. High above this snowshed village rose Sentinel Peak, a 12,600 foot mass of jagged, wicked rock with a great gash down its eastern slope that provided a perfect funnel for periodic avalanches.

When the G.W.'s ten secondhand Diesels rolled onto this demanding Division of high iron, all hell broke loose. They arrived in November, like tired streetwalkers covered with fresh paint. Their performance, with ten feet of snow at Eldorado Summit, fulfilled the most savage predictions of their bloodthirsty critics. The ground relays were faulty. Their lube systems would have disgraced a Model T Ford. And their cylinder castings, an early experimental type, cracked repeatedly in the bitter cold and plunging temperatures.

These first Diesels stalled in the most horrible places—in the center of Cranford Tunnel on a three per cent grade, on the edge of Black Rock Canyon—and one of them right out of our Belknap shops after Class 3 repairs, a general overhaul, capsized on a crossover and ripped up a hundred feet of both east- and westbound rail near Basco. But Fontaine, the G.W.'s stubborn president, stood his ground, pulled all of the pressure he commanded, which was plenty, and got fifteen brand-new Diesels delivered the following year.

With these great power units the G.W. began to lick its operation problems on the Hill—but not the men of granite who had fallen in love with Henry Hartmann's huge Mallets, designed and built in the G.W.'s own shops, and probably the last and greatest exponents of steam power in the country. These Hartmann fanatics were wedded to steam. They were picked veterans hard to replace. But they had failed to face an historic fact. Railroaders and most laymen now know that every panting locomotive in the land was fatally stabbed through the steamchest on the day the first practical Diesel rolled out of the shops. The Iron Horse has been brutally murdered, and there are many mourners. But the boys on the G.W.'s Big Hill had never faced this. To a man they regarded themselves as sacred custodians of the old days and they began to refuse service on Diesels.

Confronted with this problem in human relations, old Fontaine is reported to have roared, "To hell with the technicians and brass. Get me a redheaded diplomat who can handle these bastards."

Redheaded diplomat. Somebody thought of me. Forty-eight hours later I was on the job. Fontaine had calmed down. He was an able man with a sense of humor who had known all his "bastards" for years by their first names. And the Mountain Division was his child, a precious and exasperating one. I clinched my position on the Division by riding steam exclusively for six weeks, openly sympathizing with the veterans, and agreeing with one and all that Diesels were the final curse of an ungodly generation of castrated railroaders.

Then I showed the boys our cost sheets—and asked them what they'd do if they were running a railroad. They read the epitaph of steam and mourned. But they began to train for Diesels without another whimper.

It's characteristic of me that I discuss the railroad before getting around to Betty. While Betty's my wife, the railroad has always been my mistress. Betty didn't mind this at all. What really frightened her, to my surprise, was the possibility that I might ditch this mistress and consort with another—Art with a capital A.

I'd met Betty eight years ago. She was night telegraph operator at Mesquite, a godforsaken siding just east of Raton Pass tunnel on the Santa Fe. Right there we pulled a drawbar one night on a long drag including four Diesel units destined for San Bernardino. While the train crew sweated and cursed—I was merely nursemaid to the idle Diesels—I wandered into the renovated truckless boxcar that served as a tiny flag stop. There was Betty pounding out our predicament in fast Morse that would have pleased old Samuel F. B. himself. Betty was Irish, dark-haired and blue-eyed, pert and pretty, with a sense of humor. And she had a Silex full of hot coffee on an electric grill. I drank coffee and looked her over. What was a girl of her caliber doing out on the New Mexico-Colorado line near Raton Pass pounding out Morse to La Junta on a minor breakdown?

I talked to her and found out. Betty simply came of a long line of railroaders, Southern Pacific and Santa Fe. Her old man had been injured, pensioned, and retired. She and her family were putting a kid brother through Cornell. They lived on a nearby ranch. That's all there was to it. Or so I thought. I at once discovered Betty was coolly indifferent to all men, meaning me. This irritated the hell out of my ego for at the time I considered myself quite a lady killer, having just completed the difficult conquest of a pert blonde whose uncle ran a most convenient motel on the outskirts of Omaha.

In vain I exuded charm and trotted out all my time-tested tricks. The head shack came in and announced we were ready to shove off. Utterly routed, I headed for the door. Betty looked up and grinned.

"Good-by, mister. You're a nice boy, but you're wasting your time."

That did it. I ran through Mesquite many times during the next year and made a point of tossing off bundles of new magazines and thrillers addressed to Betty. Sometimes we stopped at Mesquite and I had a chance to talk to her.

On a certain brisk October day, after more than a year of this uncertain courtship, I pulled a stunt for which I hope the Santa Fe will now forgive me. I was headed West, nursing the Diesels on "El Capitan," the Santa Fe's coach streamliner, and keeping an eye out for Mesquite. Those were the days when every Santa Fe Diesel was padded with a traveling nurse. We were running uphill but going fairly fast. It was a little after ten in the morning. Betty had been night op and was probably home on the ranch and fast asleep.

Just the same, I was still faithful. I pushed back into the mail car with a bundle of new magazines, shoved open the door, and caught a glimpse of Betty's boxcar and a section shanty rushing towards us half a mile away. That was Mesquite. As I tossed my bundle to the short gravel platform Betty ran out of the tiny station and not ten feet away looked up at me. She waved but she wasn't smiling. Her violet eyes were wide and questioning. Then she was gone.

Like a man in a dream I hurried forward, picked my way through

17

the four Diesel units, climbed into the cab, took a deep breath, and placed my hand on the shoulder of our engineer, Billy Bascomb.

"Mr. Bascomb," I said gravely, right in his left ear, "the emergency fuel trips on units 2 and 3 are shot and we'll burn something up in five minutes if we don't stop at once. We're going pretty fast."

We certainly were, even up that grade. But Billy just looked up and nodded.

"Okay, son."

He began his air reductions at once and El Capitan ground to a stop a mile past Mesquite, slowly backed up to Betty's station, and put out a flag.

I ran into the station. Betty was alone.

"Listen, Betty," I said, as profoundly serious as I'd ever been, "I just stopped El Capitan because I had to. There's not a damn thing the matter with that train. But I've got to know something right away. I want you to come to Los Angeles and marry me. Will you?"

Betty had her finger on the key. She didn't change expression but she took a deep breath and I saw the key tremble a little. She looked up at me and said quietly, "Good Lord, it took you a long time. I'll be there on the tenth."

The whole train crew now pounded into the station in various stages of outraged astonishment. The conductor practically accused me of stealing his train. Albuquerque came on the wire and I continued talking briskly to Betty:

". . . lube systems on units 2 and 3 not functioning. Believe oil boosters need packing. Estimate delay at twenty minutes." I looked up at The Brains, our usually affable conductor named Slocomb. "Will arrive on time," I added confidently, knowing Billy Bascomb. The head shack looked relieved and Slocomb nodded.

I went to the door and turned. "That shipment will arrive on the tenth?" I asked Betty.

"Without fail," she replied gravely.

I floated through the air, floated into Unit 2, made a hell of a racket pounding some pipes for five minutes, and then floated out again, informing The Brains and Billy Bascomb that El Capitan could roll again without peril. We glided off, the Diesels roaring. Betty didn't even make a final appearance. We were twenty minutes late into Raton, but later Billy hit it up and got to Albuquerque fifteen seconds ahead of schedule. I wondered what the Brass would say when they saw our speed-recording tape. But I didn't really care.

Betty and I were married and spent a five-day honeymoon at Laguna, getting tight at Victor Hugo's and heavily tanned on the beaches. Then I headed back to La Grange for another round trip and Betty went househunting in Los Angeles, finding a small modern home convenient to the S.P.'s Taylor Roundhouse but on a hill in the Silver Lake area with a fine view.

The success of my marriage rather amazed me. After all, I'd been a roving railbird for a long time and had undoubtedly become a bit brassy and callous in my take-it-or-leave-it attitude towards women I encountered in my transient cross-country marathons. I had certainly developed a number of tenacious and selfish habits. And I also wondered how Betty would flourish under my uncertain schedules, which resembled those of a harried country doctor confronted by a perpetual epidemic, in this case a virulently contagious fever for Diesels that was nationwide.

But I needn't have worried. Betty was marvelous. She took everything in stride, for railroading was a part of her, in her blood, and how thoroughly and deeply I wasn't to discover till later.

It was the development of what I often called my Horrible Hobby, my increasing interest in painting, that brought out contradictions in Betty I'd never suspected and revealed a simple fact about her outlook that at first astonished me as much as it would have many of her friends. Betty was broad in her sympathies, narrow in her interests. We had a lot of friends, most of them railroad people. We went to ball games, company picnics, golfed a little, took in fights, movies, and the theater. Betty enjoyed them all. But in general, aesthetic interests were completely outside her comprehension. I just never realized it.

I learned quite late that Betty was one of the most literal-minded women I had ever met. What she saw existed. What she didn't see she doubted. This must have accounted for her keen interest in my technical work. She understood a good deal about machines. Everything in our world was of a solid concrete nature, from the rock ballasted roadbed of the Great Western to its signals, hurtling trains, humming offices, and, of course, our comfortable pay checks, which ran around seven hundred and fifty dollars each month.

To Betty, in the beginning, my hobby of sketching and painting was "nice" or "fun," even when I was able to study at odd times with Hans Haffer and Leland Gordon. But when the Commonwealth Club affair burst upon us, when Haffer and Gordon begged me to devote myself to painting, when the Grand Central Galleries summoned me East for a big showing during the Christmas holidays, when the Copley Galleries in Boston asked for a subsequent exhibit, and Fontaine gave me six weeks off with his blessing, poor Betty's roof fell in. I found to my dismay that Betty was all woman, a most attractive one in her own milieu, but a lost child outside it. The mere suggestion that we might embark upon a chartless sea of painting, with a livelihood dependent upon selling my work, simply appalled her.

My musings were suddenly ended as we rolled through the dank dusky snowsheds at Eldorado Summit, pierced with the colorful jewels of red, green, and yellow signal lights and the dim blue gleams from dwarf switches at crossovers. The "underground garden," the "roof garden," the "strawberry patch," with its serried rows of red lights, the boys called it. We stopped. I hopped to the ground, shouted good-by to Billings, and headed back along the train. Abruptly, in that clear bracing air, I made my decision. The male animal, after sniffing the wind and baying the moon, had subsided. I was staying with the railroad. I was going to tell Betty the good news at once.

But as I walked rapidly along that standing train some mischievous gremlin I had overlooked must have taken command of what seemed to me a simple situation already resolved by my noble purpose of self-sacrifice.

I climbed into the Azure Palace, opened the neat tan door labeled E, and went in smiling, as the train glided off for Pioneer Gap twenty minutes away.

I was looking at a picture I'd like to paint. I had braced myself for a determined opponent and found myself confronting a charming, bright-eyed, affectionate woman who was my wife. Betty had two tall drinks ready on a small table. She leaned comfortably cattycorner in her seat, smiling slightly, and looking up at me with those wide deep violet eyes of candor and pleading that I knew so well.

It was dusk and the lights were on, the room's glowing comfort intensified by the vista of towering peaks gliding by in sunset cloaks of purples and blues. It was snowing lightly. Big soft flakes floated past the train, against a deep blue background, like wisps of cotton tossed at random by some child.

The Mallet's rich mournful whistle echoed down the canyon. Betty smiled broadly, patted the seat beside her, then looked a bit saucily at me and laughed.

"Hi. You look wonderful, though a bit chilly." She indicated a glass. "It's waiting for you."

I thought she stiffened a little as if she sensed some new decision in my bearing. She drew a quick breath as I sat down beside her and then she placed a hand on my arm.

"Howie, honey, I've thought and thought. I had a lovely speech all ready and I've thrown it away. I've just one question to ask. It means so much to both of us. I——"

I interrupted her. "Let me say it . . ." I picked up my glass, raised it in the mocking gesture of a toast. The words were all nicely selected and neatly arranged. I was going to add, "Here's to Howard and Betty Bierce, and to the Great Western, now and forever, amen."

I never said them. Betty beat me to it. She said, "Please, let me finish. When this wonderful trip is over, Howie, will you make me happy and give up this nonsensical hobby and stick with your job?"

Then and there I blew up. Perhaps it was Betty's unfortunate choice of words, or the single term "nonsensical" that bit deep, or a too bright glint in her eyes, which at the same time were full of all the tenderness and feeling she could muster. I only know that all at once I was caught in a cold fury, in the bursting within me of some reservoir of hatred and rebellion I didn't know existed, and that in an instant tore all my wise and cautious resolutions to shreds.

At that moment I must have been a consummate actor. I remember downing half my drink and staring composedly out the window. The first lights of Pioneer Gap flashed by. It was snowing harder. The grind of brake shoes heavily applied vibrated through the room. I even glanced casually at my watch. It was exactly five-twelve. I touched Betty's arm, got up, and managed to smile down at her.

"I just forgot something. I've got a message for Reynolds. I'll be right back."

Betty looked surprised but lost none of her assurance.

"You'll give me the right answer?"

Again I was able to smile.

"The right one," I replied. "In two minutes."

I managed to get into the corridor and close the door. I leaned against it, shaking. I recall walking the length of the car to the forward vestibule. On the off side of the train, opposite the station, I swung back the upper half of the door, unlatched the lower half, and pulled it up. The automatic step slid out below like some magic gleaming tongue. As the train stopped I jumped to the ground, landed in a foot of slush, and remained there.

The Sierra Limited paused very briefly at the Gap, which was simply a flagstop for passengers destined for Chicago or beyond. In a few moments the train moved, glided by me, rapidly picking up speed. It was now quite dark and snowing fitfully. Glowing yellow windows raced past. The observation car was a cascade of light, flashing briefly. Two red taillights glowed steadily for a moment, then vanished in darkness. Only the Limited's Mars light, a great crimson Cyclopean eye peering back at me from the rear end swung rhythmically and mockingly from side to side, up and down, slashing high and waving ribbons of saffron light against a black snow-laden sky long after the train had disappeared.

The diminishing click and song of the rails sounded a chant—you damn fool—you damn fool. . . .

I hadn't even bothered to take my coat with me. I stumbled across slippery rails and made for a low squat familiar structure dripping with melting snow. Over a small doorway flashed a modest neon sign: G.W. HOTEL.

I went inside.

21

2

Natives of small towns who recall the appearance of any First Methodist church the morning after a disappointing rummage sale may conjure up a reasonably accurate picture of the G.W. Hotel lobby. It was simply stuffed with junk.

The hotel had been formed from an ancient and overly ambitious two-story station erected in 1887 for a traffic and mining boom that never materialized. A flowery handbill published by the Great Western on Pioneer Day, 1893, stated that the original structure had "been redesigned at great expense solely for the comfort and convenience of its faithful employees." Uh-huh.

At that it wasn't bad. I often thought of the G.W. Hotel as a mass of cunningly wrought steam pipes enclosing grateful railroad guests seeking shelter from below-zero operations on the Hill. The lobby, dark, warm, and disorderly, was commonly regarded as an enlarged entryway for the upstairs cubicles. Officially the lobby, about twelve by twelve, contained a stove, an old print of the Donner Party languishing in massive snowdrifts, three battered antique Morris chairs, a small counter, and Dan Shields, our local historian and amateur camera enthusiast, a benign, scholarly old boy, completely bald, and a permanent fixture who moved about in slow motion as mine host and clerk. Dan ruled with impassive and impartial mien in a tiny space behind the counter and directly under the key and letter compartments gathered in a fly-specked frame that hung on the wall at a rakish angle. The angle was due to Dan's two Siamese cats, who perched on top of this flimsy structure regarding all incoming and departing guests from their lofty eyrie with somnolent and impressive disdain. Off to the right there had once been a moldy dining room, long since abandoned.

Both lobby and deserted dining room were piled high with what appeared to be the miscellaneous contents of some bombed-out warehouse. For years, the hotel, as railroad property under Dan's eagle eye, had been regarded as a singularly safe depository for all kinds of personal belongings. Townspeople, transients, and commercial travelers, overcome by the desolate prospects of another day at the Gap, developed a general custom of placing their personal belongings in Dan's care, informing him they would "be right back," while they fled for solace to Snyder's Bar, the Busy Bee coffee counter, or Al Crowley's bowling alley.

Alas, many never returned at all. Through the years Dan acquired a tremendous stack of cardboard suitcases tied with string, paper bundles and bags, petrified sandwiches, snowshoes, boxes, raincoats, rubbers, shovels, umbrellas, lunch cans, bird cages, hats, shirts, dogs, and cats. This tidal wave of miscellaneous property flowed from the lobby into the dining room, to be blocked at last by the bulkhead of the far wall. Dan always found stranded pets a home and once a year held an impromptu auction for unclaimed articles, which netted him a tidy sum. But an immense amount of junk remained.

When I entered the hotel Dan was in an almost horizontal position on two chairs behind the counter. He was reading under a green-shaded lamp. His head rose just above the counter level, like a great glowing ostrich egg in a circle of mellow light. On the counter was a crudely lettered cardboard sign, obviously designed by Shields to avoid unnecessary conversation. It contained one word that stopped all debate. "Full," it said.

Old Dan barely glanced at me. "Hi, Mr. Bierce."

One of his cats rose above him, with obvious and immense effort, arched its back, and subsided with a yawn. I moved closer to a tall impressive nickel-topped stove, vintage of 1886, and long since converted to oil.

I was still dazed over my impulsive act. "Who got the last coop?" I asked accusingly.

"Mr. Reynolds." Dan went on reading. He wasn't being rude. He was an old friend of mine. Dan simply didn't care to talk unless there was something to talk about. I decided there was. Still shaken by my tantrum I realized one thing—I was in a bad spot. Betty was hurtling East across the Nevada desert, probably picturing me stopping to talk shop with someone in the lounge car, but beginning to wonder. When she woke up to the fact that I was no longer on that train—brother!

I decided I'd better talk to Reynolds. He was as cold as ice, but in my opinion very smart. I was up in some eerie unreal stratosphere and I had to come down without a crash. I felt Reynolds could ease my descent.

"What room's he in?"

23

"Eleven."

Dan's voice was mildly reproachful. I should have known. Whenever Reynolds visited the Gap, he had a permanent tag on 11, a large corner room with two windows that looked out on the yards and roundhouse. I stumbled up the dark narrow stairs, the G.W. obviously believing all its railroad guests carried lanterns. I knocked on the door of No. 11 and realized I hadn't the slightest idea of what I was going to say to Reynolds.

"Come in."

I did so. Reynolds had both windows open, though it was eighteen above outside. He sat close to one of them and in his shirt sleeves, making meticulous entries in one of several little black notebooks, which were encyclopedic in their detailed observations of road conditions on the Division. An array of steam pipes that resembled the Belknap yards boiled, hissed, banged, and talked back to one another. The power plant must have feared an eight-day blizzard.

Reynolds violated every traditional concept of the conventional railroad official. He was trim, young, and quite handsome, with sharp blue eyes the color of glacier ice, finely chiseled features, a manner of quiet gallantry, and his hair was curly, cut close, and very brown. When he first reported for work he drove up to the Division offices at Sacramento in a rakish blue Jaguar. Where he acquired it on a railroad salary we never knew.

To this day MacIntosh, the Division superintendent, has never recovered from the shock. But after hazing Reynolds for a month he discovered he had a young genius working for him. And Reynolds made a couple of concessions, giving up his Jaguar for a Buick and toning down his sartorial effects. MacIntosh poured it on for another six months, then gave him his permanent appointment as assistant superintendent at thirty-nine of one of the most difficult railroad divisions in the world.

At first I wondered about Reynolds. Later I got used to him, admired his ability, and in an impersonal way I liked him. But he was a self-contained, often silent man, living alone in a small modern house near the Belknap Golf Club, where he played once a week. He had a few close friends but I never saw him in the company of women. It often seemed to me Reynolds was a man cased in armor, a man with a fierce inner drive, a relentless and to me tyrannical element of his being that seldom allowed him to relax. I think he puzzled MacIntosh, who told me once he was convinced he had seen Reynolds somewhere, sometime, a long time ago.

As I entered Reynolds' room he got up and said gravely:

"Hello, Bierce. Lord, what you did to me last night."

Then he stared. His voice rose a little, unusual for him.

"What in hell are you doing here? Where's Betty?" He studied me for a moment. "Didn't you have a room East on 20?"

I sat down rather abruptly.

"I did have. Betty's still got it. I just took a powder, Jim, and jumped off 20."

He looked at me again and then, in the only demonstrative gesture I ever saw him employ, he placed a hand for just a fraction of a second on my shoulder.

"I'm sorry to hear that." He turned to his suitcase. "You want to talk about it?"

He flipped open the case, pulled out an unopened pint of my favorite brand of bourbon, and tossed it to me. "Take a couple of slugs. And try to relax."

I obeyed orders. The explosive effect of the bourbon told me I was still under great tension. Reynolds had never seen me like this. He stared at me gravely.

"Come on, Howie. Open up. You can't go around with the lid on like that."

All at once the lid came off. I talked in a torrent of words I've never equaled, before or since. I carried on a terrific debate—between Bierce the tough railroader, Bierce the struggling young artist, Bierce the martyred man, Bierce the magnificent husband, and Bierce the snarling male animal trapped in a tree. The biggest and noisiest debate I'd held inside myself for years. When it was all over Reynolds poured himself a drink, something unusual for him as he was technically on duty. He was usually a fanatic on Rule G. (Rule G prohibits drinking liquor on duty.) Then he smiled his rare and brittle little smile, nothing but a pleasant muscular spasm which momentarily altered the grave attentive mask he always wore.

"Man, you've had it. I wondered last night if——"

But he didn't tell me what he wondered. He added briskly:

"Come over to the Casa Alta and grab a steak. Where's your coat?"

"In Drawing Room E," I admitted meekly.

His eyebrows went up. "What were you planning to do?"

I didn't answer. He picked up a two-hundred-dollar camel's hair coat off a wall hook and tossed it at me, then grabbed a leather jacket from the bed and put it on.

"Food, Howie. Don't ever make decisions on an empty stomach."

Out in the darkness I thought of something. I turned towards the tiny station whose only light flowed from the night op's bay window. His home signal was set at clear and I heard a freight pounding up the valley from the east.

"I'd better send a wire to Betty," I said. "It will catch her at Placer and——"

"And she'll hop right off and be back here on 33 in two hours. You sure you want it that way?"

I didn't and said so. I needed more time.

Reynolds said quietly, "Let me take care of it, Howie. And stay right here. No use advertising you're in town yet."

I waited in the shadow of the hotel and watched Reynolds cross to the station and go inside. It was still snowing, but not very hard. A clock in a service station across the road said five fifty-seven. It was impossible for me to realize that forty-five minutes ago I'd just seated myself beside Betty in Drawing Room E. I hadn't even told Reynolds what to say.

Waiting in snow and slush, with the thermometer plunging, I stared somberly at the thin line of straggling ragged structures strung along Route 80 and called Pioneer Gap. It was a Tired Town —Betty and I bestowed the term on the Gap as a nickname—an exhausted town, worn with its losing fight for a man-made destiny that never came off. In eighty years the Gap had had five picturesque booms, each of them abruptly terminated in abject failure. In the early seventies came the lumber boom—ties for desert rails, timber for mine shafts. The gold boom had lasted three years. A silver boom in the nineties endured through two winters. A copper boom was a dud. Ditto for zinc and lead.

Shortly after the turn of the century the dismal truth dawned upon its inhabitants. The Gap had no future, only an uncertain and feverish past. Everyone who had the wherewithal fled. Today the black and white sign on Route 80 proclaimed, "Pioneer Gap, Unincorporated. Pop. 978. Alt. 7455."

But once upon a time Pioneer Gap had been a roaring booming mountain town of 12,000. As an outfitting center for wagon trains pausing to assail the last great ridge of the High Sierras, the Gap had been made, and wisely, the Great Western's first division point east of the Sierra summit. For a long time it had been a railhead for the Desert Division which ran hopefully up Wildroot Valley and stopped dead, waiting for the rails pushing up Missing Moose Canyon on the west slope of the Sierras while the road's first tycoons ran out of money or blew their brains out, and surveyors and engineers wondered how to get rails from the Gap over Eldorado Summit without using elevators or stepladders. Five Rogers engines on the western slope were finally hauled from Basco to Summit on ox-drawn sledges—one sledge, thirty-six oxen—and lowered by cable over Rainbow Cliff onto other sledges that pulled the engines into the Gap and placed them, to rousing cheers, on new fifty-pound rail. A year later engineers solved their biggest headache through fresh surveys and ran their rails from the Gap to Summit at a terrific cost in money and men.

For ten years Pioneer Gap bloomed and flourished. The foundations of scores of vanished homes were still visible on Pine Hill. The sturdy old stone roundhouse with stalls for sixteen wood-burning engines had been turned into shops, a pump house, and stalls for a couple of Mallet helpers. But the town itself had shrunk to a shabby string of frame houses and a block or two of shops and miscellaneous structures, many of them empty, clinging desperately to highway 80, a through route from Nevada to Oakland which never swerved an inch in its contemptuous thrust through the somnolent community.

Motorists considerately slowed down from eighty to seventy miles an hour while passing through Pioneer Gap, usually leaving a nightly crop of devastated tomcats, a dog or two, and an occasional rabbit to be picked up by old Jack Toomey, the town's dawn clean-up detail.

Yet the Gap intrigued both Betty and me. We dined there many times and often poked about its historic spots, accompanied by Dan Shields, who expatiated glowingly upon the town's golden past, which I'm sure he didn't believe had existed any more than I did. We also made a number of firm friends in the community. As in other mountain settlements, the Gap's inhabitants were divided into two distinct classes—Those Who Worked for the Railroad, and Outcasts. Among the unshriven were small resort owners, storekeepers, service station attendants, and local small fry who milked passing tourists for their sustenance.

My rather depressed and nostalgic mood was shattered by a long raucous "blat" from the Diesel-drawn freight calling for orders at the Gap. The train order signal over the op's bay window shifted to "Stop." The train snaked through the yards, slowing to about twenty miles an hour as a youngster ran from the station with his Y hi-speeder order hoop and stood close to the westbound rails. The engineer, his window open, thrust an arm through the hoop and picked up his flimsies on the string. The Diesels roared full-throated again, the train picking up speed. The boy remained where he was, with another hoop and duplicate flimsies for the head shack at the rear end, still almost half a mile away.

I was surprised by the extreme cold, unusual for that time of year. Films of ice already covered pools in the street. The sky was heavily overcast. I saw Reynolds walking briskly towards me. He joined me and said cheerfully:

"Sorry to be so long. I got talking to Summit. Fifteen inches of new snow up there. Kind of early this year."

I wasn't interested in the weather. "What'd you say to Betty?" I asked.

Reynolds smiled briefly. "Tell you later. Let's eat."

As if to explain his abruptness he added casually, "I'd like to know

27

what you want to do first. Let's wrap ourselves around Maria's steaks. Then we'll talk."

We walked two blocks to the Casa Alta, a small two-story stucco hotel run by Mrs. D'Alvarez, who provided the best food in town and a counter service that pulled in truck drivers like helpless flies. Though specializing in Mexican food, the Casa Alta had the best steak dinners in three counties. Five years ago Maria D'Alvarez had taken over a dilapidated café in a rambling, ramshackle old hotel that had been empty for years. This was just after her husband, a trackman from Sonora, had been killed in a slide at Mile 154.

Maria had a pension, a stocking full of savings, and against everyone's advice, bought the decrepit Casa Alta building and spent every nickel she had in transforming the melancholy structure. And transform it she did, with immediate success. The place had warmth and color, an intriguing atmosphere, and quickly became a favorite rendezvous for tourists and lesser brass of the G.W. In search of culinary triumphs, Maria lured an elderly Mexican chef over the Sierras straight from Cordova's, San Francisco's famous eating place. A year later she married him.

To her unusual hostelry Reynolds and I now repaired, entering the gaily painted door that led into the low-ceilinged arched lobby, warm with serapes, sombreros, and multicolored Mexican baskets on the wall. And our hostess, a woman of considerable dignity and much charm, resembling a retired opera diva who had tossed diets and cautious living to the winds, was there in person. With two gardenias poked saucily in her shining black hair, Maria met us with a broad hospitable smile that indicated she was about to swallow us both.

"Mr. Reynolds and Mr. Bierce together. That is wonderful." She had the slightest of accents. "We have a party tonight. We are opening the Sonora Room. There will be music, dancing, and free flowers for everyone. You will be my guests?"

Reynolds took over. "Sorry, Maria, no party for us. Business. How about a quiet corner and two big steaks—New York cut, medium-rare. Everything with it. Have you got a room—for Mr. Bierce?"

Maria was quick and sensitive. She caught something at once. Her smile vanished. She was all business.

"Certainly. I have the big corner room at the back. Very comfortable and quiet. And the dining room is empty. Everybody is waiting for the party. You want a drink first?"

We ordered a couple of martinis and headed for the dining room. Maria looked at me sharply, noting Reynolds' gleaming coat, then beamed at me and disappeared.

Over our drinks Reynolds and I talked a little shop, reserving our main topic until later. I began to feel much better and take an interest in my surroundings. Betty and I had discovered the Casa Alta a year ago. It was about the same time Maria had discovered Selma Ferris. And Selma was worth discovering. Through the open door to the coffee shop I watched her ministering to the urgent appetites of truck drivers and travelers who stood two and three deep waiting for empty stools at her always crowded counter.

With her I noticed for the first time a young second waitress, a striking contrast to Selma. She was dark, slender, and very pretty. And very Viennese, I decided, never having been to Vienna. Yet there was something forbidding about her, a cold detachment, and even a touch of grimness in her deft, quick, impersonal movements.

Selma was the golden sun in the glittering little world of chrome and silver over which she presided. Selma was one of those colorful flamboyant women about whom men love to weave their most intimate and amorous fantasies. With no visible effort of her own she inspired intense speculation and comment, as well as attracting a vast volume of business. She was a big, long-limbed, full-bosomed voluptuous blonde from Basco with almost classic features and a soft, sensitive, sensuous mouth that made strong men falter upon their appointed rounds. About her vivid, disturbing person clustered unnumbered legends, picturesque, lurid, charming, carnal, and alarming, one flourishing upon the other and so juggling fact and fancy that any resemblance to reality became purely coincidental and indeed unimportant.

Selma lived in men's imaginations like a popular pulp serial with everyone waiting breathlessly for the next installment. She was a Bad Girl Headed for the Rocks in the opinion of Those Who Knew, which meant the ladies' roster of Pioneer Gap. But Maria D'Alvarez was not among the latter. Pondering a problem of her own, she had made a great discovery in Selma. For many months Maria had been watching the big trucks roar by the Casa Alta, wondering how to stop them. Truck drivers consumed fabulous amounts of food, and these husky chaps with big tankers and trailers all the way from Michigan and Illinois were well paid and worth trapping. Maria not only discovered that Selma could stop any male in his tracks, but the girl was a terrific cook. Adding up her talents and brash beauty, Maria simply moved in and took possession of Selma, learning that the girl had been orphaned as an infant and farmed out to various greedy and avaricious relatives. No one in those early years, apparently, had ever treated Selma as a human being. From the age of six on she had been cuffed about, cared for other people's children, done heavy housework, and rumor had it that at the age of fifteen she had been seduced by a vagabond uncle killed in a drunken brawl a year later.

Maria saw at once that Selma needed security, comfort, and someone with a blend of guidance and discipline to look after her. Maria had all that to give. So, to the tongue-clucking of the community, she took full possession of Selma and placed her in charge of a new streamlined short-order counter behind a huge plate-glass window facing Route 80. Then Maria installed the most impressive and loudest juke box she could find—it resembled a crimson and chrome-plated version of the Taj Mahal—filled the window with yellow flowers to match Selma's crown of golden hair, announced a gala opening, and placed a neon sign on the corner visible a mile in either direction along Route 80. It said everything needed: "Selma's Coffee Shoppe. 24 Hrs."

One final stroke of genius insured the immediate success of Selma's Shoppe. At Maria's express orders all of the seductive aromas of roasts and steaks on the big modern grill were blown directly across Route 80 by a powerful ventilating fan. Only drivers of exceptional will power were able to hurtle through that fragrance without making an emergency stop.

Through the open door I now watched Selma, who seemed to float back and forth across the big plate window, always filled with flowers, like some seductive goldfish. She wore a tight, jaunty, low-cut cotton dress that beautifully limned each and all of her ample and undeniable charms. Forty eyes followed her every move like hypnotized spectators at a tennis game. Twenty jaws champed slowly, rhythmically, in no hurry at all.

I was beginning to succumb myself when Reynolds' voice competed with Selma and won a grudging victory.

"Funny thing you and I landing at the Gap together. I had no intention of coming up here. But Purdy called me at five this morning and I just made 48."

"Anything special?" I asked casually. I didn't want to butt in on anything private, and anything official was Reynolds' affair. I was on leave.

Reynolds frowned a little, then laughed. "No, I guess not. Probably just a gag. But——"

He broke off as the steaks arrived. I didn't press him and began to eat heartily. When we'd finished I pushed my plate back and announced, "Okay, Jim. I'm feeling better. Thanks for the remedy. Now what did you say to Betty?"

Reynolds gazed at me blandly. "Tell me first what you really want to do."

I still wasn't sure. I said slowly, "I need a rest. I need a little time to think things through." Then it came to me. "I'd like to sit right here for the rest of the month, battle out some decisions, then join Betty in New York."

Reynolds nodded. He said laconically, "Then I guessed right. We're in the clear."

"What did you say?" I insisted.

Reynolds smiled. "Quite a lot. I told her I'd snatched you off 20 to handle a crisis in motive power, that Wharton had been taken suddenly ill. Told her to go ahead with your plans. I'd rush you East as soon as I could. You were writing her. She could cut me up in small pieces when she got back. And a lot more gobbledygook."

Reynolds was the only man in the world who could have fed Betty that mishmash and gotten away with it. Betty always stood a little in awe of Reynolds. I said:

"I think she'll buy that for a while. And I'll write her in the morning. Thanks a lot."

I made a mental note that I could duck all the details of my upcoming exhibit and still be in New York for the opening on January 2. But I was in for a lot of embarrassing correspondence. Meanwhile Reynolds offered to drop in at our Belknap house and send up some of my clothes and painting paraphernalia. I gave him the keys and told him what I needed. Then he irritated me by remarking:

"When you head East, better tell me your plans. You know what a winter up here means——"

So he was already figuring on my successor. I cut in.

"Hell, Jim, as of now I'm holing up at the Casa Alta for two or three of the quietest and dullest weeks of my life. I'm dogtired. But I'll be back on the job by January 15. I'm staying on the Hill as long as they'll have me. I'll continue to paint on the side."

He looked at me hard.

"Then what was the big fight with Betty all about?"

"She beat me to a decision I'd made myself. And she picked some awfully wrong words."

Reynolds' expression was a bit sardonic. "So she's got to suffer awhile, is that it? Well, Howie, I guess you can stand some rest and you're entitled to it." He added with a trace of irony, "I'm glad you're staying with us."

After agreeing to pass the word around the Gap station that I'd been detailed for a special job and wasn't to be bothered by anyone, Reynolds informed me he was going up to Klamath Falls for a day to look over two rotaries the S.P. wanted to sell. We talked shop awhile until I was struck by Reynolds' absent expression. He was frowning a little and making small pellets of bread with two fingers and not hearing me any more.

"Don't let me keep you," I said. "I'm hitting the sack."

He came around quickly.

"I was thinking of Purdy's screwy phone call at the St. Francis this morning——"

31

Purdy was assistant trainmaster at the Gap. I saw Reynolds wanted to tell me something.

"Somebody steal your railroad last night?" I wisecracked feebly. Reynolds looked startled.

"You're getting psychic, Howie. You're mighty close. We had a holdup. Right on the Hill. Last night."

I stopped eating pie à la mode and put down my fork.

"Who's kidding you?"

He answered evenly, "A lot of folks. Purdy, Benson and his fireman, and two shacks in a bad-order caboose coming down the Hill. Only they weren't kidding."

"Let's have it," I said soberly. "You've been trying to tell me about it all evening."

He laughed shortly. "I guess I have."

Then he told me a fantastic little tale. Benson, a veteran engineer due for retirement in a few days, had worked on a helper from Belknap to Summit the night before. At one in the morning he started back for Belknap, running light and towing a bad-order caboose with two brakemen in it, fast asleep. At Mile 183, right above Black Rock Canyon, he ran into a flare and a red board and stopped. The signal had been tampered with. When Benson climbed down to investigate, a chap wearing a black mask and a navy peacoat with a torn right sleeve shoved a service revolver in Benson's stomach and lined up the rest of the crew, including the two sleepy shacks stumbling out of the caboose. Jesse James then made them uncouple the Mallet, run down the Hill a mile, and there he left them abruptly, climbing up the bank to a side road, roaring with laughter and telling them to get their caboose and beat it.

I listened, bug-eyed. "I know there's a lot of inflation," I remarked, "but when folks get hard up enough to steal locomotives——"

"Wait," said Reynolds. He told me the men involved had been sworn to silence. It wasn't the kind of publicity the G.W. wanted on the Hill, but the affair was being thoroughly investigated. With a gleam in his eye Reynolds asked me:

"What do you make of it?"

It didn't make any sense and I said so. Reynolds agreed.

"You know, Benson got the shock of his life. I was wondering tonight if it wasn't a gag. You remember how Benson——"

I laughed with relief. "I think you're right. Benson's retiring on Saturday. I'll bet somebody decided to give him a farewell party and scare hell out of him."

We finally decided that was it. Benson was known all over the Hill for his tall tales. He had an incorrigible imagination that had flowered through the years. He bored everyone to death with lurid accounts of impossible happenings in which he invariably played a leading role. There wasn't a crack-up, slide, or cornfield meet in railroad history that Benson hadn't been in on. He was the original "I was there" man and with a few drinks under his belt once managed to convince himself and a local reporter that he'd been held up by Jesse James.

I thought of something else. One of the boys a year ago had held out Benson's pay check and informed him the company pay roll had been hijacked from the Belknap office by a gang of masked riders. For about twenty minutes Benson believed this, long enough for him to get MacIntosh on the phone and tell him the robbery had actually taken place. All hell broke loose before the backfiring joke was run down and disposed of. Several men were disciplined. One of them, I was convinced, had decided to give Benson a taste of his own medicine and enjoy the show. Reynolds had forgotten this. He was now convinced and relieved. He said curtly:

"We've got enough work up here without having some Rover Boys in our hair. If I ever locate that pea jacket with the torn sleeve somebody's going to be in trouble."

We talked shop a little longer. Then Reynolds rose to go and put out his hand.

"Bierce, enjoy yourself. You've picked the dullest spot in the Sierras. Get all the rest you can. When the weather hits the Hill in January you'll have plenty to do. Meanwhile, you better make up with Betty and have a good fling in New York. That wire of mine will hold her just so long."

Over my protests he picked up the check and we headed for the cashier's desk. Then things began to happen and the remembrance of them is blurred. I recall now that through the door to the coffee shop I had been watching Selma and the slender young girl working with her. While Reynolds and I talked a big florid-faced chap in an expensive coat had entered, taken the only seat at the end of the counter, and promptly fastened a pair of dark brooding eyes on Selma. That was standard practice, but from the uncertain way our friend handled the menu card I was aware all at once that he was quite drunk. When Selma asked for his order he looked her over from head to toe and made a remark that brought deep color to Selma's cheeks. Her eyes snapped. She made a sharp reply. The stranger laughed and made another remark. Selma slapped his face. The party with the expensive overcoat leaned across the counter, put an arm around Selma's waist, pulled her close, and addressed a number of colorfully suggestive remarks to her. Several customers stood up, watchful and wary. Selma shouted, "Get out! Get out of this place."

Reynolds assured me later that by this time I was already through the door. I grabbed our friend by a coat lapel. Looking back, I

33

realize now that ever since leaving Betty and jumping off that train I had been itching to hit somebody. I was spoiling for a fight and didn't know it. An ideal situation was at hand. The stranger threw a left hook at me that missed completely. That was all I needed. I choked his coat collar about his throat with my left hand, and employed my right fist as a battering ram against his broad ruddy face. I finally pin-pointed a hefty right on his jaw and he went down like a felled ox. Having completely lost my temper, I leaned down and grabbed him by the back of his coat.

At that moment a young tigress leaped to the door, yanked it open, and her level gray-blue eyes blazed into mine. It was Selma's assistant, whose name I did not know. She said in a mellow husky voice, as if referring to some bit of waste paper I'd picked up, "Throw him out."

It was a pleasure. I heaved the big chap out into the falling snow, and dusting off my hands in a rather pretentious gesture I'd probably caught from some film, I turned to face an astonished and silent audience. Then came a general laugh in which everyone joined with two exceptions—Reynolds and the dark young girl, the second waitress, who had apparently just discovered one another. I remember now the sudden interest that flared in Reynolds' eyes.

"Were you going to tackle him yourself?" I heard him ask her.

She nodded briefly and walked behind the counter.

"What's your name?" asked Reynolds a little peremptorily.

The girl surveyed him coldly and turned away. Reynolds appeared puzzled and commented to me in a low voice, "Charming little thing. Probably carries a couple of pearl-handled popguns."

Then he glanced out the window at our friend reclining on the sidewalk and turned to the row of now silent statues regarding this tableau.

"Some of you boys pick him up. Take him to the first aid room at the G.W. Hotel. Tell Shields if he needs any attention to call Doc Woodruff." Then he said to me in a low voice, "Get out of here, Howie. Join me in the lobby."

Selma said to me with a dazzling smile, "Thank you, Mr. Bierce."

Her young assistant, who resembled a tense version of Hedy Lamarr, was watching Reynolds as he left the room. I joined him a few moments later in the lobby. He appeared preoccupied and led me to a couple of easy chairs.

"I never noticed that girl before," he said as if reproaching himself for a serious lapse of observation. Then he looked me over, severely.

"Listen, Howie, if you're on vacation don't start beating up strange men."

"Why not?" I asked. "You saw what he was pulling. I feel a lot better."

"Know who he was?" asked Reynolds, deceptively calm.

"Why the hell should I?" I replied. "I never saw the big goat in my life."

"I could hope you won't again," snapped Reynolds. "You just sailed into 'Jackpot' Thomas."

"Good—whoever he is," I replied. "I'd——" But Reynolds' expression stopped me. "Okay, Jim, who is 'Jackpot' Thomas? MacIntosh's brother—or Fontaine's illegitimate son?"

"Stop kidding, Howie." Then he told me, and dim memories of newspaper headlines stirred in my mind. Then I remembered. "Jackpot" Thomas. He had a curious first name I couldn't remember. Mine promoter, big-time gambler, income tax evader of course. He owned half of Antelope Inn at Las Vegas and part of the Club Cimarron at Reno. A big shot in the Florida and West Coast underworld. Former New Jersey liquor czar.

I sobered rapidly.

"What's he doing up here?" I asked. I was aware Reynolds had shown no surprise at seeing Thomas. Reynolds looked me over carefully.

"It will keep till next time. But take my advice. Stay away from him. He's a bad-order job for everybody, and maybe for the Great Western."

I got up, feeling a bit subdued, and examined the swelling knuckles of my right hand.

"I'll stay under wraps, Jim," I promised him. "I just blew my top. This has been the queerest damn day of my life."

Reynolds nodded.

"Queer day for me, too," he agreed reflectively.

"Thanks for everything," I told him. "I sure need a rest. But things will work out all right."

"I'm sure they will," he said emphatically. We were on the front steps. Reynolds looked up at the leaden sky, then across at the G.W. Hotel, fringed with icicles, the lights on in the first aid room at the far corner. There was a hint of uncertainty in his manner, something I had seldom seen in him before.

"I'll be back Tuesday. If you're going to hang around here for a few weeks you might be useful. You've got a good observation post."

That puzzled me.

"If it's Benson——" I began. But Reynolds wasn't thinking of Benson.

"That nut? Forget him. I'm thinking of you—and Thomas. Keep out of his way."

"What are you trying to tell me?" I asked curiously.

He shrugged. "Nothing. So long. I'll see you Tuesday."

35

3

After Reynolds left me the reaction set in. I was exhausted. I tried to chat with Maria for a few minutes. She had Selma's brief version of the abrupt departure of Thomas. I gave her mine without adding Reynolds' identification of our visitor. Maria had enough worries. I concluded by remarking, "That chap was obliging. I've been wanting to slug someone all day. He came along just in time."

"Don't make it a habit," commented Maria. "This is a very respectable place."

I thought of something else.

"Selma's assistant—that cold little Sphinx with the gray-blue eyes. Who is she? What's her name?"

"Lisa Maddon," said Maria, looking a little surprised and a bit wary. I repeated the name and added, "She's very pretty. But a grim little spitfire. A lot different from Selma."

Maria looked at me thoughtfully. "Not so very different," she said quietly. "Sometime I will tell you about them both. But not just now."

A tactful, discerning woman, she looked me over and laughed.

"Mr. Bierce, don't be so polite. You need sleep. So sleep. I hope the party will not disturb you."

I hoped so too but I didn't admit it out loud. I said good night and went up to my room, a large low-ceilinged comfortable affair which had once been Maria's old sitting room and still showed evidences of her personal touch. There were two or three big easy chairs, a Franklin stove in addition to two radiators, and a large dormer window over a window seat that afforded by daylight a superb view of the Great Western climbing Wildroot Valley with Sentinel Peak thrusting into the western sky.

All I could see just now, through a gentle fall of snow, were a couple of jeweled signal lights, yellow and red, gleaming in the distance against the shadowy mass of the mountains. The other window, I'm sorry to say, stared north at the town dump.

Intending to relax a few moments before taking a hot shower, I took off my shoes and shirt and leaned back on the big double bed. That's all I remember. I was out. I must have fallen asleep at once. Ordinarily I dream very little. But I recall on this occasion a vivid impression of slowly emerging from darkness and swimming pleasantly about some blue-shadowed grotto illuminated by a brilliant beam of light and with soft music in the distance. Then I woke up. The beam of light came from a headlight five miles up the valley. It swung slowly across a wall of my room and disappeared. But the music remained. Below me Maria's party was apparently in full swing and I had the impression of people dancing to a piano and a couple of guitars.

Then I turned on the light and looked at my watch. It was 1 A.M. I'd slept for four hours and felt refreshed and completely relaxed for the first time in weeks. Idly, I listened to the music. It was excellent. The musicians in Maria's Sonora Room knew their business, and music was another early enthusiasm of mine that had been pushed far in the background by the pressure of my professional duties.

In the Sonora Room below me there was sudden silence. In the lull that followed the pianist began some leisurely improvisations. He had an excellent touch and I thought for a moment of a Harvard student I'd encountered while I was at M.I.T. I wondered what had become of him. He was a homely youngster with an erratic, brilliant mind, a few close friends, and he struck me as incredibly lazy considering the talents we thought he possessed. Trying to identify some of the themes which the pianist below me so cleverly elaborated, I recognized fragments of Rimsky-Korsakoff's *Sadko*, part of a Spanish suite by Ravel, and something by Debussy that in an intriguing series of modulations shifted into a shimmering free-lance interpretation of Wagner's "Forest Murmurs" from *Siegfried*.

Flattering myself on my rusty musical memory, I suddenly recalled there was only one individual I'd met who improvised that identical sequence with such exciting results. And that individual was the Harvard youngster I had vaguely recalled. His name came to me unexpectedly. Theodore Helmholtz. Twenty years fell away and I remembered a slight wiry lad with pale blue eyes and thin blond hair on a head much too large for his slender body who had played such music as this in the basement of the old Beacon Hotel in Boston after a noisy student party. He had hypnotized us all.

Why on earth would Helmholtz be pounding an old Bradley upright in a second-rate hotel in a godforsaken Sierra mountain town?

But I was excited. I couldn't be mistaken. That pianist had to be Helmholtz. I grabbed my shirt, put on my shoes, and made for the door. I ran downstairs into the hallway filled with chattering guests. Then I spotted Maria, caught her eyes, and joined her.

"What's the name of that pianist?" I demanded. Maria beamed.

"He's terrifeek, no? He plays everything. Even Mexican music as you don't hear it up here."

"So what's his name?" I insisted, raising my voice.

Maria was exasperatingly deliberate.

"I don't know much about him. He came here a month ago. He had been sick. I felt sorry for him. Then I heard him play. I hired him at once. He brings in business. He says his name is Helm"— Maria stumbled over the two *ls* but got it correct—"it's Helmholtz. I think he's at the bar."

I pushed past her and made for the Sonora Room. Then I saw him and my last lingering doubt vanished. Helmholtz was standing by the bar chatting with another man. Pausing a moment to take in the slight figure leaning easily against the rail, I noted with dismay that my old friend had not been treated kindly by the years. He was almost bald, stooped a little, and wore large tortoise-shell glasses. He was wearing a blue T shirt, blue slacks, and an old pair of tennis shoes, while his familiar long arms and large hands rested casually on the bar. This certainly wasn't the magnetic youth I remembered. This was Helmholtz twenty years later, a long way from where he's tried to go, a man to whom many things had happened.

I walked over to him just as the man he was talking with moved away. The room was dimly lighted by candles, except for a light some distance off, and it was full of smoke. I put out my hand as Helmholtz turned.

"Hello, Ted. How in hell are you?"

Helmholtz peered at me without recognition, his pale blue eyes magnified almost owlishly by his glasses. Then I realized the room was dark and he was trying to see who it was. I moved a step or two and stood under the light and the transformation of Helmholtz was wonderful to watch. He gave a yelp of genuine joy.

"Bierce! Howie Bierce!"

I had remembered Ted as a very undemonstrative individual. But he shook both my hands, slapped my back, and gave me a heart-warming welcome.

"What are you doing in this cockeyed Valkyrie, this Copley-Plaza of the Sierras? Don't tell me you live here! Married? Making money?" He gave me no chance to answer his questions. "It doesn't matter. Good Lord, you're the first man I've met in ten years that I can talk with."

I knew what he meant. We had been great confidants in the old days. As Helmholtz rattled on I saw Maria watching us, obviously astonished by this resurrection of a former friendship. Ted turned to the bar.

"This we've got to drink to." He ordered straight double bourbons. Then we looked one another over, gravely, inquiringly, peering through the years trying to find again the golden thread of friendship we had once discovered together, though briefly, so many years ago.

"Howie," he asked me finally, tossing off his drink and wiping his broad mouth, "to what do we owe this miraculous meeting above the clouds in the unimposing ruins of the most forlorn-looking community I ever encountered?"

I shook my head. "Blessed if I know, Ted. You're the exclamation point to the queerest damn day of my life. And I was going to ask you that—what on earth are you doing up here?"

An innocuous, casual question. But I was shocked at its effect. Helmholtz reacted as if I had struck him. I tried to undo a little of the damage I had caused. I said quickly:

"When can we talk? Can you grab some beer after this party's over and come up to my room?"

His expression was still grim and haunted, as if my sudden appearance and unconsciously pointed question had summoned too many ghosts from the past and he was struggling to herd them all into some forgotten cellar again. For the time being, I think, he succeeded. His eyes lightened and he smiled quizzically at the ancient upright piano, mantled with beer bottles, guttering candles, and paper party hats.

"I've got to batter that poor helpless bastard for another hour or two. Are you game to stay up?"

"Until dawn, if you want. I'll be right here."

The party went into high gear again with a rush. The room vibrated with the dancing. Maria studied me for a moment, politely but fiercely curious.

"You know him, eh." It was a flat declaration and not much of a discovery by this time.

"I certainly do. You'd better hang on to him if you can. He's the best damn pianist west of Horowitz." That's all I said and Maria, after pouting a bit, left me with Alice Livingston and moved majestically away.

Alice was one of our local schoolteachers, very young and attractive. She would have made a good cover girl for any magazine and her coloring reminded me of my wife. We danced and talked together for quite a time. The boys, behind her back called her the Battling Virgin. She had been teaching on the Hill for two seasons but was engaged to a young engineering student at Berkeley, a native

39

of India named Lal Besar, and was marrying him in two months and moving to Karachi to make her home.

Alice isn't important to this story but she had won undying fame on the Hill for her fiery tactics on behalf of her pupils. During a big blizzard a year ago she had flagged down our snooty streamliner streaking up Wildroot Valley and demanded and obtained two dozen eggs and a quantity of ham, bread, and coffee from an outraged dining-car conductor. Four of Alice's pupils were snowed in a short distance away without food and there was no way to get into town. Instead of making capital out of this human-interest tale the Great Western indignantly huffed and puffed through a gilt-edged investigation of the unlawful flagging down of their pet train, only to hurriedly fold its tents and steal away when Alice's first vocal blasts concerning the plight of her pupils and the indifference of the railroad made page 1 in every San Francisco newspaper.

I thoroughly enjoyed myself with Alice, danced with several other ladies, and at 5 A.M. helped Ted and Maria sweep up. Our last charitable act was to move the sleeping form of Chief Brown, the Gap's bulky custodian of law and order, close to the radiator. The launching of the Sonora Room had been a huge success. Raiding the icebox for the last of the beer, Helmholtz and I went up to my room, leaving Maria counting the gate receipts with a most satisfied expression on her pleasant face.

I built a small fire in the Franklin stove—the radiators were getting rigor mortis—and we made ourselves comfortable. There was a rather pregnant silence as we gazed at one another over fresh bottles of beer. Helmholtz lounged in shadow on the window seat. I sat before the stove, my feet on a straight chair. And I made a discovery. I had thought I only wanted to talk to Helmholtz about myself. That had been my familiar role in the old days when I'd felt a bit guilty at tossing overboard my mother's somewhat hazy plans for a musical career for me. But on this occasion, noting many changes about him, I wanted Helmholtz to talk about Helmholtz.

Helmholtz was an ugly man of great charm. When I first knew him he possessed an array of unusual and contradictory enthusiasms which attracted the few who recognized his indisputable talents. Many people openly disliked him. But Helmholtz and I had found a number of common ties in our background and interests. His ancestors had lived for generations close to my own home in South Glastonbury, on the banks of the Connecticut River a few miles below Hartford. Here the first enterprising Bierce built a small shipyard, launched privateers, and smuggled an immense amount of rum and other Caribbean contraband into a thirsty New England, founding the first and only Bierce fortune of any magnitude. His descendants had spent it as fast as they could.

Helmholtz's maternal grandmother was a cousin of Theodore De-hone Judah, another native of Connecticut and the engineering gen-ius who surveyed the first practical route of the old Central Pacific, now the S.P., over the Sierras, contracting a fever in Panama and dying in New York before the first western rails were laid. Thus Helmholtz, also impressed by my father's career as a bridge builder, had taken a natural interest in my own budding ambitions in the engineering field.

Moreover, he came from Colorado, where his mother had gone from Connecticut to marry a mining engineer. Helmholtz was ex-ceedingly reticent concerning his family and his personal life. I vaguely recalled that his father, after a lot of hard luck, had been killed in a railroad accident. Helmholtz had to leave Harvard at once to aid in supporting his family, while his mother struggled to operate a rooming house at Grand Junction and gave piano lessons to a few youngsters. Ted and I corresponded rather desultorily for a year. Then he moved. I had never heard from him or seen him since.

No one could have predicted too confidently that Helmholtz would have carved out a brilliant career as a concert pianist had family tragedies not interrupted his plans. But I, for one, think he would have. He was a sensitive musician with many unique points of view, with sharp insight, and a profound ability to portray in tone what he saw and felt. Music formed almost the sole basis of his friendships, so that those who knew him best were a curiously diver-sified lot.

Musing over the mysteries of twenty vanished years, I noticed Helmholtz almost covertly glancing about the room. It seemed to me he noted with some relief the total absence of personal belongings.

"Are you just staying here overnight, Howie?"

I thought that over and watched him closely. "I'm not sure. I may be here two or three weeks. I've sent for some things."

Again that uneasy, worried expression that so clouded his whole countenance. But he relaxed a little and peered at me gravely through the thick lenses of his glasses.

"Twenty years—that's hard to bridge," he said slowly, in turn taking inventory of me. "You still look lean and pretty fit. I'd say you were doing the things you like to do and you've got that married expres-sion. Still pretty sure of your world, aren't you?" He hesitated a mo-ment and frowned, studying me some more. Then he smiled. "Something's bothering you, but it doesn't seem too vital. And," he added enviously, "you've kept your hair. Are you still building bridges?"

"Pretty good. But one error," I commented cheerfully. "It's always

41

been railroading. No bridges. Don't you remember my early brain-storms?"

I flipped him one of my cards. He picked it up, read it, and looked at me with a curious expression. There was a bit of the small boy in his face. I think he was recalling the days when I used to show him snapshots of my father, Arthur Bierce, the bridge. designer, who was then flinging some daring spans across the Kicking Horse River in British Columbia. Even then I was a determined railroad fan but Helmholtz had apparently confused my ambitions with my father's profession.

"Railroading of course. Funny I forgot that." He stared at the card again. "Somehow I figured you in your father's shoes." He turned the card over and over, as if it contained a key to some mystery. " 'Road Foreman of Engines.' What the hell is that?"

"A Road Foreman of Engines," I announced solemnly, "is a rail-road's private eye in the motive power and operating departments. He spies on suspicious-looking locomotives, steam and Diesel, and the men who operate them. He's called a 'traveling grunt' by his colleagues, though seldom to his face. He's the railroader's Sherlock Holmes, Sam Spade, and Mike Hammer. As a snooping gumshoe tailing engineers and firemen, he climbs into engine cabs at the most unlikely spots, often in the dead of night, and rides glumly about his Division seeing to it that his engineers don't fall out of cabs while the trains are in motion, and that amorous firemen don't keep fallen women in the tender tank."

"Cut it out," protested Helmholtz, smiling a little.

"Okay. There's a little more to it than that," I conceded. "I hire firemen and train engineers for both steam and Diesels. I watch Nervous Nellies on their first runs and qualify them for Diesels after five trips. I diagnose the incredible ailments of our engines for the master mechanic's benefit, study the quaint habits and customs of our engine crews, report violations of rules, and every month or so forward my dossiers, with commendations and reprimands, to our local Brass Collar, the Division superintendent, by name, John Ramsay MacIntosh. The bodies are usually removed by sundown. I'm a stool pigeon, informer, and heel. But I like the job."

I expanded my theme a bit. A Road Foreman of Engines was about on a par with a trainmaster but he had a great deal of authority in an engine cab, an authority which he tried to use with great discretion. He was out on the road most of the time. "A Road Foreman's day in the office is half a day lost," was the G.W.'s slogan. In short, the R.F. of E. was a roving general inspector who could halt any train any-where, toss off or discipline the engine crew, and raise general hell if he wished. Not a wheel could turn until his conditions were com-plied with and he gave the word. But in actual practice the Road

Foreman seldom exercised these powers. You don't handle veteran engineers like errand boys. Courtesy, ceremony, and protocol are customarily practiced in the engine cab. I had to be a blend of diplomat and inspector-general, and reported to the Division superintendent, who reported to the president, who reported to the chairman of the board, when he felt in the mood, and the chairman reported to the directors, the stockholders, and God.

"All of the operating officials of the G.W. come up from the ranks," I explained to Helmholtz. "Fontaine, the president, began as a freight clerk. And up here on the Hill a lot of responsibility is delegated to individuals. Our mountain engineers are the best. Any man who can handle a heavy train on the Hill can handle any problem encountered on any stretch of rail anywhere. Up here it's tough, informal, direct, and nobody makes an important mistake twice. Once is enough. He's through."

"And this Brass Collar, MacIntosh," asked Helmholtz, "he plays God on the mountain?"

"He sure does," I said soberly. "He's personally responsible for the safe movement of passengers and freight over one of the toughest divisions in the country. He's colonel of a regiment in wartime—and it's war up here eight months of the year."

I quoted from the G.W. bible again. "Each Division Superintendent shall have charge of his respective Division, and of the real estate, shops, stations, structures, and other buildings: the telegraph and telephone lines, Centralized Traffic Control installations, if any: signals, equipment, and all other property connected with the operation thereof: he shall have charge of the discipline of the forces, the maintenance of the roadway, track, bridges, buildings and signals, the safe, prompt, and economical movement of trains and traffic, and the general conduct of business on his respective Division, and shall be responsible for the expenses connected therewith. He shall, with the approval of the General Superintendent, appoint the necessary employees within his jurisdiction."

I paused for breath. Helmholtz raised both hands.

"Kamerad! And what does the Great Western pay such a genius— fifty bucks a week?" He looked impressed. "You learn all this stuff by heart?"

I nodded. "Not forgetting the G.W.'s rule book and bible—981 rules, three prefaces, a foreword by Fontaine, plus definitions, exceptions, general rules and Division timetables, passenger and freight, for employees only. Ask me."

"You know 'em all?" asked Helmholtz with mock awe.

"Like my house number," I replied and meant it. "But you can boil 'em all down to one simple axiom, paramount on every pike. 'Do not allow two trains to occupy the same piece of track at the same time.'"

43

"I trust you succeed," commented Helmholtz dryly.

I crossed my fingers. "We have for the past five years."

I finally told him why I was temporarily occupying a room at the Casa Alta, and mentioned the rising threat of my hobby, painting. Helmholtz was genuinely astonished over my tiff with Betty and I was piqued a bit that he hadn't heard of my Commonwealth Club award, for a snowstorm of San Francisco papers blew into Pioneer Gap every day. I mentioned this, but Helmholtz said acidly, "I never read those disgraceful embers of our dying culture. It's a murderous world we live in, Howie, and I make no point of keeping up with current affairs. I know that Coolidge is dead and World War II is over. That's about all."

I blinked and wondered if he wasn't telling the truth. Part of Helmholtz's personality had always impressed me as that of a clever, charming child. I remembered his eloquent bursts of enthusiasm and bitter criticisms of contemporary events in his student days when his disregard of realities was both reckless and obvious. Perhaps he hadn't changed so much after all. He was smiling at me now.

"Engineer and artist, eh? Well, it's been done. But it's worrying you. I can see it."

"You had the same problem once," I retorted carelessly, thinking of his early ambitions for a scientific career. I regretted the words at once. I had a terrible habit of voicing what was uppermost in my mind at the wrong moment. But Helmholtz's expression of engaging candor remained unchanged.

"That problem was settled for me," he said quietly. "And it's your turn, Howie. What about me?"

I smiled and leaned back, determined to be cautious. What I saw in my friend's face both interested and disturbed me. Only the pale blue eyes retained the power and glint of mocking vitality that were among his great charms. The rest of the man had taken a beating. His skin was very white, with a mildly bluish pallor where shadows fell across his face. The face was a long oval, the flesh full but a bit puffy. The scholarly high-domed head was still large for the slight frame which supported it. I saw the face and head of an unworldly philosopher surmounting the figure of an adolescent youth. There were times, and this was such a time, when Helmholtz suggested to me an ageless engaging gnome who had roamed too long among the leprechauns of fancy and the fascinating inner realms of a fertile and undisciplined imagination.

What had happened to him? For the first time I became acutely aware of an aura of tragedy about the man. It was difficult to define, impossible to pin-point in a concise phrase or two. I said casually:

"I'm looking at an old friend and my favorite pianist, bar none."

Helmholtz gave me a friendly but mocking smile.

44

"Your old habit of playing safe hasn't deserted you, Howie. But in this instance I don't blame you."

There was a hint of challenge in these words that I suddenly accepted.

"Just a minute," I went on. "You're after something. Hard. You're protecting yourself against disappointment by preparing to be resigned if you don't get it. You've had some rough deals that hurt. But you're here for a purpose, Ted. And there's a finality about it that I can't define."

He went white at that. The expression of guilt, so marked after our meeting, returned. The soft fleshy lines of his face seemed to dissolve and his features were haggard. Then the expression vanished as quickly as it had been created and I wondered if I had seen it at all. But I had.

"Bravo," he said in an unexpectedly mild voice. "You have more insight than I had reckoned on. You're right. Old man reality, at whom I've scoffed all my life, has finally caught up to me."

For the moment he didn't elaborate. He took a drink of beer from the bottle and frowned a little. I had the strange impression that this slender man was walking a tightwire across some bottomless chasm. I was startled at how vivid the image was to me. Helmholtz leaned forward, suddenly tense. His voice was harsh, grating.

"Hell, Howie, what's the use of kidding? You called the turn beautifully. No, no, don't say a word. I asked for it. My life was messed up for me and I've successfully completed the job. Always, always, I've walked forward looking back at the past. Never learned how to discipline myself. Always fascinated in all the many facets of the big show going on about me. But I could never realize, until much too late, that I was part of that show."

"What happened?" I asked abruptly. I didn't like his assumption of pathos. He brooded over that for a moment and I didn't think he would answer me. But he did.

"A youngster killed my father through carelessness," he said suddenly. "My father was riding in the rear car of a train to Leadville for the first big job he'd been offered in five years. That job meant everything to my mother, to all of us. This youngster neglected to protect the rear of the train. He went into some place for coffee when it stopped. An engine roared around a curve and plowed into the caboose where my father was sleeping. Four men were killed, including my father and the brother of a friend of mine named Pete Gustavson. The boy disappeared. He was never seen again.

"As you remember, I went home. My mother never recovered from the shock. I wasn't even equipped to support myself, let alone a family. Then came the depression. A certain corporation gobbled up our home, the homes of neighbors, friends, and a particular friend of mine. And within two years both my mother and this close friend of mine were dead. As direct results of what happened. To me they were murdered. My father, my mother, this girl. She left a child, a daughter. The husband, a mining engineer, lost his nerve and committed suicide. I looked after the youngster for a while. Then a wealthy aunt in California claimed her."

Helmholtz got up and walked about the room, finally staring through the dormer window at the distant signal lights. I was angry at myself for so carelessly prying into this unhappy past that I had never known existed. I didn't know what to say or how to stop this flow of old pain remembered. Helmholtz continued, his face again white and drawn.

"Act Two. I taught music and starved in a handful of small colleges for ten years. Then I got t.b. I went up to Aspen, Colorado, got my health back, but lost my nerve. I was broke and had about decided to finish myself off when Gustavson ran into me."

He had already mentioned the name. "Who is he?" I asked carefully, trying to ease Helmholtz off this dangerous path.

"A first-rate mining man. A friend of my father and the family. He insisted on staking me. I found he hadn't forgotten that rear-end crash either. I opened a small studio in Berkeley and surprised myself by making a go of it. Three months ago Gustavson popped in on me. I paid him back every nickel he's loaned me—and added two thousand dollars, all I'd saved, for an investment he outlined."

"Ted," I said gently, "stop it. You don't have to tell me all this."

He jumped back to reality with a perceptible jolt. He drew a deep breath and looked calmer and again he drew about him like an invisible but potent cloak his bland manner of detached observation.

"Sorry to throw this at you," he said. "But I feel better."

He looked better, much better, and he managed a smile.

"Let me get it off my chest, Howie, so we can forget it and go on from here. I'm ashamed to say I put it over Maria a bit. She's a jewel and convinced I'm a broken-down waif she's consented to shelter. It's not quite as bad as that. But I am here for a purpose. You're right about that. Meanwhile, take a look at this. Gustavson and I are partners." He cocked an eye at me and added almost regally, "We own a silver mine, with a dash of gold thrown in."

To my astonishment he handed me a legal document and lease informing all and sundry that Theodore Helmholtz and Peter Gustavson had obtained restricted rights from the owners of a certain piece of property in Virginia City, Nevada, to operate a limited portion of No. 7 gallery in the long abandoned workings of the old Ophir-Mexican mines, the Ophir being one of the first great bonanzas among the fabulous shafts that gutted the Comstock Lode some ninety years ago. I studied the document with some incredulity. It

46

was about as daft a venture for a penniless pianist as I could imagine. Especially so as I dimly recalled that all work on the old tailings and diggings at Virginia City had virtually ceased during World War II, a decline precipitated even earlier when gold was pegged at thirty-five dollars an ounce.

So Helmholtz, the talented young student of my Cambridge days, owned a bit of the Comstock Lode and spent his evenings pounding the piano for a handful of transients passing through Pioneer Gap! I decided it was all part and parcel of Ted's unstable existence and uncertain life. I tried not to betray my mood and said fervently: "I hope the firm of Helmholtz and Gustavson wrings a fortune from the Comstock."

"Thanks, Howie." There was an overtone of irony and he added shyly, "After all, you find it confusing to mix painting with your professional career. I hope you'll forgive a pianist's flyer in an abandoned silver mine. At least," he concluded wryly, "I can see what I haven't got."

I made no attempt to read the riddle of his words. Nor did I wish to. I strolled over to the dormer window. A glowing, cloudless, incandescent sky greeted me. A pale pink haze filtered over the pre-dawn blues and purples that still mantled the mountains. Even as I watched, a single rosy ray of sunlight touched the topmost pinnacle of Sentinel Peak. In the cold blue haze of the valley below a crimson signal light stabbed through the darkness. Much closer I saw the golden gleam of another board, indicating that 502 was eastbound down the Hill from Summit. As an exception to somewhat standard practice, both east and west rails of the Great Western were block-signaled in both directions, affording the road for all practical purposes two single-track railroads over the Sierras, an expensive provision that had long since paid off in many winter crises.

Moments later, far up the mountain and miles away, I caught the faint high whine of the Diesels, set for regenerative braking down the heavy Sierra grade and holding back the sleek train.

I wasn't sleepy at all. But in the growing light my friend's pallor worried me.

"Turn in, Ted. You're tired. We've got all day ahead of us."

Helmholtz nodded and rose just as someone knocked at the door. Maria, clad in a pink quilted wrapper and clucking her tongue at our late hours, handed me a telegram, addressed to me in care of Purdy, the trainmaster.

"It just came. I paid Purdy for it," she said, and went away.

Sent collect? That meant Betty. I opened it slowly, read it quickly, and relaxed as Helmholtz went to the door and paused.

"I'm driving over to Virginia City at eleven. I wish you'd come along. And see how badly I got swindled. Can you make it?"

47

I was still digesting Betty's telegram, but I saw Ted's request was important to him.

"Sure," I replied. "I'll be in the lobby at eleven."

His tension vanished. He smiled warmly.

"Thanks, Howie. You won't regret it. I'll show you something you won't forget."

Then he quietly closed the door.

4

I read Betty's wire again. The wretch had simply forwarded me one of her typical letters by wire—at my expense. I noted the charge. Six dollars and eighty-seven cents!

"MY POOR DEAR BOOB . . ." That's the way it began. ". . . YOUR DRAMATIC ALIBI FROM REYNOLDS FOOLED ME FOR ABOUT THIRTY SECONDS. AS SOON AS WE LEFT THE GAP AND YOU DIDN'T RETURN I REALIZED JUST WHAT I HAD DONE. FORGIVE ME, HOWIE. I NOW KNOW YOU HAD ALREADY MADE THE DECISION I HOPED FOR. MY STUPID INSISTENCE ON INTERRUPTING YOU AND MY AWFUL CHOICE OF WORDS WRECKED EVERYTHING. IN PRESENT IMPASSE I PROPOSE FOLLOWING BARGAIN: I WILL CONTINUE TO EAT CROW, ARRANGE YOUR NEW YORK AND BOSTON EXHIBITS, KEEP YOUR FRIENDS UNDER CONTROL, WHILE YOU ENJOY THREE WEEKS' VACATION. BUT JOIN US FOR HAFFER'S NEW YEAR'S PARTY, YOUR HONOR. I LOVE YOU. QUARREL WAS SHEER NONSENSE. PAINT THE REST OF YOUR LIFE IF YOU WISH. BUT NO MORE PHONY MESSAGES, PLEASE.

"GET A GOOD REST. YOU PICKED DULLEST PLACE IN THE WORLD FOR COMPLETE RELAXATION. WIRE ME DEARBORN STATION, CHICAGO, CAR 238, TRAIN 26, AND WRITE QUICKLY NELSON HOTEL, NEW YORK. ALL MY LOVE. YOUR OWN STUPID BETTY."

I went to the writing room and penned an appropriately forgiving message to my repentant wife, agreeing almost too enthusiastically to her one-sided bargain. Then I took my telegram over to the station. An earnest youngster I'd never seen before was on duty that quiet Sunday morning. It was not quite seven o'clock. He read my telegram without a quiver and the charge was over four dollars. "Mark it collect," I said airily, and walked out into the crisp clear air.

Strolling over to a favorite spot of mine, the old stone bridge that spanned Wildroot Creek, I stood there for a while watching the

49

morning light sweep up the valley. Far away the faint exhaust of a Mallet vibrated on the quiet air. Sparkling snow covered the hills and peaks to the west, but a mile to the east the lower foothills were barren of snow and still bright with late autumn reds and yellows. The colors everywhere were magnificent. Light mist rolled upwards in delicate clouds from the clear cold waters of the creek, covered with thin sheets of ice in hollows and shallows. The urge to record some of this on canvas was strong and I began to plan a week of leisurely work ahead of me.

While I walked slowly back to the station an ancient blue coupé rattled up beside me and stopped. Out of it leaned Alice Livingston, her face pert and rosy in the frosty air.

"Mr. Bierce! What on earth are you doing up and out at this hour?"

"I might ask the same," I retorted. "Just going home?"

She laughed. "Heavens, no! But now that I've almost run you down I've a big favor to ask."

I tried to look forbidding. Everyone in and around the Gap seemed to be determined to involve me with everyone else.

"What is it?" I asked crisply.

Alice laughed at my expression. "You won't have to punch a time clock," she assured me. "But we're planning a pageant and party Christmas Eve to raise money and dedicate the new district school at Summit. The program will be in honor of some Truckee children coming down as guests. And we need a scene painter. We're trying to elect you. Maria put me on your trail."

She added the pageant would celebrate in song, story, and drama some highlights of Sierra history. I tried feebly to beg off, but the job did sound like a bit of fun and I felt I owed it to Maria to help out. So I said yes. Alice was delighted, blew me a kiss, and drove off.

Back at the hotel I ran into Maria, who joined me for an early breakfast. Over stacks of buckwheat cakes, scrambled eggs, bacon, and coffee she stuffed me with local items as well as food. Everything at the Gap seemed quite normal. Purdy's wife had just had her fifth baby. Selectman Woodruff had been drunk again in Snyder's Bar. Three other selectmen still opposed a new concrete walk to replace the ancient wooden deathtrap before the Town Hall. Four more houses were empty. The Gap's population annually diminished by about this rate.

Maria told me Alice and the school board, led by a Mrs. Gaines, were about to battle the Great Western again. This annual struggle revolved about the problem of transporting youngsters, legally entitled to the state's educational facilities, to and from schoolhouses from remote and snowed-in ranches. There just wasn't any solution.

The county highways and side roads were impassable for months at a time. The Great Western, taking into consideration its heavy schedules, snowfalls, slides, rains, floods, blizzards, and other acts of God, adamantly decided it wasn't going to transport groups of children every day up and down portions of the Hill in the dead of a Sierra winter. Frankly, I couldn't blame the road.

But every year irate board members picketed the Division offices and hurled appeals and petitions at harried officials. Every year MacIntosh, the Division's Brass Collar and a favorite in local communities, came up on the Hill, made a speech or two, attended a church supper, and went back to barricade himself in his office for another winter.

Maria never mentioned my little fracas of the night before. But behind her chitchat I knew she was dying to know about my former friendship with Helmholtz. And of course she wondered what the devil I was doing at the Casa Alta without Betty when I had been announced in the local press as a visitor to eastern parts for the next six weeks. She was surprised but pleased when I told her I intended to be her guest until the last week in December. Then I told her something of my early friendship with Helmholtz, toning down his personal revelations and omitting his flyer at Virginia City. She listened gravely and I sensed vaguely that Helmholtz posed some problem for her.

Maria possessed an enormous capacity for affection and sympathy where it was most needed. While absorbed in the problems of her friends, she seldom meddled in them. And her kindness and generosity also battled with sound business instincts, and an unquestioned ability to make money. I thought of last night's events and casually inquired about Selma and Lisa Maddon. Maria was silent a while. Then she said quietly, "Let me tell you something about Mr. Helmholtz first. He is not well."

"What do you mean?" I asked.

Maria shrugged. "He had influenza the first week he was here." She appeared momentarily puzzled. "Why he came to the Gap at all I do not know. I called in Dr. Woodruff. He asked me questions about Mr. Helmholtz and his family that I could not answer. Then maybe a week later he came over when he had had some drinks— he drinks a lot, you know—and got me alone in the office and told me it would be nice if I could keep Mr. Helmholtz at the Casa Alta as long as possible because he did not think Mr. Helmholtz had too long to live. He had the nerve to say it would not cost me much for Mr. Helmholtz's music brought in quite a lot of customers." Maria grew very indignant. "Cost me anything! I do not do things for people for money. Never!"

Offhand, I didn't put too much stock in Doc Woodruff's diagnoses.

He was garrulous, he drank, and he was often careless. Just the same I was a bit startled.

"What did he say was the matter?"

"He wouldn't tell me, except that he hadn't said anything to Mr. Helmholtz. Then he told me to forget it. Our friend might live a long, long time. What do you think, Howie?"

I recalled Ted's old bout with t.b. and wondered if Woodruff had found some new symptoms. Aloud I made light of Woodruff's remarks but promised to corner him at an early date. Then I prodded Maria again on the subject of Selma and Lisa.

Maria took my cue with a rush. There was irony and humor in her comment about the girls, and there was something else, some undercurrent of concealed drama. Maria, before meeting Selma, had swallowed most of the rumors that clustered about this striking blonde. Happening to become friendly with Selma, she was astonished to find that each and all of the colorful tales of Selma's two husbands, countless lovers, and innumerable lurid episodes were based on nothing but widespread male frustration and wishful thinking.

"She had a bad childhood. She is nothing but a frightened kid," said Maria emphatically. "Nobody ever fooled me so. I would question her over and over before I believed her. She is really afraid to death of men. Her uncle beat her regularly when she was little. But he never seduced her. That is nonsense. And you know something?" Maria leaned close, her eyes round and wide, her voice an awed whisper. "I think she is still a virgin. She is also very religious, very devout. And Catholic, like me."

If Maria presented this portrait of Selma as authentic I had to accept it. But it made Selma's position in the community pretty sardonic. Every lusty male that entered the coffee shop considered Selma his lawful prey. All kinds of stories made the rounds. Selma herself encouraged them, dressed with outrageous boldness, and was an artist of double-entendre and innuendo in her flippant repartee with the customers.

"What about Lisa? Where's she from?" I asked.

"That is curious, too," replied Maria, deftly spearing a perfect circle of buckwheat cake and waiting until she had carefully swallowed it before continuing. "She is a puzzle. I do not know very much about her. Just before Mr. Helmholtz came here I needed an extra girl for the coffee shop and put up little cards advertising for a waitress. Selma was with me when Lisa came in the next day. She looked pale and unhappy and would only say she came from Oakland. Also, she had no experience. But Selma liked her. It is funny" —Maria tapped her forehead—"something told me up here not to take her. But of course I did. I am soft with people like that. She learned fast, but she does not belong in this work. Anyone can see that. Then last week I find out things that are not my business. But——"

She paused and her expression so resembled Reynolds' when he was trying not to tell me something that I smiled.

"So she's a puzzle," I reminded Maria. "Why?"

"More than a puzzle—a mystery," said Maria, looking a little startled and adding thoughtfully, "I will tell you. I gave Lisa a little room next to Selma on the third floor. Then a few days later she rented two big rooms from Mrs. Enfield, who is a very deaf old lady. Most convenient, that deafness, as you will see. About this time Mr. Helmholtz came here, and as I told you I employed him.

"Then many little things happen. First, a piano goes into Lisa's two rooms. Somebody tells me she plays very well. Then another piano into those two rooms. Two grand pianos! Old ones. But still, two grand pianos. Next, Mrs. Enfield tells me Mr. Helmholtz is giving Lisa piano lessons every day. Every day! For hours. And now Lisa has given me notice. She is leaving the coffee shop next week. She needs all the time she can get for her music. That is what she says. But I say to myself, Who pays for these two big rooms, for the two big pianos, and maybe for Lisa's living?"

Although I shrugged I was more intrigued by all this than I cared to reveal. Maria went right on without waiting for any comment from me.

"Just last week I came home early when I am supposed to be in Reno. I look for Selma, here, there, finally in the Sonora Room. Selma is not there. But Mr. Helmholtz and Lisa are. He was sitting at the piano, on the bench, and looking very upset. Lisa stood by the window, very stiff and angry. I heard her say, 'I can't wait that long, Ted. I won't stay in this awful place more than a few weeks.' Mr. Helmholtz looked at her as if she had beaten him. 'I'm doing all I can, Lisa. Don't push me any more just now . . .'"

Maria looked at me inscrutably. "Then I went away," she said simply. "I don't know what to make of it. So I make nothing. Let's forget it. I think I am becoming an old snoop."

Ted had emphatically confirmed my guess that he had definite business at the Gap. But Lisa as part of his plans had never occurred to me. Instinct and caution told me to halt Maria's little investigation at once.

"Let's keep out of it," I said firmly. "Ted's over twenty-one. Lisa's a very capable-looking girl, capable and grim. I'm more anxious about Ted's health. I intend to see a lot of Ted while I'm here. Maybe he'll tell me about this. If not—it's none of our business."

"You're right, Howie," agreed Maria, and we dropped the subject. Later I went for a walk, strolling around Pine Hill and spotting two or three scenes I intended to sketch, and on my return detoured by the station to glance at the thermometer. A barometer, protected by a wire screen, hung beside it just outside the operator's window. The temperature was forty-eight and rising. But the barometer was down, way down, for such a sunny day. I looked up at a flawless sky except for a faint hint of whiteness in the crystalline blue to the northwest. At least Helmholtz and I had a clear day for our trip.

When I entered the lobby of the Casa Alta, Ted was waiting for me, bundled up in a leather flying jacket and a jaunty red ski cap. My anxiety over Woodruff's remarks temporarily vanished. Ted looked extremely well, with as much faint color in his pale face as I'd ever seen.

"Just saw Dan Shields," he announced. "We were talking about your one-round decision last night. Congratulations! But I'd dye my hair blue and grow a shovel beard if I were you. Do you know who you knocked out?"

"Unfortunately I do," I replied, and relayed what Reynolds had told me. Helmholtz listened with uncommon attention. Then he said soberly:

"Forget it, Howie. Shields told me he didn't think Thomas had an idea who hit him. He was too drunk. When he came around he drank a lot of coffee, never said a word, and drove a big lavender Cadillac east at two this morning. I wouldn't worry."

I really wasn't. I was thinking of something else and very foolishly ventured a random shot at Helmholtz just to see if it registered.

"Who's that little spitfire working with Selma?" I asked casually. "She was going for Thomas herself but I got there first. Reynolds took quite a shine to her. Somebody called her Lisa."

Have you ever lit a quick fuse on a small firecracker that almost went off in your hand? That's the effect I got from Helmholtz. He turned white. His eyes cut me to pieces.

"Reynolds!" he said gratingly. "What's he got to do with Lisa? And her last name's Maddon, Howie," he added savagely. So it was Lisa, as intimately as that, and not even Lisa Maddon, or even remotely Miss Maddon.

"Forget it, Ted," I said abruptly. "Reynolds and I just noted that Miss Maddon's a very pretty girl. Reynolds is crazy about Selma. Didn't you know?"

Helmholtz looked at me suspiciously, but he seemed somewhat reassured and I breathed easier. We went to a row of garages behind the hotel and Ted brought out a car belonging to his partner Gustavson, a Hudson Hornet that his friend frequently drove to Oakland on business. I was surprised to find that Ted was an excellent driver. The car was very fast. We drove the fifty-six miles to Virginia City in forty-five minutes.

54

We sped across Carson Valley, past the sparse and sad remains of that famous old pike, the Virginia and Truckee, and then spiraled up the highway through Devil's Gate, Gold Hill, and on into the mute and time-worn tumble-down structures of Virginia City, tossed like a bundle or two of old shingles against the steep flanks of Mount Davidson. We drove past cement ruins and ancient tailings and slag piles, stopping sharply before a small new galvanized iron office shack bearing a neat sign: "Gustavson & Helmholtz, Inc. Ophir No. 3, Lease B6594. Office."

Unusually solemn, Ted ushered me out of the car.

"Welcome to the Comstock, Bierce," he said gravely. I stood beside him, struck by his expression, as he briefly pointed out to me some of the famous old town's familiar landmarks to the east and south—Robbers' Roost, Sugar Loaf, Six Mile Canyon, Seven Mile Canyon, the ancient cemetery to our left, and to our right the still impressive old Occidental mine structures on a distant slope.

"Those with memories tread softly here," continued Helmholtz. "The ghosts of Ralston's Ring, the shades of Gould, Curry, Flood, O'Brien, Mackay, of Hale and Norcross, Best and Belcher, of the Yellow Jacket, the Chollar-Potosi, and the Savage, hover around us."

He really seemed to believe it and solemnly doffed his hat. Partly for Ted, and partly out of respect for that vanished and amazing throng who had created Virginia City and its incredible legends, I did the same. After this brief ceremony, Helmholtz ushered me into a sparsely furnished office.

A morose-looking young clerk was studying a blueprint tacked to a draughting table. But before us stood a huge, stocky, towheaded individual that Helmholtz introduced as his partner. Gustavson crushed my right hand to a pulp and gave me a gold-tinted toothy smile that almost blinded me. I liked him at once. Helmholtz made a little speech.

"Howie, this is Pete Gustavson. Likes to tear the earth apart. South African gold mines. Chilean copper mines. More recently, from the Flin Flon mines in upper Manitoba, near The Pas. Knows every rock and shaft in Colorado. He drives cars like a madman, flies planes, once owned a snowmobile around Hudson Bay which he palmed off on some hotel owner in these parts. And he still wants to own a fruit ranch back home in Colorado."

This was no transient mine promoter with a sucker list. Gustavson had a pair of remarkably large and clear gray eyes. His broad heavy face seemed carved from some ruddy Scandinavian granite. He was roughly dressed and waiting for us. Above all, he impressed me as a man who knew at all times exactly what he was doing. A strange partner for Helmholtz, I reflected, and then caught what seemed to me an affectionately paternal role that he assumed towards my friend. Gustavson informed Ted they were expected at a law office in Carson City within two hours. A deal had been made to purchase some used drilling equipment in Oakland. Once the papers were signed we would drive back together and Gustavson would drop us off at the Gap.

Helmholtz was now a figure of bustling efficiency and animation. "Fine. Fine. But give us an hour, Pete. I want to show Bierce our gallery—and what's under that hill."

He pointed out the window at the gaunt slashed flanks of Mount Davidson, and the serried staggering rows of Virginia City structures that clung to it. Gustavson grinned.

"Sure. I have some letters to write." He looked at me. "You'll get wet. The dam shaft leaks like a sieve."

He walked over to a steel locker, opened the door, and tossed out galoshes, two sou'westers and oilskins, typical fishermen's outfits. Helmholtz and I put them on while Gustavson picked up a Coleman lamp and lit it for us. He called to the clerk and turned to us.

"Better take Harry along to work the winch." He introduced us to Harry Sherman, a local boy, who looked completely bored with his job. Gustavson also gave us a couple of small electric torches and another gold-toothed grin as we started off across unfenced lots of slag and tailings, shattered timbers, and the weather-beaten wreck of an ancient lift. Helmholtz was as excited as a small boy. A hundred yards from his office he directed me into a small timbered horizontal shaft leading directly into a lower flank of Mount Davidson. Turning on my torch, I plunged in, allowing Sherman to walk ahead with the Coleman lantern. My interest in our little expedition rose at once. I had visited the tourist side of Virginia City, aboveground, on several occasions, and both Betty and I had long been interested in the picturesque past of the famous old town. But for the first time I now realized there were two Virginia Cities, one aboveground and once upon a time an extraordinary concentration of wealth and men, the other an underground city burrowing into the bowels of a fabulous mountain. Both communities had been feverishly busy a generation or two ago.

The amazing Comstock Lode, the greatest mass of precious metal ever discovered by man, was not, as many still believe, a single solid body of gold- and silver-bearing ore. The Lode was a tremendous mass of clay, quartz, rock, porphyry and volcanic materials, over two miles long and much of it barren, but with fabulous bodies of precious metals scattered through it, as old John Mackay put it, "like plums in a charity pudding." And the search for those plums, as shaft after shaft was sunk into the Lode, east, west, north, south, the frustrations and failures, the small pickings and the great bonanzas created the vivid epic of Virginia City and the Comstock.

The Ophir bonanza, whose ruins we were entering, was discovered in 1859 close to the surface, creating a sensation although never a millionaire. But it led the great parade of shafts bearing famous names that bored into the Lode from north to south all the way to Gold Hill—Consolidated Virginia, Best and Belcher, Gould and Curry, the Savage, Hale and Norcross, Chollar-Potosi, Imperial, Yellow Jacket, Kentuck, Crown Point, Belcher, and many others.

Close to the Ophir and part of the Ophir bonanza was the old Mexican mine, worked by Mexicans who never timbered their diggings but left pillars of ore in the stopes to hold up the roofs. These finally crumbled and the whole mine caved from top to bottom in 1863, seriously damaging the Ophir works. A new joint Ophir-Mexican shaft was sunk later but produced nothing but floods of hot water.

It was Gustavson, salvaging metal during World War II, who stumbled on a choked incline leading down into the combined wreck of these two all but obliterated mines, spotted a fragment of rich vein in No. 7 gallery, and for almost a song obtained a year's lease from an absentee owner of the property. A small power generator, low wattage bulbs, six men, and a marine hoisting winch now comprised the Gustavson and Helmholtz venture.

Their domain, as we stumbled down the treacherous incline, was dank, dark, muggy, full of dripping water and fallen rock. Helmholtz finally stopped beside some rough cribbing. A hoisting cable disappeared down a jagged bottomless hole.

"We're going down there?" I protested.

"That we are," replied Ted shortly. And down we went, with a sickening rush, cowering on a small slippery wooden platform and clinging to the cable. We stopped abruptly at a massive loading platform and entered another low tunnel, dimly lit by a few small bulbs. There was blue-black muck and humid heat all about us. It was getting hotter all the time. I caught a little of Ted's excitement. I had never really visualized what it meant to tear out the rocky heart of this remarkable mountain. Far above us, on the wind-swept Washoe slopes, had risen Virginia City in the days of its glory with opera, theater, and culture rubbing shoulders with miners, drovers, brokers, gamblers, and thousands of Chinese. There above us once stood the International House, boasting the first elevators west of Chicago, jammed with celebrities, with Mark Twain and Dan DeQuille extolling its glories while hard-rock millionaires enthusiastically ordered carloads of oysters, carefully iced, all the way from Long Island a week after the first transcontinental railroad was completed.

Far below this fabulous town and out of this black volcanic world we were exploring, the wealth had poured. I touched a wall of solid rock and it was like a warm stove lid. Helmholtz was watching me.

"The first hinges of hell," he commented. "The whole region was once a chaos of lava and volcanic fires. What remained raised hob with the mines. Hot springs flooded them. At some levels the miners worked in half-hour shifts in 130 degrees of heat. Sutro's great tunnel to drain and ventilate all the shafts was the answer. But it came too late."

Pete's small leased gallery opened suddenly to our right. Here half a dozen men, the entire working force of Gustavson & Helmholtz, picked the last crumbs of the Comstock, loading loose rock into a single bucket car perched on pitted rails. Stripped to the waist, bearded, spiritless, and ghostlike, they looked like tired bindle stiffs to me as they slid about in a blue-gray paste of muck and hot water. Helmholtz greeted them briefly and then turned to me. I sensed some inner tension had increased within him.

"My two thousand bucks is right here, Howie. Pete spotted the remnants of a rich vein in that right wall. It's good for a few months, that's all, but it will fulfill its purpose."

He said this grimly, as if its purpose meant far more than a pleasant profit for the little firm. Then he beckoned to me.

"Come through this tunnel. I'll show you something few men of this generation have ever seen—a portion of the world's greatest single memorial to man's profit motive. Keep your head down."

Swinging the Coleman at his side, Ted plunged into a low unlighted tunnel shooting off at a sharp tangent from the working gallery. We stumbled through this half-ruined shaft, full of rock, loose gravel, and pools of stagnant water. It twisted, turned upon itself, wandered about like a drunken man. It was propped, shored up, lined and jammed with huge ancient beams, some of them twenty-four inches square. They stood horizontal, vertical, at every conceivable angle, bolted and spiked, torn apart, crushed, and bent here and there by tremendous internal pressures. These great beams had been slashed from the Sierra forest, hauled from Lake Tahoe and more distant points down into the Carson Valley, up the windswept Washoe hills, then cut, squared, angled, and thrust by the tens of thousands into these shafts to hold up the remnants of a gutted mountain.

Every few feet we passed abandoned galleries and drifts, some of them boarded up, others with crudely lettered signs of warning: "Keep Out"—"Closed"—"Dangerous"—"Caved In." And always "Keep Out!"—"Keep Out!"

A bad cave-in confronted us, almost filling the tunnel. A muddy footpath crawled across the flank of this mass of fallen rock. A larger more official sign announced: "Closed! Passage By Permit Only."

We had no permit but Helmholtz crawled on for a short distance. I followed with real misgivings. I had had enough of this mole-like

58

existence. I came up to Helmholtz noticing he had stopped abruptly. So did our tunnel. It simply fell away in shadowy darkness. A splintered rail, showing traces of ancient red paint, barred our way. I heard water dripping far above us, and far below. Helmholtz held the Coleman high.

"Stand beside me, Howie," he said. "Flash your torch over there and look up."

I did so. The Coleman's steady white light and the slender shaft of my electric torch thrust back the shadows above us and showed me one of the most magnificent and profoundly funereal spectacles of utter and impressive ruin that I had ever witnessed. The effect was beyond description.

Far above us, tier on tier, in ragged grandeur, the gaunt dripping skeleton of an underground skyscraper, abandoned in midconstruction, rose in a vast and colossal web of timbered levels, a forest of squat squared timbers, a formidable latticework that rose and rose from level to level until there seemed no end to it. The whole mass vanished in shadow so far above us that our puny illumination could not expose its limits.

The spectacle astonished me so that I stepped back and grasped Ted's arm.

"What in God's name is it?"

Helmholtz said soberly, "That, my friend, is where the Ophir bonanza once slept for centuries. There stood a portion of the Comstock Lode, the greatest mass of precious metal ever raped by man. Two miles long under Virginia, Gold Hill, and Devil's Gate. Forced up by volcanic fires and hot springs between hanging walls of granite. From forty to a thousand feet wide. Higher than cathedral towers. The Comstock Lode. Gone, gutted, torn from its embryo. Sierra forests, sawed and squared—a chap named Philip Diedesheimer invented the method in the sixties—fill the void and buttress and support the remains of a ravaged mountain.

"Looks like the clean picked bones of some colossal skeleton, doesn't it? Well, it is. All through the Lode men hacked out more than thirty miles of galleries and stopes. Thousands of muscled miners crawled up and down those ladders, blasted their way through miles of drifts and tunnels, digging and dying in floods, quakes, cave-ins, scalding water, and in falls down bottomless shafts. Out of this empty forgotten womb was hacked the Comstock bonanzas, in the strange alchemy of our society to be translated into mountains of currency that helped pay for the Civil War, that altered relations between dozens of nations, that built Nob Hill, the Palace Hotel, and most of San Francisco: that founded fortunes, telegraph companies, newspapers, transportation systems, Fifth Avenue mansions, yachts, and art galleries; that pushed into the world's financial currents like the

Johnstown Flood with a thunderous impact felt to this day. And the solid core of all this fabulous wealth once slept for countless ages right before you."

I was now profoundly aware that this venture of Helmholtz possessed a strange and powerful significance for him, that its spell and attraction sprang from sources within him, deep, obscure, and completely concealed from my own limited vision.

Helmholtz remarked casually, "That's one view of Virginia City you won't find on a post card. Now step forward, not too close, and look down."

He swung the Coleman over the lip of the broken gallery where we stood. I looked down and flinched. There was complete chaos a hundred feet below us and beneath the man-made mountain of timber rising above us. The great cave-in of '63 and a great underground shift or quake had shaken this forest of timbers at its base and flung masses of heavy logs about like shattered toothpicks. Battered mounds of earth, rock, and broken timber had been forced into fantastic shapes by tremendous pressures. Against a wall of solid rock huge timbers lay shredded, shattered, matted together. Others were bent like bows. Below and to the left a mass of rock and timber bulged out like a tortured bubble about to burst. To me it seemed likely to explode at any moment with destructive force, though the original disturbance had probably occurred half a century ago or more. I looked, but not for long.

"That's enough," I said firmly. "I want to get out." I had seen the empty ravaged womb of the Comstock. But I was not anxious to see it again.

Helmholtz silently led the way back to the lift, an apparently endless trip. He rang the bell and we started up that interminable dripping shaft. I said nothing. There was something terribly depressing about these dripping sweltering ruins. I began to feel as if we were riding our own coffin through an endless grave. Then we saw gray light and finally the blank face of the young clerk looking down at us. Fifteen minutes later we emerged into sunlight. I blinked, dazzled by the blinding light, and breathed deeply, wondering what incredible impulse turned sane men into miners. I was covered with perspiration, dirty water, and blue-black mud to my ankles.

"Ted," I said seriously, though I managed a smile, "you're madder than the Mad Hatter. The Comstock's gone. The Ophir's a wreck. Can you honestly make a sound dime out of that mudhole?"

"I think so."

"Well," I said grimly, "it's one hell of a way to make a living."

Ted's features hardened unexpectedly. I was astonished by the change in him. "Is it?" he asked sharply. Then he said something very strange. "I'm rolling the stone away from a tomb, Howie. I failed once. But now I'm going to do it. Nothing can stop me this time."

I had no idea what he was talking about. I didn't ask him. His whole mood was beyond my limited powers of analysis. I realized, too, that his mood was one into which I had no real wish to inquire. I preferred Helmholtz and his music and conversation aboveground, not Helmholtz as he was now, groping about, I suspected, in the shadow of some haunting past, his own or another's.

There were crude showers and hot water behind the office. We washed up. Then with Gustavson we started back to Carson, facing a bitter Washoe wind blasting up through Devil's Gate. Gustavson spoke only once. He must have sensed my mood.

"It is something to see and remember, that Comstock."

I nodded. Gustavson continued, "Down there many of the old mines run together. There have been great cave-ins. I found one shaft that comes out through the old Mexican mine, closed down in 1867, not far below our office. But"—he shrugged—"it is no place to go."

I felt strangely subdued and glanced at Ted's expressionless face. Something was driving my friend. He was deadly and intensely serious about this mine, far and above the concern motivated by the modest sum he had invested. Briefly and elusively, I felt as if I had encountered some dark boarded-up shaft in Helmholtz himself. But it was a shaft, I decided, I had no desire to explore.

We stopped in Carson City for an hour and I draped myself over the Cowboy Bar while Helmholtz and Pete visited their lawyers in offices on the second floor. Their conference lasted quite a while and I got through two or three drinks. The bartender, noting my boredom, struck up a conversation.

"Friend of Mr. Gustavson?" he inquired. I confirmed this casually.

He nodded. "A smart man. The only engineer who has taken any money out of Virginia City since before the war. We thought he was crazy—until last month."

"What happened last month?" I asked.

"You'll have to ask him for the figures," smiled my new acquaintance, "but he told several of us right here they took out over fifteen hundred dollars a week, absolutely clear, for six weeks. And Pete's no liar."

I agreed, and thoughtfully considered what I had seen. When Ted and Gustavson finally walked in I set up drinks for them and then made a brief address.

"Mr. Gould and Mr. Curry," I said gravely, "I want to invest three grand in that hole of yours."

Gustavson took it as a joke, but Helmholtz regarded me intently.

"Are you serious, Howie? What's happened?"

61

I absolved the bartender but told them what had occurred. Both men laughed and glanced at one another. Helmholtz seemed embarrassed.

"Look, Howie, I didn't drag you up here to salt some old diggings and rope you in. That wasn't the idea at all. I wanted to show you those ruins of the Comstock."

"I know that," I retorted.

Helmholtz still balked. "That remnant of a vein Pete spotted can peter out in forty-eight hours."

Gustavson grunted dissent, but he qualified his disagreement with Ted by adding:

"It is a small vein, Mr. Bierce, and it won't last too long."

"But if it lasts six months you'll make a small fortune. Can you use more capital?"

"Absolutely," said Gustavson before Ted could reply.

I pushed hard. I just happened to have about thirty-three hundred dollars of idle money lying around, and the whole venture with Gustavson's solidity to back it up caught my imagination. I couldn't lose at the rate they were going, and I might pick up some easy and pleasant velvet. And Ted gave in unexpectedly, turning to Gustavson.

"Is it all right, Pete?"

Gustavson nodded, smiling warmly. "Sure it is. I'm for it."

Helmholtz looked me over soberly. "All right, Howie, we'll fix up the deal in a day or two. You're in. Pete really spotted something."

"Maybe. Maybe," said Gustavson carefully. "You won't lose a penny, Mr. Bierce, but it is hard to say how long that fragment of vein will last."

Excited by the day's tangible communings with the ghosts of the Comstock, we celebrated our deal with several drinks and then piled into the Hornet with Gustavson at the wheel. Pete seemed untouched by four double bourbons, put the speedometer needle at eighty-five, and held it there with a colossal indifference to curves, grades, or speed restrictions. When we arrived at Pioneer Gap the clear sky had vanished. It was dark and beginning to snow. Gustavson looked soberly aloft.

"Ted, I'm going to cut over to Truckee and take Route 40. It's faster. And it's going to storm. If it keeps up I may leave the car at Oakland and come back by train Tuesday." He turned to me. "And welcome to the firm, Mr. Bierce."

Gustavson looked at the sky again, then at us, and a warm and friendly smile creased his broad face.

"Yah," he said with sudden accent, "it is going to snow like hell. I think."

5

Gustavson was right. It snowed all night. But I never knew it. All the tensions of recent weeks caught up with me and I slept around the clock and more. It must have been eleven the next morning when Maria came up to investigate my unending slumber. She brought coffee and corn bread with her and announced that some of my things had come in on the morning train and she would send them up. She even urged me to stay in bed all day and commented accusingly as she went out:

"I never saw you so tired. Rest here all you can."

I intended to. I wasn't only tired. As I glanced out the dormer window and saw snow still falling in a white silent world, I suspected I had been close to a bit of nervous exhaustion. And that weird trip to the Comstock with Helmholtz hadn't helped matters any. This reminded me that I was a pledged partner in his crazy mine. What Betty would have thought of my latest aberration was best left unexplored. I was certainly operating on some queer tangents. Crawling over to the mirror near the window, I recoiled from my own reflection. I preferred the face of nature, and for some time studied the view from the west window looking towards Sentinel Peak.

But Sentinel Peak wasn't visible. I was gazing at a curtain of soft slowly falling snow against a gray background. The depth of snow was surprising. I looked at a caressingly silent scene. Two cars moved without a sound up the short stretch of visible highway. All the world was muffled, purified, serene. A Mallet whistled in the yards. The deep rich tones seemed filtered through cotton wool. Winter had struck early at the Hill. I could imagine what had been going on while I slept. Shovelers called out. Men on the extra board ordered to stand by. Probably several flangers, spreaders, and a rotary plow or two headed up the Hill in case it continued to snow. But studying the sky, I judged the present storm was about over.

Then a maid knocked at the door and handed me my things with a message that Reynolds was arriving later and hoped to have supper with me. I guessed he was coming in on 20. He had done a good job, packing everything I would need for a month in a couple of suitcases and a valet-pack. I was also amused as I watched the maid come in a second time with my snowshoes, which Reynolds had added to my inventory. I hadn't used them in years and smiled at this extreme presentiment of his. Later I had occasion to recall that smile.

Unpacking my paints and heavy clothes, I began to pick up energy. As soon as it stopped snowing I planned to take a sketch pad and push up the tracks past Rainbow Cliff to Gunnison Gate, a grim cutting through lava rock by which the G.W. thrust into the upper reaches of Wildroot Valley.

A couple of miles to the west squatted a picturesque yellow shanty at the west switch, usually inhabited by a grizzled old Killarney chow named Flanagan. I had always wanted to sketch Flanagan and his pipe against the magenta-colored rocks of Gunnison Gate and far-off Sentinel Peak. There was something in Flanagan and his shanty, at least to me, which symbolized the isolated drama and winter struggle between the Great Western and the High Sierras.

Sure enough, by two o'clock it had stopped snowing and a little later, with more coffee and a trio of Selma's scrambled eggs under my belt and a sketchbook under my arm, I was trudging up the rails under an astonishingly dark and lowering sky, a great gray mass of solid cloud moving rapidly out of the west. Twenty minutes more and it began to rain, a steady soaking rain. I swore and pulled down the ear flaps of a heavy hunting cap.

In a usually colorful scene there was almost no color at all on this dark day. Nothing but stark whites, light and dark grays, shading from white to black, and the somber bleak lines of pines and dark rocks under the heavy overcast. Almost every form of Sierra tree seemed to flourish here in Wildroot Valley. Alders and willows along the stream, recently golden with autumn yellows, were now slim black skeletons etched against snowy backgrounds. On the lower slopes rose fir trees, with beautifully tapered cones, their thickset needles holding pillows of snow. Above them the cedars, flexible, pliant, often bending low beneath their heavy burdens of snow but determinedly sloughing them off until they stood proudly upright again. The yellow pines, with beautifully designed thin needles that sifted falling snow, wet or dry, straight to the ground, appeared as fresh and green as they did in summer.

Highest of all, high on the far heights and timberline frontiers, like distant relatives of the cedars, rose the tall slender tamaracks, the lodgepole pines of Yellowstone and Jackson Hole, and nature's most beautifully designed tree for high altitudes. The tall tapering tamaracks fought the full force of every storm. Frequently they bent in tight arcs all the way to the ground under heavy weights of snow, only to fling this snow violently into the air in prismatic showers, released like long bows and springing upright again with only a powdering of glittering crystals upon their needles. They lived vigorously, triumphantly.

Plodding onward, studying these trees while the rain came down harder than ever, I reached a section shanty and stepped off the rails to watch a work train pass. A light engine with a pilot plow, hauling a flanger, crew car, and caboose chuffed by me. The plow thrust two plumes of flying snow to either side. Heavy smoke billowed high from the stack, then fell quickly back and drifted heavily along the flanks of nearby hills, filtering in gray wisps among the pines. That meant a low barometer and more snow, I reflected, wondering how soon I'd have a sunny day for painting.

I trudged past Rainbow Cliff, a stratified colorful bluff, but a dirty gray today, just south of the rails. I now looked straight up Wildroot Valley to Eldorado Summit. In my humble opinion this was one of the most ruggedly dramatic views in the High Sierras, far surpassing the genuine grandeur of Donner Summit. Those familiar with the steep eastern approach to Tioga Pass, leading up from Mono Lake to the Yosemite hinterland, may have a rough idea of the scene confronting me. As the crow flies, Eldorado Pass—the railroad always called it Eldorado Summit—and Sentinel Peak were less than six miles away. But by rail it was more than twelve miles to the smoke-filled snowsheds that crept over the backbone of the Sierras.

Directly ahead of me was a two-hundred-foot-high wall of dark magenta-colored lava rock, so symmetrical and evenly leveled that it resembled man-made masonry. In its exact center in recent centuries Wildroot Creek had slashed a savage little canyon, perhaps sixty feet wide, through which the G.W. thrust its rails into the steep valley beyond. This rocky passage was called Gunnison Gate. Through this natural gate a striking optical illusion confronted the spectator. Across the broad flank of Sentinel Peak, two or three miles away, he saw three tiers of rails, each several hundred feet above the other, and with no apparent link by which traffic could make these tremendous leaps. The key to this impossible ascent lay in three long narrow V-shaped valleys which cut far south of Wildroot Creek. The rails followed each valley a couple of miles south, always climbing, then back again on a higher level. Without these providential valleys the ascent would have been impossible. As it was, it remained a heartbreaking climb.

As I approached the yellow switch shanty the rain slacked off to a cold drizzle. The spectacle was all I could wish for. The shanty was a bright yellow hexagon, of ancient vintage, trimmed in black with a red stovepipe and black cap projecting at a rakish angle from its roof. From this diminutive stack wisps of light blue smoke drifted lazily away. The shanty looked for all the world like a cocky Irishman smoking an impudent pipe, and Flanagan, I was sure, was inside taking his ease. As I looked up at Sentinel Peak the work train that had passed me puffed up the first high level of rails like a child's train on a toy railroad.

One item interested me at once. Sentinel Peak resembled a ghostly volcano. A long spectacular plume of wind-driven snow leveled straight off the summit towards the southeast. I looked over at Mount Rogers and Mount McGregor and noted the same effect. A tremendous wind must be blowing up there a few thousand feet above this silent snow-mantled valley.

I shouted at the shanty. "Hi, Flanagan! Anybody home?"

Someone answered me. Then the door opened. But it wasn't Flanagan. A pleasant-faced young Mexican lad I had never seen before looked out, seemed surprised to see me, and greeted me shyly. He was wearing a red ski cap, an unbuttoned great coat, blue denims tucked in high rubber overshoes, and he had been cleaning a pair of snow glasses that dangled in one hand.

"Where's Flanagan?" I asked. "What's your name?"

"My name is Ricardo D'Alvarez. Flanagan is sick. He has the flu. I'm working his shift for a few days. Anything I can do?"

I told him who I was. I could see he couldn't figure out what a Road Foreman of Engines was doing at this lonely spot with a lot of drawing equipment under one arm. I didn't blame him. He hesitated, then invited me in to get warm if I wished. It wasn't a bad idea, and I entered the little shanty and sat down. The shanty was neat and snug. It contained a bench covered with black oilcloth, a small potbellied stove, a coal and wood box, two chairs, and several shelves stocked with canned goods, flares, torpedoes, lanterns, Y hi-speeder hoops, and other gear. A pot of coffee and a pan of bean soup simmered on the stove. All in all, a snug retreat from the stark country outside. I looked at the young switchman with interest.

"D'Alvarez? Any relation to Mrs. D'Alvarez of the Casa Alta?"

The youngster smiled.

"Yes, sir. She is my aunt." I told him what I was up to, as he looked curiously at my sketchbook, and he became friendly at once. He was a handsome boy, and as he talked with animation about Maria I realized he was an excellent subject for a sketch. Ricardo was only one of many Mexicans—and Nisei, too—carefully selected by the G.W. for section gangs and track maintenance work. You would never believe Mexicans, from a subtropical country six hundred miles south, could become such confirmed and enthusiastic mountain dwellers. Whisked from their palm-fringed southern homes they suddenly found themselves perched in eagle-like eyries, clusters of company cottages connected by snow tunnels, and clinging to the sheer sides of Sierra peaks at high altitudes with avalanches and slides often thundering down nearby slopes. Both Mexicans and Nisei throve on the life. Ricardo, studying husbandry during his evenings on some correspondence course, was returning to Sonora in another year to run his family's fruit ranch. But at the moment I certainly puzzled him. A road official with a sketch pad and nothing else on his mind was something that seldom appeared at the west switch, on the G.W. or any other pike.

Again it rained hard, beating such a tattoo on the shanty roof that I knew I wasn't going to do any outdoor sketching. Ricardo was a willing subject and I went to work. Eldorado Summit, he informed me, looked for more freezing and a lot more snow that night and I figured Reynolds would be in for a busy week on the Hill.

We thoroughly enjoyed ourselves. But at four o'clock I knocked off. The light was bad and it would be dark in half an hour. At the same time I heard a steam drag coming down the Hill and Ricardo got up. He looked eagerly at my sketch pad, and smiled shyly. "Can I see them?"

"Sure," I replied. "Pick any one you want. And one of these days I'd like to do a small painting of you for Maria."

He was delighted and looked over my half dozen pencil sketches critically and with no self-consciousness at all. One, the first, was no good and he spotted it at once.

"I don't look like that. I don't really feel like that."

"Right," I said, and tore it up, to his dismay. The rest weren't bad, and he promptly picked the best of the lot.

The Mallet, quite close, whistled loud and long for the passing track. Ricardo put on his gloves and went out to line up the rails. As he did so he informed me this was 484, a regular eastbound freight. It would take the siding to allow two other eastbound trains to pass—a superior train, Extra 52, a fast special drag of eastbound reefers full of Central Valley fruit, and No. 20, the Sierra Limited. Both trains would run around 484 at the Gap. I decided to stay inside the shanty. Some of the engine crew might recognize me and wonder what in the devil I was doing out here.

The Mallet rumbled past and took the passing track, shaking the shanty with its weight. A half mile of swaying clanking boxcars, their brake shoes red-hot from the sudden descent from Summit and clouds of acrid blue smoke rising from smoking wheels in the cold air, followed the Mallet into the siding. I looked through the west window at Sentinel Peak and saw the novel sight of Extra 52, Diesel-drawn, halfway down the mountain in the fading light just as the sleek orange cars of the Sierra Limited slid out of the snowsheds on the top tier of rails. Reynolds was aboard it, no doubt.

I went to the door. The rain had turned to light sleet. Over Sentinel Peak a great wall of black cloud, edged with white, was driving towards me. We were in for some rough weather. The train passing me had slowed to ten or fifteen miles. The caboose was still a long way from the shanty. I quickly made up my mind. I wasn't going to walk back to the Casa Alta in this weather. I tossed my sketchbook and pencils on the bench and called to Ricardo.

"I'm hopping a ride, Ricardo. Look after this stuff, will you? I'll be back tomorrow or Wednesday. Okay?"

Ricardo flashed his white teeth. "Sure thing, Mr. Bierce. Any time at all. It was nice to meet you."

I walked close to the train and waited for a couple of tank cars headed my way, seized the grab iron on the first one, and swung off the ground with no difficulty at all at that low speed. I pushed back and sat down under the overhang of the tank, which protected me against the driving sleet. We rattled leisurely along for about a mile or more and then stopped. I figured the Mallet had parked under the water spout just east of the station and we weren't going any farther. So I got off almost opposite the Casa Alta and at the west end of the station platform. As I did so I saw Lisa hurry out of the hotel and cross the street, heading towards me and the station with a handful of letters. She saw me and smiled briefly. On an impulse I greeted her and offered to mail her letters. She actually smiled a little.

"Oh, I need the air," she replied.

"Mind if I go along?" I asked.

She glanced up at me. "Not at all. Where have you been?"

"Just sketching a bit. Look out for that ice." We were walking along the blacktop platform, raised in the center for drainage and slanting off to the rails on either side. It was still sleeting and freezing fast. Behind us 20's rich whistle echoed down the valley, quite close. Just at that moment I got a surprise.

On the far side of the station to our left a lone Mallet helper pulled in from Placer, and down from its head-end cab climbed Reynolds and several trainmen. I had thought Reynolds was coming in from Belknap on 20 just behind me. Reynolds caught sight of us at once, probably recognized Lisa, and headed our way, walking rapidly with the westbound rails between us. I looked back and saw 20's headlight bearing down on us not two hundred yards away on the eastbound rails. I took Lisa by the arm and walked her carefully in the center of that ice-sheeted platform. It should have been sanded a long time ago.

Then a dramatic little scene occurred so unexpectedly I could hardly grasp it. No. 20 was pulling rapidly abreast of us, to our right. Across the rails to our left hurried Reynolds. I heard him call, "Hi, Bierce, get your stuff all right?" He suddenly jumped from the snow and slush between the rails to our platform. I yelled, "Look out for that ice, Jim."

I was too late. Reynolds hit that ice-crusted blacktop on our platform and kept right on going—towards No. 20, not a score of yards away. He almost stopped, but not quite. He half caught his balance, then slowly slid, like a skater vainly trying to recover from a certain fall, his arms and legs flailing the air, headed for the rails and 20's oncoming pilot. The huge bulk of 20's helper, its headlight throwing a white glare on Reynolds and the gleaming platform ice, loomed over us.

I stood there, paralyzed. Lisa didn't. She hurled herself away from me like some projectile, her letters scattering like forgotten leaves. She rushed straight at Reynolds, her arms extended, her hands outspread. Her hands caught Reynolds in the small of his back and gave him a tremendous shove. He was simply propelled at high speed right across the rails not ten feet in front of the fast-moving pilot of 20. Lisa, unable to stop, flung herself across the track right behind him. Then the black bulk of the engine pounded past me and cut them from my sight.

With my heart pounding I took my own chances and snatched at the grab iron at the rear of the tender as it ground by me. I made it with a terrific wrench of my right arm and then scrambled across the buffers between tender and mail car, leaping to the ground on the other side. I was frankly terrified. I couldn't believe the girl and Reynolds had missed the huge bulk of that engine. And I had a final shock. At first I couldn't see either of them. Then, looking back I saw two figures lying flat on their backs in the shallow drainage ditch filled with two or three feet of slush. I was sure they had been tossed there by the pilot. I ran towards them. As I did so Lisa sat up and so did Reynolds. They were both a bit dazed and Reynolds was as white as the snow about him. He got up by himself while I pulled Lisa to her feet. Neither of them was even scratched. I was breathing hard and shaking. None of us said a word for several moments. I remember looking up at the bulk of the halted train behind us and seeing several astonished passengers peering down at us, their faces outlined in the glare of lights behind them, pressed against the windows. We must have looked like three drunks. We walked shakily towards the rear of the train. Reynolds finally said something.

"Well, Miss Maddon, for what it's worth, you saved my life. Do you always think as fast as that? You all right?"

"I'm all right, I guess," she said in a low voice.

They were both soaked to the skin. We got around the rear of the train and walked forward to try to find Lisa's letters. As far as I could see there hadn't been a witness to the incident. Later I learned the fireman had his head in the cab, and was working the injector.

We recovered the letters and I advised Lisa and Reynolds to get into dry clothes at once. Then I headed for the mail car. When I got back to my room Reynolds was taking a hot shower. I laid out an outfit for him. He dressed slowly, looking very sober. A little later he glanced a bit guiltily at me.

"One slip on a railroad is all it takes," he observed. "Damn stupid thing I did. I even heard you yell before I jumped."

"That platform is usually sanded. I'm going to give someone hell," I replied, then added, "I thought you were coming in on 20."

He didn't answer me at once. He had plenty to think about. He put on a shirt and tie, then sat down and lighted a cigarette.

"Brother!" he said at last, expelling a cloud of smoke. "That was close. That girl's got a head on her shoulders."

"And a lot of nerve," I added. "I was sure you'd been hit."

"The cylinder head brushed my ears," said Reynolds roughly. Then he added in an almost irrelevant and much milder tone, "I'm buying Miss Maddon the biggest steak in town. Then we're going to the early show. I want to talk to you later."

This was a development and a fast one. Reynolds was almost notorious in his avoidance of women. True, this girl had just saved his life. But I was surprised all the same. I said nothing.

Standing in the lobby a little later, Maria and I watched Lisa and Reynolds walk out together, heading for Marco's, a flashy little restaurant at the other end of town. Maria didn't mind. The fates completed this little tableau by propelling Helmholtz down the main staircase just in time to see Reynolds take Lisa's arm and disappear down the street. Helmholtz froze on the second step from the lobby floor, the color draining from his face. He glanced uncertainly at Maria and me and then, like a stricken man, he slowly turned and walked upstairs again.

Maria touched my arm. "Have dinner with me," she said gravely.

I was very glad to.

6

Afterwards I went up to my room. I hadn't seen Helmholtz again and was in no mood to look for him. I read and puttered around. Shortly after nine Reynolds knocked and entered. His face was a study in frustration. He tossed my coat on the bed and sat down, staring moodily at me. Looking at him with mild inquiry, I said nothing whatever. But I wasn't prepared for his first question.

"What's the matter with that girl?" he demanded abruptly.

"Steak no good?" I asked casually.

"I'm serious, Howie. We had a terrible time. She would hardly talk to me. I'm no gift to women but I tried to put myself out. I'm grateful, damn grateful, for what she did. Haven't done anything as stupid as that since——" He stopped, his eyes darkening. "Something's eating that girl. Deep."

I felt like adding, "And you too, my friend." But Reynolds went on. "She wouldn't even let me take her home. Left me flat in front of the hotel. It was grim, believe me. What's the matter with her?"

"Shock, probably," I suggested. "You'll feel it yourself, later. That wasn't funny, what happened this afternoon."

"It's more than that," said Reynolds thoughtfully. He looked up at me. "Somebody's sewed that girl in a strait jacket."

"Are you going to try to take it off?" I asked mildly. Again Reynolds surprised me.

"By God, I might at that. I might at that," he said with sudden force, staring across the room and rubbing his chin. He had blotted me out. He had the look he always had whenever he was suddenly called out on the Hill. A summons to battle. I was astonished by his reactions and decided I wasn't going to follow them up.

We switched to a small drink apiece and he explained that instead of coming in on the 20 he had had to fly to Reno that morning, then

71

drove to Placer on business, and came in on the westbound helper I'd seen.

"Did you hear from Betty?" he asked, lighting a cigarette while I poured more Old Grand-Dad into my faucet-water highball. I summed up my situation, assured him everything was fine, and thanked him for his services. I made no mention of my trip to Virginia City. Or of Helmholtz. Reynolds, I decided, was going to do most of the talking.

"Only one thing wrong with your layout here," he observed wryly. "You better not hang around too long. Somebody will put you to work. Maybe me. For instance, I wish you'd talk to Rykoff in a couple of days." Old "Run-Around" Rykoff was one of our best engineers, handling streamliners east and west. "Wharton bumped into something. Rykoff ran 501 a mile past Battle Canyon last week. Had to back up to make his stop. Not reported."

"Who covered him?" I asked sharply. Running a streamliner past a designated stop was something new for Rykoff. Reynolds told me The Brains, an old conductor and friend of Rykoff, had covered for him and swore the train crew to silence. Rykoff was due to retire in three weeks and everybody liked him. I told Reynolds that I would talk to him. I was curious myself.

Reynolds finally got up, looking very restless and tired. He ran a hand over his hair, then stretched out his arms and clenched and unclenched his fingers several times, as if taking limbering-up exercises. When he straightened his back he grimaced. As if he changed his mind he sat down again.

"She's got strong hands," he said out of nowhere. "My spine's up front." He was looking right past me. Then he took another tangent. "You know, Howie, I seldom get hunches—but I think we're in for a mighty rough time on the Hill."

As if to emphasize his observation the wind suddenly boomed about the eaves. Snow and sleet drove with new force against the dormer window.

"You mean weather?" I asked.

"Weather. Traffic. A lot of things," he snapped. "We've still got eleven engines in the shops, figuring things would hold off till January. A while back the War Department gave us three weeks' notice to move two full divisions—thirty-three thousand officers, men, and equipment—over the Hill between December 10 and 24. Headed for West Coast camps. That's seventy-five trains for each division, my friend. A real headache. On top of that——"

Reynolds eyed me speculatively. "Fontaine say anything to you last week?"

"What about?" I asked in some surprise. The alert expression on Reynolds' face died away. "Then he didn't," he observed. "Well, you'll probably hear about it. There's a queer deal coming up soon. I'm a bit worried about it."

Reynolds seldom worried about anything. His present mood made me curious, but I said nothing. Already I could feel the octopus arms of the Great Western reaching out for me. I stiffened. Nobody was going to put me to work until I reported for duty on January 15. Reynolds must have read my thoughts.

"Don't worry, Howie. You're safe. But I've got a lot on my chest these days and you're vulnerable. Mind?"

"Nope, I'm open for drinks, steaks, conversation, and advice, when and if requested. All on one condition. Don't ask me to go back on duty until my leave's up." He nodded and I added, "This weather bother you?"

"It's a minor problem just now. Trouble is, this is only the first one, according to the dope."

"Weather Bureau piling up advance predictions?"

"I've got my own weather bureau," said Reynolds with his old cockiness. "Like to meet him? He's a kid in town here."

This was something new to me and I said so. Reynolds smiled for the first time that evening. "I found a radio ham that's a real weather hound," he announced. "Name's Jack Morris. He's a Korean vet, navy radio and electronics. The kid has a house full of radio and electronic equipment that would knock your eyes out."

"What's he got to do with the weather?" I asked curiously.

"It's his hobby. He talks to ships and stations all over the Pacific and started feeding me bulletins a few months ago that had the jump on the air stations and regular forecasts. I see him regularly. He lives on Fort Street. Want to run over with me?"

I agreed but informed Reynolds I was due for a canasta game with Maria, Helmholtz, and Selma at ten-thirty. Reynolds looked at me hard, then laughed.

"Selma, too? Bierce, you sure are on vacation."

"I am," I said firmly. "And I'm going to stay on it. What else is promoting your old age?"

"Lack of sleep," he announced. "We bought those rotaries at Klamath Falls. They'll be down Saturday. But I was up most of the night with Fontaine and MacIntosh." He added absently, obviously thinking of something else, "About that deal I mentioned. We never had anything like it on this pike. It will take some handling." He glanced at me sharply. "You see Thomas around today?"

His apparent shift of subject disconcerted me. I passed on what I had heard. Reynolds nodded and gave me a hard smile.

"You gave Thomas what I'd like to give him tonight. He's trouble. His lawyers were with Fontaine last night. Thomas has just won a suit against the G.W. and Fontaine's fit to be tied. Thomas has his hotel ready to open at Rainbow Valley, has a ski festival planned for January, and just dropped a pile driver on Fontaine by getting final approval for his concrete retaining wall a quarter of a mile long right above our rails. Worst slide area on the pike, too."

I thought of that great and solitary valley, just west of Eldorado Summit and overlooking half of California. It was high, isolated, beautiful, and remote, but full of ideal ski slopes with easy access from the G.W. I wondered all at once why someone hadn't beaten Thomas to it a long time ago.

"What's Fontaine worrying about? Thomas is paying for his wall. He can put it in by June."

"He's putting it in now," retorted Reynolds.

I sat up. "You mean he's excavating and pouring concrete in the middle of a Sierra winter?"

"That's right. Says he'll have it completed in a week. It's costing him fifty thousand dollars. But he doesn't seem to care. I think it was a personal feud with Fontaine. And Thomas won. That's all that matters to him."

"What's the purpose of the wall? Can't the hotel stand up by itself?"

"I don't know why the hurry. But I think he's going to demand a station there when business picks up."

There was something fishy about it to me and Reynolds was as puzzled as I was. He told me Thomas was the front man for an eastern syndicate of big-shot gamblers with interests in Miami and Las Vegas. They had been singed in some Florida deal, were reported in financial difficulties, but they were pouring money into Rainbow Valley, rushing their work to squeeze some money out of the current season.

"Another thing," said Reynolds broodingly, "I don't like these crooks sitting on top of our pike with what's coming up."

By this time I was getting impatient. "Look, Jim, what in the devil *is* coming up? You sound like that radio guy, The Whistler, telling everybody the town's haunted. What's really cooking?"

Reynolds was silent a long time. Then he said contritely, "You're right, Howie. If I can't talk, I can't. I got no business mentioning it at all. Forget it. Let's walk over to Jack's. Then I'm going to turn in."

We buttoned up, walked downstairs and out into the street. I wasn't prepared for the stinging blast of wind and snow that struck us when we rounded the first corner. A forty-mile gale was tearing straight down the valley. Driving snow seemed to be pumped out of some vast bellows. Visibility was about fifty feet. There wasn't a sign of traffic on Route 80. Just a long ribbon of white unmarked velvet. Two trucks, their lights dimmed in a world of swirling white, were parked in front of the coffee shop.

We hunched over, pushed two blocks across town, and then

Reynolds led the way to the side door of a modest frame house. He rang and the door opened at once, though I saw no one open it. We stepped through a small vestibule into a brilliantly lighted study, laboratory, and living room with no rugs, only highly polished linoleum. A good-looking, black-haired chap, with headphones loosely adjusted, sat before rows of panels and controls. He swung about and greeted Reynolds warmly. Then I noticed that he wore heavy braces on both legs and occupied a swivel chair equipped with small rubber-tired wheels. A row of buttons on his desk made me guess he had used one to open the door and others doubtless controlled many other gadgets. I knew little of radio and electronics. But Reynolds was right. A small fortune was invested in this equipment that lined an entire wall of the room. On an adjoining wall hung a series of maps and weather charts, principally of Alaska and the North Pacific all the way to the Kurile Islands and Kamchatka Peninsula.

As Reynolds introduced me to Morris I liked him at once. He waved us to a couple of deep leather chairs, put down his headphones, and lit a cigarette, lounging back in his chair. He said cheerfully:

"Well, Mr. Reynolds, you're in for some fun on the Hill this winter."

Morris emphasized this comment by blowing a cloud of smoke through the room.

"How long's it going to snow, Jack?" asked Reynolds.

"Tomorrow afternoon, probably. But this one's only a starter. Take a look at this."

With a flip of his wrist Morris sent his swivel chair noiselessly spinning across the linoleum to the side wall lined with charts. Using a pencil, he started at Kamchatka Peninsula and Bering Strait and gave us a concise lecture on that fertile weather embryo that generates the great storm fronts creating our western winters.

From Vancouver Island to Kodiak and all the way to northern Japan he had penciled in isotherms and four big circles labeled "Low."

"I'm not kidding, Mr. Reynolds," he said soberly. "There's a lot of ships in that area this week. I've talked to them all. There's one cold front after another—clear across the Pacific. Big ones. Earliest I've seen them like this. They're rolling east like fast ground swells. The weather's not waiting until January. It's on its way now. And it's blowing fifty-five at Summit. You'll have a bigger one next week."

Reynolds looked glumly at me. "You better head south, Howie." He turned to Morris. "Let me talk to Summit, will you?"

"Sure," said Morris, and rolled back to his desk where he handed Reynolds a small pilot phone. He flipped two or three switches on a board before him and added, "Go ahead."

Reynolds picked up the phone and began to talk.

"That you, Gerson? Reynolds. What's the dope? . . . Yep, I just dropped in. He's fine." He listened for a few moments, nodding now and then. "You holding 87 for Second 24 at Placer? How late is 501?" That was the pride of our pike, the westbound streamliner. Reynolds whistled. "Four hours late, huh? Yep. Every plow is out. I'll be up on 87 myself . . . He is, eh? Tell him I'll be there."

Reynolds hung up and smiled ruefully at me. "I hope you enjoy your canasta game. MacIntosh is on his way. Put his car on 502 at Sacramento. Everything's rolling, but late. A work train split a frozen switch at Soldier Canyon and held 501 for three hours. Lost another hour into Placer. This blow is clear into Utah."

Morris nodded. "It's worse up north. I talked to Bill Ensign at Bonner's Ferry. The Great Northern has called out everything they got."

"The hell with it," spat Reynolds disgustedly. But he thought of something, got out one of his little black notebooks, and made several entries in his fine copperplate writing. Then he looked up and grinned at Morris. "Before coffee, Jack, how about showing Mr. Bierce the works?"

"Sure thing," said Morris. "This way to the cellar, gentlemen." He pressed a button, another door opened, and Morris rolled his chair towards a gentle ramp leading down to a brilliantly lighted workshop that extended, unbroken by partitions, the length and breadth of the house. A third of the space was devoted to a beautifully equipped machine shop, with a compact turret lathe that must have cost a small fortune. Shelves against the wall contained a dozen model locomotives, superbly detailed in HO scale, and obviously Morris' handiwork. I examined them with some awe and a great deal of admiration. Each locomotive was a scale model of a Great Western prototype, and each was a little masterpiece.

Walking about the workshop, I encountered more marvels. Morris, with some young enthusiasts aiding him, had constructed a 35- by 20-foot HO scale model layout of the G.W.'s rails over Eldorado Summit. Three years in the making, and the results were startling. Enjoying the impression he was making, Morris sat down at his switchboard and showed us some train operations in miniature. The plastic Sierras were realistic to the last degree, backed up by superb colored photo-murals on the walls. Through snow-covered valleys, past lighted homes, with block signals operating perfectly, Morris ran half a dozen model trains, streamliners, freight drags, limiteds, and a work train replete with lighted windows and two shacks clinging to the rear platform of the crummy. A lighting system created dawns, sunsets, night, and dazzling day. The miniature Placer yards were jammed with rolling stock. There was another small fortune tied up in this scale-model pike.

Then Morris sprang his surprise when I ran out of superlatives. This HO pike was to be his Christmas gift to the new schoolhouse and he told me Alice already had a room prepared for it, built by voluntary labor as the regular school funds did not provide for model railroads or any other unexpected hobbies.

"We're moving it up in sections next week," he informed me. Then we went back upstairs while Reynolds whipped up coffee and toast. By this time Morris had me really interested. I learned he lived with his uncle, Frank Gerson, one of our three CTC or Centralized Traffic Control dispatchers at Summit, the man with whom Reynolds had just talked. Mrs. Gerson, an elderly lady in delicate health, was in Florida for the winter. I gathered that Morris conducted various electronic studies for a West Coast research lab, some of them highly confidential. But aside from this and his expert model work it was his radio contacts that fascinated me. Here on the isolated slopes of the Sierras sat a partially paralyzed young man, up to his ears in work, but bringing half the world into his living room every night where he chatted with an army of friends.

He told us some amusing anecdotes, one of which had occurred that afternoon. A friend of his named Cunningham was radio editor of the San Francisco *Eagle* and lived in Oakland. His office tried to get Cunningham but couldn't, and then learned from the phone operator that Cunningham's receiver was off the hook. What to do? The city editor called Morris who, on a good guess, called a radio ham named Billings at Point Barrow, Alaska, two thousand miles due north. Sure enough, Billings was chewing the fat with Cunningham on another wave length. Morris, from Pioneer Gap, issued orders to Point Barrow.

"Tell Cunningham his phone receiver is off the hook in his Oakland living room and to get the hell over to his office right away. The Air Force has a big yarn breaking."

Morris laughed. "Half an hour later, on instructions from Billings in Alaska, Cunningham was at his Market Street desk. His editor made quite a story over it and is sending me a box of cigars."

"Nobody's safe any more," I observed. Morris grinned but commented, "I don't know. I've helped out a lot of people. In a crisis radio hams can get medical supplies and any kind of help into remote spots in a hurry with these contacts. It sure shrinks the world."

We were drinking coffee when the doorbell rang. Morris pushed the button on his elaborate switchboard, the door swung open, and Selma glanced in without entering. Her eyes fastened on Reynolds. She wore a big red sportcoat, was a little out of breath, and looked extraordinarily handsome. I introduced her briefly to Morris, who was duly impressed, while Selma hurriedly informed Reynolds that MacIntosh wanted him to call as soon as he had checked on some train orders waiting for him at the station. Reynolds got up impatiently.

"Thanks, Selma. That's our cue, Bierce. Come on."

Selma dashed off ahead of us as we walked out into the weather again.

"That's a nice guy," I said.

"He sure is," replied Reynolds. "That boy's spirit makes my own troubles look small. Brother! it's really blowing."

It was. The ramshackle town looked like an outpost in the Arctic. It was snowing heavier than ever, a massive fall driving straight before a bitter wind. Drifts were rapidly piling up in hollows, against fences, house walls, and parked cars. We struggled over to the station and glanced at the instruments. It was ten above. The barometer was way down. The platforms were a hive of activity in contrast to the deserted town. Tower floodlights, shining through crystal curtains of snow, illuminated tracks and platforms filled with milling crowds of snow crews and shovelers. A string of work cars, their stove chimneys smoking heavily, stood on a siding behind a white-coated Mallet. The wind here was terrific. A Diesel horn blasted right behind us and we both jumped to the center of the platform. The Diesel, hauling two rotaries, a flanger plow and caboose, slipped by like a ghost train heading up the Hill.

We went into the station. The storm desks were up in the waiting room, manned by two girls. The place was blue with smoke and jammed with trainmen, shovelers, and extra men, most of them in heavy boots, galoshes, high-collared storm jackets, and caps with ear flaps. Shovels and brooms were stacked in the corners. Three linemen, their snowshoes tossed on a bench, warmed themselves over a pounding radiator. Hanging high above the tables, where the men checked in and out, were the usual winter storm boards, big black and white signs labeled "Pioneer Gap Shovelers"—"Extra Men" —"Helper Crews"—"Sweepers"—"Switchmen"—"Extra Board"—"Plow Crews"—"Work Trains"—"Enginemen, Extra."

The first stages of a big winter battle had begun.

As we walked over to the ticket window a tall man, coated with snow, opened the outside door and shouted into the waiting room.

"Okay, boys. Work crews for Extra 21. All aboard. We're moving. Step on it."

There was a rush for the door as the work crews grabbed shovels and brooms and pushed for the crew cars. Reynolds called over to Purdy, the trainmaster, and got another fill-in on operations. So far, no real trouble. But there was six feet of new snow at Summit and a small slide being cleared at Mile 124. Otherwise east and west rails were open and working.

"Where's 87?" asked Reynolds.

"Still on the rails," said Purdy, trying to be facetious. He was a worried-looking harried little man, but he knew his business. "Left Placer at six fifty-two. Due here in twenty minutes. We're pushing 21 up ahead of them."

Reynolds nodded. We heard two sharp blasts from the work train, which moved slowly off as last minute shovelers climbed aboard. Through the operator's bay window I saw a vague blur of slowly moving cars and yellow lights from a few small square windows. Then the train vanished and I noticed that Reynolds was scowling at his watch. He next comment gave me a jolt.

"I'm tied up, Howie. Do me a favor. I made a date with Lisa. For lunch tomorrow. Tell her I can't make it." He must have caught my expression for he said abruptly, "What's eating you?"

A warning bell sounded deep within me. "Nothing at all," I replied blandly.

Reynolds looked at me a bit suspiciously but said nothing. You had to know Reynolds to appreciate the startling nature of his interest in Lisa. He was cold, austere, even snobbish in his attitude towards women. Once in a while he went to a company party and was impartially attentive to half a dozen wives or eager daughters. He lived alone in a small modern cottage in Belknap near a golf course, not far from the yards, and in a fairly fashionable neighborhood. To my recollection I had never seen him in the company of a woman. Yet I now nursed an impression that far more than mere gratitude dominated his sudden interest in Lisa. I was musing over this while Reynolds got on the phone and talked with MacIntosh. When he joined me again he burned the air with a blast of profanity.

"I'll be tied up all night," he concluded. "Beat it."

I did so, feeling like a GI ordered from a field of battle. I was already late for our canasta game but I decided to see Lisa first. So I ducked over to Mrs. Enfield's, hugging the buildings in the roaring wind. When I got to her front hall I heard the piano upstairs. I went up and rang the bell of Lisa's apartment. But I wasn't prepared for the poised young woman who opened the door. Lisa was wearing a smartly tailored suit of soft tan with a powder-blue blouse that enhanced the striking quality of her eyes. These were shaded with long dark lashes and she looked up at me gravely and questioningly. She was very, very pretty, and my astonishment at Reynolds' sudden interest in her seemed rather infantile. She invited me in and I gave her Reynolds' message as well as my own tribute for her quick thinking that afternoon. Lisa poured me a small brandy and one for herself. Her rooms weren't too warm and I listened to the wind rattle the ancient windowpanes. Her reply to my remarks was shaded with anxiety.

"Mr. Reynolds should rest after his experience."

"Sorry," I informed her, "but he'll be out in this weather for the rest of the night."

She regarded me with a good deal of grave speculation.

"You are a good friend of his?" she asked me. I assured her I was. Then she inquired, "Why is he so difficult to talk to?"

"You know," I said lightly, "he intimated as much about you."

It was almost a faux pas. I saw she didn't like the fact that Reynolds had discussed her with me. She said rather somberly, "I don't think he has lived much with people. He lives among them, but not with them. He tries to be so hard. But behind that hardness he is hiding something. I would like to know what it is. I would also like to know why Mr. Helmholtz dislikes him so."

That was quite a broadside and I had to ignore it, offering a rather lame invitation to our informal canasta game. To my surprise Lisa accepted, almost eagerly.

"Thank you very much. I have some things to do first, but I will be over in an hour."

Returning to the Casa Alta, I noticed a State Trooper's car covered with snow and parked at the corner. In the lobby I encountered Captain Edwards, a living small-town edition of Gary Cooper, same figure, same expression, same drawl. Sam Edwards was a P.C., a privileged character in Nevada and California, having been a Reno cop and a highway official in both states before moving to the Gap and receiving his commission in the California State Police.

"No lodge meeting?" I asked. Edwards grimaced.

"Hell, no. Not tonight. They're closing Route 8o for a few hours. Too much ice. A tanker's in the ditch at Millvale and a bunch of trucks are stalled at Summit. All our patrol cars are out." He thought of something else. "Say, Bierce, if you're worried about Thomas, forget it. I talked to him at Rainbow Lodge today. He doesn't remember who or what hit him."

"Glad to know he isn't stalking me," I commented, wondering what Edwards was talking to Thomas about. He almost answered me.

"I thought I'd check on him. He's got a lousy record and we don't like his crowd. Did you know about that big retaining wall he's putting in just above your pike, in this weather?"

I nodded. Edwards added, "Too many of his kind are moving into these resort areas. They don't make good neighbors."

"Your problem, Sam," I said cheerfully. "I'm playing canasta tonight with the two prettiest girls at the Gap."

Edwards said something very naughty and went out. I spruced up a bit in my room and then joined my impatient hosts waiting at a card table near the bar. There was no mistaking a lot of tension in the air. Helmholtz examined me as if I had just stolen his mine. Selma was too professionally chipper and Maria was humming to herself, always a bad sign when she was with others. When we were settled, with Maria dealing, I said casually:

"It's a good night for canasta. There's ten feet of snow at Summit. I just talked on the phone with Reynolds."

That remark produced a variety of reactions. Maria opened her eyes wide and dropped a card. Selma had the nerve to kick me under the table. Helmholtz snapped out harshly, "Reynolds at Summit? He's in town with Lisa—and you know it."

I managed to stare down Ted's bitter glance. "That's not true. I just left Lisa myself. She's going to join us. And Reynolds went up to Summit long ago."

Ted didn't believe me. That was obvious. We played in profound silence for a while. And then Lisa joined us, cheerful, composed, and wearing a casual house dress under her heavy winter coat. Helmholtz was really rattled. With an air of grim triumph I set up a round of drinks while Maria went off to help Miguel, and Selma and I paired off with Lisa and Ted, who grudgingly relaxed. For a time we really enjoyed ourselves and Selma played like an angel. We defeated our opponents in two games and started a third with a fresh supply of bourbon. I began to be warmly conscious of Selma, who exuded a kind of radiant vitality and sheer animal magnetism that often proved universally disturbing. Again I found myself questioning Maria's estimate of this vital creature as a maligned and virtuous innocent.

Selma had just made our fourth canasta when I heard the phone ring in the lobby booth. Maria went to answer it. I had to look at Lisa, for I was sure the call was from Reynolds for her. I was only half right. It was Reynolds all right, but Maria stood in the doorway beckoning me with a curved forefinger. She said quietly, "For you, Howie."

"Who is it?" I asked. I knew and I think Lisa knew, for she looked at me with quick anxiety. Then I saw Helmholtz was also watching her.

"Mr. Reynolds," said Maria.

There was dead silence at the card table as I got up and went to the booth. Reynolds was curt and businesslike.

"Sorry to bust in on your little game, Howie, but I need your help. Right away. Wharton's sick. So is Gerson's relief. We're in trouble up here. Come up on 109. Put on all the clothes you got. I'll only keep you a few hours. Okay?"

"Okay," I said flatly, and hung up. I went back to the table, threw down my cards, and looked accusingly at Maria standing beside Helmholtz.

"Fine spot you've got for a vacation," I snarled. "Reynolds is putting me to work. I'm leaving for Summit right away."

Helmholtz burst out laughing. Almost savagely, I turned on him. Definitely, I didn't like Helmholtz tonight.

"What's so amusing?" I demanded. "Did you ever see Summit in this kind of weather? I prefer company. If you had any guts you'd go with me, just to see the show."

Helmholtz surprised me as he often did. He said mildly:

"Okay, Howie, I'd like to go, very much. Will you ladies forgive us?"

The ladies, nonplused by this exchange, silently nodded at us like charming marionettes. Maria had just rejoined us and said, "We will have hot breakfasts waiting."

Helmholtz and I went upstairs to get some heavy clothes. We came down, buttoned to the ears, and while Helmholtz said something to Lisa, Maria managed to get a word with me. "You think it good to take him out in this weather?"

"I'll keep him under cover all the time," I promised her. Maria still looked worried.

"I think this is wrong. Please keep him away from Mr. Reynolds," she said quickly and walked away.

Pushing over to the station, Helmholtz and I heard 109, an accommodation train from Placer, whistling for the yard as we ducked into the waiting room, still filled with milling shovelers. Some were going to Summit with us. Helmholtz looked at the busy scene with rising interest but neither of us said much until we had shoved our way forward to the Mallet's head end and climbed into the cab. I had authority to issue cab permits to certain individuals at my discretion, and several days ago had seen to it that Ted signed one of the G.W.'s standard forms that guaranteed if anything happened the deceased's relatives would claim the remains, pay the freight, and forever hold their peace. So up we went.

Already the cab was comfortably filled with minor officials and the engine crew. I managed to install Helmholtz in the jump seat on the fireman's side and I crowded in behind him. The shovelers were aboard the single coach at the end of several mail and express cars and we started off. Helmholtz stared soberly at the cab windows ahead, plastered with snow except for two small arcs cut by the swinging wipers. The muffled blasts from the engine's stack sounded behind us and we moved up the Hill. Nothing could be seen ahead but a wall of white driving snow caught in the glare of four-hundred-thousand candle power from our frustrated headlight. Bill Belton was handling the train and began to pull back sharply on the throttle as we bit into the heavy grade past Rainbow Cliff. Helmholtz glanced at the snow blasting against the windows and shouted up at me:

"You call this railroading? I can't see a thing."

"We'll see plenty before we're back at the Casa Alta," I promised him. He nodded, and I decided to ask him a leading question then and there. I plunged in without warning.

"Ted, what in hell have you got against Reynolds?"

He looked at me with an expression I didn't like at all.

"My life, Howie. Just my life," he said mildly, and turned to examine the snow-covered windows that rattled in their frames as we roared through Gunnison Gate and on up the Hill.

7

Helmholtz's melodramatic reply to my leading question really floored me. I also had to face the fact that a Mallet cab full of trainmen plowing up the Hill in the teeth of a winter storm was no place to conduct any further inquiry into the subject at the moment.

Visibility was absolute zero. Most of the boys stood close together by the boiler head while Belton and Ed Tilton, our engineer and fireman, with their heads cocked up against the snow-covered panes, cleared in small arcs by swinging wiper blades, called off the signal boards, the briefest blinkings of dull green light flashing dimly over the cab roof in wind-driven blankets of snow.

"Clear," called Tilton in a low flat voice.

"Clear," came Belton's rumbling confirmation.

Blasts of wind drove particles of snow up and about the cab through pipe fittings in the deck boards. When we reached the last high tangent of rail on the flank of Sentinel Peak, just before entering the snowsheds, I thought some of the cab glass would cave in under the screaming gusts of winds. The pilot plow tossed heavy sheets of snow halfway up the cab windows. There was a minimum of talk. We were slipping a little and taking it easy. Belton had his throttle in the second notch, doing about thirty miles an hour.

We plunged with a shattering clatter and roar into the snowsheds. The headlight burst through the last curtains of snow and shot a beam of white light a thousand feet ahead, silhouetting endless dark timbers wreathed in flying mist and streamers of snow.

A yellow board, a steady eye of gold, showed up. Belton had his foot on the "forestaller," a trip device that prevented the automatic setting of brakes when an engine passed a caution or stop signal. As we passed the signal there was a raucous warning *beep* from an air whistle under the cab roof. Belton released the forestaller and a little later slowed the train. We were approaching the yards at Eldorado Summit.

The next board was red, went quickly to yellow, then green. We rolled slowly into a passing track. Gloomy tunnels of timber over gleaming rails shot off at tangents in all directions. Cement structures pierced with small lighted windows, like underground bunkers on some battlefront, flowed by. Crossovers and passing tracks spread out in fanlike formation before us, with lattice-like footbridges over the tracks here and there. This was Eldorado Summit's "underground garden"—a forest of flowering lights, red, yellow, green, white, dim blue, sparkling like clusters of blossoms or jewels tossed into the timbered shafts of some gigantic mine. Storm crews and shovelers, throwing ghostly shadows on the timbered walls of the sheds, surged to and fro like a restless living river.

Some two hundred employees and several families lived the year around in this underground community of mist, steam, dripping timbers, and eternal dusk. Light bulbs blazed twenty-four hours a day. Over the sheds lay ten to twelve feet of snow, increasing hourly. High above all this, like distant surf on some remote shore, roared the Sierra storm.

With short warning blasts on the horn for a crowd of shovelers and linemen, many of the latter carrying snowshoes, we pulled up beside the main structure housing the Centralized Traffic Control installations. It was a vibration-proof cement structure housing a small fortune in electronic equipment. I was watching Helmholtz. For once he was profoundly impressed and fascinated by our railroad and the scene before him. He had a theatrical mind, and the action and drama, above all the setting, were pure theater. We climbed stiffly to the ground and stood for a few moments watching our train disgorge its work crews, colorful in plaids, multicolored ski caps, and storm clothes of every hue, many with snow glasses fastened to their belts, as they made for the platform carrying shovels, picks, and gear.

"Beautiful. Macabre. Superb," said Helmholtz slowly, with a great deal of feeling. "The Nibelungs at work in an underground wonderland."

We stumbled across the rails as the rumble of a heavy eastbound drag pounding through a tunnel far to our right reverberated through the sheds and shook down fine showers of snow from the roof timbers.

Under present conditions I was sure Reynolds was out on the road and out of our way. I decided to defer reporting to MacIntosh until I got Helmholtz settled where he could see the show. Also, we were both chilled. We walked through a low squat building, glancing through open doors into a series of dormitory rooms filled with army cots and sleeping men, their storm clothes loosened as they flung themselves down for a brief rest before tackling the snow-clogged rails again. The lunchroom, one of those ancient truckless coaches called "Donegans" by rail employees, was permanently parked between the CTC shack and the pump house. Two Chinese brothers, wise, witty, and excellent cooks, presided over its popular counter.

As we downed scrambled eggs and coffee Helmholtz watched the scene and listened to the shoptalk buzzing about us. He was really enjoying himself. Later in the CTC building I gave him a five-minute dissertation on that structure's functions. Basically, Centralized Traffic Control is exactly what its name implies, a simplified method of automatic train control operated by one man, the CTC dispatcher, over a designated stretch of rails, usually in a strategic or troublesome location, in this case eleven miles each way east and west of Eldorado Summit.

Above an impressive array of interlocking levers and electric controls rose a narrow ten-foot-long illuminated track diagram—background yellow, eastbound rails blue, westbound red, switches, signals, vital structures, and slide areas marked in multicolored lights for eleven miles on each side of the Hill.

Every train movement over these twenty-two miles of rail was controlled from this room by one man. Train orders and flimsies were null and void once an engine entered CTC control. The superiority of one train over another meant nothing. Engineers simply followed track routes and signals as set up by the dispatcher in this command room jammed with electrical equipment.

We spotted MacIntosh at once, talking to Frank Gerson, the CTC man on duty. Even in this restricted sanctum before the diagram board there was quite a crowd of minor brass, signal engineers, a couple of trainmasters, and several B. and B. boys. MacIntosh was a stereotype—the living embodiment of a magazine-cover portrait of a Sierra Division superintendent. Six feet three and heavily built, he had a voice like a bull, a massive grimly cheerful weather-beaten face, shaggy brows, and sharp blue eyes behind big brass-rimmed spectacles.

At the moment he seemed ready for a dash to the South Pole with Shackleton, wearing an enormous storm coat of violent plaids, a fur storm cap, and rubber storm shoes. I gathered he had just come in from the Hill, for his coat was covered with snow and he was demanding the latest report on traffic from Gerson. Frank read off a lot of items from his cumbersome train sheet in a flat clipped voice:

"Not too bad, Mr. MacIntosh. East and west rails are okay. Two

86

rotaries working Jade Canyon. There's a flanger derailed at Mile 115 but Melton says he'll have it rerailed in an hour. Extra 44's stalled at Basco on the passing track. The Mallet ran dry. They're taking on snow. If they don't get out we'll send some 'dog catchers' after them." ("Dog catchers" were relief crews for stalled engines.) "Extra 604, that fresh-fruit hot shot, is two hours late at Calico Mills. 501, the streamliner west, is three hours late out of Battle Canyon. And it's rough to the east. Wyoming's got it bad. The U.P. has two extras stuck on Sherman Hill."

"Glad to hear it," rumbled MacIntosh, who didn't like the U.P. for some obscure reason buried in his past.

When our Brass Collar had a free moment I reported in and introduced him to Helmholtz, defining Ted as a mining man from Virginia City and my guest. MacIntosh was cordial but his mind, as usual, was on the Hill and its problems.

"Glad to know you, Mr. Helmholtz. Look around. Bierce, we'll only need you a few hours. The storm's beginning to break already. But this damn flu epidemic has raised hell with the help. As soon as that phone's free put these orders through to Belknap." He shoved a sheaf of memos in my hands. "When that's done take a helper down to Reynolds and his work train, around Mile 118. We'll have some relief crews up here by 5 A.M. You can knock off then. And thanks for helping us out."

Shelton, the trainmaster on the Belknap wire, seemed to be engrossed in phoning his life history to someone. The line would be busy for a while. I cornered two camp chairs and Helmholtz and I sat down in comparative privacy beside a welcome radiator that was just short of red-hot. Helmholtz had complained of a stiff back and again showed signs of a slight head cold.

But he was fascinated by MacIntosh, who was now in the doorway bellowing orders at some officials on the platform. A snow-covered engine pushing a flanger plow clanked by the window.

"Tell me about him," said Helmholtz. There wasn't much but I summed up our Brass Collar as best I could. He was married, lived in a big frame house in Belknap with his wife and four children, played golf, belonged to half a dozen civic groups, boasted an ego as high as Sentinel Peak, and knew almost nothing of the world outside the Mountain Division. But that Division he knew like the back of his hand. He often reminded me of a precocious, gigantic child. The Division had been his toy, his alarm clock. For thirty years he had taken it apart and put it together again, examining all its minute parts, until everyone was convinced old Mac could identify every tie and fishplate from Belknap to Placer.

"Where's he from?" Ted asked idly.

"Colorado," I replied, and then remembered Helmholtz also came from Colorado. "Maybe you heard of him in the old days. He's a mountain man from way back. A protégé for years of Big Dan Cunningham, the Rio Grande genius who died a few years ago. MacIntosh started firing on the old Moffat road out of Tabernash and over Corona Pass on to Craig. Went up through the ranks. On the Denver and Salt Lake, the Rio Grande, Colorado Southern, and some of the narrow-gauge pikes. But Cunningham made him. He's got a fistful of stories to curl your hair, and most of them true. He's a Paul Bunyan of the rails and thinks he's God's gift to the Great Western."

"Is he?" asked Helmholtz with sudden interest.

"Yes, I guess he is," I said slowly. "He's limited as hell in ways that aren't important to a railroad. But he's a genius in getting out of bad jams on the Hill. He can smell January trouble on a mid-summer day. The road hasn't been closed over the Sierras since he came here. Not even the Southern Pacific can make that boast. He's old. But he's made of iron. He knows exactly what every man and machine on the Division can do. And he sees that they do it. I'd say the Hill is his playground, his religion, his life. He'll be dead and buried a month after he retires. He knows it."

Helmholtz was puzzled by something.

"How'd he pick Reynolds?" he asked. "That's a queer combination."

It was. I tried to explain.

"Attraction of opposites, I'd guess. The old boy picked Reynolds on his record, sight unseen. Had apoplexy when he met him. But he had to recognize Reynolds' unquestioned ability. They fight like hell at times. Reynolds has contempt for the Old Man's colossal self-worship. And MacIntosh once referred to Reynolds in a fit of temper as 'that Colorado bindle stiff.'"

Helmholtz said blandly, with a queer tone in his voice, "So he knows Reynolds comes from Colorado."

Here we go again, I thought. Shelton was still making noises on the phone. I decided to plunge in.

"Come on, Ted, what's this all about?" I asked casually. "MacIntosh thinks everything good and bad comes from Colorado. So he's mistaken. We all know Reynolds got his start in New Mexico. At Tucumcari for the Santa Fe or Rock Island. But you've told me you hate Reynolds' guts. Why? You seem to have known him. Get it off your chest. I'm a safe listener."

"Are you?" asked Helmholtz, as if to himself. He drew in his breath sharply. "All right, Howie. I'll tell you a few things you don't know. Among other reasons, I came to Pioneer Gap a couple of months ago to kill Reynolds. Don't jump. I couldn't do it, of course. Not the killer type, I guess. But God knows I wish I were. In the first place, his name isn't Reynolds. It's McInnis—James Michael McInnis. He's

88

not from New Mexico. He was born in Grand Junction, Colorado, and lived two blocks from my home." Helmholtz paused, as if to brace himself. "He was the young brakeman who killed my father and Gustavson's young brother. He disappeared an hour after the crash."

Quite abruptly a lot of walls and partitions fell away in my mind. "How did you find all this out?" I asked quietly.

"His picture was in the Oakland papers when he got his job. When I was a kid it was in the Colorado papers after that wreck. I recognized him at once." With a queer feeling I recalled MacIntosh's comment that he, too, felt vaguely that he had seen Reynolds' face somewhere or other. Helmholtz continued.

"I phoned Reynolds. When he got on the wire I said, 'How are you, Mr. McInnis?' You should have heard his reaction as he hung up. Later I saw him and knew I was looking at a murderer."

"Wait a minute," I protested. "That was a slip made by a kid long ago——"

"For me there's no time or distance to these things, Howie. It led directly to other tragedies."

"All right," I said sternly. "A rookie brakeman on a rusty branch line thinks his way freight is in the clear and ducks in for coffee. An extra engine crashes the rear end. That's a fatal mistake, gross neglect of duty, a lot of other things. But it's not deliberate murder."

"To me it was and is," snapped Helmholtz.

"How does it happen Reynolds doesn't know you?" I asked irritably. "Wasn't your father's name mentioned?"

"Not for several days. And McInnis took off at once. He would have been lynched if he hadn't. Nobody saw him again. My father was traveling under another name. Gustavson's brother wasn't identified for a week. His family lived way down near Ouray. All the play was on the three trainmen killed."

"And you really wish to see Reynolds hanged for a twenty-year-old blunder?"

Helmholtz was grim. "It would be a pleasure."

I had obviously missed a great deal in the mental processes of my friend. I glanced at the phone. Shelton showed some signs of concluding his marathon.

"And Lisa Maddon?" I asked abruptly. "Where does she fit in?"

Helmholtz almost choked on that one. He said indistinctly:

"If Reynolds and Lisa ever——" He dropped it. Hot hatred filled his eyes.

"Who is she, Ted?" I insisted sharply. "Colorado, too?"

"Yes," said Helmholtz softly. "But later. Much later. I was in love with her mother." He looked as startled as I felt. He added:

"How did you know I'd known Lisa before I came here?"

"Maria. Besides, it was obvious."

Helmholtz looked dumfounded. "Maria knows, too? How?"

I told him of Maria's observations, of the little scene in the Sonora Room she'd run into. Helmholtz looked crushed. He said in a low voice, "Things are getting too thick for me, Howie. Let me tell you something. I'm not in love with Lisa, but I'm determined to see her launched on a musical career. I'm determined to finance her studies with Walter Stolzing in Geneva. He's a great teacher, the greatest, and was a close friend of Paderewski and the finest pupil of Leschetizsky. I once planned to study with Stolzing myself. I'm determined that Lisa will."

"That must take money," I observed.

"Plenty," retorted Helmholtz. "Look. Let me try to explain this. I was terribly in love with Lisa's mother, Mary Turner, a beautiful woman and a fine musician. But it was all one way. Mary married Tom Maddon, a mining engineer——"

On impulse I interrupted him.

"Did Gustavson know Maddon?" I asked.

Helmholtz stared at me. "That's right." He drew a long breath. "Listen, Howie"—as if I wasn't—"the depression and a land steal in the early thirties ruined a lot of families in our valley. Maddon among them. He's the chap I once told you about. He committed suicide. Mary died a little later. Of a broken heart, I'm sure. She left Lisa, a year old. We cared for Lisa awhile. Then a wealthy aunt from California took her to Berkeley to live. The aunt quarreled with her last year, then died and cut her off without a cent. I dropped into Berkeley to lecture and ran into Lisa. She was a waitress in a restaurant."

His voice was bitter. So that was part of the picture. But I couldn't put it together at all. What was the significance, if any, of this Colorado reunion twenty years later on the slopes of the Sierras?

Helmholtz added a great deal of detail. The gist of it all was that he had heard Lisa play at a small recital in Oakland, decided at once she had to have a concert career, picked up the old threads, began to give her lessons free, and became convinced she had to continue her studies with Stolzing in Geneva. But how to finance such a project? And at that moment, like an answer to a prayer, Gustavson appeared on the scene, on a business trip to the Bay area.

Then I saw a burst of light. What occurred to me seemed fantastic but I knew it to be the truth. "Then this mine of yours is your method of financing Lisa?" I asked a bit incredulously.

Helmholtz looked relieved. "That's all there is to it. Gustavson hasn't forgotten the past either. It was his brother who was killed with my father. He had just leased the Ophir gallery and made me his partner at once with an understanding that fifty per cent of our joint profits would go to Lisa. All of mine, I decided, if she needed it."

The supreme irony of Reynolds' interest in Lisa at this moment, just as Helmholtz believed he was about to realize his fondest dream, wasn't lost on me either. What to do about it, if anything, was something else again. And Helmholtz was keeping up with my train of thought. His face was white and strained. Over his shoulder I saw Shelton put down the phone.

"If he falls in love with Lisa," said Ted in a strangled voice, "I couldn't take it. I'd do something desperate. I've invested my life in that girl."

I said quietly, "You'd better face something, Ted. Has she invested her life in yours?"

That stung. I had already started for the phone. But I was struck by the indecision and helplessness in his voice. And I wanted to help him. The best I could do was to say, with what I felt was sudden inspiration:

"Why don't you and Lisa go East with me in ten days? Get her out of here. Gustavson can run the mine. And Reynolds is going to be damn busy."

He followed me over to the phone and stood thoughtfully beside me as I put in a call for the Belknap dispatcher. The lines were busy and I had to wait. I looked up at him.

"Have you got enough money for what Lisa and you want to do?"

He didn't answer and he didn't look too sure. Just then I got Ben Stallings at Belknap and jumped back into my own familiar world while Helmholtz returned to his seat by the radiator. I leafed through MacIntosh's orders and began to talk.

For the next four or five hours I was intensely busy on the phones helping to shake up the extra board and get a lot of engine crews over the Hill to Placer, where traffic was piling up. Some of the boys were astonished to see me, believing me East, but they were all too busy to talk much about it. At first I worried a little about Ted but I soon had him typing up extra copies of traffic records and storm memos ultimately destined for our Market Street files. And as I had hoped, Reynolds was out on the road working far down the Hill.

But at 1 A.M. MacIntosh told me to take a Mallet helper down to Mile 113 above Basco and haul Reynolds and his work train back to Summit. That meant I'd be gone some time, and learning an east-bound extra would be along in an hour, I wrote out a pass for Helmholtz and advised him to head back for the Casa Alta. I didn't want him to run into Reynolds, and I think his interest and curiosity in our operations had already been long satisfied.

I went out to the Wye track, where 6570 was simmering like a samovar. MacIntosh told me the storm had broken and we'd have clear skies in an hour. It was hard to believe as I rattled through the sheds and plunged out into a screaming hurricane on the ledge high above Black Rock Canyon. The whole cab shook and vibrated with the rush and roar of wind. The powerful headlight didn't penetrate six feet in those slashing curtains of snow. Neither rails, markers, nor signal posts were visible. Using eight and ten-pound reductions of air, I crept down the mountain. After a mile or so I noticed a strange glare from above that passed by on the fireman's side. I called across the cab and asked him what it was. He told me it came from Thomas' floodlights on top of his new retaining wall. He also informed me the last concrete had been poured three days ago. About the craziest construction job I'd heard of in the dead of winter. I wondered what Thomas' reasons were.

We entered the long circular descent through Cranford Tunnel and when we came out at the lower end I could hardly believe my eyes. I felt as if someone had suddenly switched reels in a storm scene I'd been watching. MacIntosh was right. The weather had broken abruptly. A full moon racing through fleecelike clouds threw a wonderful silver sheen over a glittering massive world of ice and snow. We rode between big banks of snow, twelve to fourteen feet high, recently drilled out by the rotaries. Streamers and whorls of snow, like fine grains of white quicksilver, raced before the wind through hollows and piled-up drifts. The dark crossbars of telegraph poles were only two or three feet above the snow level in many places, the crusted, frosted wires frequently sagging out of sight in high drifts.

Above Basco, on a passing track, I noted Extra 44 stalled there, as reported by Gerson. The Mallet at the head end, short of water, had pulled ahead of the train to a big drift under a towering overhang of ice and snow. Four trackmen were on the tender shoveling snow into the tank. I stopped beside them and learned that another helper, down the mountain and around a curve at the rear end, was ready to give them a shove. They expected to be under way in half an hour. Engineer and fireman were inside the tender tank shoveling loose snow tossed into them up against the tank heater.

I started up again and swung around a curve that gave me a full view of the storm-swept right of way for three or four miles. Far down the canyon I caught the lights of Reynolds' work train. They had been shunted into Perry Siding to aid some plows and flangers clearing a long stretch down to Jade Canyon, where other crews were at work.

We rolled into the siding and coupled on. Most of the boys had stopped work and were lined up for coffee in the cook car. Others, dog-tired, leaned on their shovels and stared up at the great white peaks silhouetted by moonlight against a blue-black, star-studded sky that looked like a theater backdrop. The moon raced through huge masses of piled-up white wool, these cloud masses themselves racing across the peaks or flinging themselves like surf against their flanks. Each high peak was tipped with a long flying spume of wind-driven snow gleaming with silver.

I stayed in the cab with the windows tight closed. The cold was bitter, the wind high and piercing. Somebody knocked on the cab door and shouted. I pulled it open and in piled Reynolds, Purdy, and two signal engineers. All looked exhausted and half frozen. Frost clung to Reynolds' eyebrows and his stubble of beard. He rubbed the tip of his nose, which was too white, grunted some greeting to me, took off his mittens, and held his hands close to the warmth of the boiler head. The others did the same. Someone else cleaned off the cab windows. Five minutes later I got a highball and started to move out the work train. It wasn't easy. There were only six cars, including a flanger plow. But they'd been standing there for hours and were frozen fast to the rails. I worked the Ragonnet reverse wheel and throttle until I was sweating, pushing back, taking up slack, lunging ahead, but not too hard for it was a cinch for the Mallet to pull out a drawbar or two. After five minutes of this I managed to get rolling, though I heard afterwards that I had turned the cook car into a lurching mass of cursing men and spilled coffee.

After we had pulled out on the main and started up the Hill, Reynolds, who had thawed out a bit, yanked over a toolbox and sat down beside me. The other men had gathered at the windows absorbed in the sudden clearing of the storm and the panorama of silver shadows and white vistas so abruptly revealed.

I was astonished by the rapidity with which Reynolds returned to normal. His physique was not impressive. Like many nervous men he quickly showed tension and the effects of fatigue. But he also recovered far faster from physical ordeals than much heavier and huskier individuals. I briefed him on what had been going on since he left Summit. He nodded.

"Looks like we're in fair shape." Rounding the curve at Basco, we looked along Black Rock Canyon and up at the lights of 44. Ahead of the train the tiny figures of the trackmen, clearly limned in moonlight, were still shoveling snow into the Mallet's tender. Reynolds stiffened and snapped out, "What the hell did he run under that snow nose for? He ought to get out of there."

"Plenty of snow at tank level there," I replied. "And they're about ready to go."

Then we hit a reverse curve, lost sight of 44, and came out on a high promontory with a sweeping view of the valley and the eastbound main above us. It was worth the whole storm to me. Everyone crowded to the right side of the cab. With reason. In the brilliant moonlight about two hundred yards above us two rotaries were headed towards one another, one drilling out the main, the other working on Binns Siding, a long hundred-car passing track. No one in our cab missed the stunning effects wrought by those rotaries. Each rotary was pushed by a Mallet belching black plumes of smoke and white steam high into the moonlit air. From the black snout of each plow, forced up by the whirling blades, rose a great geyser of flying snow, fifty to sixty feet high, flung far to one side across the rails and falling slowly down the canyon side in luminous curtains of silver such as one sees at an elaborate fireworks show. Powdered snow from these cascades eddied and drifted about us. Even Reynolds was moved by the spectacle.

We swung around a left curve through a rocky cut and caught sight of 44 and the Mallet again, much closer. Reynolds scowled. "I wish that Mallet would get out of there."

That's as far as he got. He stopped suddenly. I heard a sharp exclamation from one of the other men. I looked at the Mallet and what I saw is cut indelibly in my mind. We found later one of the trainmen, not the engineer, had climbed in the cab and started to move the engine close to fresh snow for the tank. We saw the Mallet move, its stack billowing big puffs of smoke against the mountain flank. I think now the sudden exhaust set up enough vibration to start the snow rolling. Perhaps a thousand feet up the slope above the Mallet we saw a small whirling mass of snow rolling downhill. With sudden acceleration it picked up more snow. All at once a whole portion of the slope seemed to give way, slowly at first, then faster. Above it a fine cloud of snow dust billowed up into the wind. Then the whole mass of snow and ice directly over the Mallet broke loose, seemed to hang suspended, like one of those slow-motion tricks on film, then dropped right on the engine and kept on going, headed straight for Black Rock Canyon.

At first we thought the slide might have passed right over the Mallet. Then to our horror we saw the big engine, four hundred and fifty tons of steel, rolling with it. On its first overturn a huge mass of live steam burst from the shattered boiler and rose like a miniature atomic blast, mushroom cloud and all, above that flying mass of ice, snow, rock, and tumbling engine.

We were hypnotized. Profanity and harsh urgent exclamations were wrung from us. The avalanche, bigger, wider, faster, growing in force and volume, bearing near its crest the shattered remains of the Mallet, like a huge log tumbled about on some tidal wave, swept down a steeper slope, left the Mallet capsized on a final ledge of rock, and then crashed to the bottom of the gorge in a thundering roar of flying snow and updraft that flung masses of ice and rock far up the other side of the canyon.

Two thousand feet from her rails lay the dying Mallet, a last plume of steam and smoke issuing from the remains of her fire box and flues. The tender lay on its side five hundred feet away and almost buried. I wondered how far down the canyon the broken bodies of those four snow shovelers had been swept. For a few seconds, as we ran through rocks that cut off our view, the whole disturbance vanished. I had a fleeting impression that nothing had happened at all. I hadn't moved a muscle. My left hand was frozen on the air-brake lever. But I hadn't moved it. Then Reynolds whirled on me.

"Give her all you got. Get going, Howie. Spot her by the crummy."

Everybody was now cursing, myself included. I yanked back on the throttle. The Mallet lunged forward, the double exhaust roaring. Reynolds yanked down on the whistle lever and held it down. A quarter of a mile more, the whistle still blasting, I made an abrupt stop just past the passing switch and opposite the caboose and helper. Startled faces peered at us from the rear platform of the crummy as 44's train crew poured out. The train stood on a long curve with the head end out of sight. Believe it or not, they'd been in a card game, hadn't heard anything, didn't even know their head engine was lying shattered halfway down Black Rock Canyon. Dazed by our quick briefing, they crowded into our cab and we hurried up the track to the scene of the slide. The helper cut out and followed us. We found the day of miracles was far from over. Neither main nor passing track had been touched. The avalanche had simply picked up the Mallet and hurled it over the outer rim of rock without disturbing a spike or tie.

We piled out on the rails, clawed our way over a mass of tangled rock and snow at the lip of the slope, and stared down at the smoking remains of the Mallet. All of us were awed and shaken. Behind us came running a lot of shovelers from the work train. Purdy broke a shocked silence.

"You going to get the Big Hook?" he asked Reynolds.

"What for?" snapped Reynolds. "She's broken apart. Junked. And she's a quarter of a mile into the canyon. Let's get down there."

We slid, slipped, stumbled, and half fell down the deep broad gash torn out of heavy snow by the avalanche. What we saw wasn't pretty. Halfway down I noted the leg of a shoveler sticking straight up from a mass of snow and ice. Two men stopped to dig him out. I knew it was no use. I kept on going. Then we came to the engine. The Mallet's great boiler, broken apart, was almost upside down. Torn and twisted flues stood up like jumbled jackstraws. The cab had disappeared. The forward pony truck had gone, too. The forward set of drivers had been torn from their frames, guides, and

95

crossheads, which were twisted like paper. The engine was completely wrecked. With sudden shock I reminded Reynolds that the engineer and fireman had been inside the tank. Probably pulp by now. We floundered over to the tender, followed by Purdy and several trainmen. When we got there, pushing through loose snow up to our waists, Reynolds shook his head. Torn loose from the engine, the front end of the tender was pushed in and crumpled like cheap wrapping paper. The tender was on its side. I managed to reach the inlet cover to the tank and yanked it open. A man's face, streaked with blood, appeared.

"What the hell's happened?" he said weakly, and then scrambled out and sat down suddenly in the snow. That was Alders, the fireman. A second man, without a scratch on him, crawled out in dead silence, leaned against the tender, breathing heavily, and finally said, "Christ!"

That was Travis, the engineer.

Alders had two scratches on his face. Beyond a few minor bruises, that was absolutely the only injury suffered by either man. Both men were drenched, their clothes already stiffening in the bitter cold. We couldn't believe it. We poked them, felt their bones, looked them over, wondering at this second miracle, and then burst into congratulations. I asked Travis, "How'd you do it?"

"Heard it coming. Both of us. Grabbed the braces about the heater and hung on. Ever get tumbled about in a big smashing wave at your favorite beach? That was it. I thought we'd never stop rolling. Snow inside also cushioned us, I guess."

Travis looked up at the moonlit mountain, hanging glittering, massive, and menacing above us. He paled suddenly and sat down beside Alders. The shock was getting him. He glanced over at the broken remains of the Mallet.

"You mean—we rode it down this far and got out?"

I nodded, adding quickly, "Don't sit down. Your clothes are freezing. Make it to the crummy. We'll help."

It took us twenty minutes to get up to the rails again. Alders kept saying to himself, "It was the hand of God! The hand of God! I'm going to church every day and twice on Sunday till I check in."

I didn't ask him why God's hand had deserted the four dead shovelers. Two of them weren't found until the late spring thaws. We put the men in the caboose, coupled on to 44 with the helper sent back to the rear again, and after another struggle got going. Half an hour later we crawled into the sheds at Eldorado Summit. Everybody was waiting for us. The wires had gone out and the board recorded a big slide. We had passed repair crews on our way up.

So the Great Western was minus four trackmen, a brakeman, and one Mallet. It put a bad damper on the success with which the storm had been handled elsewhere. Travis and Alders were sent down to the road's hospital at Belknap, but after a checkup and some sleep they went home. Neither man could show a substantial bruise. It was uncanny.

We were all upset. Five men dead. True to form, Reynolds scarcely mentioned the missing men or their families. He was determined to identify the guilty party who had spotted the Mallet under that threatening snow nose. That's all he seemed concerned about. We found later two of the trackmen had persuaded Travis to spot the engine where he did. Both men were dead. MacIntosh roared and cursed and sent down a track crew to check the rails. He couldn't believe they had been left untouched by the slide.

And it was MacIntosh, not Reynolds, who rode an engine down to Emerald Camp, where the shovelers lived, and told their families just what had happened.

In the midst of all this uproar I found to my relief that Helmholtz had left Summit shortly after I did, riding a helper to the Gap on my permit. Reynolds ate a big meal, slept for an hour, and then just before five we caught a string of deadhead sleepers bound east to Denver and part of the car pool being assembled there to transport the two army divisions to the Coast. On board were several extra engine crews, which meant that I could knock off. We climbed into the rear Pullman carrying several porters and trainmen. We were both dog-tired but sat there and couldn't even doze.

I finally began to talk as our train slipped slowly down the flanks of Sentinel Peak between walls of freshly plowed-out snow higher than the car windows.

"I brought Helmholtz up to Summit with me tonight," I began, "and put him to work typing. He got quite a kick out of it."

"A pianist ought to make a good typist," commented Reynolds offhandedly. "Maria says you used to know him. Where's he from? Boston?"

I made sure I was looking out the window, which showed nothing but a dark reflection of the plush seats across the aisle. I said just as casually, "He's from Colorado. Grand Junction and Leadville. Come to think of it, didn't you start railroading up there?"

That registered. There was a moment of ominous, pregnant silence. I didn't look around. A moment later Reynolds bit off his words, each one a particle of chilled steel. "I started railroading in New Mexico. At Tucumcari. I told you that. What are you getting at, Howie?"

The quality of his voice startled me so that I turned quickly and looked at him. I had the vivid impression that Reynolds was peering at me through narrowed eyes over a couple of six-guns. His eyes probed and searched me, through and through. It was lucky indeed that my surprise was genuine, if momentary. I said quickly, "That's right, of course. There are so damn many Coloradans up here I wondered if you weren't one of them once."

Another moment of significant silence. "Who else is from Colorado?" Reynolds finally asked. I still puzzled him but this time his voice was quite normal.

"Miss Maddon," I replied. "She lived on a ranch near Grand Junction."

"Is that a fact?" commented Reynolds, and his voice was colder than the walls of white flowing by the window.

"And Helmholtz," I reminded him, as lightly as an afterthought, "he's from Grand Junction, too."

There was no answer this time. Not a word. Just a dead, murderous silence. I knew I had gone as far as I had dared. I knew I was sitting beside a very disturbed man and that the reactions of Reynolds completely confirmed for me the story of Helmholtz.

We were a long time getting down the Hill, stopping half an hour above Gunnison Gate for some plows. We finally managed to break our oppressive silence and confined ourselves to shoptalk. Reynolds swore again over the loss of the Mallet, never mentioning the five fatalities. Then he jumped to the feud between Thomas and Fontaine and swore all over again at Thomas and that ponderous concrete retaining wall just installed above Black Rock Canyon. When he was all through he said abruptly:

"Howie, I'm going to break my official word for the first time since I came to this pike. Only Fontaine, MacIntosh, the general counsel, and a couple of the top brass know about it. The fact is the Great Western, in the week before Christmas, has agreed to transport in three shipments, special cars, armed guards, and all the Hollywood trimmings, somewhere around eighty-five million dollars in gold bullion, currency, negotiable bonds, and registered securities, from San Francisco dockside to New York.

"The consignors won't take a chance on planes. Fontaine got his pride up and promised a running time to Chicago of thirty-five hours flat, four and three quarter hours faster than the streamliner."

I whistled and began to react to this fantastic information. Eighty-five million dollars! It was the biggest transshipment in one gulp I'd ever heard of.

"Who are the consignors?" I asked.

"Three banks—in Hong Kong, Manila, and Singapore, I understand. The stuff is coming in on three ships due in San Francisco shortly. That's all I know now. But MacIntosh and I are making final arrangements this week. There's a lot of detail."

Reynolds now showed so much fatigue and strain that I tried to cheer him up. "Don't worry too much. You've got enough plows up

98

here now to take care of any weather that comes along. But eighty-five million . . . !"

"It's not just the weather," snapped Reynolds. "I guess I'm getting old and jumpy. That fall of mine last night and the Mallet today put the skids under me. Fontaine loves this Hollywood stuff. I don't. And the fact is, Howie, I don't like Thomas and his crowd sitting on our rails with this kind of a deal coming up. Furthermore——"

This reaction of his astonished me.

"Are you serious? What could these mobsters do? And who wants registered securities—or gold bullion?"

Reynolds laughed. "Last year somebody yanked eight hundred pounds of gold off a Toronto platform. It hasn't been found since. What really worries me is how we're going to handle all this traffic in one month. We'll have to run these specials against the troop movements, along with ten thousand cars of fruit heading East. Brother!"

He gave me a few more details. The ships, two from Melbourne, one from Manila, would dock a few days apart, the dates at present known only to Fontaine. There would be three special trains, three or four express cars apiece, armed guards provided by the road and the banks involved, and picked engine and train crews all the way to Chicago. We discussed a lot of items. The specials would be lined up on the Embarcadero, routed south over the S.P.—an ironic touch —to Teca Junction, thence into Belknap and on up the Hill on the G.W.'s rails. MacIntosh had suggested the specials run five minutes ahead of our streamliner, 502, from Belknap to Placer, which was as fast as any train could get over the Hill, and then the specials could take off on their own across the desert, a three-pronged dash that meant plenty of extra trackwork and even spiked switches in some localities. MacIntosh had hinted the trains would run on or about December 18, 22, and 24.

Thirty-five hours to Chicago in midwinter. That was really rolling. No information was to be given to anyone except the engine and train crews selected. I wondered if the ICC had sanctioned it.

Reynolds and I dropped stiffly off the train at the Gap, both of us dog-tired. We'd been an hour creeping down thirteen miles from Eldorado Summit. There was a bright orange sky over Wheeler Ridge to the east. Even as we stumbled along the platform a pale yellow sun flooded above the horizon.

A tremendous fall of snow at the Gap, far more than had swept in at Summit, had added five feet of new snow to old, had clogged the streets, buried parked cars, and drifted to the second-story windows of Dan Shields' stubborn little hotel. Two bulldozers were already at work on Route 80, which lay white, unmarked, and silent.

Reynolds staggered into his retreat at the G.W. Hotel. I stumbled over to the Casa Alta. When I got to the lobby and shook a shovelful of snow from my feet, only Maria was up. She met me accusingly. Helmholtz had gotten in, soaking wet, at 3 A.M., and was coming down with a cold. I gathered I had presented it to him personally. Selma was angry because she didn't know what was going on. Lisa, very unhappy, had wilted early and gone home as soon as we left. I learned the kitchen roof was leaking again and as an old friend interested only in my welfare, said Maria, she had to inform me I looked like the battered remains of a tired old roué.

Then I told her what had happened, with the exception of Reynolds' disclosures, of course. Maria grew very grave, almost apologetic, and got me a hot buttered rum. Next, she ordered me to my room. Then, minutes later, I was fast asleep.

8

Quite suddenly, after all the turmoil of personal revelation and confession, blended with the uproar of our storm on the Hill, everything, and more important to me, everybody, quieted down. The weather turned idyllic, with golden dawns and jade-green and scarlet sunsets. In this superb and dramatic mountain setting, with weather now ideal for outdoor excursions and painting, most of my gloomy presentiments blew away and all but vanished.

I was even pleased to see that our local weather genius, Jack Morris, could falter. Two of his heralded storms, blocked by unexpected highs to the south, had folded up and scurried east over the Canadian prairies, leaving us to sunlight and calm. Everyone seemed to take his cue from this sudden truce declared by the elements. Reynolds was safe, busy, and—more to the point—silent in his Sacramento office. Selma continued to bloom, warming hearts and stomachs indiscriminately in her popular ministry to human comfort. Maria went contentedly about, indulging in occasional picturesque squabbles with Miguel to which everyone was an audience, trying to digest a dual stream of explosive Spanish, of which no one understood a word. Only Lisa baffled me. She was more withdrawn, tense, and taciturn than ever and had already deserted the coffee shop.

On the first of these idyllic days I rose with the sun, as I did every day thereafter, prodded Helmholtz out of bed, and half an hour later, having breakfasted, we were off on an exacting schedule of painting and sketching. Ted had once sketched a little, borrowed a pad of mine, and went to work more to keep me company, I suspect, than to produce any startling display of talent. Occasionally we used skis and snowshoes to reach desirable points of vantage in the neighborhood.

Our favorite haunt was Pine Hill, a gentle rise south of the town with a sweeping view of the Gap, the valley, and Eldorado Summit to the west, while far to the east rose Wheeler Ridge and in very clear weather a V-shaped glimpse of the distant desert. Here I could keep an interested eye on the railroad as it wound for miles through this rugged winter country while Helmholtz sketched a little and talked a great deal. There was now ten or eleven feet of level snow at the weather-beaten Gap, a mere introduction to the real winter ahead in the eyes of the hardy natives, who read with scorn of the disruptive effects of a thirty-inch snowfall in the East. Bulldozers charged noisily up and down Main Street and Route 80, piling mountains of snow up to second-story levels. Occasionally, some overnight customer of Snyder's Bar who had forgotten where he had parked his car could be observed poking through the big drifts with a ski pole or longer timber trying to locate the family Ford.

During this period I thought a good deal of what Helmholtz and Reynolds had told me. But in that luminous mountain air and sunlight it was impossible to sustain any mood of anxiety very long. And I would be gone in less than two weeks. So I painted day after day, talked with Ted, and enjoyed an experience I've not forgotten and never will. Ted spent his mornings with me and his afternoons, I gathered, at the piano with Lisa. Once we reached Pine Hill before sunup and watched Pioneer Gap wake to a new day with rhythms of its own.

Reveille for the community usually sounded with the swift eastward passage of the streamliner shortly before six as it raced through the yards with frosted windows and dim night lights still glowing in corridors and vestibules and plunged on towards Placer in a final swirl of sparkling snow against the sun-tipped hills to the east.

A little later the yards came gradually to life. Two or three puffing Mallets, breathing heavily like prehistoric monsters after a restless night in their stalls, clanked up and down the rails seeking water and fuel for the day's work. From their stubby stacks steam and smoke rose in lazy rings and spirals.

About this time, from his neat yellow cottage near the water tank, Purdy, the trainmaster, emerged holding the door open for his constant companion, a fat scrofulous black and white Springer spaniel named Jezebel. Purdy began the day with mysterious rites of his own. After a brief conference with Jezebel, during which both of them indulged in a deal of scratching and shaking down, Purdy would stand with arms akimbo, gazing right, left, forward, back, up, and down, as if to assure himself that everything in his immediate and distant environment was securely in place before he dared plunge into his daily duties. He then felt around in his coat pockets, usually found the two-inch stub of an old cigar, which he handled with the deference due a dollar Corona, lighting it with confidence and aplomb. Then Purdy carefully buttoned his coat, settled his cap, waved at his cluster of pajama-clad kids behind a frost-covered windowpane, and finally made determinedly for the station as if he had at last embarked on a final dash for the Pole, though the structure wasn't six hundred yards away.

By this time the whole community reluctantly came to life. Behind the walls of silent homes one could almost hear the sighs, grunts, wheezes, protests, and fond farewells to warm beds and quilted comforters as stalwart citizens climbed shivering out into the frosty air of another day. Chimneys belched streamers of blue smoke, redolent of frying ham, wood smoke, and fragrant breakfasts. Denizens of Snyder's Bar, a back room illegally open all night, shyly poked bleary faces from the side door and pulled hastily back, glaring in astonishment at the sun, recoiling in horror from the sharp cold air. A through freight, hammering up from the east, whistled for orders. A truck and trailer, covered with frost and snow, drew up to the Coffee Shoppe while driver and helper, stiff and tired, got down slowly, shook themselves out, and made for the door.

At six-thirty sharp Dan Shields opened the lobby door of the G.W. Hotel and tossed his two Siamese cats, Up and Atom, out in the snow, promptly slamming the door behind him. His cats invariably walked straight back to the closed door and sat down in truculent attitudes of stubborn waiting. Dan always let them in five minutes later, informing me profanely on several occasions that he was continually astonished at their persistence in ignoring the usual demands of nature.

As for the majestic background of this waking community there arose beyond and above the Gap, to the west, a vast panorama of glittering snow-clad peaks tipped with cadmium and madder rose in the dawn, towering above shadowed valleys and gleaming dark green pine forests bowed under sparkling canopies of snow. Twisting like a steel river through these peaks flowed the rhythmic life of the railroad, its billowing plumes of smoke from hard-working Mallets looking from a distance for all the world like the puffing pipes of invisible and noisy giants marching up and down the Hill.

Helmholtz was fascinated by the railroad's colony of canines. They were a disreputable lot, with here and there a trace of proud parentage all but lost in a sea of uncertain ancestors, crawling recklessly in, around, and under rolling stock, moving or stationary. Most of them limped. Many were three-legged. Almost all were marred and scarred by personal encounters with Great Western traffic.

Only Jezebel was different. She was a privileged character, spending most of her days seated squarely between the westbound rails and staring expectantly at the eastern horizon. With good reason, too. Twice a day the Golden Gate Limited and the Sierra Special, from Denver and St. Louis respectively, pulled in, and Jezebel, who had spotted accurately the stopping place of each diner, got a royal handout of steak, scraps, and filet mignon that would have brought tears to the eyes of any bindle stiff.

Jezebel disappeared one morning. If the Purdy children had been kidnaped in broad daylight by a group of sinister men in a big black limousine the uproar could not have been greater. Once Purdy was convinced that Jezebel had gone, the Great Western's operations, at least in the immediate vicinity, practically came to a halt. Train crews left their engines and tried to console Purdy. What this mournful-looking spaniel meant to the harassed, silent little man I had never known until now. Curiously enough, Jezebel returned in a fine wooden crate from Oakland a week later, consigned to a nearby hunting lodge. An innocent citizen had bought her in good faith from a stranger he met in Oakland, for twenty dollars, a price that outraged Purdy. By coincidence the dog was shipped to the Gap, near the hunting lodge. There was a great celebration. We passed the hat and reimbursed the embarrassed stranger. Jezebel got a steak dinner, Purdy enjoyed a tearful hang-over, and the incident passed into Gap history.

Another uproar occurred when O'Brien's caboose disappeared. O'Brien was a gay, eccentric Irishman, a veteran brakeman with top seniority who a few years ago had latched onto a caboose in the Belknap yards that caught his fancy. This crummy, with the passage of time, became a masterpiece of modern comfort lavished upon it by the sybaritic tastes of O'Brien. Into it went an Armstrong linoleum floor, a compact deep freeze filled with game and venison in season, a radio, a ten-inch TV set, leather seats, fluorescent lights, and a couple of passenger trucks from our Belknap shop equipped with wrought-iron wheels, far quieter than the usual cast-iron pounders, that made O'Brien's miniature palace ride like a Pullman.

This impressive vehicle, the envy and awe of rival crews, had been christened the "Blarney Stone" and this name had been blazoned in gold letters on its venerable sides. And it was hijacked one night by an eastbound freight in charge of a jealous rival, a grizzled shack named Two-Bit Mason. The FBI couldn't have put on a more uproarious and extensive search for O'Brien's caboose than the G.W. did as the wires burned, east, west, north, and south, demanding immediate return of the stolen Blarney Stone. The crummy was found two days later, under a hasty new coat of boxcar red, tacked to the rear of a local freight on the distant northern branch that tapped some Montana cattle ranges. By the end of the week the Blarney Stone was back at the Gap, due for a paint job, while Mason was fired and several trainmen, confederates in the dastardly crime, were suspended for two weeks.

These incidents delighted Helmholtz. Anything that upset normal

G.W. routine apparently excited his admiration. But then came a minor break in our routine that momentarily jarred the serenity of this pleasant week. One morning I drove Maria to San Francisco to place some Christmas orders for the Casa Alta. We borrowed Gustavson's car, started at dawn, and cut the train time to Oakland in half. On Market Street we parted on separate errands and got together for lunch at Cavello's, a terrific eating place on Mason Street. Cavello's was a big ornate place, full of tables, mirrors, and high-backed, semi-curtained booths that rambled through three odd-sized rooms. Maria and I picked a corner booth near the big mahogany bar and close to the entrance to a smaller dining room off the main floor. We had just tackled brandied cherries on ice cream for dessert when Maria glanced over towards the bar, put down her spoon, and looked strangely at me, growing paler by the second.

"What's the matter? Are you ill?" I demanded anxiously.

"Maybe. Look in that mirror, up by the television set. But don't lean forward."

It took me a few moments to get the view that had rocked Maria. There were three ornamental mirrors set at angles about a TV set high above the bar's shelves of glittering glassware. The right mirror gave me a shock, affording as it did a direct view of two booths in the inner room, just around the corner from us. In the first booth sat Reynolds and Lisa leaning towards one another over untouched food and engaged in a quietly murderous discussion that seemed to charge the atmosphere about them. In the next booth I noticed four middle-aged people frankly listening openmouthed to our two friends and looking thoroughly alarmed. A waiter stood some distance away, regarding Lisa and Reynolds with a watchful worried expression.

Lisa was doing most of the talking. I could hear the steady murmur of her voice, though nothing was intelligible at that distance. All at once she reached out with her right hand open and deliberately and slowly pulled it sharply down the length of Reynolds' left cheek. Even at that distance I saw the three pink lines she left, deep scratches actually, that came quickly to scarlet life. Reynolds didn't even change expression. He pulled back, took out his handkerchief, placed it against his cheek, and examined the bloodstains with mild curiosity. Then he got up, nodded his head, left a bill on the table, and walked out passing directly by our booth. But Reynolds wasn't seeing anything.

Maria had my wrist in a grip of iron. "Don't go to her," she commanded. We watched Lisa gaze blankly about the dining room and then burst into tears. The maître d'hôtel went to her, said soft soothing words, and eventually led her out a side door into Mason Street.

I mopped a damp forehead. Maria let go my wrist.

"Madre de Dios!" she said softly. "Those poor kids."

She shocked me. "Poor kids!" I retorted. "They're two adults who hate each other and will probably commit mayhem if someone doesn't stop them."

Maria gave me a pitying glance. "They're very much in love, Howie."

"If that's love—— What's she doing down here?" I asked abruptly.

"Howie," she said patiently, "wake up. Lisa has been driving to Belknap, to Oakland, to Reno, even to Truckee, for many days now —to see Mr. Reynolds. She has been to dinner with him, to the theater, to Reno twice. I know this. Miguel knows it. Selma knows it. Mr. Helmholtz knows it, and is badly upset. Where have you been?"

I couldn't tell her because I didn't know. As if to concede me something Maria said in the biggest understatement of the day:

"They cannot go on this way. It is not a healthy situation."

Afterwards, driving across the Bay Bridge, and reviewing the little scene we had witnessed, I asked Maria a number of questions, especially about Ted's mine, for Maria saw much more of Gustavson than I did.

"Up to now, as you know, it has done much better than they expected. But I felt this week as if Pete was worrying a little. It is really a gamble. They have been lucky so far."

Ted had carefully avoided giving me any inkling of how long he intended to remain at the Gap. I told Maria of my plan to take Lisa and Ted East with me, if I could persuade them to go. She looked at me thoughtfully.

"It is a good idea, Howie." She added doubtfully, "It will either clear the air—or start a lot of trouble. Lisa and Mr. Reynolds——" She shrugged. "There are things hard to predict."

I decided to talk to Gustavson as soon as I could in order to obtain a clearer idea of where Ted stood financially. I even decided, inwardly, to loan him some money if I could extricate Ted and Lisa from the impasse that I was sure was now impending.

In the midst of these musings Maria started talking about Selma. She had decided, just recently, that Selma was in love. But she was baffled and frustrated by being completely unable to identify the object of Selma's affections. I teased her a little.

"Then it must be Dan Shields. He's only seventy-six and probably has a secret penthouse on the roof of the G.W. Hotel. They'd make an ideal couple."

Maria reproached me and gave me an itemized account of Selma's emotional disturbance. I became a little curious myself as to Selma's final choice among the sea of transient suitors that swirled about her.

When we arrived at the Gap, I dropped Maria at the Casa Alta and decided to pay Morris a quick visit to obtain some late weather

106

bulletins. I got the surprise of my life. I went up Jack's ramp and rang the bell—but it was Selma who opened the door.

"Darling, you're late——" she began, and then her shining eyes opened wide with shock. Her handsome face crimsoned, one hand went to her throat, and she simply stood there, numb and disarmed. I had never dropped in at Morris' quite so early. Selma and Jack Morris! I certainly had a scoop on Maria. I gently closed the door, looked sympathetically at Selma, who was beginning to tremble, and then took one of her hands in both of mine.

"Selma," I said warmly, "my apologies for butting in like this. And my congratulations. I mean that with all my heart."

I thought Selma was going to cry, but all at once she laughed. "I told Jack we couldn't keep it a secret much longer. We——"

The bell rang and I knew it had to be Morris. I opened the door myself and Jack's astonishment at seeing me was as great as mine had been at running into Selma a few moments ago. Then he rolled his chair merrily into his house, took in the situation and Selma's confusion at a glance, and said gaily:

"I was right behind you, Bierce. We got engaged last week and were going to tell Maria the big news at a cocktail party she's throwing Saturday. But you beat us to it. Congratulate me."

I beamed. "I congratulate you both. I think it's wonderful. Made any plans yet?"

The last barrier to the good news went down and both Selma and Jack talked at once. We threw a little party then and there and over drinks toasted one another and everyone else we could think of. The wedding was going to be in early spring; I was to be best man, for after all I'd introduced Selma to Jack when she ran over with MacIntosh's instructions for Reynolds. They were going to live in Jack's house after some extensive alterations to that cozy structure. They swore me to secrecy until Maria's little party and I finally departed in a fine glow, feeling something warm and heartening in their unexpected romance. It had been Selma's good fortune, and something else, to make fools of all of us and our fantasies woven about her. She and her heart had gone unerringly to a man who had mastered his own tragedy, who was sure of himself, who knew where he was going and could successfully take her with him.

To cap this eventful day I began to think about Gustavson and his mine. I even resented my investment, created by sentiment and the mood of the moment, though I stood to lose nothing. As if in response to my psychic contacts the substantial form of Pete suddenly emerged from the phone booth in the lobby. He continued to anticipate my mental processes by handing me a document in a long envelope.

"There is last month's statement on the mine and up to the tenth of December," he told me. "I am going to Oakland right now, but we can talk about it in a couple of days."

Something in his voice caught my attention.

"Fine," I said cheerfully, putting the envelope in an inside pocket without opening it. "How are things going?"

His steady eyes regarded me gravely.

"The mine? So far, so good. You will make a little profit. But the vein will not last too long, Howie. It is only a fragment." His glance conveyed a mild warning. "I have said nothing to Ted." His eyes shifted momentarily to the phone booth. "Besides, there are other things wrong. Maybe we can talk about them when I get back."

Without another word he walked stolidly out the front door.

9

I've never regarded myself as fundamentally superstitious, but during this pleasant period an incident occurred that deserves to be recorded. It concerned Rykoff, the engineer I had promised Reynolds to interview, and the event serves to demonstrate some of the more subtle human problems encountered in train operation.

I had actually forgotten about Rykoff. But Reynolds mentioned him again when I agreed to meet Jim early one morning at Millvale. We planned to ride the streamliner together to Placer to check some engine crews for Fontaine's confidential specials soon to roll eastward. Looking over Purdy's train schedule I saw Rykoff was handling 502 that morning. I decided I'd kill two birds by riding the cab with Rykoff from Millvale to Placer and getting to the point as to why he rolled his train a mile past Battle Canyon station a fortnight ago.

Reynolds and I had business at Millvale before the streamliner arrived there so I borrowed Maria's blue coupé for the short trip down the valley and for some obscure reason breakfasted in Al's Diner, several blocks from the Casa Alta. It was still dark. Plowing through my sausage and scrambled eggs, I happened to glance up at a big chap next to me running a hard eye down the front page of a local sheet. I almost fell off my counter stool. It was Jackpot Thomas, the man I had knocked out at the Casa Alta, and looking twice as large as life. He caught my eye and pushed part of his paper at me.

"Something to read?" he barked, and went back to the rest of the sheet. With great relief I realized he hadn't the slightest idea who I was. I told Al to hurry another cup of coffee and mentioned I had to be in Millvale in half an hour. Thomas got up when I did. He grunted that he was going to Millvale himself and would take me there in fifteen minutes flat. I didn't doubt it but I demurred. Thomas insisted. When we got outside he tossed a scornful glance at Maria's decrepit heap, which I was approaching. Then he politely but firmly propelled me into the wine-colored interior of a modest little Cadillac, of solid lavender hue with gold trim and mother-of-pearl monogram, and all of two blocks long.

At first amused by this novel encounter, I was now thoroughly alarmed. But it was soon obvious that I had nothing to worry about. Thomas was simply accustomed to having his own way. He didn't think I could make it in Maria's car. He had a car that would make it, but fast. Ergo, I was going in his car. Just like that. My only compensation was the hope that Reynolds would be on the Millvale platform when Thomas deposited me there. I wanted to see the Iron Man's face.

Our ride was a remarkable one. Thomas was a type I'd read about but seldom encountered. I knew he was a big-time gambler and a political crook with power in three states, Florida, Nevada, and California. What really amazed me was the fact that Thomas, in appearance, mannerisms, and approach, actually resembled in all details a carbon copy of his fictional prototype in films, pulp yarns, and comic strips.

He didn't talk much at first. His big ruddy pock-marked face, under a flat-brimmed hat, was poised about two inches over the steering wheel. He did ninety-one, not eighty-five, down Route 80. And his face looked like cast iron, pitted from a too hasty and too violent molding. His eyes were his worst features. Two small, black, hard, uneasy eyes set so close together that they seemed to be holding a perpetual conference, not on pleasant things, over the battered bridge of his prominent nose. I began to make mistakes with Thomas' first question. He asked me where I lived. Quite casually I told him I was hanging around the Gap for a few weeks' vacation. That interested him. He gave me a buzz-saw scrutiny.

"Say, that red hair of yours reminds me of something. You want to make a grand? Couple of weeks ago somebody slugged me, knocked me out cold, in that Casa Alta coffee shop. The one on the corner where the big blonde works." Thomas continued. "I was tight as hell. Didn't get a good look at the punk. But he had red hair, darker than yours. I want to know who he is. When I came around in that lousy railroad hotel I had half a mind to go back and drill him. I always pack a rod." He proved it by patting one in a holster under his left arm.

I held my breath. "Probably some half-cocked bum or truck driver," I commented hopefully.

"Nope. I don't think so. And I intend to get him," snapped Thomas. To my complete astonishment his right hand pulled out a wallet, deftly extracted a thousand-dollar bill—yes, that's right, one thousand dollars—and laid it on the seat between us. "That's yours, mister, if you finger the guy that socked me. I'll be through the Gap off and on. Where you staying?"

I didn't dare lie. "The Casa Alta," I said feebly. Thomas grinned. "Yeah? Well, here's some easy dough."

I wondered what would happen if I retorted, "I'll take it. I'm your man." I decided not to find out. I handed the bill back to him. It looked and felt genuine. Thomas began to talk, spitting words like bullets, firing casual questions at me that weren't so casual, that streamed at me as if he had suddenly squeezed the trigger on a fighter plane.

I lied my head off as to personal questions and finally told Thomas on the spur of the moment that I operated a small mine at Virginia City. Unfortunately, that also interested him. I gave him a brief description of what the gutted Comstock looked like, mentioning I'd gone into one of the old Ophir galleries. When I told him what the mine made, tripling the figures, he looked disgusted. "Peanuts," he remarked.

But Thomas was flattered that I knew a good deal about Rainbow Valley and his lodge. He told me something of his problems. I finally discovered that fabulous retaining wall of his contained two elevator shafts, empty at the moment, and he was determined to get the G.W. to put in a flag stop and station there within a year. He had worked up a real hate for Fontaine and I believe now had rushed his wall to completion just to enrage our Big Noise. He had certainly succeeded. His final items of information revealed his resort costs, especially labor, were way over estimates, and he was on his way to Reno to raise two hundred thousand more capital. I thought he looked a little worried.

"Much of a job?" I asked.

"Couple of hours," he said casually. Then he added a sudden switch that startled me. "That big-breasted blonde at the Casa Alta dump is a swell piece of flesh. I'm planning to make her a hostess at the lodge one of these days."

Then he shut up. So he'd really tagged Selma for himself. I glanced at him with new and violent distaste. He sat frowning at the speedometer, now at ninety-three, as if he wished General Motors had installed a jet engine under the hood instead of this feeble sewing machine. I decided Mr. Thomas was not a funny man at all. He might resemble a caricature of a lot of gangland stereotypes but he wasn't one. He was the real thing. Deadly, humorless, and playing God or Lucifer, or both, in his own distorted little world.

I felt relieved when we pulled up at Millvale station. It was just getting light and I realized my fondest wish. There was Reynolds pacing the platform and glancing at his watch as we stopped beside him. He didn't look our way until I was out on the platform. Then his face practically fell apart. I made the most of it.

"Thanks a lot, Mr. Thomas," I said loudly. "It was pleasant talking to you."

"I enjoyed it myself, Mr.—— Say, I didn't get your name," he replied.

"Reynolds," I said clearly. "Jim Reynolds." Standing beside me, Reynolds started violently.

"Okay, Reynolds. Drop up at the lodge any time after Wednesday. I'll be glad to show you around. So long. Get a tab on that guy who socked me and the grand is still yours. And remember me to that blonde."

His mouth gleamed momentarily like a gold mine. Then Mr. Thomas and his car vanished together, leaving a soft purr on the quiet air.

"Hi, Jim," I said nonchalantly, and paused to light a cigarette. It was a pleasure to see the Iron Man drop his mask and to watch the conflict of expressions that played across his face. I think he was actually a bit awed as he finally looked me over, shook his head wonderingly, and commented, "You sure get around, Bierce. You really get around."

Then we went into the station and talked shop. Having made some decisions, Reynolds got on the company wire and transmitted them to Belknap. By this time it was almost time for 502 and we agreed to ride the cab while I sized Rykoff up and talked to him when we got off at Placer. I hadn't seen him in weeks. I began to think about him now. Rykoff was one of our best. Fifty-three years with the road. He was known all over the Division as "Run Around" Rykoff, a title richly deserved, though I had always called him Whitey.

Running around a freight ahead of you can be an art in itself, and Rykoff was a master of that art. A popular practice on many pikes, running around a train operating in the same direction ahead of your own is a valuable seizure of priority, translated into additional wage dollars and increased time on the road for the lucky crew. One of his firemen once remarked that Rykoff could get a thirty-five-hundred-ton train over the Hill on a pint of oil and a quart of water. At any rate, for years Rykoff burned up the rails with hot-shot freight before he went to the streamliners. Never, to my knowledge, had he run out of water on the Hill.

A long weary drag would pull into the Gap and take on water while a hungry train crew headed for the diner with the cautious inquiry, "Where's Rykoff?" Rykoff was like a shrewd race horse who dawdled on the far turn before storming down the home stretch.

Invariably, Rykoff was reported far behind, taking on water at some desert tank. But invariably the first train crew had no more than donned the feed bag when Rykoff and his train, with a long tricky whistle blast known far and wide, would come charging up the pike, screaming for a clear track, roaring and clattering around the halted train ahead of him, while he waved a mocking hand from the cab, and the captives in the diner cursed roundly and swore never to stop their drag again, anywhere. Rykoff's train would vanish up the Hill in a cloud of smoke, which meant his crew got first place on the board at Belknap—and would be the first crew out again, a definite financial advantage to all concerned. The train that stopped slipped back a notch on the call board.

Rykoff was solid, brainy, capable, efficient. I added up the score. Not a mark against him in five years. Happily married. Two married children. Three grandchildren. Comfortably off. Top seniority. A fat pension coming up. Popular with everyone. In perfect physical condition two months ago. What in hell had happened at Battle Canyon? I was even more intrigued when Reynolds informed me he had turned up another choice bit. Rykoff had executed an opposite maneuver by stopping the Sierra Special a week ago at Sinclair, a desolate zinc mine in the desert. Stopping a first-class train there was like a millionaire pausing for a stale beer on Skid Row. Train reports indicated a leak in the air lines. But Reynolds believed it was another cover-up. Man failure or machine failure. Which? I decided at once that Rykoff had something on his mind. Either that or a sudden heart condition he might have concealed.

We were standing by the stove as I lit another cigarette when things began to happen. Five-o-two was due in about six minutes. The agent, a pudgy youngster, was on the phone. All at once he yelled excitedly at us through the window gate. We ran inside his office. He had just hung up.

"Something's screwy," he exclaimed, trying to look calm and being damn jittery about it. "Five-o-two went by the Gap doing seventy. Raymer just called. They passed there doing eighty or better."

Raymer was nothing but a siding and lumber mill. But there was a 60–40 speed restriction down Wildroot Valley between the Gap and Millvale where we were. Sixty for passenger trains, forty for freight. I caught the agent's excitement. So did Reynolds. Something was wrong.

"Where's the next track phone?" I snapped. Reynolds knew at once.

"Foreman's shanty. Section 5. Dalvero's the man. Buzz him. It's 254."

The agent grabbed the company line again and got Dalvero at once. He made inquiries, then with a startled expression held the receiver towards us. We heard a brief rising hum, a rush and clatter, then silence. The agent listened again. He hung up abruptly.

"That was it," he said. "Same thing. Five-o-two by like a bat out of hell. Dalvero figures they were doing ninety. What'll I do, Mr. Reynolds?"

"Put up your red board," snapped Reynolds, making for the door.

"I set it ten minutes ago," retorted a now frightened young man.

I pushed hurriedly after Reynolds, the agent following me. Something was going to happen fast. Dalvero's section house was only three miles away. If Rykoff was doing ninety there he wasn't going to stop at Millvale unless he changed his mind mighty fast. Reynolds was already out on the platform, listening hard, staring up the track, thinking of something I'd forgotten. Then I remembered. The G.W.'s rails swung into Millvale on a very sharp twelve-degree curve that swept in almost a semicircle about a big plywood mill that concealed the rest of the right of way from us. The speed restrictions on that curve were 35–20. Nobody could get around it doing ninety—or even sixty. Below that he might get by.

The agent, already looking white, joined us. The three of us stared west at the sharply curving rails that disappeared half a mile away behind the long bulk of the plywood mill. Then we heard the train. In fact, a long blast from its horn echoed normally down the valley. The red board above us, and there was an interlocking one around the curve, temporarily reassured me. Born of wishful thinking, I figured for a moment that Rykoff might have been delayed and had been making up lost time, exceeding speed restrictions and a lot of other rules. Maybe he had his train under control and was simply . . .

But Reynolds knew better. So did I as I heard the rising rumble of a train going very, very fast. We were the only people on the platform. Reynolds suddenly yelled:

"Get on the other side of the track. He's not going to make it!"

We leaped across the rails, in short to the safer lee side of that waiting curve. And then it happened. Like a dream. Like a fast clip of film running out of control. We found later that when Rykoff hit that curve the tape speed recorder on the Diesel registered ninety-two miles an hour. The orange and silver nose of the Diesel shot past the plywood mill and kept right on going in a straight line off the rails, dragging a streamlined baggage car and "combo" with it. The four-unit Diesels shot through a twenty-foot mass of piled-up snow, hit a hundred and fifty neatly piled ties, tore up two hundred feet of blacktop used as a parking area. Then the Diesels turned over on their sides but kept right on going. Twenty parked autos were pressed together in one compact mass of accordion-like pleats, demolished completely. Welders a few days later had to cut them apart.

The sky was full of flying snow, ties, blacktop, bricks, debris, and showers of sparks. With a grinding, ripping series of crashes the Diesels slithered over two sidings, demolished a boxcar and gondola, and then with a thunderous roar, piled up against an abandoned brick warehouse, bringing half the building down in another great column of dust and snow.

Spectacular was the word for it.

And the nineteen cars of 502? The train itself? I don't think it could ever happen again. Not the way it did. They had barely entered the curve when the Diesels shot off the rails. With the air lines torn apart the brakes set. The entire train sailed safely around that curve, spitting showers of sparks from brake shoes and fire-rimmed wheels. On these high-speed trains we used anti-slide wheel decelerators which allow heavy applications of air, even emergency stops, without sliding the wheels. The wheels didn't slide but the brakes bit deep. Through the big frosted sunglass windows of the double diner I caught a flash of lurching, falling passengers and flying dishes. The entire train rocked and rolled past us, holding to the rails, grinding half a mile past the station, and stopping abruptly with a final perceptible shudder.

There were a few moments of complete silence, as if someone had stopped a camera and frozen the scene before us. My legs were shaking. Reynolds was white, saying over and over in a tight voice, "Jesus H. Christ—*Jeesus* H. Christ." The agent didn't say a word. He stood there trembling, shaking his head and staring at the prostrate smoking Diesels. Under the third unit a dull red flame showed and a small column of black smoke from burning fuel oil rose towards the sky.

Then, of course, all Millvale erupted into an uproarious din. Whistles from the plywood mill, the shops, and a yard engine split the air. A few moments later fire alarms, bells, ambulance sirens, and auto horns joined the swelling chorus. Reynolds dived into the station to call out the Big Hook from Placer and all the wrecking and rescue apparatus available. The agent and I ran pell-mell for the Diesels. People, crowds of them, sprang out of nowhere. I dreaded looking into the forward cab, which other men had reached before me.

Even as I ran a vision of that broken Mallet in the mountains flashed before me. And now four Diesel units, shattered and smoking, with Rykoff and a fireman somewhere inside. Two accidents in a week, the first black marks for the G.W. in two faultless years. There would be a third, according to legend, and I had many occasions to note the legend seldom failed.

To sum up this curious and spectacular accident: Rykoff lived, with two broken legs and multiple bruises. His fireman, checking some ground relays in Unit 3, had been killed instantly. Even the baggage and mail clerks were only bruised, though badly. Not another crew man or passenger was even injured. Passengers in the two diners had been piled by the sudden stop against the head ends of the cars, in a welter of food, dishes, and napery. The company claim agents were amazed, mystified, and relieved by the comparatively small grist for their mill. If the train had left the rails there would have been a catastrophe. As it was, this was the worst mess the G.W. had had in ten years of a remarkable safety record. Like all railroaders, I didn't relish seeing the pictures in the papers.

Reynolds and I were busy at the wreck scene until midafternoon. But in two hours the shaken passengers of the streamliner were whirling East again behind fresh Diesel units hurriedly whisked into Millvale from Placer. The fire had been promptly put out, the blackened Diesels righted and rerailed on a siding by three o'clock. They would be dragged by night back to the Belknap shops and I knew the repair bill on the Diesels alone would run into six figures, with another fortune tacked on for damages and personal claims. While we worked a great crowd gathered. Various owners of parked cars stood about, looking with awe at their compressed pancakes that a few hours ago had been the family pride. They cursed loudly and fervently at everything associated with the Great Western. At the moment I couldn't blame them.

It was four o'clock before the doctors at the little emergency hospital, supported by the mills, let me talk to Rykoff. I had been doing some hard thinking. He was still in a state of shock and they gave me five minutes. Rykoff was a good friend of mine. He was in a small private room, and I sat down quietly by his bed and for a few moments silently studied his big handsome head with its unruly thatch of white hair. His left leg was in a traction splint. His eyes were closed. I was afraid he was asleep and I hated to waken him. But then he turned his head and looked straight at me.

"Hello, Howie," he said in a flat, expressionless voice.

"Hello, Whitey," I answered, and placed my hand in his for a moment. I was embarrassed when tears came to his eyes. I said nothing more.

"They tell me Mickey was killed. No one else injured. And most of the train never left the rails. That right?"

"That's right, Whitey. Half a dozen miracles rolled into one."

Rykoff was silent a moment. I don't think he believed in miracles. Then he said in a matter of fact voice, as if dispassionately discussing some detached portion of his being, "I blew my top, Howie. I should have quit last month. I sure figured it wrong. Seniority, pension, a life's work—down the drain."

He sighed. He had a right to a great deal of pride in his record. I felt terribly sorry for him.

"Just tell me what happened, Whitey. We'll talk about it later. The boys are all damn glad you came out of it. They all sent in their best."

For a moment I thought Rykoff was going to weep. Thank God he didn't. He said finally, "It's my wife, Howie. I've had her on my mind. I worried more than I realized, I guess. I don't understand it. I think I'm on the job, not worrying. Then something happens. Somebody else has to notice it first. I—I ran by Battle Canyon a while back. Did you know that?"

I nodded and said gently, "And stopped at Sinclair, I hear."

He sighed. "Edith lived there once. I must have remembered that."

I thought of Edith Rykoff, a tall, quiet, white-haired genial woman. Finally I got the story. I think I had figured it might be something like this. A month ago the doctor told Rykoff his wife had a brain tumor, might not recover, and would have to undergo dangerous surgery the first week in January, the very week he retired after fifty-three years of service. They weren't going to tell his wife until after Christmas. They had been happily married for forty-three years. A big family party had been planned for the holidays.

There it was. Rykoff trying to maintain and create some gay Christmas spirit and planning party details with his wife, who might not live a week past his own retirement. Trying to play a part. Trying to conceal all his gnawing anxiety from her and from himself, while every day he hauled our crack trains over the Sierras and hurled them over the Nevada desert. Of course he should have climbed down from his cab weeks ago. He certainly should have confided in someone. In MacIntosh, Reynolds, or me, all old friends. But pride is a fearful thing. Most of us are convinced we can control a conflict of this kind. So Rykoff fought on, trying to make his deadline of January 1, and at last piled up his Diesels in the Millvale yards.

When I left him I told him, "Whitey, you're the best damn engineer this pike ever had. I'm making you a promise. I'm getting you your pension. And we'll look after Edith."

I doubted my ability to make good on that promise. But eventually the story had a happy ending. The investigations and reports had to center blame and responsibility on Rykoff of course. Officially, and with universal regrets, he had to be wiped from the G.W. roster and he was. But Reynolds and I personally went to Fontaine and told him the whole story. We got results. The operation on Rykoff's wife was a complete success and some G.W. special funds paid for it. And without any public or private record of the transaction, Rykoff has been getting his pension from that day to this. The G.W. as a corporation may be no better than it is. But George Fontaine, I decided, had his moments of understanding.

After I left Rykoff I went over and had a drink by myself. Rykoff's story had shaken up a lot of memories, experiences, and impressions of my work. The role of a first-class engineer is never overestimated. Sit in an engine cab day after day and watch the minute decisions and multiple emergencies, great and trivial, that arise week after week, month after month, year after year, all of them different, all of them demanding, all of them confronting one man handling a high-speed projectile of several thousand tons containing several hundred people with families and friends awaiting them—and you'll realize why only a trained, picked, well-balanced man, with a stable temperament and an ability to think fast and decide twice as fast, and with years of tested experience behind him, is allowed to sit on the right-hand side of an engine cab.

I remembered when I first became a Road Foreman of Engines how I used to sweat it out when some emergency put a rookie fireman and a freshman engineer on a major run for the first time. I thought of a reporter who once asked Jimmy Henderson, who loved to roll them fast, what he was thinking about when he was tearing along on the Pennsy through crowded communities and scores of grade crossings at ninety miles an hour.

"I'm usually thinking about a mile and a half ahead," said Jimmy.

In my job I've had to study men as well as machines. Both are fascinating. I've known good, bad, and indifferent engineers, tense engineers and relaxed engineers. Good engineers without a worry of any kind, placid at home and in their cabs, but quietly alert. Each reacts differently in different situations. I thought back, a long way back. Once, for three months, I filled in for a Road Foreman on an Ohio division of the New York Central. I aged ten years. I had come out of the great open West. But here towns, villages, entire cities rushed by a few miles apart. Scores of grade crossings. And high-speed schedules. One of the best engineers I rode with had a minor nervous breakdown after every run on the Knickerbocker Limited. He tensed and relaxed after every grade crossing like a magnetized rod. I didn't blame him. You tried to get used to giddy motorists playing tag with the engine pilot or trying to beat the crossing bell. Sometimes, if there were safety gates, they plowed right through them.

Another engineer I knew was a complete fatalist. At a crossing near Elyria, in Ohio, one sunny day, the track visible a mile in either direction, we saw an olive-drab army car stop at a country crossing. Wigwag and warning bell, both operating. No gates. We were doing seventy-five. A quarter of a mile from the crossing the car started up. Our fireman tied the whistle down. I saw an army sergeant driving. A blond kid who waved to us. I remember the grin on his face. He drove right on the tracks—don't ask me why. Then we hit. The car came down in pieces five hundred feet away. So did its occupants, three officers in the back seat. Every man jack killed instantly. We made an emergency stop and backed up a mile. Our engineer climbed down, chewing gum, and soberly surveyed a gory terrible mess. I was feeling sick. Then he looked at me and said in a conversational tone:

"Well, sir—I guess he just didn't make it that time."

Then I started to think of a cornfield meet I'd been in on the Rock Island—but by this time I'd had enough of this line of thought and went out to look up Reynolds. He was at the station, having just completed his final report. The station had been roped off. The brass had arrived and were conducting two separate investigations. We managed to get loose. Reynolds had to stay over. He would be up half the night. As I was technically on vacation I decided to duck out and get back to Pioneer Gap as quickly as I could, and I saw by the clock, with a great deal of pleasure, that 23 west was due in ten minutes.

But it was not to be and that momentous day was to haunt me for a long time. I left Reynolds and waited alone on the platform, idly watching cleanup crews at work on the wreck scene under floodlights, with railway dicks keeping the camera hounds and public away, when I saw a Nevada police car and a familiar California State Trooper car whirl up and stop by the station. Several police and detectives got out of the first car. My friend Captain Edwards emerged from the second. They piled into the station just as I caught the headlight of 23 coming in from Placer.

Whatever it is I'm well out of it, I thought, urging 23 on by sheer will power. The train pulled in and I was heading for the coaches when someone grabbed my arm. It was Reynolds. There was a tired sardonic grin on his face.

"Not so fast, Howie. The police want you. And Edwards will drive you home. Come along." He didn't let go my arm.

"What the hell is this?" I demanded angrily.

Reynolds' little smile vanished. His face was gaunt with fatigue and the shock of Rykoff's wreck. "Come in the office, Howie."

I went. As I did so Reynolds added with profound feeling, "My friend, I'd give five grand to put you on the first plane East and forget you. You have a genius for getting involved—just involved, that's all."

In the agent's office I faced several Reno police and Captain Edwards as I moodily listened to 23 blast away from Millvale. Edwards looked at me curiously. I still figured a bit vaguely that they were making some kind of checkup on the wreck and Reynolds had told them I was a witness. Though why the police were—— Then Edwards really jolted me.

"Did you ride into Millvale with Jackpot Thomas this morning?" he asked crisply.

"I sure did——" I began. Edwards stopped me.

"Okay. Howie, we'll have to ask you to run up to Reno with us and answer some questions. It'll take a couple of hours and I'll drive you home."

"Wait a minute. Wait a minute," I protested violently. "What in the devil has Thomas got to do with this wreck?"

"Wreck?" repeated Edwards. "We're not interested in your wreck. Get a load of this."

He pushed a Reno afternoon extra at me, and over its edge I saw Reynolds grimly watching me. Then I read the headlines, in boxcar type. It was the topper to an extraordinary day.

ARMORED CAR LOOTED was the top line. A heavy bank below read: Gang Gets Half Million in Daring Daylight Robbery—Bystander Shot in Gun Battle—Police Dragnet Out for Jackpot Thomas.

That was all. I didn't even bother to read any more. I just looked helplessly at Edwards. Five minutes later I was driving to Reno in his car while under the dome light I read the lurid details. They had a familiar ring, following the pattern of similar robberies in the East. But this was Reno's first experience. As I read on I began to wonder if some armored-car drivers aren't recruited from homes for mental delinquents. This particular car, carrying at high noon exactly $560,-860.17, including the pay rolls and receipts of a prominent night club, had pulled up to the curb by the driver's favorite lunchroom. Everybody flounced inside, leaving the car absolutely unattended. While they dawdled over coffee and a track sheet a chap wearing a company uniform, and thoughtfully equipped with the proper keys—he had been fired a month ago and hung on to them—casually unlocked the rear doors, moved half a million in several sacks to a nearby sedan, a blue Buick, and started to drive off. He left a lot of silver. Too heavy.

The shooting started because the driver remembered he'd left his favorite cigar on the front seat. He went out after it, saw his rear doors open, the Buick pulling out, and fired five brave shots from his pistol. It was fine shooting. He broke a plate-glass window a block away, shot a spectator through the shoulder, and the other three bullets chipped granite off the Washoe County Bank.

But what poignantly interested me was Edwards' revelation that Thomas' lavender Cadillac had been found in Virginia City an hour later. No sign of Thomas. I felt chilly.

"How in hell did you know I saw Thomas today?" I asked suddenly.

"You leave souvenirs around, Mr. Bierce," said the Captain kindly. He handed me an ancient crumpled engineer's time slip with my signature that had tumbled from my pocket to be found in Thomas' car.

"Reynolds confirmed that Thomas brought you to Millvale," added Edwards.

"Okay, Sam," I said disgustedly. "You want a full confession now?"

Edwards laughed shortly. "You're among friends. Give us every word you can remember."

To the best of my ability, I did. Edwards looked at me hard. "You mentioned a tie-up with that mine of Gustavson and Helmholtz?"

That startled me. I told him the extent of my investment and asked, "What's that got to do with it?"

Edwards shrugged. "But you mentioned it. And we're trying to figure what Thomas' car was doing in Virginia City."

"I hardly said a thing——" I began indignantly. Then I stopped. The hell I hadn't. I'd not only posed to Thomas as a mining engineer, I'd even mentioned the name of the mine and my trip through Ophir No. 3. So I told Edwards some more. He looked at me quizzically. "You sure get around," he said, echoing Reynolds.

Then he summed up what he knew. Thomas had lunched early at the Riverside Hotel, had dropped in at the Cimarron Club, and had been seen by several acquaintances. The grapevine informed Reno police that several members of his eastern syndicate had arrived in town only the day before, obviously for a conference. Thomas and all of his cronies had vanished into thin air just before or after the robbery. Nobody had seen Thomas or any of his crowd after twelve noon. The big job had been pulled at twelve-twenty. Privately, I thought it nonsense that Thomas would personally engineer anything so spectacular after driving openly into town in that lavender chariot, and after telling me he was hard up and looking for two hundred thousand additional capital. It didn't make sense. Edwards agreed with me after I aired these observations. But he said, "Tell it the way you see it to the Reno boys. Let's go."

So I told my story all over again at the police station. But I left out all references to Virginia City. And Edwards didn't prompt me. I was grateful. Finally I signed five copies of my statement, told the local gendarmes where I was staying, and then at 11 P.M. Edwards started home with me. In a complete state of exhaustion I threw myself in the back seat and woke up in front of the Casa Alta. Edwards, like a seeing eye dog, kindly led me into the lobby and left me there.

10

Rykoff's wreck and the Reno robbery marked for the time being a violent conclusion to my painting, my leisure, and my peace of mind. I think I realized this the morning after the robbery as I finished breakfast, watched snow driving past the window, and noticed Helmholtz and Lisa locked in a tense discussion, in a corner of the writing room. Then I observed Captain Edwards enter the lobby, shaking the snow from his sheepskin collar. I joined him and he summed up his latest information by remarking that he had a report that someone had driven Thomas in a great hurry to Sacramento about the time of the robbery. Thomas, he was convinced, had flown to L.A., boarded a plane there for Mexico, and vanished. Not one of his visiting delegates from the syndicate had been picked up.

Edwards agreed with me that Thomas himself, after such an open approach to Nevada, would not be likely to execute such a glaring job personally. "But," added Edwards, "he was in on it somewhere. I have a funny hunch he'd planned it for a later date and some of his crowd double-crossed him to put him on the spot. They sure did that."

Edwards had his coffee and told me he was going up to Rainbow Lodge with four Troopers to comb the place.

"I don't think there'll be any ski festival there next month," he said genially, and went out.

I had a hectic few hours, practically holding informal court all morning in the writing room before a big log fire. Then Maria came in with the mail and two long letters from Betty. Betty begged me to get to New York by the twenty-eighth and indicated rising excitement over our exhibition as she helped unpack and plan the position of my canvases. The Boston exhibit was all arranged for, and I now found Betty's excitement contagious.

So I wrote a quick note telling Betty I was bored to death and very lonely, that nothing at all had happened at the Gap, and I couldn't wait to join her. This last point, at least, was completely accurate. I had begun to miss Betty terribly. I'm not built for bachelor life.

Next, Alice Livingston arrived, brisk and rosy, full of agendas, reports, and plans. The school pageant committee, composed of Alice, Dan Shields, Mrs. Gaines, and myself was to meet right here at 4 P.M. Alice and Mrs. Gaines had conceived of the pageant as a tribute to the school children of Truckee and the Lake Tahoe area. They were coming over in droves, returning a similar exodus of youngsters from the Gap to Truckee the preceding year.

We finally decided to feature in a simple manner some of the historic highlights of Donner Pass: a brief tableau of the tragic Donner Party snowbound at the head of Donner Lake in 1847; the first stage line over Donner Summit; the coming of the pony express over the two-summit Tahoe trail; the first railroad survey and final laying of the rails—this was going to be good on a twenty-foot stage —and a final community celebration of Truckee patriots observing the union of East and West. I saw I was going to be painting impossible snow-clad mountain peaks and pony express stations at a terrific rate for several days.

Mrs. Gaines then asked me if I would introduce the pageant and read a new ballad, *The Legend of Donner Pass*, by Mrs. Frances Llewellyn Clancy, the Gap's uncrowned poet laureate and valued contributor of poems, jingles, and saccharin sentiment to an obscure column in the *Enterprise*. I agreed to introduce the pageant, but after digesting three verses of Mrs. Clancy's epic I flatly refused to read it aloud to anyone. Mrs. Gaines laughed and said she'd find another victim.

Then I had an inspiration. I discovered half of Alice's youngsters were Mexicans. And Maria had been a moving spirit in raising funds for the new school. Moreover, I had often been oppressed by the sameness and dullness of many school affairs such as this one.

"Let's do something a bit different," said I to the others. "Who's the leading spirit that keeps alive a spark of civic pride in this prostrate community? Maria. Make her your guest of honor—and make her talk, though somebody will have to halt her with a stop watch. In short, let's wind up the party with a Mexican *posada*. It will open the eyes of these snow-blind Anglos up here. And it's a lot of fun."

I described the *posada*, which was a re-enactment of the journey of Joseph and Mary to Bethlehem, including a colorful candlelight procession according to Mexican custom. The ladies were enthusiastic. I agreed to invite Maria, and Alice and Mrs. Gaines finally left until our afternoon meeting.

At Alice's insistence the affair was to be held in the new school auditorium. I thought that over. The building was just off Route 80, sheltered by a high peak to the north, and it was quite close to Rainbow Lodge. Watching the driving snow for a few moments, I began to wonder just how much of this white blanket there'd be up there by Christmas Eve. If Route 80 was snowed in we'd have to hold the ceremonies at the Elks' Club in town or the Casa Alta and greatly cut down the crowd. On an impulse I picked up the phone and called Jack Morris, demanding to know what it was going to do, weatherwise, for the rest of the week.

"Snow," was the laconic response.

"And next week?" I asked.

"More snow. And I mean snow, Howie. I'm just an echo of the Weather Bureau today. Read your paper. Three big lows converging on Washington and Oregon. A big polar front moving down from Coppermine. A lot of things are going to happen, my friend. I've just scared hell out of Reynolds."

Morris sounded really enthusiastic, as most prophets of doom do when they get a chance to sound off. After his flop in predictions a week ago I gathered he was determined this time to show us just what he could do in conjuring up imposing proofs of his prowess. I hung up. There was certainly going to be a white Christmas in the Sierras.

I was aware all this time of Lisa and Helmholtz conducting their interminable tug of war in an alcove off the writing room. Lisa, her hands clenched, her lips a thin line, paced up and down. Helmholtz finally got up with an impatient gesture and walked into the Sonora Room. Lisa followed him. Then came some angry discords on the piano. More silence. At last a door slammed and I gathered Lisa had had enough of their argument. A moment later Helmholtz began playing the piano again.

I remained before the fire, sketching out some rough ideas for our Donner Pass settings and wondering how many old bed sheets I could wangle from Maria for our scenery and backdrops. Then I heard someone enter the lobby stamping snow from his feet. I looked up just in time to see Pete Gustavson confer briefly with Maria behind the counter. Then they entered her office and Maria closed the door. Both developments were unusual and Maria almost never closed her office door.

Perhaps half an hour later Gustavson emerged, looking very solemn. Then he saw me and came over, offering to buy me a drink. I agreed without any prodding at all and we went into the bar, one of those small warm retreats in almost total darkness with curtained booths just off the Sonora Room. I had already noticed that Gustavson's yellow hair was carefully combed flat. He was also wearing a neatly pressed blue serge suit and gave me the distinct impression of a family undertaker who was no bearer of glad tidings.

Meanwhile, in the adjoining room, cut off by heavy curtains, Helmholtz was solidly launched on an impressive rendition of one of his favorite compositions, Schumann's "Dedication," I believe. We listened for a few moments, and as my eyes got more accustomed to the darkness I was surprised to see Doc Woodruff two seats away and drinking alone. At my invitation he moved over and joined us. He already knew Gustavson and we chatted a bit about the robbery. Gustavson also inquired formally about our Millvale wreck, but his mind was on something else. I asked him how the mine was doing.

"Fine. Fine," he said without enthusiasm, and I saw his eyes were intently regarding Doc Woodruff. Then I got the first of several jolts that morning. Gustavson said to me abruptly, in a low voice:

"Ask him about Ted. He knows what's the matter with him. I don't. And Ted isn't well, that I know."

For some reason I found that I couldn't question Woodruff in front of Pete. Woodruff was a plump, almost cringing little man and one of two mediocre doctors at the Gap. The other got the pickings. Woodruff got what was left, and looked it. So I paid for a couple of double bourbons, and Woodruff and I went over to the first booth. Gustavson understood. The music was loud and Woodruff and I had to raise our voices. Doc was grateful for the free drinks. I decided it was now or never.

"Doc," I began, "I want to ask you a hell of an unprofessional question. Maybe your ethics won't let you answer me."

In the dim light I saw him smile wryly. "Ethics? I remember hearing that dusty word a long time ago. What is it?"

"You were called in a while back by Mrs. D'Alvarez to attend Mr. Helmholtz, who's playing in there now. Ted Helmholtz is a very dear friend of mine. You said something pretty serious to Maria at the time. Did you mean it? In all friendship, Doc, what's the matter with him, if anything? A touch of t.b., or what?"

Woodruff was about to answer when the music stopped abruptly. He said nothing. We sat in silence. Ted had forgotten a difficult sequence of chords and we heard him explore the passage until he had it down to his satisfaction and swung into the flow of melody again.

Woodruff examined his drink, downed it, and stared a moment at the stove in the corner. "He's your friend?" he asked, as if to convince himself of something.

"A very close friend," I said emphatically. "I want to help him."

Woodruff looked at me hard. "You can't," he said. "He's got cancer, not t.b. Cancer of the spine. He's got about a month to go. I shouldn't have talked to Maria. I was probably tight." He looked at me with sympathy. "You asked for it, Bierce."

I sat in stunned silence for several moments. Almost mockingly the tide of Schumann's music, alive, vital and eloquent, flowed about us.

"You didn't tell him?" I asked finally.

"What for?" asked Woodruff. I decided there was no answer to that. I thought of the stiff back Helmholtz complained about at Eldorado Summit that night. And I had taken him up there. I got up slowly and went back to the bar, Woodruff following me.

"Thanks for telling me, Doc," I told him. He nodded, finished another drink, then buttoned up his coat, thanked us for our hospitality, and left.

I was still dazed. Gustavson was eying me cautiously. His glass was clasped in his right fist.

"Well?" he asked gruffly. The music stopped again.

"Wait," I cautioned him. I was afraid Helmholtz had left the piano and might wander in on us. But it was Chopin this time, a harsh crisp étude that sparkled through the room. It was then I told Pete what Woodruff had told me. His big ruddy face went white. He apparently swore in Swedish, violently. Then in a voice both angry and sorrowful he said, "Christ, to happen to a man like that, after what he has already suffered."

We sat there in silence, listening to the music of the man of whom we were thinking, and who was playing the music of another man who had suffered his own tragedies. To me, and I am sure to Gustavson, this stark pronouncement of Woodruff's was poignant and painful to a peculiar degree.

Gustavson shattered my train of thought by striking the bar rail with his fist.

"She is killing him, too!" he exclaimed angrily. "She has got to be told."

"Who are you talking about?" I demanded, completely mystified. He turned to face me, his features flushed, his eyes hard.

"Lisa. Who else?" he almost shouted. I tried to quiet him down although the music was quite loud. He rushed on.

"You do not see things as they are, Mr. Bierce. I have known Lisa. I have known Ted, for many years. You think Lisa is just a pupil of Ted's, a quiet little girl who plays the piano well, maybe better than he"—he nodded towards the Sonora Room—"but you don't understand. It is the other way around. It is Lisa who pushes him, drives him, takes everything he has—always, since she was a child,

126

she has wrapped Ted around her little finger. Someday she will toss him aside—and finish him, maybe, before this other thing."

"What's your evidence?" I demanded, watching him closely. Gustavson scowled and mopped his forehead.

"Look," he said grimly, "I have known them both since Lisa was born. Very early she found out Theodore loved her mother. You know that, eh?" I nodded. "So. She used this knowledge early. She was to be the big artist, the great pianist. I can only tell you this. Everything that Lisa wants and thinks she has to have, everything life cheated her out of, she has decided Helmholtz can give her. Must give her, says Lisa. Who pays for her clothes, her two pianos, her rooms? That sick man in there. And like a club, a sword, she plays on the memory of her mother."

"Maybe," I observed. "But maybe you're forgetting Ted's love for music and his discovery of it in Lisa. Nobody but himself is forcing Ted to all this. He could have told Lisa to go to hell. The important thing is, he didn't."

Gustavson grunted his rejection of this comment. He believed his own thesis and nothing else. He was intensely excited. I decided it was time to put some cards down. I showed him one he didn't know existed. I told him about Lisa and Reynolds. This really horrified him. Quite aware of Reynolds' real identity—after all, he'd lost his brother through Reynolds' youthful blunder, as Helmholtz had his father—he abhorred as much as Helmholtz did the possibility of any serious relationship between Reynolds and Lisa.

"You think Lisa knows the identity of Reynolds?" I asked.

"No," said Gustavson roughly. "But I am going to tell her."

I was greatly alarmed. "No, you're not. Don't do it, Pete. Let them alone. There's enough explosive lying around here now to raise plenty of hell without lighting another fuse. There's only one thing to do," I added quickly. "Get them both out of here. I've just decided to take Lisa and Helmholtz East with me in two weeks. Once in New York maybe I can let Lisa have it between the eyes. I don't think she's as tough on Ted as you do. I think she'll come to her senses and show him some real sympathy and understanding, once she knows what has to happen."

In strong language Gustavson didn't think so. But he agreed heartily with my suggestion to get them East. Like Helmholtz, I discovered he had a profound hatred for Reynolds. But at least his hatred was more objective. He had never plotted any infantile personal revenges against the man but he was just as determined as Helmholtz that Reynolds wasn't going to get Lisa. Then he surprised me by saying he intended to return to Colorado if I got Helmholtz and Lisa East.

"What about the mine?" I asked. He said a bit vaguely, "I will probably hire a manager, an engineer I know." He added quickly, "Your money is all right."

I hadn't even thought of that and said so. Gustavson then told me Helmholtz had little ready cash. He said Lisa got it all. We talked quite a while and I spoke of getting a comfortable room in New York at Doctors' Hospital as soon as Helmholtz showed signs of needing care. Gustavson nodded. "It is good he has such friends as you and me," he said without a trace of self-consciousness. In the midst of our talk the music stopped and a moment later I heard the outer door of the Sonora Room slam loudly.

"He's left," I announced. Then I thought of something MacIntosh had once said to me.

"Just when was that rear-end crack-up?" I asked Gustavson. "Can you remember that?"

"Of course I remember," said Gustavson savagely. "Why would I forget? March 14, 1932, on the Salt River branch, near Phantom Springs. Why?"

I shrugged as if it weren't important but made a mental note and tucked it away. We talked shop awhile. I told Pete about Morris' weather predictions, the troop movements coming up, and Reynolds' anxiety over the G.W.'s shipments of gold and currency in the offing. Gustavson looked grim.

"The Great Western!" he exclaimed. "Pfui! I would like to see the damned road closed down for the winter. Smashed. Kaput."

His vehemence astonished me. "Not much chance," I retorted. Something in his expression stopped me. "What the hell's the matter with the Great Western, Pete?" I demanded a bit sharply.

I got another jolt when Gustavson hit the bar again, his face purpling. He shouted, "The Great Western is a dirty, lousy, son of a bitch of a corporation." And out came another piece of this Colorado puzzle. It was a familiar story in railroad history. In a rich valley near Grand Junction some twenty years ago the Great Western and a big land syndicate it controlled had battled a handful of small farmers, bankrupted them in corrupt courts, drove them off their lands, and took over—wrecking a number of obscure lives and small fortunes in the process. The Gustavsons had lost their fruit ranch, just beginning to pay off. Lisa's father lost land he had homesteaded, went bankrupt, shot himself a month later. The Helmholtz family lost a hundred and fifty acres of valuable but unimproved land as the G.W.'s juggernaut rolled over them.

I listened with my eyes popping out. It seemed to me that just about all the survivors of this economic holocaust, avidly sharpening their knives, had gathered in convention at Pioneer Gap. For once I began to understand some of the obscure currents that had swirled about me since I arrived at the Gap.

Gustavson and I made a final summary of our moves. He agreed not to see Helmholtz until I had first talked to him, and we planned to lunch together in a couple of days. Then he left.

Determined to move fast, I went up to Helmholtz's room. He wasn't there. I was now worried and upset, the weight of all this new knowledge pressing in on me. If Helmholtz isn't home, I thought, maybe Lisa is. I started out, wishing to decide for myself, as quickly as possible, what her attitude really was and how much of Gustavson's harsh criticism of her, partially supported by my own observations, really stacked up.

The storm had steadily increased. This day in history, though I didn't know it at the time, marked the official beginning of what became known in local and even state annals as the Big Snow—two weeks of almost continuous downfall. At the moment it simply meant fresh snow piled on old.

When I entered Mrs. Enfield's front hall I heard Lisa practicing upstairs. I went right up and knocked. It struck me as a coincidence at the time that she was playing the same Schumann composition, "Dedication," that Helmholtz had been playing at the hotel. By the time I knocked on Lisa's door my self-confidence was wilting. Just what was I going to say? And what did I hope to gain by this frontal attack?

The music stopped and Lisa opened the door. Clad in black slacks, sandals, and a sky-blue blouse, she looked pale to me and made no bones in her attitude that she had been interrupted in the midst of a hard practice period. But she invited me in and stood in the center of the room waiting. Her gray-blue eyes were unusually cool this morning. I noticed her coat and a blue muffler on a divan. Something struck me about that coat, but I didn't think about it until much later. She was undoubtedly surprised to see me, for I had never dropped in on her alone.

"This is a pleasure, Mr. Bierce," she began formally.

"Lisa, it's important. I wouldn't interrupt you like this if it wasn't."

She looked at me sharply, then indicated a chair and seated herself, her feet under her, on the end of a divan and lit a cigarette.

"Is it about Jim?" she asked with a directness that made me jump. Reynolds was far from my mind.

"No," I said, showing my surprise, I think, for she suddenly flushed. "It's about Ted and you. If you think I'm butting in, I guess I am. I've got some serious news."

She saw that I did have and her manner changed.

"What is it?" she asked gravely.

I said slowly, "I care a great deal about Ted. I think you do, too. I wondered if—did you know he's not well?"

She looked relieved, as if she had expected something else. She blew a cloud of smoke from between half-parted lips, then said almost briskly, "I've known that for a long time. He has to be very careful. I know the trouble he had, at Aspen. But he's getting along quite well up here. And I think you've helped him a great deal."

"I wish it were true," I replied. Then I told her, cautiously but pretty directly, all that Woodruff and Maria had told me. It must have been a very great shock to her. She got up and stood very stiffly, looking down at me, her eyes trying to read me, trying to deny my words.

"Is this really true?" The words were a whisper.

"I believe it," I said. "So does Gustavson."

She was very pale but hardly changed expression as she walked over to the window and stared out at the driving snow. She dropped her cigarette on the rug, picked it up, and then turned sharply on me.

"What can we do for him?" she asked. I thought to myself, If that's her first question she can't be as bad as Gustavson made out. Carefully, I suggested my first solution. In a week the three of us would be rolling East. I told her everything Gustavson and I had planned for Helmholtz's comfort and added that she could help us immensely. But on no account was Helmholtz to be made aware of the truth. I then added that once in New York she would at last be in an excellent position to go ahead with her plans. I was watching her carefully, curious to see what her reactions would be. But I wasn't prepared for what happened.

"Yes, of course, it's the only thing to do," she said at first. But there was no relief in her manner. It was as if some new and terrible problem suddenly loomed before her. And from it she shrank back, terrified.

This poised, cool, self-possessed girl suddenly began to wring her hands like a helpless child. She cried out, "What am I going to do? What am I going to do?"

"We're discussing Helmholtz at the moment," I said heatedly. She was walking up and down the room, clasping and unclasping her hands. When she turned to me I was startled to see tears in her eyes.

"You don't understand. You don't understand at all," she cried, and then looked frightened. "Suppose he knows all this already—has known it."

"Impossible. Woodruff never mentioned the nature of the trouble to anyone until today. Just tell me, before I see Ted—will you go East with us?"

"Of course. Of course. But I——" She was standing by the window, the victim of some inner disturbance far too much for her to control.

"Mr. Bierce . . . !" The words were wrung from her in a tone of blind pleading. Then she ran to the divan and crumpled on it, bursting into tears and crying hysterically. Anyone in the house but deaf Mrs. Enfield would have come running. There was more than Helmholtz in this collapse. I thought of Maria. All at once I thought of Reynolds, and I was watching Lisa's face. A flash of insight hit me. I sat down beside Lisa.

"Lisa," I said. "I'm poking around in the dark. But you're in love with Jim Reynolds. And you don't want Ted to know. Isn't that it?"

She looked at me, hating to trust me but feeling she had to. "Only part of it, Mr. Bierce. Only part of it. There's so much more."

She began weeping again and it was some time before she could stop. Then, quite suddenly, she began to talk.

I was there an hour before I had the picture from Lisa's point of view. Lisa confirmed a good deal of Gustavson's estimate of her, but not all, and I couldn't help but feel a good deal of sympathy for her. Here was a talented, self-centered, hard-driving girl, off to a bad start and a broken home, with an all-consuming talent and ambition fanned by everyone who knew her. Helmholtz's attitude of devotion to her, the legacy of affection carried over from her mother, and Ted's conception of Lisa as a musical Galatea fulfilling his own thwarted life fitted beautifully into her own self-portrait. I think she put the screws on Helmholtz almost unconsciously.

But the best laid plans of women, as well as of mice and men, are often a gamble. Like many another before her, Lisa had failed to take into account the force of her own passions and the needs of her nature. By an irony of fate, and Ted's failure to anticipate such a bizarre contingency, it had to be Reynolds, of all people, who tripped her up. She exclaimed over and over, as if Reynolds had deliberately uncorked some diabolical scheme, "He has interfered with all my plans."

Maria was right. Lisa was terribly in love with the Iron Man of our railroad and the more determinedly she tried to shatter his spell the more enmeshed and confused she became. I gathered both of them had recognized a mutual attraction at once. And both had fought against it.

I said little until Lisa was through. Then I remarked as casually as I could:

"Look, Lisa, there's no use tearing yourself apart over this. Under that mask of his Jim feels just as deeply as you do. Why not try to find out what you have in common—instead of building up these differences? No reason you can't continue your studies and enjoy a possible musical career and at the same time be Jim's wife."

The word "wife" seemed to terrify her. "I couldn't! I couldn't! I've got to get away from him."

"That's quite simple. What follows isn't."

"I don't understand," she said, frowning hard.

"You're only running away from yourself. Reynolds proves it."

"You mean"—abruptly she slowed down and picked her words carefully—"you mean I would—would run into the same situation with someone else? That I'm denying an important part of myself? And can't?"

"Something like that. No one lives alone in this world and gets away with it. Helmholtz has already proved it. You're trying to. Maybe Reynolds is, too. And you seem to be terrified by the force of your own feelings. Forgive me, but I think, like Reynolds, you're afraid to trust anyone. Did you ever stop to think that you're also interfering with his plans?"

That registered. I don't think she'd ever thought of Reynolds' point of view at all. She looked like a bewildered child and her manner changed abruptly. She gazed at me very thoughtfully.

"What frightens me about Jim is his cruelty, his hardness," she said. "Only performance and obligation seem to matter to him. There's no softness or feeling for people in him anywhere. People don't exist for Jim."

"Do they really exist for you?" I asked bluntly. "Reynolds is trying to make up for something. So are you. You're both denying yourselves a whole lot. It's just possible you might make some important discoveries together."

"What is he trying to make up for?" Lisa demanded.

"I don't know," I lied to her. "But you both want to run your lives with a slide rule. It can't be done." I made a slight concession. "You're quite right about Jim. He's all you say he is and blind in many ways. But you see more than he does. Maybe you could help him—and help yourself at the same time."

She went back to something else.

"Why does Ted hate him so? They scarcely know each other. But Ted's hatred of Jim frightens me. I've always felt it."

I had to lie again. "Ted is ill. He's disappointed. But he recognizes and lives in your talent. He's afraid Reynolds will take you away from him."

"But Ted isn't in love with me."

"Isn't he? Not in your terms. But to Ted you're music and Mary Turner. You're the possibly brilliant career he never had himself. You're a part of Ted, so important he's determined absolutely nothing is going to interfere with the course you've both charted."

Again she looked frightened. Her expression was very solemn. I was convinced she had never examined all this from Ted's point of view, either.

"Is everyone really like this?" she asked wonderingly.

She was silent a long time, and then got up and leaned against the piano looking down at me. Her expression was still confused but she seemed to have reached some conclusion.

"You understand more than I do, Mr. Bierce. You've made me see something. I'm grateful. But let's not discuss this again, please. I'll—I'll go East with you and Ted. As to Jim"—she shook her head—"it's impossible. I'll have to tell him by the end of the week."

I had gone as far as I could. "All the luck in the world," I said. "I'm a Road Foreman of Engines, not a competent advisor on personal affairs, my own included. Think it through in your own way, Lisa. But take it easy. I'm around any time—and let's do what we can for Ted. He deserves it."

She nodded gravely, opened the door for me, and I went out.

I went straight back to the hotel and headed for Helmholtz's room. As I entered I had a moment of panic. This time he was there. I'm a poor actor. I was suddenly fearful I would give myself away. Ted had hauled a big easy chair in front of the window, had his feet on the cushions, with several bottles of beer within easy reach, and was staring up at the window, which revealed nothing but hard-driving snow, which he was watching with close interest. His natural pallor was enhanced by the white glare from the window. To me he looked white and drawn. Even defenseless. He barely turned his head.

"Hello, Howie. Join me in a beer and watch this snow. It fascinates me."

I opened a bottle and sat down on the window seat, facing him. Then he startled me.

"Are Lisa and Reynolds in love?" he asked with no preparation at all. I carefully put down the beer bottle.

"How would I know?" I demanded. Helmholtz regarded me closely.

"Cut it out, Howie," he said easily. "We haven't any secrets"—then he looked at me with his old slyness—"or have we? I think they are. I'm going to stop it."

It was time for me to move fast. I tried to match his deceptive poise and ease of manner.

"Look, Ted, if you're convinced such a situation exists—leave my opinion out of it—I've got a simple solution. We're in for a lot of lousy weather and your anxiety is getting you down. Come East with me on the twenty-fifth—Christmas Day. And take Lisa with you. It's time you both got out of here. Also, I think Betty can do a lot for Lisa at this point and I want you to see my exhibits. You'll both enjoy the change. In fact, if I can, I'll arrange to stick around New York awhile longer. There's something even more important. Just forget Reynolds. Forget him."

I shut up and waited. I was waiting for that familiar negative shake of his head, that slow sardonic smile. But he surprised me.

"I think you're right. I've been communing with myself a bit in the same direction. To tell the truth, Howie, I can't endure the problem that Reynolds presents. And the mine is doing well. The real question is: Will Lisa go?"

"She will if you ask her." But I couldn't conceal my astonishment and pleasure at his quick acquiescence in my proposal.

"You haven't talked to her?" he asked, watching me. I did my best to register surprise. "Hell, no. Why should I?"

He smiled faintly. "All right, I'll ask her." His face was suddenly hard, and I suspected he was thinking of Reynolds again. "I think she'll go. If she doesn't——"

I said quickly, "I think she will, too."

"I'll see Lisa tonight," said Helmholtz. "I just left Gustavson," he added, and again I felt he was watching me closely. For some reason I held my breath. But Ted went on easily, "Gustavson's moving into the Casa Alta tomorrow. Did you know that?"

"No." I was genuinely taken aback. "I had a couple of drinks with him earlier but he didn't mention that."

"Where were you?" asked Helmholtz.

I grinned. "In the bar. And we enjoyed your concert."

"Oh." There was the slightest hesitation in Ted's manner as his mild blue eyes regarded me with curious intensity. "Did he tell you about the mine?"

"What about it? He said it was doing fine."

"Yeah." Helmholtz carefully opened another bottle of beer. "It is. But we're closing down for two or three weeks over the holidays. Most of the boys want to be home. And there's too much snow in the offing. So Pete will be here for a while."

That appealed to me. Gustavson must have decided to move fast. I relaxed a little. But Ted had leaned back in his chair and closed his eyes. To me, with my new apprehensions, he looked ill and tired, with deep shadows under his eyes. Yet there was strength and even a touch of grimness in the set of his features.

He finally opened his eyes and smiled at me, and his mood had changed. "I've got a small bone to pick with you," he announced, and let it be known he was deeply hurt that he and Lisa hadn't been invited to sit in on our pageant committee. I assured him they were both bona-fide members as of now, informed him of the afternoon meeting, and then told him of my plan to have Maria appear as the guest of honor and wind up the party with a genuine Mexican *posada*. Helmholtz came alive at once and insisted that Lisa perform a fantasia on Mexican folk themes on which she had been working. This was news to me, and I was enthusiastic over his proposals.

134

So we talked and planned and discussed many things and drank a good many bottles of beer. But watching the relentless drive of that snow outside and nursing the knowledge I had, I could only fervently wish the next few days were over.

11

As a small boy once interested in polar exploration, I had wondered what an arctic winter was like. I was now beginning to think I knew. Our major storms usually didn't roar in over the Sierras until after the holidays. This year the weather was in a hurry. My room faced a northwest exposure, which meant the driven snow piled up rapidly against this side of the Casa Alta. When I looked out my dormer window two mornings later the snow had mounted to within three feet of my second-story window and the west end of town resembled Peary's last camp at the Pole. Route 80 was a miniature Grand Canyon plowed out by those three-auger bulldog rotary highway plows, junior cousins of the big railroad rotaries.

I was up very early, and after a cup of coffee pushed my way over to the station to mail some letters, including a long one to Betty apprizing her of some late developments and the news that Lisa and Ted would accompany me East. The streamliner was about due and picked up a sackful of Gap mail on the fly each morning. On the way over I noted idly that the Gap had taken on the appearance of a few battered beleaguered buildings crouched behind mountains of snow, now piled high above the second-story levels by the town's three tired bulldozers.

But at the station there was enough evidence of an emergency in the making to open my eyes. It appeared that MacIntosh, studying his weather data and stroking a rabbit's foot, had ordered out all available storm equipment and then gone overboard for more. He was one of our few officials who never hesitated to spend money in a hurry to stave off a crisis that might never arise.

The first eye openers I saw were two Denver and Rio Grande rotaries, six hundred miles from home, being towed into a siding by an ancient Mikado usually confined to the Utah Division. Two long drags were being held on the passing tracks and shorter sidings were jammed with work cars, flanger plows, cabooses, and spreaders. Purdy told me a track gang was going to slap down a half mile of temporary siding east of the station to take care of more rolling stock.

"What the hell's MacIntosh expect, the return of the Ice Age?" I asked him in astonishment.

"Just about," replied Purdy. "He's burning up the wires to Ogden and Denver yelling for everything they can spare."

"It snows over there, too," I observed.

"Not for MacIntosh," retorted Purdy. "The S.P.'s got plenty of trouble in the Cascades already. They also got a derailed Mallet between Dunsmuir and Shasta, with seven trains held at Redding for the rails to clear."

I was turning to leave when Purdy gave me a knowing look.

"Stick around," he said in a close approach to a stage whisper. "Fontaine's ghost train is due here in five minutes."

I had momentarily forgotten all about the specials and their dates. This was the twenty-second.

"On time?" I asked.

Purdy looked at his clock. "Thirty-two minutes late. Not bad in this weather. They just about pulled everything off the rails west of Summit to boost her over the Hill in a hurry." He looked at me with a question in his eyes. "They really pushing her to Chicago in thirty-five hours, Mr. Bierce?" He was asking for more information than that, so I just shrugged.

"So I hear," I replied, and went out on the snow-clogged platform just in time to see the silver gleam of a headlight coming down the valley. It was quite light but the G.W., like many western roads, burned headlights in daylight hours on moving trains. In open country, in bright sunshine, they can be seen for miles. So the silver eye approaching heralded twenty or thirty millions rolling into the Gap. After all the hoopla and tension it looked pretty prosaic. One of our G-S Mountain engines, plastered with snow, simply ground to a stop beside me towing four regulation mail and express cars. Then I saw MacIntosh's business car on the rear end and watched a yard goat detach it and place it on a short siding behind the station while a shack placed markers on the new rear-end car. MacIntosh was paying us another visit.

But there were a few touches that weren't so prosaic and betrayed the unusual nature of the occasion. The special hadn't quite stopped when, with military precision, a dozen guards carrying Winchesters jumped down, six to each side of the train, and began pacing back and forth at the ready. At the same time I noted Edwards and some of his Troopers stationed unobtrusively in and around the station.

The scene reminded me of the prankster with the sleeve-torn pea-coat who had hijacked Benson's engine the night before I came to the Gap. He had never shown up.

The special remained at the Gap for less than two minutes while car knockers or "car toads," those boys eternally squatting before wheels, trucks, and journal boxes, hurriedly checked over the four cars and decided everything was in order. A highball was given, the guards climbed quickly aboard, and with an easy staccato exhaust the engine whisked Fontaine's first special out of sight between high banks of snow. At the same time I heard the streamliner whistling down the valley to the west. I had decided to pay a brief social call on MacIntosh and was headed for his car just as Reynolds climbed down from the observation end without bothering to open the gate. He joined me with a warning.

"Don't drop in on the old boy now. He's fit to be tied." Reynolds' phrase was a good deal more primitive and direct. "He's on the phone trying to explain why we lost thirty-three minutes into the Gap. Flanger derailed at the west portal of Cranford Tunnel. We got her on the rails in twenty minutes and shoved the crate, with a broken drawbar, all the way to Summit doing over forty. And there's some more foolishness being cooked up. Got a minute?"

We entered the station, where Reynolds got off some company wires. He was busting out all over with more news and I just waited. We watched the streamliner slip through town like a scarlet ghost train, and then Reynolds talked.

"Howie, you want to hear a queer story?" he began. "Fontaine has been having the jitters over these bullion shipments. He's worried over the final shipment. Talking with him the other night, I jokingly suggested that he ought to put the last shipment on the streamliner if he was that much worried. Nobody would touch 502. Well—he took me up on it! News of his specials has leaked all around. Know what he's done? His third special, on Christmas Eve, with twelve armed guards, mind you, is running empty from Belknap to Placer."

I was slow. "Where's the swag going?" I asked in surprise.

Reynolds grimaced. "Believe it or not, on the streamliner. Fontaine grabbed at my idea. He's ordered the switch at Belknap. The whole shipment goes back on the special at Placer. But over the Hill Fontaine's decided the streamliner is the goat. He's putting just two G.W. guards aboard. MacIntosh told me in private that Fontaine has a big G.W. money shipment for his Chicago bankers aboard. Over a million. So Fontaine's running the special as a deadhead pilot train for the streamliner, three to five minutes behind. It's all right if he gets away with it."

"What do you mean?" I asked, completely mystified.

"Hell, Howie. Fontaine picked up my idea and is doing this strictly on his own. The consignors don't know about it. Suppose the stream-liner drops into Black Rock Canyon—and an empty special pulls into Chicago. I'd be shot, and they'd hang Fontaine from Sentinel Peak."

It was none of my business, but I thought it over. It was highly irregular, to say the least. But Fontaine was levelheaded. He must have had his reasons for accepting Reynolds' idle and only half-serious suggestion. Between the weather and the alarms and excursions over Thomas, I figured that Fontaine thought to double the pike's safety factor by running the special train as a pilot train over the riskiest section of rail. If anything happened to the special the streamliner could always get back to Belknap. But still—I agreed with Reynolds that Fontaine was putting his head in a big noose if anything went wrong. Reynolds and I talked some more. I decided Reynolds didn't look as if he were enjoying life at all. He hadn't slept much lately, hadn't shaved, and looked as if he'd been living on a diet of old razor blades.

"Got time for a cup of coffee?" I asked him.

He shook his head. "I'm heading for Lisa," he said grimly.

"This early?"

"By special appointment," he replied with an edge to his voice. "Maybe I'll see you later."

We were out on the platform. I saw Edwards approaching as Reynolds left me, heading doggedly for Lisa's apartment with all the pleasant innocence of an infantryman stalking a machine-gun nest. The tall figure of Edwards plowed up beside me and he cast a speculative eye at Reynolds.

"What's eating Jim?" he asked me. "I used to like him. But he's got so touchy I can't talk to him any more. Weather and job getting him down?"

"Worse than that," I said, idly wishing I had a tape recorder in Lisa's rooms when Reynolds arrived there. "At thirty-nine he's got real woman trouble for the first time. It's tough at that age—or didn't you know?"

Edwards seemed startled. "Yeah. I guess you're right. I saw them having a real hassle in Reno last week. The Maddon girl, isn't it? I'd say she's giving him a tough run for his money."

"Maybe it works both ways," I suggested. "Got time for coffee?"

I must have been determined to have company that morning. Edwards agreed and we got a small table in the coffee shop, almost empty at this hour. Selma waited on us and glowed so visibly that the usually phlegmatic Edwards fidgeted like an amorous schoolboy and confided in me, "If I was ten years younger I'd make a play for that."

"You're too late," I informed him. "She's already tagged by a local boy. It's a hell of a surprise and the announcement in a few days will shove Thomas right off page one of the *Enterprise*."

Edwards forgot all about Selma at my mention of Thomas. He came to life in a hurry.

"We've had a break, Howie. One of Thomas' syndicate boys, a chap named Friskin, was picked up on a dude ranch ten miles south of Reno. Dyed his hair, was a good spender, and popular at the ranch. But a sore girl friend tipped the Reno people off. She was right. Friskin has begun to talk and he's shaking in his shoes."

"What's he say?" I demanded.

"Not too much. He's waiting to see how much the cops have on him. He lent some support to my theory that the Reno robbery, planned by Thomas, was pulled in advance to put him on a spot."

"Why?" I asked.

"We got the impression Thomas had an even bigger job coming up that the syndicate people turned thumbs down on fast. It scared them to death. Thomas wouldn't back down. They decided to stop him quick."

"What was he going to do? Knock over one of the big clubs in Reno?"

"Bigger than that. We asked Friskin about Fontaine's special trains. Friskin clammed up, but he sure showed us we were on the right track."

I was astonished.

"Then Thomas is nuts. Nobody could get away with such a job. I don't wonder his boys blew up."

"Somebody's always trying the impossible," replied Edwards. "Sure it's screwy. But what's more important—Friskin's whole behavior convinces us Thomas is right in this area, with the Reno loot stashed away for a quieter day. Friskin is panicky. When I asked him where Thomas would stay in Mexico he blurted out, 'Jackpot would never go there!'"

I thought this over while Edwards drank more coffee. He looked up and added, "I think Thomas is right in Reno or Virginia City. I think he's still boss and going right ahead with his plans. Anyway the Nevada people were jittery enough to put guards and special track details across the Humboldt desert and up Battle Canyon to protect the remaining two specials."

I said soberly, "Even Reynolds is getting jumpy about this deal."

Edwards laughed shortly. "I read the papers. Nothing surprises me any more. Look at that Brink robbery in Boston a few years ago. So eighty-five million dollars goes East in three trains, and there's been no real secret about it. It's a silly way to move that much money, I say. Why shouldn't somebody like Thomas and his mob, if he had a brainstorm or a hot tip, make a play for it?"

I insisted there hadn't been a major train robbery in years but reluctantly I shared some of Edwards' views. But he was now intrigued by something else.

"Just why would Thomas' car be picked up in Virginia City?" he mused. "Nobody in his class hangs out in that human cemetery."

Edwards was a little hard on Virginia City, having once been slugged in making an arrest there some years ago. But I, too, was thinking hard of something else—of my pose with Thomas as a mining man working an old shaft of Ophir No. 3. And I was thinking that mine was a fine place to hide anything, from a person to half a million dollars.

"Did you ever search Pete's mine that I mentioned to Thomas?" I asked Edwards abruptly.

"We sure did," he answered. "And we put new locks on it. Ask Gustavson."

Pete hadn't told me about that.

After Edwards had left me I picked up some mail at the desk. There was a note from Betty and a long envelope from Grand Junction, Colorado. I ripped open the letter thinking of the query I had forwarded there ten days ago. Three yellow newspaper clippings dropped out. One of them showed me a one-column cut of a faded young face—and the face belonged to Reynolds. The caption read: "James McInnis: Grand Junction youth is wanted for questioning in Phantom Springs wreck." The stories corroborated everything I'd been told.

Just as I put the clippings in my pocket Maria joined me and began talking at once about our Christmas Eve party. I had already started the construction of some simple scenery and saw I was in for a good many hours painting backdrops. Maria was enthusiastic about details of the *piñates* and *posada* and told me Alice was determined to hold the party on the Hill. She was buttering Edwards and the highway patrols every five minutes to keep the road open to Summit until Christmas Day at any cost. Maria also relayed the information that Alice wanted a half dozen rolls of clothesline, rope or wire variety, for scene-shifting purposes, and hoisting the *piñates*.

After Maria had gone I phoned around and discovered a curious situation. Someone had bought twenty rolls of clothesline, all they had, at Morgan's hardware store the day before. I called Hardy's general store at Millvale. The same thing had happened there. Somebody was getting ready for a big spring washing, or some lumber company was stocking up its camps. Just for fun I called another store, Bagley's, over near Raymer. I announced myself to Mrs. Bagley and said, "I suppose somebody bought up all your clothesline yesterday."

"How did you know that?" asked Julia Bagley in surprise. I told her and then had to phone down to Placer, where the big clothes-line shortage hadn't hit yet. They promised to put my order on 23 that afternoon and charged it."

I wandered back to the bar, wondering who was stripping the country of clothesline in late December, when I saw Reynolds cross the lobby. One look at his face made me join him with the suggestion "Let's go up to my room." I guess he heard me but I practically had to steer him upstairs. This time he didn't refuse a drink and I poured him a big one. He sat down on the bed wearing his most impressive six-gun expression again.

"I think I'll kill that goddamned piano-playing friend of yours," he said icily. "You'd better get rid of him quick. Get him out of town."

"What's happened now?"

To my astonishment Reynolds began to tremble and shake, first his arms and hands, then his whole figure. He got up suddenly like a tense spring uncoiling.

"I'm shot to hell, Howie. Lisa just told me off. She said Helmholtz is taking her East with you on the twenty-fifth. That he insisted and she agreed to go. Is that true?"

I thought fast. Lisa sounded as if she'd left me out of this. I sure hoped so. And I'd better find out at once.

"Yes, I guess it is. They told me they wanted to go to New York in a few days to see about her scholarship. And Gustavson told me privately that Ted is a very sick man. So I put in an order for a couple of compartments. I thought you'd been informed."

Reynolds ripped off several searing lines of unprintable profanity. He also whirled on me, his fists clenched.

"What the hell's going on here? Don't try to cover up on me, Howie. By God, I'm going to get to the bottom of this tug of war between Lisa, that damned pianist, and me. Damnit, I must have missed a lot of things right under my nose. I went over to ask Lisa to marry me, for the tenth time. I got the shock of my life."

I knew a good deal. But how much to tell Reynolds in his present condition was a problem. His hatreds needed no prodding. But his sympathies did. So I told him bluntly of Helmholtz's death sentence and Doc Woodruff's diagnosis, something of Ted's feeling for Lisa's mother, and all the elements from his own life that went into his self-centered relationship with Lisa.

My disclosures took the starch out of Reynolds. He was being very quiet, trying to digest what I had told him. All at once he said abruptly, "Howie, did you ever spend any part of your life trying to live down just one mistake?"

For a moment I was fearful he was about to open up his Colorado disaster. But he skipped it by commenting, "I made a hell of a mistake as a youngster. I've lived with it night and day. It won't leave me. But I can't go on living the way I have. I grabbed for Lisa because I sensed something in her I need and never had. She was a way out of myself. And she loves me. I am sure of it. But something's all wrong. Something I don't know about."

He finished his drink and set the glass down with a crash.

"I may be a damn good railroader, Howie, but I realized last year —and I'm getting older—that I'd locked myself in 'solitary' long ago and thrown away the key. Lisa calls me ruthless, cold, cruel. Maybe so. Maybe I can't understand people. Lisa says I never will. But I can see myself once in a while. Good old Reynolds. The self-made solitary man. Not a close friend. No social life. No women. Not even a healthy vice."

His voice was rasping and bitter. Behind that trim well-groomed mask he wore I saw that Reynolds had had more bad moments than anyone knew. But it was news to me that he was aware of it. I didn't think he had that much insight. I knew, too, that he was going to regret this outpouring of confidence. It would put a strain on our friendship from now on.

"You've still got a little time. Four or five days," I told him, and added a little brutally, "Helmholtz won't be in the way long."

"That's enough," he said, actually wincing. I had the feeling Reynolds wasn't going to like me for a long time. He got up to go, appearing very shaken. "It looks as if I'm too late," he said cuttingly. "It looks as if I'm getting the works from Lisa, from you, and maybe myself. Thanks for everything, Bierce." He walked across the room, scowling. "And Merry Christmas," he added savagely, slamming the door as he went out.

There was a bitter taste in my mouth. I wanted to blot out the days remaining before my eastward flight on the twenty-fifth. It occurred to me that I had better inform MacIntosh of my planned departure and add another assurance I'd be back on the job by January 15. It was also a good excuse to get out of my room.

When I reached the business car I found the Great Man was in a jovial mood, having just demolished a big T-bone steak while listening to some encouraging reports from a couple of signal engineers and the assistant chief of motive power, who were present. After they left I told MacIntosh my plans. I could see he was puzzled by my unexplained stopover at the Gap and I suspected he thought Betty and I had separated. He was immensely pleased to hear everything was in order. After chatting a while he looked at me sharply and asked:

"Do you feel like some exercise today?"

I didn't. Visualizing another ascent of the Hill and plowing around in wet drifts and high wind, I shook my head emphatically. I wanted a binge, not another bout with the elements. "No, sir. Not if I can help it. I want to stay off the Hill until I report back for duty."

MacIntosh laughed. "You got me wrong, Bierce. We're short as hell everywhere with this snow and troop traffic coming up. I thought you might like to run over to Battle Canyon and Benning on Second 20, and come back with some army brass, riding the head end with a freshman engineer. This is the first of the army drags and I'd like to have an old hand along." Then he dangled a big bunch of carrots before my nose. "I thought of you because you'll have one of the Nine Thousands, the Northerns, coming back. I hear you like those babies."

That got me. An answer to a prayer. In my mood a chance to get out of the Gap with a glimpse of open country and a high-speed run with one of our Northerns was just what the doctor ordered. And I was a fall guy for the Northerns. The finest engines on the G.W.'s impressive roster and operated out of Big Bend, Nebraska, through Colorado and Utah to Benning, east of Battle Canyon. I hadn't ridden one for a long time. MacIntosh was amused by my expression.

"That's different, huh? Okay. It's out of our Division area but Davis and I" (Davis was super of the Utah Division) "are making a lot of swaps, and switching crews all over the damn map. I'll wire him you'll be along. Your train is Extra 77 west from Benning, baggage and army brass. Come right on up to Summit tonight—you're due there about eight-fifty. And roll 'em if you want to, Bierce. We'll put the tape speed recorder in a museum."

He rather tossed this off, and I wondered if he meant it, but I had already decided to enjoy myself. I also learned another reason for MacIntosh's good humor. Fontaine's first special east was already well into Utah, only ten minutes late, was expected in Denver at midnight, and planned a final run to Chicago in thirteen hours flat. Even some of our old-timers were getting excited about the run and it was leaking into the newspapers.

I went over to the Casa Alta for some heavy clothes and returned to MacIntosh's car to wait for Second 20. The first section had just left. Then we heard Second 20's horn and watched her headlight emerge through the driving snow. I mentioned the height of the trackside drifts to MacIntosh. He was tilted back in his big leather chair, a long unlighted cigar between his lips, as he made occasional notes on a pad and stared through his brass-rimmed spectacles at the snow-clogged yards. He removed his cigar and looked at me quizzically.

"I usually clam up on weather, Bierce. You know that. But I think, my boy, this may be It."

"It?" I repeated.

"It," replied MacIntosh, pounding in the word. "I think we're in for the heaviest continuous fall of snow since '89. That December, fifteen feet came down in four days. Twenty-seven feet in two weeks. A level snow pack of forty-two feet. A season's total of eighty feet at Eldorado—sixty-four at Norden. Or take 1906-07—a record 884 inches at Tamarack. But at Eldorado, 1020 inches! That's eighty-five feet of white stuff from October to April. They tell me the snow pack on level ground at the base of Sentinel Peak was forty-five feet in February. Sixty- to seventy-foot drifts in the canyons. I wasn't around yet. But the newspapers of that time record the G.W. was snowed under for five weeks. Not a wheel moving from Placer to Calico Mills. Three freight drags lost and out of sight for a month. Two engine crews froze to death. Three hundred passengers taken down from Basco on sledges. It damn near bankrupted the road."

"You planning to close down for a month?" I asked kiddingly.

"I'll say this," he replied, "but not outside my car—we'll be damn lucky to stay open. Take a look at the weather map when you get back to Summit tonight. It's a dilly. We're dickering now with the S.P. to route some of these troop trains south to Barstow, Mojave, and over the Tehachapis, but they don't want to. Got their hands full."

I got up to go, as Second 20 pulled in.

"Thanks for the assist," said MacIntosh, and then gave me a quick glance. "Just stay on the rails. I know what those Northerns do to you."

As I walked forward to the Diesel I noticed it had begun to sleet and would soon rain. In spite of dusk it was getting warmer. All we needed was a nice fast thaw for a day or so, on top of all this snow, and half the Sierras would be sliding down on our rails.

I found my old friend Billings handling Second 20 and he couldn't repress a smile when he saw me. After all, I had ridden up to the Gap with him on the momentous day I'd ditched Betty and jumped off. He never knew just what had happened but he did know I'd been holed up at the Casa Alta ever since.

"Hi, Mr. Bierce. Going to make New York this time?" he asked blandly.

"Afraid not," I retorted. "I'm just practicing. Going to Benning and coming back on Extra 77, with the first of the military. Several of the Nine-Thousand class are coming over here."

Billings knew my weakness and smiled.

"Going to do a little rail scorching with the Northerns," he observed accurately. "Well, I'm going through to Benning myself. A lot of crews on both Divisions are pretty scrambled."

Ordinarily Billings got off at Placer, our Division point. At Placer we found snow had turned to drizzling rain with only a few inches of melting snow on the ground. And just once the sun shone briefly through scudding masses of clouds.

I was also surprised to see the collection of motive power Mac-

Intosh had gathered at Placer to boost swollen traffic over the Hill at this critical period. In the big yards had been assembled a cavalcade of steam power representing developments in power and design for the past fifty years, and now mobilized for a last mournful historic fling prior to the final burial of the Iron Horse. There were the usual Diesels and Mallets, but over by the roundhouse and fuel tanks were samples of about everything that had ever moved under steam on the G.W. for the last two generations. Antique Mikados and some heavy new Berkshires. Mountain types, Baldwin and Alco, dating back thirty years. A lone, ancient, hulking Lima-built Decapod, a curiosity. Sleek Pacifics, the most graceful of engines in my opinion, backstopped by half a dozen old Consolidations, probably used at the time of the Pharaohs, resembling teapots against the looming hulks of three big 2-10-2 Santa Fe types. And over by the pump house stood two small immaculate ten-wheelers, like flappers of a bygone day, outshopped by Baldwin in 1909 for high varnish on the Kansas plains.

The real monstrosities were the Mikados. Originally put out by Alco in 1912 they had been twice rebuilt to increase their power and steaming qualities. The result was a frightful tangle of plumbing and ponderous gadgets plastered all over the boiler and head end. Over the pilot rose a maze of cluttered compressors, pumps, feed water heaters, superheaters, and jigsaw fittings attached thereto which made these plumbers' nightmares look as if they were about to topple into the ditch at any time. I had driven them and there wasn't one that didn't suffer from half a dozen pulmonary ailments. They were all boneshakers equipped, I was convinced, with square wheels. But I looked over Placer's collection of engines with a good deal of nostalgia and much interest.

We got out of Placer eleven minutes late, heading over snow-free desert with the Sierra peaks gleaming a deep blue-white forty miles behind us against a flaming sunset sky. When Billings got rolling at about seventy he called over his shoulder:

"Like to take her, Mr. Bierce?"

I decided I would. I thanked Billings and we changed seats as I nodded to the fireman, a young Mexican named Parera who called off the signal boards in a rich tenor voice. Very shortly we came down to a crawl at a bad-order stretch of arroyo that was being ballasted. But there were ninety-five miles of straight level track ahead, no snow, no Pioneer Gap, no problems, and I was on my own.

Across the arroyo the board was green and I pulled the throttle lever back a couple of notches, watching the load meter on the control panel. With eight notches on the usual Diesel throttle, the lever moves back about a quarter inch per notch, the numbers showing up in a lighted slot as more or less speed is called for, accelerating the Diesels through a governor. We rapidly picked up speed, the Diesels yowling behind us. Every time the needle on the load meter dropped down near the red area I clicked up another throttle number and kept six hundred amperes or better reaching the traction motors.

There's a myth that Diesels hum. They don't. They growl, blather, whine, scream, thunder, and snarl at each other like a pack of enraged cougars during their starting speeds. But at about forty-five m.p.h., with the motors "in parallel," they ease off to a steady hell-raising racket. I soon got up to throttle notch 7—about eighty miles an hour—and held it there. I was saving my real fun for the return trip with the Northern. But I did enjoy the speed. On the Hill nobody but the chaperon of a streamliner ever made over forty-five. Top speeds of twenty-five to thirty-five for passenger trains and fifteen to twenty for freight were about standard. The Diesels I was handling, three powerful brand-new EMD E-8 units, were geared to a maximum speed of ninety-eight miles an hour. But farther east on the plains we had a lot of Diesels factory-geared to 117 m.p.h. Needless to say, they were seldom operated at anything like that speed.

We arrived in Benning at five-fifty on the dot. I had time to see Davis, a few old friends, and stow away a hot supper in the station dining room. Even over here there was concern at the steady driving falls of snow on the Hill. Then at six-forty I heard a train roll in and Davis, finishing coffee with me, looked out the window.

"That's Extra 77, Bierce. She's all yours. Kiernan's okay but he hasn't ridden west of Utah in his life. And don't steal our Division on the way back. We got to live here. She's carded to clear at six-forty."

I put on my coat and shook hands.

"Let's go," I said.

12

I hadn't seen one of our big Northerns for almost a year. I walked slowly across the tracks and studied No. 9060. She was showing the white feather, a tall straight column of live steam roaring up from her pop valve into the night air. The valve closed with a sound like a hard cough and the engine simmered peacefully again. To me she was a 440-ton poem in motive power, a masterpiece of design from every angle, and one of the greatest mobile powerhouses ever mounted on wheels.

The Nine Thousands are worth a brief digression. They were the third of a series of G-S or General Service 4-8-4 heavy-duty Northerns designed by our own chief of motive power, Henry Hartmann, and built by Lima in 1947. Physically they provided a most remarkable contrast to their creator. Hartmann, with a perpetual slight stoop from his draughting boards, was a trim, slender, white-haired little man, a kind of merry genius with a cherubic ruddy face and close-clipped white beard. He was also a protégé and rumored kinsman of the late Otto Jabelmann, the Union Pacific's chief of motive power who designed many of the U.P.'s great postwar engines.

In their big boilers, long clean lines, and high drivers, Great Western engines bore basic similarities to the U.P.'s finest. But in these last great Northerns he designed Hartmann surpassed himself and everyone else, in my opinion. Back in Ohio he had driven the Lima people half crazy with last-minute refinements and changes, chiefly in exterior design and appearance. An artist insisting on his finishing touches. I was sure that Hartmann, facing the devastating triumph of Diesels, was determined to sing a last magnificent swan song for the Iron Horse. And sing it he did. If steam had to die, Hartmann determined it would die in a blaze of glory.

Thinking of Hartmann, I walked all around 9060 before climbing

148

up into the big lofty streamlined cab, a functionally designed laboratory, weatherproofed and sound-deadened with masonite, with adjustable foam rubber seats, clear-vision windows with air defrosters, adjustable windshield wings, and the entire cab supported from the boiler to prevent shearing or distortion due to expansion and contraction of the 9060's huge barrel, 115 inches in diameter just forward of the firebox.

I was a Diesel expert but I had to pay a profound tribute to these monsters. Hartmann's masterpiece flowed in one long almost unbroken line from pilot to tender coupling—112 feet, 6 inches—and tipped the scales at 1,310,000 pounds, with Ragonnet power reverse and Schmidt superheaters. The small amount of outside plumbing was artfully concealed or molded with care under the running boards. The huge boiler overhang at the head end seemed to be in a hurry. Low streamlined twin stacks, one for each cylinder; graceful smoke lifters; and twin sand domes in tandem emphasized the over-all impression of great speed and power. Hartmann had placed heat indicators on every journal and driving box, all ball-bearing. His toy worked at three hundred and fifty pounds steam pressure with eighty-inch drivers and forty-four-inch leading wheels.

As an artist in steel Hartmann also made every use of modern metallurgy to cut down weight and step up power. Driving axles, main and side rods, crankpins and piston rods were made of heat-treated, low-carbon nickel steel. Pistonheads were of lightweight alloy steel with three T-section combination bronze and cast-iron piston packing rings. The crossheads were manganese-vanadium alloy steel castings, operating in multi-bearing guides surfaced with pure tin. Hartmann also used novel cushioning devices on all driving axles to insure great flexibility and steadiness. The weight of the reciprocating parts on each side of the engine reached nearly a ton, and Hartmann designed his own secondary or cross-balancing devices in addition to careful counterbalancing of the conventional type.

For this huge powerhouse Hartmann provided a semi-Vanderbilt tender, 4-10-2 wheel arrangement, carrying 25,000 gallons of water and 6,400 gallons of fuel oil in 48 feet of length. Contrast that with a 60-ton engine of 1893 carrying 3,000 gallons of water and six tons of coal.

But you had to see these machines in motion, at work, alive in action, to appreciate their beauty. Old William Mason of Taunton, Massachusetts, who made cotton-textile machinery for a living and for sheer fun and love designed the finest proportioned engines in locomotive history a century ago, would have bowed in admiration to Hartmann. These modern giants possessed an ease of operation at any speed that delighted everyone who handled them. Built for a top speed of ninety-five m.p.h., one of them on its test run stepped twenty-two old-style Pullmans along—almost two thousand tons—at 108 miles an hour. And might have done a lot more if our Master Mechanic had said the word. He didn't. He was satisfied. These Northerns bowed to no other engine in the matter of horsepower per pound of engine weight. They were also marvelous steamers, economical, and seldom in the backshop except for scheduled overhauls.

In short I was feeling pretty good when I introduced myself to our freshman engineer, Kiernan, a cheerful Irishman from Topeka, who had fired six years and put in two at the throttle on our Montana branch. The fireman, Elwell, I already knew. The Brains had given me the line-up or consist, fourteen baggage and express, one diner, and five Pullmans full of army brass. Twenty in all. Something over eighteen hundred tons.

I decided to check Kiernan a bit and take over later. Kiernan made the usual standing test of air brakes, bleeding the train line of fifteen pounds' pressure, and watching the gauge while "car toads" along the train observed brake action and other mysteries of the "secret works" under each car. No leakage. Everything okay. Kiernan relaxed and crossed his feet to hold down the "dead man's control" pedal. If he jumped out the window or keeled over with the train in motion, the released pedal automatically set the brakes.

Kiernan glanced at his watch as we got a highball from the rear end and the air whistle overhead blurted its familiar *beep-beep*. Then he switched off the overhead cab light and tugged at the big throttle lever as Elwell sounded two short blasts on 9060's rich baritone whistle. We glided off, 9060 walking away with a pleasant sharp chuff from her twin stacks as if we were heading leisurely for the roundhouse. I sat on Elwell's side for a while, then stood in the semi-enclosed gangway listening with sheer pleasure to the measured breathing of this superb machine which rode like a Pullman while hauling twenty cars up a 1.8 grade to Cardinal Summit at sixty-five miles an hour. Kiernan knew his stuff and so did Elwell after a first few minutes when he poured a lot of black smoke over the landscape. 9060 didn't need that much fuel and the boy soon found it out.

We slowed to forty at Cardinal as we snatched a "19" order from the operator's Y hi-speeder hoop and rattled by a long line of reefers clattering east on a passing track. It was then, with an exchange of courtesies from Kiernan, that I took over.

While I was picking up speed and getting the feel of 9060 Kiernan voiced his own enthusiasm for the Nine Thousands and gave me five good reasons why he preferred them to Diesels. I agreed with him emphatically, but told him our accounting department turned up figures that canceled out all our arguments.

"I know," said Kiernan sadly. "These babies may be dead ducks tomorrow—but they sure can fly today."

"Okay," I told him, "we're going to find out how fast this baby can fly right now."

Kiernan grinned as I began to feed steam into the 9060's big cylinders. In five minutes we were doing eighty. I opened up a little more and glanced a bit guiltily at the tape speed recorder box locked just behind the speedometer. The tape speed recorder, signed by the last engineer, was always removed at Oakland by a machinist's foreman and delivered to the Division superintendent's secretary. Its graph gave an experienced reader a close picture of the entire trip, usually convicting the guilty and exonerating the innocent in any squabble over rules violations. I decided to give our G.W. brass something to think about and I was passing the buck to John Ramsay MacIntosh if anyone yelled. Also, speed restrictions on this stretch were a generous ninety-five for passenger trains, with plenty of allowance for making up late schedules.

At eighty-five I leaned out the cab in the chill night air, listening to the music of the rails, and took a good look around at the whirling valve gear, the flying drivers, the trailer truck under me, the long swaying train behind me on a slight curve, the five lighted Pullmans and diner looking like a Christmas tree towed behind our dark express cars. Everything seemed in order. I also looked at the country. Ordinarily, under a blazing noonday sun, the scene was desolate in the extreme. The rails ran through a dismal barren alkali valley bordered with low crumbling buttes and white salt cliffs, about as dead and dreary a landscape as ever depressed bored passengers and train crew alike.

But on this clear luminous night the scene caught me in its spell. A great golden full moon hung halfway up the sky behind us flooding the barren valley with a ghostly silver sheen. What it did to those crumbling bleached buttes was sheer magic. They were transformed into superb etchings in black and silver, ruined fortresses, grotesque castles, turrets, gleaming minarets, all touched with white fire against a blue-black, star-studded sky, as far as the eye could see.

I was grateful to MacIntosh for this welcome treat. We roared at ninety past the maintenance camp at Dry Coulee. Somebody paid us a tribute by running out of the foreman's shanty. A white blurred face looked up at me with something like real concern as he flashed past us into the shadow of the rushing train. Then we thundered through a mile of cutting, some of it quite deep, and the cab reverberated with the crashing echoes of battling sound waves. At a siding called Trotter we were rolling at ninety-seven, and again I thought of Hartmann and his draughting boards. Of Lima, too, and the men who had built his masterpiece. The 9060 ran like a greyhound—the exhaust a subdued throttled thunder, practically no side sway at all, only a gentle up-and-down motion when we hit a bit of track that could stand some manicuring. But in general the roadbed was perfect. I thoroughly enjoyed myself. We made the next fifty-one miles in thirty minutes. Over a hundred miles an hour.

Then we entered twenty miles of double track and I slowed to seventy for the only substantial curve near Battle Canyon station, where Rykoff had missed his stop. Only we weren't stopping. *Whap-whang—whoop-whoop—clatter-clatter-clatter—zzu-upp!* Tank, pump house, cars on a siding, station, and warehouse were gone. Then we rushed into Battle Canyon curve with an eight-pound air reduction, leaning heavily to the left. I was going pretty fast for that bend.

I was aware all at once of a cone of light to the left. Elwell called over, "Four-eighty coming up." Of course, on my side of the cab, I couldn't see the opposing rails more than a couple of hundred feet ahead. Suddenly a steam-spitting, smoke-belching, one-eyed monster with a long jointed body rushed right at me, crowding the curve with a terrific racket. The illusion of any engineer on the inside of a sharp two-tracked curve filled with two opposing trains is an abrupt conviction that you're both on the same rails and due for an immediate head-on crash, in this instance with a clattering swaying mass of drunken boxcars headed by a maniacal monster threatening to boil off the rails.

A thin two-inch flange, grinding on curved rails, is all that manages to tear you apart and prevent catastrophe. Thump, rattle, grind, scream, clatter-clatter-clatter. *Whap!* Boxcars, gondolas, hopper cars, reefers, flats with farm machinery, big black rolling cylinders—oil cars—bulky automobile cars, more boxcars, more flats, more of everything. Dust and thunder. Then the quick flash of green and cadmium caboose markers. And 480 was on its way east. You were free of its terrible embrace and plunged on into the desert night in a sudden cessation of uproar that seemed like complete silence to me.

Coming out of Battle Canyon curve, I really opened up, determined to crowd this great machine to the limit. Far across the Humboldt Desert, forty-three miles of absolute straightaway to the west —the boys called this the "Race Track"—were the twinkling pinpointed lights of Placer, lonely and isolated against the serrated fringe of Sierra peaks another forty miles distant.

The canyon cliffs fell away. We were streaking over empty moonlit desert, the rushing air filled with the spice of sage and dampness from the first traces of snow. I watched the speedometer needle climb—80–85–91–97–102. I glanced back at Kiernan. He wore a broad smile and made a gesture of cutting his throat.

"She's a son of a bitch," he shouted in my ear. He was right. I hoped the army brass were enjoying the ride as much as I was. I learned later a plump major had slid off a lounge chair into the aisle when we hit Battle Canyon curve. He was convinced for five minutes that the train was out of control. I adjusted the valve travel a bit and tugged hard at the throttle lever in a final gesture of triumph. We hit 116 miles an hour and stayed there for five minutes.

This was it. This was my binge. Then I began to cut down the speed.

I had my head in the cab a moment studying the brake pressure gauge when Elwell called suddenly across the cab: "Yellow!" I repeated the word and looked out. Brother! There was a yellow board rushing up a mile away, a red board beyond it, and the whole town of Placer pouring up out of the desert less than five miles away. My celebration was over. Kiernan had enjoyed it too. I dropped my hand to the air-valve handle, nursed the lever, and watched the needle until it was down about eight pounds. It was just as if 9060 ran into a strong head wind, checking its rush. I made several more service applications and we ground to a stop before a final red board, just out of town. What the hell was holding us? I knew the tower boys and I was in a hurry. I called to Elwell, "Give 'em the works."

Elwell's teeth gleamed. He, too, had had a good time. He grabbed the whistle lever and called for clear, four short blasts, repeated over and over, that ripped through the night like the voice of a dictator. For two minutes we bellowed there like a balked bull. Later Rudy Silver in Tower B told me everybody thought we had a bunch of dying generals aboard. The trouble was nobody expected us that early. We weren't due until eight-twenty and it was just seven forty-three. A yard goat and some coaches were still on the main. They were cleared in a hurry, and three minutes later we eased to a halt beside Placer's big ugly frame station.

An informal reception committee straggled over, headed by Ellis, the trainmaster. His eyes were popping, his expression not too approving.

"What the hell's going on, Bierce? Your home on fire?"

"Just wanted to see if this boiler was good enough to get up the Hill," I said soberly. "What's the matter?"

He just looked at me, then at 9060, breathing easily, high, handsome, and huge, with hot oil gleaming on her piston guides, her semi-streamlined jacket towering over us, polished and shining in the moonlight.

"How come the wheels are still on?" he asked with heavy humor. "Okay, okay," he continued as I started to say something. "But you'd better tear out that tape speed recorder and throw it away. Cut loose on your own Division after this. You probably scared hell out of the Army. And you hung up a record, if you want to know—sixty-three minutes out of Benning. Five minutes faster than Fontaine's special

153

going East. Maybe the Commonwealth Club will give you another medal," he said acidly, and turned on his heel.

That was all. 9060 gulped up fifteen thousand gallons of water and we started off again. But sedately, with dignity. No more rail scorching. Kiernan took over and I coached him on what was ahead. And here came the snow. Into the Arctic again. We passed through Pioneer Gap at an even forty-five and I looked over at the familiar lights of the Casa Alta. Once more I was startled at this sudden transformation to massive peaks and endless snows so close to the moonlit snowless desert. So was Kiernan. And sure enough, in Wildroot Valley the weather clouded up at once and, to keep the pattern, just past Gunnison Gate it was snowing!

So I was home again. I enjoyed watching Kiernan's face as we marched up those heavy grades without a helper through plowed-out white-walled canyons, often high above stack level, to Eldorado Summit. Telegraph lines along the rails frequently sagged out of sight or seemed to skim the surface of the snow. Kiernan had never rolled west of Utah. He was simply struck dumb.

"This stuff ever melt?" he finally asked in an awed tone.

"Once a year. On the Fourth of July," I told him. He shook his head, but I almost think he really believed me.

At Eldorado Summit I got down and bestowed a final parting glance on 9060 in tribute to Hartmann's brain child just as MacIntosh and George Esmond Fontaine, himself, came over. Fontaine's appearance at Eldorado Summit meant things were getting serious. We shook hands. I gestured at 9060 for Fontaine's benefit.

"You can scrap everything you've got, Mr. Fontaine. But don't scrap these Northerns. Put them on pedestals when we're through with them. There's nothing on wheels to compare with them."

Fontaine nodded gravely. He knew what I meant. But MacIntosh was looking at his watch and rumbling ominously. He said to me, sotto voce, "Bierce, you bastard, you're not due here for another hour. You took advantage of me. The ICC will hang me."

"I don't understand it," I said solemnly. "We had the brakes on all the way in from Benning. I've got two witnesses."

MacIntosh looked at me reproachfully. But Fontaine wasn't even listening. "Come over to my car, Bierce," he said. "I've got something to show you."

The Big Hill's gears were beginning to mesh again. I told Kiernan he had nothing to worry about and walked away with Fontaine. His private car was on the Wye track, with a phone connected, and I got his permission to call Alice Livingston who, I happened to know, was staying overnight in the old schoolhouse a short distance away. She was still busy with a pageant rehearsal and I made a date to run over and see her in half an hour. Then I rejoined Fontaine in his drawing room.

Fontaine's car, "El Gobernador," was the former "Maricopa" built for Bruce Hodges, the San Francisco millionaire who disappeared in the early forties. Although renovated along utilitarian lines for official railroad usage, the car remained a sumptuous palace on wheels with two master bedrooms, a small office, dining room, kitchen, and a twenty-two-foot observation-living room with a color décor of blue brocade and gold, and boasting a genuine mid-Victorian black marble fireplace, a memento of the old Flood mansion, with a coal grate almost always glowing a cherry red, as it was now. All this luxury under a stark snowshed on the summit of the Sierras, with the roar of the storm muffled and distant, seemed a bit incongruous. Fontaine referred to it himself.

"I don't use this car too much," he said dryly. "It gives me a false sense of security. It was made for the Florida beaches and that's where it belongs."

He was even more worried than MacIntosh, both by the weather and the responsibility of the special shipments, and reminisced a bit about the past decade in the Sierras. The five-day stalling of the S.P.'s "City of San Francisco" streamliner near Emigrant Gap in the big snows of 1952 was still fresh in his mind.

"We can all get caught in this kind of jam," he observed. "We had six or seven very mild winters in the forties—and all the railroad brass in the West seemed to get an impression that it wasn't going to snow any more. Everybody started tearing down snowsheds, snow fences, cutting storm budgets, and putting storm equipment in storage. Well, the U.P. got it first in 1949 over in Wyoming. What a tie-up! Streamliners stalled for days. Freight drags scattered all over. I'd hate to tell you how many top officials went to the guillotine. My Southern Pacific friends were distantly sympathetic but told me how impossible such mishaps were in the Sierras, where we are always on guard.

"So 1952 rolled in with the City of San Francisco frozen in solid just above Emigrant Gap, and the road closed down for days. You know what it was like."

I sure did. Fontaine flicked the ash from his cigar and scowled at the massive snowshed timbers outside his window.

"Maybe it's our turn now," he continued somberly. "We've done all we can. We've got to fight it out. But if I had fifty fingers and fifty toes tonight I'd keep 'em all crossed until after the first of the year. . . . Oh yes, I've got a bit of a Christmas gift for you."

He got up, disappeared in his office a moment or two, then returned with two big ornate loose-leaf books, handsomely embossed. He handed them to me.

"Take these along for a day or two," he suggested. "The first concerns the 'Cloudbuster,' a new two-decker all-vista dome train dropping into Pioneer Gap on her first trip West in a few days. Last word in modern, functional, streamlining. Our chairman's baby. But here's something you don't know about. Take a look. That's my baby."

The book he indicated consisted of a big sheaf of handsome color plates, luxuriously bound, from the Pullman-Standard Car Company. I opened them up and almost toppled off my chair. A gold-embossed card announced the inaugural run of the "Golden Age," a fast, de luxe masterpiece of modern mid-Victorian décor, inspired by the golden decades of San Francisco in its prime—and thirty-eight hours between Oakland and Chicago. The interior of each car was a period masterpiece representing a prominent decade of San Fancisco's earlier days. All decoration by the New York designer, Beauchamp. Exterior color was royal blue and gold from coupler to coupler, with handsome coats of arms in Tuscan red, jade green, cobalt blue, and gold affixed to each car. The cars had exceptionally high clearance, with wide imposing clerestory roofs. I was stunned to note that the "Palace Bar" in the forward lounge car, filled with beveled mirrors, red and gold brocaded easy chairs with hassocks to match, boasted four paintings by "Howard Bierce, noted railroad artist of the High Sierras." I was just about speechless.

"You mean—this is ready to roll?" I asked in a small voice.

"It is," said Fontaine, a bit grimly I thought. "It's on exhibition at Grand Central Station, January 6 to 13. Leaves the thirteenth on its inaugural trip. Arrives at Oakland the fifteenth, 7 A.M., fifty-five hours out of New York. I just about had to buy up the ICC to schedule that timecard. And you and Betty can have your pick of rooms right now. It's on the house. And you'll be back on the job, on time."

I got off the usual inane expressions of astonishment, joking about a probable suit from the B. & O. over the blue and gold trim, and wound up by remarking, "It looks like a string of private cars, sir."

"That's what I want it to look like," said Fontaine emphatically. "I'm glad you were tight that night, Bierce. Every crack you took at these functionally designed hygienic steel tubes we're operating hit home with me. I've been mulling over a train like this for years. You convinced me. After two years I finally jammed it through the board with a bare quorum. If it doesn't take—I'm hung. But I think it will."

I leafed silently through the plates showing each car as resplendent as a millionaire's study, full of fine fabrics, rich brocades, superbly shaded lamps and more beveled mirrors. The library car, with oak-paneled wainscoting after an English club, must have cost a fortune. And the final touch floored me. Both lounge cars boasted small marble fireplaces with coal-burning grates. Good Lord, the cost—and the cleaning bills and upkeep! I dared to hint at this. Fontaine nodded grimly again. He began to rattle off statistics and concluded:

"The walls and ceiling of every car contain over fifty-three thousand feet of electrical wiring. Your beach cottage may boast twelve hundred feet. Circulating ice water, phones, and radio in every room. Fluorescent lights, electronic doors and weather control. Any one car, at $150,000 apiece, would more than cover the entire cost of our eight-car 'Western Trail,' including engine and tender, that we placed on the rails in 1898. You're right. Cleaning and upkeep will cost a fortune. But I believe we've got the luxury trade to support this train. I think it will run the Cloudbuster into second place. The New York Central brass went over it in the Pullman yards last week and have been pawing the air ever since." He laughed. "I think they may junk the 'Century.'"

In astonished silence I leafed over each plate again, each superb car named after famed San Francisco haunts: "Knob Hill," "Coit Tower," "Cliff House," "Embarcadero," "Fairmount," "Twin Peaks," "Telegraph Hill," and so on.

"Half of San Francisco will ride this train every season," I said at last.

"They'd better," replied Fontaine grimly. "And there'll be a Christmas check in recognition of your contributions to this project. Not a word to anyone for the present."

Fontaine's boldness in creating a train that flew in the face of every trend in modern design for the past thirty years greatly surprised me. But as I left him I had a hunch the "Golden Age" would be the sensational success it has since proved to be.

In excellent spirits after this extraordinary day, I picked my way through the sheds and down the long snow tunnel that led to Alice's old school building.

Space permits but few words concerning the old Summit School that practically straddled our rails. I doubt if any schoolhouse ever occupied such a location or operated under such impossible conditions. Summit School was created in 1909 to lead eight or ten youngsters of railroaders into the perils of education. In a burst of generosity, as no funds were available in the community, the G.W. contributed the remains of an ancient company store, about to collapse. The roof was tightened, the walls shored up, and a few gallons of company paint, drab yellow and brown, were slapped over the cracked clapboarding—and the school was turned over to its first appalled staff of one young lady teacher from Reno.

The building stood midway in an open hollow between two sets of snowsheds, each about eighty yards distant from the school, and connected to it by wooden snow tunnels. With each passing train the structure practically toppled over to a thundering racket that rattled timbers, shook down showers of dust, and brought all educational activities to an abrupt halt. Class and teacher froze in a kind of still-picture pose until the train had passed. So conditioned did everybody become to these interruptions that recitations left in mid-air were picked up two minutes later without a word lost in the process. Over the single big classroom were crude living quarters, a kitchenette, and a second small coal stove, rooms where teachers formerly lived and where Alice once in a while now spent a night or two if the lane to her nearby cottage at Summit had not been plowed out.

It was in the classroom that I found Alice winding up a gay rehearsal of the Mexican *posada* and giving final instructions to ten or twelve excited young participants, due to return to their homes by special bus in a few minutes. Our two leading characters were a limpid-eyed mischievous Mexican youngster of twelve, Billy Garcia, and a freckle-faced Irish kid, Tommy O'Brien, both of them born actors. The schoolroom was a chaos of pageant props and gear for the party. After the children had gone, running and shouting through the sheds, Alice made some coffee and we sat down. I looked at the snowbound windows, rectangles of opaque white, protected from pressure by heavy wooden bars. The snow was already up to the second-story windows.

"Are you still determined to hold that party in the new auditorium?" I asked. Alice gave me a bland confident glance.

"Absolutely. The highway boys have sworn to hold back the heavens until midnight, Christmas Eve. I'm going to dedicate that building if we have to shovel our way in and out."

I laughed at her assurance. "Okay. But I have a hunch we'll be digging out your guests all next May."

"I'll be in Karachi, then," retorted Alice. Her warm eyes glistened. "Can you imagine me a housewife in far-off India after this? I can't believe it."

We listened to the wind roaring over the quaking structure. The potbellied stove panted unevenly under an erratic forced draft. Alice leaned back and stretched out her arms.

"Don't tell Lal Besar" (that was her young engineer-fiancé) "but I hate to leave the Hill, Mr. Bierce. I've been up here two years. I think it's been the most glorious time of my life. I'm afraid my pioneer blood is really up. I feel sorry for everybody that has to live below eight thousand feet. Spring, summer, brief autumn, and winter on the Hill—they're all glorious."

"If working in this ramshackle wreck is your idea of glory," I said cheerfully, "you'll adjust to Karachi or any other locale."

"You know what I mean," she retorted accusingly. "And don't

hide behind that blasé official air of yours. I've watched you. You wouldn't trade your job on the Hill for ten million in cash. Would you?"

I smiled and shook my head. "No I wouldn't, Alice."

"You see?" Her dark blue eyes sparkled. "Everybody feels the same up here. It's clean, fresh, bracing. I hate to leave. It's been my Shangri-La. And I think it's yours."

We drank more coffee, went over final party details, and gossiped a great deal. Then I glanced at my watch and grabbed Alice's phone, calling CTC and getting Gerson. It was 1:10 A.M.

"What time's 58 by?" I asked, inquiring about a leisurely accommodation train for Placer, usually an hour or two late, but nominally due at one-two.

"You kidding?" snapped Gerson. "She left here six minutes ago, right on the nose." Then he must have figured my predicament for he added too cheerfully, "Last bus went down at midnight, Howie. Route 80's closed till 6 A.M. You at Alice's?" He actually sniggered into the phone, "Have a good time, my boy," and hung up.

"Alice," I said gravely, "may I have the honor of spending the night with you?"

Alice's eyes widened. Then came a peal of laughter.

"Don't tell me—are you really stranded up here?"

"Completely. I could hammer on Fontaine's private car but I don't think he'd appreciate it. I just missed 58, on the dot for the first time in years. Route 80's closed down. There's a cot at the CTC office but I——"

Alice rose to the occasion magnificently. "This is most intriguing, Mr. Bierce, though there are only two spare blankets. I'm afraid," she added with great composure, "the double bed's too small for us both. But the guest room is always ready."

"The service is excellent," I replied in kind. "And don't worry about Lal. I won't boast about my conquest until you're safely in Karachi."

I stoked up the stove and we sat around shooting the breeze until after two. Then the phone rang and startled me. Alice picked it up, frowning.

"Oh but he is here," she said into the phone, and handed it to me, adding in a whisper for my benefit, "Pete Gustavson."

Gustavson? At two-thirty in the morning? What was cooking?

"Bierce, Pete. What's up?" Then I listened.

"Howie? I been phoning all over. Gerson told me where you were."

I hastily explained what had happened. He laughed, but there was urgency in his voice.

"I figured something like that. Listen, Howie, can you help me out at nine tomorrow morning? I need help bad, and I don't want to ask Ted. He's in lousy shape. I got a lot of heavy stuff at the mine to move to the Gap. I can't handle it alone and I can't get anybody else. You'll be back at the Gap by eleven. I wouldn't bother you if it wasn't important."

Another morning shot to hell. But to Pete I had to say yes. I could catch 502 at Summit before dawn and Pete would meet me at Placer with his car. He thanked me fervently, added without any innuendo, "Give my best to Miss Livingston," and hung up. I briefly explained the call to Alice and then we both decided to turn in. It occurred to me we had gaily advertised our little adventure all over the Hill through Gerson and Gustavson, but I didn't think it would go any farther and wouldn't hurt anyone if it did.

It also occurred to me that, along with puttering around with paints and preparations for Alice's party, I had better find out a bit more about my mine investment. Pete's call at this hour had disturbed me.

13

With the first gray streak of light, and with half an eye on my watch, I stole out of Summit School and caught 502, downing some toast and coffee in the deserted diner. An hour later Gustavson picked me up at Placer and we headed for Virginia City, another hour away.

I saw at once that Gustavson was far more disturbed by Helmholtz's illness than I had realized. After each of several long silences he would say abruptly, "You think that Doc knows his business, eh?"

Pete also surprised me by announcing he was returning to Colorado to look after some other mining interests soon after the first of the year. He let me know he had hired a manager for our own modest Virginia City project on a year's contract. I questioned him closely on the recent financial statement he had given me. It appeared that within a month or two I would realize a few hundred dollars' profit on my impulsive investment, but the general outlook wasn't too bright. I asked Pete how long he thought the gallery would produce. He pondered that question for some time.

"Not too long," he said finally. "I didn't figure as good as I thought. Maybe six or eight months. We got most of that vein out now."

He sounded glad to be leaving. He had no interest in remaining here without Ted.

It would be hard to imagine a more forlorn place than the tailings of Virginia City under a foot of sooty slush and a leaden sky, with that backdrop of decrepit structures draped against Mount Davidson, their loose boards and shingles rattling in the Washoe winds. The wraiths of yesterday, the echoes of a haunting past, swirled about us in wind and snow.

Gustavson and I worked fast loading pieces of mine equipment, most of it junk to me, into a small trailer standing by the office.

The big job was sliding the old marine winch I had seen used as a hoist up into the trailer on an incline of boards. That winch was heavy. Pete informed me he was replacing it with one of more efficient design. While we labored I noticed a small blue coupé that stopped near us. The driver watched us awhile and then drove on. After an hour's work we were ready to go. We drove up into town, as Gustavson had to leave some papers at a law office. The wind blasted out of the west and I recalled Mark Twain's pungent description of these Washoe zephyrs. Hard snow stung our faces as we got out. I noticed the blue coupé sliding into the curb a couple of blocks away. The driver emerged and also seemed headed for the Boston Bar. In fact he entered it as Gustavson and I stood talking by the curb. I had never seen the man before. He was wearing a faded blue mackinaw. Gustavson swore at the weather.

"This is one damn winter I've had enough of," he growled. "Why don't you wait in the Boston? It's warm there. I may be a few minutes."

We separated. Pete climbed a flight of outside steps with gingerbread railings to a shallow veranda and disappeared in some dingy law offices on the second floor. I went into the Boston Bar. My friend in the blue mackinaw wasn't around. Ordering a double bourbon, I hung around the famous old rendezvous of miners and millionaires of two generations ago, listening to a couple of truck drivers discussing conditions on the Geiger Grade. Gustavson was upstairs quite a while and I strolled about looking at some old posters and ancient music boxes. Then I noticed an "Out of Order" sign on the men's room door and went over to the bartender.

"Take the back stairs and clear to the end of the hall. Watch your step. It's kinda dark. This'll be fixed today."

Thinking hard about Gustavson and Ted, I absently found and mounted the rickety stairs, went down a long gloomy hall, unlighted, saw a crack of light under a door to my left, and mechanically pushed on in. I got the shock of my life, and I was completely unprepared for it. I was inside a ramshackle little bedroom with faded pale paper peeling from the wall, a single light bulb hanging from the ceiling. Two good suits hung on wall hooks. There was a suitcase on the floor. Half a bottle of liquor and a pile of newspapers sat on a small table. Behind the table, facing me, sat Jackpot Thomas, his hard eyes staring into mine. He never moved. Standing beside him was the driver of the coupé in the faded blue mackinaw. This was Thomas' hide-out. No doubt about it.

The man in the blue mackinaw whirled, saw me, and had me covered with his gun all in one instant. I heard the click of the safety catch.

"Not here," said Thomas firmly, rising slowly over the table, his eyes never leaving mine. "Sit over there, Bierce." So he had my name right. Paralyzed by fear, I sat down on the edge of a straight-back chair. "Frisk him, Fred."

Fred did so. I had never carried a gun in my life. Thomas studied me. "How'd you come in here?"

I told him. I don't think he believed me. But it didn't matter. "That's too bad," he said grittily. "It's at the end of the hall."

I could almost hear him thinking fast and hard. And I think I sensed at once the decision he had already made. He stood menac-ingly over me.

"You got too big a nose for trouble, Bierce. It's bad enough you sock me cold in that coffee shop. Great kidder, huh? Jim Reynolds, huh?" He said savagely, "Why you dumb son of a bitch, my friends straightened me out on you right away. And I read your statement to the coppers. All of that you mighta got away with. But not when you walk in here."

He suddenly pistol-whipped me—two blows across each cheek, cutting me almost to the bone on my left jaw. I felt warm blood run down my cheek and neck. I was dazed and tried to get up. Fred shoved me back on the chair. Far away I heard Thomas in a low voice barking clipped orders at Fred.

"Get him down the back way. Take my car. Take him to the old shaft and get rid of him there. He'll keep a long time. Don't come back here. Shack up with Jimmy in Reno until you hear from me."

Then my heart jumped. All the way from the front of the build-ing I heard Gustavson shouting, "Hey, Bierce! Bierce!"

Thomas stiffened. Fred's gun muzzle rose an inch. Thomas picked up the suitcase and handed it to me. "That'll keep your hands busy, mister. Okay, Fred. Get going."

As I stumbled out into that dark hallway with Fred's suitcase and Fred's gun muzzle in my back, I knew death was walking with me. For an instant I even had a crazy idea that Gustavson was in on this somewhere. I couldn't help it. There was something too neat about all this. That early-morning phone call from Pete. This guy in the blue coupé watching us. Pete bringing me to the Boston Bar. His line about "hiring a manager" while he took off for Colorado. What went? I had a chill sinking feeling about it all. One thing stopped me. Pete hadn't ever suggested I look for the men's room and walk into Thomas' hide-out instead.

We turned to the right, away from the staircase I'd come up. There must be another one. The suitcase I carried was a good one, of heavy cowhide, and with plenty of weight inside. It could be a shield, a weapon, or both. But I couldn't turn in that tight hallway. And that prodding gun muzzle pushed me along. I passed four or five closed doors. I was dizzy from Thomas' blows and my face felt damp. I realized I was sweating. We approached a door on my right, a battered door ajar a couple of inches and the light through the crack wasn't artificial. It came from a window somewhere.

As I came opposite that door a brainstorm hit me. I wasn't ready to die. I snapped the suitcase up behind me, just as hard as I could, in the general direction where I thought Fred's arms and face would be. At the same instant I jumped sideways through the door, almost snapping it off the hinges.

A lot of things happened almost simultaneously. The roar of a gun deafened me. I kept right on going across the room, crouched low, heading for the window. Out of the corner of one eye I had a split-second glimpse of a dirty kitchen, a terrified panic-stricken old woman, and Fred and his gun coming through the door behind me, half tripping over the suitcase on the sill. I dove through the window as he fired again and missed. I took frame and glass with me. Multiple cuts and scratches, they call it in the papers.

To sum up this excitement, I sailed across six feet of sagging veranda covered with slush, through a rotten railing, and dropped nine or ten feet into a mass of shoveled snow just as another shot roared out above me. I scrambled back under the veranda and cowered in a doorway.

Fred's gun really woke up Virginia City. It must have seemed like old times. The town came to life like a shooting scene for the Cisco Kid. Gustavson, the bartender, and three frightened patrons of the Boston Bar rushed into the street. Windows and doors snapped open. People peered out. Some shouted.

To my astonishment Gustavson yanked a heavy service revolver out of his overcoat—I never knew he touched a gun—aimed it up at the veranda, and fired. There was a yell of pain above me, then the sound of running feet. Gustavson and the bartender ran over to me. Just about the whole population of the old mining town was now pouring into C Street.

"Did he get you?" yelled Pete, appalled at my bloody face.

"Hell, no," I said. "Never mind me. That was Thomas' man. Thomas is upstairs. They got a car out back. Go after them."

Then I passed out.

It may have been five minutes later when I came to under a stiff drink of brandy in the Boston Bar. Gustavson, still white and scared, gave me the dope. The blue coupé was still out front. But in the uproar both Thomas and Fred had gotten away in another car in the back alley. But nobody thought they could get far. Gustavson had obviously winged Fred, for there were small bloodstains on the veranda. I told Pete about the old shaft, location unknown, where Thomas had consigned me. He ran out to pass the word and returned with the local sheriff and some deputies, to whom I quickly told my story. They rushed off to search the old shaft areas below the town. Road blocks would be up at once—and there weren't many roads out of Virginia City.

Then Pete called Edwards over at the Gap and gave him the story. If Thomas by some rare chance did get away I didn't want to find him waiting for me at the Casa Alta. Meanwhile a local sawbones patched up my cheeks, sprinkled mercurochrome on my minor scratches until I looked like a pinto pony, and told me I'd limp for a day or two from a pulled leg ligament.

And that was my memorable and quiet little morning in Virginia City.

As Pete and I crept down the grade with that heavy trailer behind us and went through a State Police road block we were both pretty quiet. Pete was more shaken than I was. Why I had insanely doubted that grim-jawed softhearted Swede in a few heady moments was now beyond me. At first he couldn't digest the fact that Thomas had actually decided to kill me. But when I emphasized I had walked right into his hide-out, and when I summed up the specific fears of Reynolds and Edwards that Thomas might well be maturing plans aimed at Fontaine's specials, he got the point but shook his head wonderingly.

"He just don't look like such a reckless fool. He's smart. And it would take an army to pull such a thing. There are no big train robberies today."

"Maybe not," I retorted, "but Thomas may think he's in a class by himself."

Then I told him about Reynolds' change in plans for the streamliner, accepted by Fontaine, in the final Christmas Eve shipment. Pete never said a word. But again he looked incredulous.

During the last five miles into the Gap we wove in and out of plows, scrapers, and road equipment. The canyon walls of snow hemming in the narrow road must have been eighteen to twenty feet high. When we got the trailer into the Highway Department's garage, the only one open, Gustavson started to unpack his equipment while I went over to the station for a few minutes to pull myself together a bit before going to the Casa Alta. I was also curious to get a glimpse of the Great Western's fight for life.

It was quite a sight. Under a windy leaden sky that promised still more snow a pall of smoke from the struggling troop trains, thundering West at approximately forty-minute intervals, drifted down Wildroot Valley like a dark threatening canopy that became a dense mass around the Gap's yards and fuel tanks.

The Women's Auxiliary and the Ladies of the Eastern Star had two coffee stands, one at each end of the platform, for the boys on those trains that made brief operating stops and two troop trains were now holed up waiting for the Cloudbuster. Already the yard boys had coined a name for the new train after examining its press pictures. With its elaborate new-style glass-enclosed vista domes, simply extended for the length of the train, the G.W.'s new creation had aptly been dubbed the "Greenhouse," a name since adopted by many tourists. We heard its horn sounding two or three miles down the valley.

Meanwhile I experienced a bit of nostalgia as I looked over the two waiting troop trains. GIs crowded open vestibule doors and grabbed steaming coffee and doughnuts from the Gap's hospitable ladies. But the rolling stock intrigued me. It gave me a start, twenty years out of Cambridge and M.I.T., to see Boston and Maine coaches with New Haven and Pennsy diners laced in among tourist Pullmans, New York Central, and Boston and Albany express cars, and a lone Central Vermont baggage combine, standing on these snow-walled sidings in the Sierras. The GIs were goggle-eyed over the arctic scenery. Frosted windows were scrawled with finger-marked items such as "North Pole or Bust," "Take Me Back to the Tropics," "The Donner Party—Company M." I didn't wonder. Behind the trains a fleet of trucks and bulldozers were chiseling out mountains of piled-up snow and dumping it in the frozen gully of Wildroot Creek a few hundred feet away.

I was still idling around the platform when Fontaine's second special pulled unobtrusively in from the West. After a two-minute stop, with the usual display of armed guards and exacting inspection, it sped on its way. I couldn't for the life of me see how Thomas, in new trouble with an eleven-state alert raised for him, could even make his way to the rails anywhere, let alone try any interference with a fast train. Just the same, I decided to talk to Edwards at the first opportunity.

Five minutes after the departure of the special the road's new Cloudbuster pulled in from the East and got a verbal going-over by interested onlookers. This train of low-slung streamlined Pullmans seemed to be surmounted by gleaming oblong sunglassed goldfish bowls—they were vista domes extended the full length of each car—and full of fluttering inmates all armed with cameras. I never saw so many mechanical eyes clicking away at us gapers, at the mountains, the troop trains, the banks of snow, the icicle-canopied station.

All of the lounge, dining, and observation areas of the new train were "on top," as well as a series of de luxe staterooms and compartments equipped with ingenious sliding panels of opaque glass to cut down light and sun as desired. It was frankly a bold experiment and I asked a prosperous-looking tourist who had dropped down beside the train what he thought of it up there. He grinned broadly.

"The kids love it. I'm impressed. My wife is jittery. Those tunnels

166

and bridges! My wife's sure we're all going to lose our heads. The illusion is terrific. Anybody looking up simply ducks."

I'd seen that before on our vista-dome cars. Well, the accounting department would tell us the good or bad news in a few months. The train finally pulled out to a few scattered cheers and a few moments later one of the troop trains scrambled out on the main and blasted after it.

I turned to leave the station, wondering how I would explain my patched countenance to Maria and then realizing the story was probably around anyway, when I ran into Lisa. Or rather, she had seen me from across the street and came hurrying over. She looked pale and worried and my battered appearance did not register at first.

"Mr. Bierce, I must talk to you. Can we go inside?"

I took her into the trainmaster's office, which was empty. Lisa turned, sat on the corner of Purdy's desk, and then digested my appearance.

"What's happened to you?" she asked.

"I had a bad fall this morning. I'll tell you about it later. What's the trouble?"

She had to steady herself a little before she spoke.

"I want to ask a favor, a most important one. Can we possibly get out of Pioneer Gap today? You and I and Ted?"

"What's happened?" I asked, studying her troubled face. I've often wondered how many lives would have been changed had I accepted Lisa's challenge and placed her and Helmholtz on No. 20 that afternoon, with or without my company. Lisa's expression astonished me. There was genuine fear in those blue-gray eyes.

"It should be done," she said emphatically. "Oh, I know all the objections. No reservations, the party, and all that. And the talk if we left so suddenly. But that is nothing. For once in my life I'm deathly afraid, Mr. Bierce. Something is going to happen. Ted will not speak to me. He will not believe that I'm all through with Jim. And I have given him my word." She drew a quick breath. "I ran into Ted's room this morning, without knocking, to beg him to behave. He was cleaning two revolvers on his table. When I demanded to know what he was doing he just shouted at me, 'Get out! I may have to use these. You should know why.' I tried to talk to him. It was no use. I have known Ted a long time. I have never seen him like this. And I—I think Mr. Reynolds should be warned."

She went on at great length and I tried to weigh carefully every word. But it was pretty obvious that Helmholtz's personal situation was approaching a crisis. I summed things up as best I could.

"Look, Lisa. We'll be out of here in forty-eight hours. But we can't get out today. It's impossible. We've all got too many commitments.

I have two compartments East on 502 for Friday morning, if the rails are still open." Lisa looked panicky at that reservation. "I'll talk to Gustavson right away and have him keep Ted in tow. Reynolds is busy on the Hill and may not even show at the party. But if I see him I'll make him steer clear of Ted. And I'll keep an eye on Ted myself."

Helmholtz could get pretty theatrical when he became excited. Just the same, cleaning a couple of guns at the beginning of his last days at the Gap wasn't funny at all. Very reluctantly Lisa had to accept the fact that we had to go through another two days at the Gap.

But as we walked slowly over to the Casa Alta I realized how frightened Lisa really was. In front of the hotel I caught sight of a familiar figure entering the lobby ahead of us and aiming for the coffee shop.

"Stick close to Maria and take it easy," I said to Lisa. "We'll be headed East very shortly."

She nodded rather wanly and left me. Then I joined a tired-looking Captain Edwards in the coffee shop. His eyes roamed with interest over my mercurochrome-stained face, but I spoke first.

"Have they got Thomas yet?" I demanded. Edwards shook his head and swore fluently. No one answering the description of Thomas or Fred had even tried to crash a road block. Instead, the Buick they'd gotten away in had just been picked up in Gold Hill, a couple of miles below Virginia City, the second car Thomas had dropped in that area. Somebody had phoned that item to Edwards less than ten minutes ago. It was my turn to be disturbed.

"Thomas talked about some shaft——"

Edwards nodded. "Bierce, they're checking everything. The Nevada people have gone through every haunted house and boarded-up mansion in Virginia City. At least they're not holed up in town."

I felt increasingly uneasy. "I'm on my last lap here, Sam. Just keep Thomas out of Pioneer Gap until I'm gone."

Edwards looked at me oddly. "That's taken care of, Howie. You've got a personal chaperon until you leave. Right behind you. It's Peters, a plain-clothes dick who knows the ropes. Tell him your plans. I don't want to pick you out of Wildroot Creek some morning with a switch stand tied to your feet. I don't think Thomas likes you."

I looked around. Peters was a big round-faced man in a leather coat. He sat tilted back in his chair and gazed vaguely about the room with a folded newspaper in his lap. He looked capable.

Before I left him Edwards disclosed that guards all along the G.W. as far as Denver had been doubled. At Fontaine's request. Obviously a lot of state and local employees in California and Nevada weren't going to spend Christmas Day at home. In the lobby I picked up an

Oakland morning paper. It was crowded with weather news, all of it disturbing, but a front-page bulletin announced that Fontaine's first special had arrived in Chicago with a new world's record of thirty-four hours and forty-seven minutes from Oakland to the C.&N.W. Station. Amid the huzzas, the report indicated the ICC might order an investigation. The run had been made without proper consultation with the ICC brass. I had just decided to go upstairs for a good long nap to restore my frayed nerves, wondering meanwhile where Maria was, when in walked Gustavson. He didn't look so good either. For some reason he started at seeing me. I think he had come over to see Helmholtz. But he invited me to the bar and I joined him. Some fresh development was definitely bothering Gustavson. His frank blue eyes now avoided mine and concentrated on his glass. In the dim light his usually ruddy face looked quite pale. Then I saw my body-guard come in and sit down unobtrusively in the first booth near the door. It gave me a queer feeling. Pete remained glum and silent. I'm not good at subtleties but I picked my way with him this morning as carefully as I could.

"Pete," I began, "I want to make a deal with you. That guy in the corner is my bodyguard assigned by Edwards to protect me from Thomas. Do me a big favor. Take on the same kind of job and look after Ted until I get him out of town. Will you? He's heading for trouble."

Gustavson gave me a queer look. He didn't seem a bit surprised, only curious as to what I was after or how much I knew.

"Yah. Ted is pretty upset," he said noncommittally, and drank some beer. I saw he was waiting to hear more. So I told him what Lisa had told me. That got a rise out of him, especially when he heard about the guns.

"The damn fool!" he exclaimed. "She saw that?"

"She sure did," I confirmed. "And this nonsense has got to be stopped."

I told him of the violent conclusion to the hectic two weeks' court-ship of Lisa and Reynolds. I said that Lisa had sworn to me she would go East and stay with Helmholtz until the end. Reynolds was out of the picture. If Helmholtz wanted to go hunting for Reynolds at this late date, I concluded, he was plain crazy. And it violated every promise he had made to me.

All this time Gustavson kept nodding absently, as if he only half heard me. But I saw he was thinking hard. He stared a long time at his glass. When he picked it up I was astonished to see that his hand shook. What was eating this big solid guy? He drained the last of his beer, wiped his lips with the back of his hand, set the glass down with a thump, and then turned to me with a grim expression in his eyes.

"Howie," he said, "stop worrying. Nothing will happen to Reynolds.

I promise it. Ted is a sick man. But I'll look after him. I'll put him on that train myself. I give you my word. Are you satisfied?"

"Satisfied?" I repeated slowly. "I won't be satisfied until we're rolling East. But I feel better. I think you can handle him. But tell me something. What's hit Ted so suddenly?"

Pete looked up and down the bar, then back to me.

"Yes, you should know," he said, as if half to himself, and then let me have it. "Look, Howie, that morning we talked here with Doc Woodruff—Ted heard everything. He was sitting by himself in that booth back there. You understand? He heard everything. He told me so, and then proved it."

That really bowled me over. "How could he?" I demanded. "He was playing the piano all the time Doc and I talked. We shut up when he stopped."

Gustavson shook his head. "No. We were all fooled. That was Lisa playing. Ted quarreled with her. He came in and sat down here, alone. We did not see him."

"Nuts," I said sharply. "I know his playing——" Then I stopped. A couple of very belated double takes overtook me. My visit to Lisa right after hearing Doc Woodruff pass sentence on Ted. Something about her coat lying on the divan in her apartment had impressed me momentarily. I now remembered what it was. Traces of snow, fast melting, on the hem. But Lisa had given me every evidence of being interrupted in the midst of a long practice period. Point two. She was playing the same Schumann piece we'd heard in the Sonora Room. I even noticed the coincidence at the time. Pete and I had certainly heard a door slam in the Sonora Room, thinking it was Lisa who had left. But it might have been either of them closing a door for more privacy while they went on quarreling. All at once I knew Gustavson was right. In the Stygian darkness of that bar a small army could have listened in on us without our knowledge.

Gustavson saw I believed him. He got up with an obvious effort.

"Just get them on the train, Howie. I will keep Ted out of trouble. Believe me, Mr. Reynolds will have nothing to worry about."

His eyes narrowed as he seemed to remember something.

"Yah. I will see Ted right now." And with that he left me.

14

The Big Day came at last. The twenty-fourth of December. And twenty-four hours before my Escape. That's the way
I looked at it by this time. And my next to last night at the Gap
had been a rough one. I had tossed, turned, taken aspirin, and dozed
on and off, wakened every hour or so by the thunder of that never
ending parade of troop trains assaulting the Hill.

When my dormer window turned dull gray I got up. Then I discovered something. I couldn't see out. The window was blocked with
snow. From a closet in the hall I obtained a broom, raised the glass
a foot or so, and poked my broom into solid snow. I finally got the
window clear. The spectacle was unforgettable. There was a brief
lull in the storm, a few flakes flying by under a leaden lowering sky.
I hope to be forgiven this constant emphasis on snow. The Gap can
be idyllic in spring, warm and lush in summer. And mild winters are
not too rare. But the historic fall that year was vividly impressed upon
everyone. It played a vital overpowering part of our own daily life in
that phenomenal month. Over 83 feet of snow fell during the season.

I had often seen old prints of the seventies and eighties showing
the rims of engine stacks protruding from enormous drifts, or the
roof gables of two- and three-story buildings barely visible. I had
always believed these pictures to be deliberately exaggerated, a
poetic license granted enthusiastic illustrators of popular magazines.
But no more. On this particular morning I grabbed my camera and
took pictures wherever I went. I knew I'd never see anything like
it again.

From my dormer window drifted snow was absolutely level with
the second pane of glass. A one-story pump house behind the hotel
had completely disappeared. West to Sentinel Peak, Wildroot Valley
was a frozen drift-filled arctic waste. Over it all, over the deep-walled

plowed-out snow canyons carrying the Great Western's rails, rose an even heavier pall of dense black smoke, rolling slowly before the wind, roughly marking the railroad's steep ascent to Summit, weaving about distant peaks and curves—the smoke from tens of thousands of gallons of fuel oil blasted through the boiler flues of battling engines boosting those trains over the Sierras. A block away, as I watched, a householder with his two small boys calmly climbed out a second-story bedroom window and marched down a packed slope to another narrow path, all that was left of Oak Street. Amused, I had an impulse to put on my snowshoes and walk out my dormer window. It would have been quite simple.

Instead, I dressed and went down for breakfast, finding a lot of people in the coffee shop matching storm statistics and betting on how long the Great Western could keep going. I wondered myself as I watched Miguel and two youths bracing a kitchen wall with two-by-fours, a wall that bulged inward from the weight of an enormous mass of snow. I heard that westbound trucks and trailers were stranded and parked all over town. Edwards had Route 80 open to Eldorado Summit. But nothing rolled west of that. Local business was at a standstill. Somebody tossed me an Oakland paper. I ran through the black headlines: "West Coast Lashed by Great Storm"—"Thousands Homeless"—"Eureka and Crescent City Cut Off by Floods"—"American River over 1938 Mark"—"Six S.P. Trains Held at Klamath Falls"—"Big Slide at Dunsmuir Halts Traffic"—"Great Western Battles Blizzard. May Route Trains South if Crisis Grows"—"Weather Bureau Warns Storm Peak Due in 24 Hours."

So there was more coming.

Pioneer Gap's sidewalks had dwindled to cramped footpaths between canyons of snow. A single side street was open to local traffic, one way only. Maria told me a couple of helicopters were being flown in from Sacramento to take out several stranded families in the Tahoe and Echo Summit areas. There was a lot of concern for other people holed up in remote places and a careful check was being made by a number of agencies. Selfishly, I thought it would be just my luck to have the road close down before my little party managed to catch a train East.

For the past several days at odd times I had been feverishly painting backdrops and scenery up at Summit School, getting volunteers to type up some simple scripts for the action, and otherwise aiding Alice and our committee in preparations for the party. I was just wondering how long Route 80 would stay open when the tall figure of Edwards materialized briefly beside me. He must have been wondering about the same problem.

"If that party comes off at Summit tonight," he announced, "I'm not responsible for the bodies dug out next spring. We may get everybody up there, Bierce, but I sure don't know if we'll get them down again. Why in hell can't that affair be held right here?"

"Ask Alice," I said. "She wants to make a lot of money tonight and the Casa Alta can't handle the customers."

Edwards snorted and stalked out while I went over to Peters and told him my plans for the day. Those involved in the Christmas Eve pageant were going up to the new school in a motor convoy at two in the afternoon for a final rehearsal. We would stay up there until the party was over. A busload of early Truckee visitors would probably accompany us. The rest of the guests were due up at Summit around seven in another convoy. Everybody would start down the Hill shortly after midnight, no later—the Lord and Edwards willing and able.

As for myself, I decided not to turn in that night at all, not to relax until I had my unpredictable charges safely eastbound on 502. The rest of the morning I puttered nervously about my room. Helmholtz came in for about five minutes. I think he was as relieved as I was that we were leaving the Gap. He seemed to me as tense and nervous as a bird poised for flight. The subject of Thomas seemed to fascinate him but I told him the man had disappeared completely. Then I mentioned the G.W.'s anxiety over the specials with Thomas still at large and told him about Reynolds' suggestion that Fontaine move the treasure over the Sierras on the streamliner, an almost facetious suggestion so unexpectedly adopted by Fontaine. Helmholtz grinned sardonically.

"So they're really scared. What would happen to Reynolds if Thomas did snatch some loot off that streamliner?"

I told him. "Reynolds would probably be shot at sunrise, along with Fontaine and the entire board of directors."

Ted laughed. "Too bad Thomas' chances are so slim. And these aren't days for successful train robbers." He was very restless, mentioning twice that he was all packed and ready to go and looking forward to the party. Then he left me, and a little later I went over to the station for a final glimpse of the Great Western's struggle to keep its lifeblood flowing.

Train after train thundered West at hour intervals. But in spite of the impressive cavalcade of steam and Diesel power that MacIntosh had assembled, freight drags were piling up at Placer. The Hill was simply choked with traffic. And under terrible conditions. The vast pall of heavy smoke now covered Wildroot Valley, east and west, as far as the eye could see. At eleven o'clock a dark, dirty sky started to spit snow again. With it came a high bitter wind. Purdy told me the S.P., anticipating more trouble, had already sent three of its crack trains around the southern route through Barstow, Mojave, and over the Tehachapis into Bakersfield. And the S.P. and Santa

Fe had finally agreed to handle a dozen of our troop trains over the same route. From the Cascades and the Sierras to the Rockies and the Great Plains, every railroader was getting worried.

A local mail and accommodation arrived four hours late out of Oakland with first editions of the morning papers. I got a bundle, went back to my room, and looked them over. Quite a picture. It was snowing above four thousand feet—three thousand feet in our area—from Prince Rupert in British Columbia to Mount San Gorgonio east of San Bernardino in Southern California. It was pouring rain from San Diego to Vancouver. A polar blast of blizzard proportions was also sweeping down out of the Canadian prairies into Montana, Wyoming, and the Dakotas, destined to hit Utah and Colorado and points east tonight. Every Sierra pass was tight closed except Route 40 over Donner Summit and that was faltering. The S.P.'s westbound track was in trouble. So were our own eastbound rails. The brass on both roads were up on the Hill with every man and piece of equipment that could be mustered. And the crashing expense of it all! I could visualize unhappy stockholders wringing their hands from coast to coast.

The Weather Bureau referred technically to two great storms, one traveling southeast from the Gulf of Alaska, the other outbound from the Pole, colliding over the Sierras. I wondered what Morris thought about what was going on and decided to find out after lunch. And I lunched alone. Even Maria was gloomy and preoccupied, telling me briefly she and Lisa were taking some of the school board and Helmholtz up the Hill in the afternoon convoy. I had the impression she was avoiding me. I hadn't laid eyes on Helmholtz, and I wondered where he was.

So, after lunch, over to Morris' I went. It was the same old story. Driving snow, bitter wind, and a blind howling arctic uproar raging through the deserted town, with a few blurred windows and roofs rising out of mountains of snow. I found Selma with Morris, both gay and oblivious of all storms, external and internal, being waged on the Hill. I was glad I'd come. Morris had some steaming hot toddies at hand. He was profoundly in love with Selma and his spirits were soaring. Selma informed me they were getting married on New Year's Day—to be announced at the party that evening—and they planned a week's honeymoon at the Palace Hotel in San Francisco.

At last I managed to get a word with Morris and demanded a layman's explanation of the atmospheric monster tearing over the western states. Morris went off like Old Faithful geyser.

"It's a humdinger, a masterpiece," he enthused, as if he had created the disturbance himself. He yanked a couple of weather maps across his desk. "Here's how it happened, and you won't see it again in a dog's age. The S.P. can't stay open. I'll say that right now. And your

174

pike may not, either, Bierce. You may be here awhile—and you might even have a lot of golden doubloons stuck at Summit tonight."

In the rush of my own preparations I had momentarily forgotten all about Fontaine's last gold-bearing special. The only thing that concerned me was the ability of the G.W. to get my train through early in the morning so that Lisa, Helmholtz, and I could make our getaway. I said all this to Morris. He looked dubious.

"Maybe," he said without confidence, and then gave me a little summary on the storm which he had dubbed "Operation Overall."

"'Overall,'" he said, pointing to the Sea of Othotsk, "began way over here ten days ago. It's been a sizzler and a fast traveler from the beginning, overtaking and merging with another big disturbance."

His map was full of penciled figures, curving isobars, and other cabalistic symbols. Briefly, a huge storm roaring out of the Gulf of Alaska was now confronting a great mass of polar air centered over the valley of the Yukon. In a grandiose collision this polar air was feeding new supplies of heavy moisture into the storm now centered over Oregon and rapidly approaching the Sierras. To add to this violent picture a large mass of tropical air was slowly moving east from Hawaii. For twelve days the resulting cocktail had poured its frozen contents on the Sierras.

Morris got off a lot more technical mumbo jumbo and concluded cheerfully, "I don't think a wheel will be turning in the Cascades or Sierras by dawn tomorrow."

"Thanks, pal," I growled. "Now what about the party?"

Morris shrugged. "I think it's pretty crazy, holding it up there in this weather. But Edwards swears he can get a convoy down if the joint closes by midnight. After that, he's throwing in the sponge."

I told him I was going up right away and would look for them later. I went back to my room, changed clothes, bundled up, and went down to the lobby just before two o'clock. There was a big crowd of excited youngsters there, just in from Truckee after a rough trip down 395 and up Wildroot Valley. They were waiting for Edwards' convoy to be formed, chattering about the storm, and hoping as kids always do that they'd be snowed in for weeks up at Summit—and to hell with school. Most of them had brought skis and snow equipment along. They were never used. It was already blowing a hundred-mile gale at Summit.

Our fifteen-car convoy, with a highway rotary and bulldozer with a shovel plow heading the parade, started off just after two. It took us two hours to make the thirteen miles to Summit. Four times we stopped while the plows bit through new drifts. At last we pulled into a snow shelter behind the new school building. Highway 80 ended abruptly just beyond the school in a twenty-foot wall of unbroken snow. Every resort but two at Summit was closed. It was a disastrous season for resort owners.

But as usual, once inside the new school building, warmed and comfortable from its own central heating plant, everyone forgot the storm or simply used its stimulation as a prod for the evening's adventure. I won't spoil the party by describing the afternoon rehearsal. It was a hectic affair, as such things always are. Part of our cast was snowed in and couldn't get over. The youngsters were all greatly excited. There hadn't been this much snow in anyone's memory, and when the huge colorful *piñata* sack, jammed with gifts, was hoisted into place high in the center of the auditorium ceiling there were cheers and yells of approval.

We ran through our rehearsal and finished just as Lisa, Helmholtz, and Maria appeared from another room. It was now about four o'clock. All three were very quiet and composed. I had the feeling Lisa had delivered some kind of ultimatum to Helmholtz. He barely greeted me, looking very pale and subdued as he busied himself getting the piano set up near the front of the stage and then standing in the back of the room listening intently as Lisa ran through some preparatory chords, from pianissimo to very loud. Helmholtz looked pleased. He said to Alice, "The acoustics are fine." He called out to Lisa, "Forget the hall, Lisa. It's perfect. Don't worry at all. Go ahead with the *Fantasia*."

There was a lot of noise as Lisa began to play. Ladies buzzing about setting up box suppers in a new classroom. A loud argument backstage over some missing props. The roar of wind outside. People carrying chairs and tacking up last-minute decorations. Kids in another room trying to get closer to Morris' model railroad, heavily guarded by some older boys. But as Lisa played on she began to gather an impromptu audience and the noise gradually subsided. I had never heard her *Mexican Fantasia* and supposed that Lisa had simply strung together half a dozen popular Mexican folk songs. I got out a couple of folding chairs and Maria and I sat down together, while she told me the names of the ancient melodies as they appeared in Lisa's musical tapestry.

The composition was brilliant, and brilliantly played, concluding with an old song of the Seri Indians, "Winds Blow Swiftly," played in an exciting passage of double octaves. For once I understood Ted's passion for Lisa and her music. There was a roar of excited applause when Lisa finished. She appeared startled, as if she had been unaware of her audience. Then she smiled briefly and ran off stage. I felt I understood Helmholtz completely. Lisa was his lodestone. But she was more than that. She was a much greater artist than he could have hoped to be. I think he knew it.

We were all exclaiming over Lisa's performance when Edwards

came through the door, spotted me, and crooked a beckoning finger. Peters was with him and I was sure they had some new bulletin about Thomas. I couldn't have been more mistaken.

Edwards said genially, "If you're not too busy, Howie, Reynolds would like you to lend him a hand over at the CTC building. Your toy railroad's in trouble. I can drive you over in the jeep."

"My God, what is it now?" I asked in exasperation. I thought Reynolds was far down the Hill busy with the plows.

"Just plain grief," retorted Edwards. "There was a twelve-hour thaw yesterday that raised hell. A lot of slides have begun and Summit's drained of help. Anyhow, Reynolds asked for you. You should have headed East long ago, my boy."

I certainly agreed. We drove through a screaming wind up the slight rise to the covered footbridge leading down to the snowsheds. The jeep lurched and swayed. Edwards parked it right against the fence. When I got out and carelessly let go the jeep I got an immediate idea of what high wind at Eldorado Pass could really do. I sailed right across a patch of ice on my fanny and brought up against the fence, clawing my way back to the shadowy shape of the jeep not ten feet away.

"Wait a minute," said Edwards, trying not to laugh. "Make a dive for the bridge when it lets up a bit."

We waited, then dove for the bridge and made it. The bridge quivered like a taut violin string. The wind sounded like a huge orchestra playing off key.

"Goddamn that party," said Edwards. "I should have put my foot down a week ago. This is the worst I've ever seen, Howie."

I certainly agreed with him. We took a final look around as we plunged down into the snowsheds. There wasn't too much to see. The sheds had disappeared under a single even blanket of snow, now thirty to thirty-five feet deep on level ground. Off to our right through driving snow I saw the gable and chimney of a three-story resort hotel apparently sticking out of the ground. Only the "ground," on this occasion, was the surface of a fifty-five-foot drift. The whole scene was unreal, overpowering.

Even in the sheds snow had drifted a foot deep across the rails. Down here the storm was the muted thunderous roar of continued surf overhead. We went directly to the CTC shack. It was almost deserted but the tension was high. An alarm bell was ringing. Two red lights, marking slides, blazed on the diagram board. Gerson, on duty, cut the alarm. Several signal engineers and linemen were grouped about a cluster of phones. Then I caught sight of Reynolds, a dead cigarette between his lips as he sat at a corner desk and rapidly flipped through a bunch of teletype reports. Another signal engineer, Ben Dutton, was chewing out somebody on a company phone. The language was obviously lurid at both ends. Two more linemen, one with a cup of coffee and his snowshoes stacked behind him, stared glumly up at the diagram board.

Then Reynolds, at a corner desk and in a nasty temper, glared up at me.

"Listen, Howie, we're all in a goddamn jam. Slides have taken out all our wires east. Those boys"—he indicated the group of linemen—"have patched a circuit clear to Klamath Falls, Alturas, down to Reno, east to Truckee, and into Placer to get us hooked up to Pioneer Gap again. Three hundred miles of wire to jump ten miles. And I need a couple of your precious hours. Take a look." He threw me his teletypes and added coldly, "You'll be on time for your goddamn party."

I ran through the teletypes and began to get an idea of what he meant. The joint was really jumping. Calls for help, yells of distress, trivial, so-so, and important, were buzzing both ways over the company wires. Here were a few samples:

4Z-3 FOR REYNOLDS: MALLET 5118 LOST RIGHT BOTTOM GUIDE FORWARD CYLINDER, BUCKING DRIFT HOBART SIDING. PISTON NOT BENT. DISCONNECTED AND BLOCKED. PROCEEDING BELKNAP.

ROGERS 2 TM

4Z-4 FOUR HOPPERS LOADED WITH SCRAP IRON OFF RAILS IN TALBOT SHED ON PASSING TRACK. SHED TIMBERS ON FIRE BUT CREW SAYS UNDER CONTROL.

TURNER 3 TM

4FM ROCKS LOOSE IN TUNNEL 11, EASTBOUND BORE CLOSED FOR TWO HOURS.

JACKSON

3XN 1 SLIDE AT MILE 97 CARRIED AWAY SIXTY FEET OF SNOWSHED ABOUT 5 P.M. BLOCK SIGNAL 0543 OUT. RAILS TORN UP BUT MAINTENANCE CREWS EXPECT TO CLEAR BY 6 P.M.

FELTON JX

211J REYNOLDS URGENT SUMMIT: MAIN BEARING JOURNAL, ROTARY 818, BURNED OUT ON WESTBOUND MAIN MILE 109. NEED NEW BACK END BRASS AT ONCE. CAN YOU OBTAIN?

MACINTOSH

Then I encountered a dilly. It read:

REYNOLDS, URGENT: ENGINE 2342 [one of our Mountain types] JUMPED

TRACK AT COBALT. LEAD TRUCK RAN HALF MILE ON TIES. ENGINE
SWERVED LEFT OFF RAILS. BRAKEMAN RIDING PILOT THRUST THROUGH
WINDOW OF SECTION HOUSE WHERE FOREMAN'S WIFE WAS SLEEPING.
PLEASE ADVISE.

BROWNING 3M

I showed it to Reynolds and asked, "What did you tell him?"

Reynolds had to smile. "I told Browning if the brakeman didn't
know what to do he ought to be fired. What else could I say?"

That thawed us out a little. "What about the journal brass for the
rotary—you located one?" I asked. They were scarce items this side
of Belknap.

Reynolds nodded. "I sent D'Alvarez down on 388 to 'Culver City.'
There's one in the storehouse there. But he'll have to walk back."

That threw me. "Four miles back in this stuff?" I said. "That's no
cinch." The brass weighed plenty. "I thought D'Alvarez was at the
west switch."

"He was, for thirty hours," said Reynolds. "Got frostbite in his
hands and came up here for treatment. I had to send him down. He
was the only guy available."

So the Iron Man was on the job again. Incidentally, Culver City,
probably so designated by some homesick Californian, was a nickname for the big road camp perched high above the rails on a steep
flank of Mount McGregor and four miles east and below Summit.
It was also in a notorious slide area, a community of a dozen one-
story company homes and store, linked by wooden tunnels, the outer
walls supported on stilts, the rear walls practically driven into the
mountainside.

I was thinking about D'Alvarez.

"How long's he been gone?" I asked. Reynolds squirmed a little.
"Over two hours, Howie. But it's a long haul in this stuff."

"You didn't even have a scooter?" I demanded.

Reynolds looked mulish. "Howie, I told you this pike's in a jam.
Culver's scooter is down near Gunnison. Everybody's out, busy as
hell, and half dead on his feet. We'll be lucky to stay open, and you
know what's coming through." He looked up at the clock. "That
streamliner and special leave Belknap at nine-five."

It was now five-twenty. Then a phone rang and Gerson picked it
up. I watched him. He said nothing but listened very intently.

"I'll sure tell him. Right away," he said finally and hung up. He
came quickly over to us and addressed Reynolds:

"That was Carrera at Culver City," he said brusquely. "He's no
alarm bell. Jim, he wants everybody taken out of Culver City as
quick as possible. Says an hour or so is the limit. He claims half the
side of Mount McGregor is ready to let go. There's a hell of a snow-

179

nose fifteen hundred feet up the mountain. I noticed it myself this morning. The women are scared stiff. They had two small slides this afternoon. That's an east slope and that thaw yesterday raised hell. He pounded my ear plenty and——"

Reynolds was staring out the window. He said deliberately, "Nothing doing. We haven't got an engine or a wheel up here. Everybody's clearing the eastbound for the special. If Carrera thinks it's that bad tell him to put his people in the work cars on the siding."

Gerson looked upset. "Hell, Jim, what good'll that do? They're located right under the camp."

Reynolds threw him a brutal look. "You heard me. I'll have an engine up here by seven. Then we'll see. I gave that area a once-over this morning. It didn't look too bad to me."

Gerson stared at him and then went back to his board without a word. At that moment a snow-covered figure entered the shack and announced, "By God, he made it. He's got the brass."

Right after him came a couple of shovelers helping D'Alvarez to a chair. One of them had relieved D'Alvarez of a gunny sack containing the heavy journal brass for the rotary. D'Alvarez had crawled up the plowed-out rails with the sack on his back, doing four miles in a little under three hours. I hardly recognized him. His eyes were sunken, his drawn stubbled face covered with frost and snow. When he took off his mittens I saw both hands were crudely bandaged. He leaned back with his eyes closed, just about out. And Reynolds never even thanked him. Right then and there I butted in. Edwards was still in the back of the room. I turned to him.

"Take this man right over to the school, will you, Sam? There's first aid stuff there, hot food, and Alice has some brandy. This boy needs attention."

Reynolds stiffened. Then D'Alvarez opened his eyes and looked at me. His voice was thick, but he said, "You better get those folks out down there, Mr. Bierce. It don't look good. And they're scared stiff."

I tried to reassure him. "We know all about it. We'll try to figure something. You go along with Edwards."

D'Alvarez stumbled to his feet just as Reynolds said angrily, "I'll handle this, Howie. We got everything right here. I've got to put him back on the west switch later on."

That really got me sore. I said nothing and simply helped D'Alvarez to the door and turned him over to Edwards, who was looking distastefully at Reynolds. They went out. Reynolds was re- garding me with his best cast-iron look.

"You're kind of feeling your oats tonight, aren't you?" he asked.

"For God's sake, Jim, that guy's been up thirty-eight hours by your own count——"

"I've been up forty-five," Reynolds angrily interrupted me. Then we both stopped. The thunder of a train coming in from the east rocked through the sheds. A few moments later a snow-covered troop train, Extra 581, rattled in and stopped. Steam and vapor poured by the windows. I was shocked and looked accusingly at Reynolds. That train was in from the east, not five minutes behind D'Alvarez. The irony of it.

"Did you know that train was on the Hill?" I demanded. "They probably passed Culver City less than twenty minutes ago. They could have picked up D'Alvarez and brought him right in."

Reynolds never batted an eye.

"Sure I knew it was on the Hill. What the hell do you think my job is? I thought D'Alvarez would make it long ago. Besides, we're not stopping a twenty-car troop train on a heavy grade for any damn journal brass. Is that clear?"

So that's the way it was. Reynolds was back in harness all right, only it promised to turn out to be a strait jacket for everybody. The phone rang again. Gerson picked it up, listened, and barked, "I don't know yet." Then he hung up and looked over at us, more worried than ever.

"It's your decision, Mr. Reynolds. That was Carrera again. He wants to know when his crowd can get out. They're getting panicky."

Reynolds looked deliberately up at the clock and compared it with his watch. He could be pretty insufferable in this mood.

"Okay," he said finally. "I'll have a ten-wheeler here by six-thirty. A Mallet helper at seven. We'll go down then."

Almost two hours away. Gerson picked up his phone. All at once I was getting damn jumpy about Culver City. I said sharply:

"No ten-wheeler's going to start that work train. Maybe not even the Mallet. Those cars have been frozen in for days."

Reynolds looked at me coldly, with cutting hostility. "I'll handle this. You're on leave, Howie. Remember?"

That did it. I slammed the teletypes down on his desk and got up.

"I sure am," I said angrily, almost shouting at him. "From here on, count me out. You row your own boat, Jim. You're heading for some rocks. I don't want to be around."

I walked out, heading for the lunch car, and feeling a silence behind me that sizzled. Maybe I was twenty minutes in the lunch car, brooding over a cup of coffee. The place was crowded but the talk was subdued. Nobody had been through anything quite as prolonged as this. Everybody was exhausted, on edge, about knocked out. Idly, I watched the troop train's helper rumble through the sheds and pull up on a short siding a few feet away. I was getting madder by the minute. No engine until six-thirty or seven? Hell, Reynolds had an idle Mallet here right now. I knew Culver City. I knew Carrera, a quiet, efficient, almost stolid man. If he said the crisis was immediate I believed him. I decided I might as well lose my job right now. If anything happened at Culver City I'd never forgive myself. Fortified by a couple of cups of java, I picked up a notch in my belt and headed back to the CTC shack determined to battle it out with Reynolds. When I got there I had a surprise and a lot of support.

The diagram room was crowded, with D'Alvarez, some trainmen, Maria, Lisa, Alice Livingston, and several of the older boys from the school. All of them were looking at Reynolds. I soon learned what had happened. With his first gulp of Alice's brandy D'Alvarez had blown his top about Culver City. Maria and Alice knew everybody there. Two of the camp's kids were taking part in the pageant. Over they came in a body. I looked at all those solemn faces and then at someone far in the rear, standing by the door. It gave me a start. Helmholtz stood there, somber, detached, remote, like an avenging angel.

I looked back at Reynolds. And I realized I had never really seen so clearly as I did now the side of Reynolds that shocked Lisa. I thought I was used to Reynolds. Sure, he was hard-boiled, efficient, and all the rest. So were a lot of other road officials. But I saw something else in this situation—Reynolds could really be a sadistic bastard, a man who enjoyed keeping worried people on tenterhooks, a man who posed as a big shot with everything under control and didn't really care whether it was or not. Reynolds, at the moment, was actually enjoying himself. It was unmistakable. And it was a great shock to me.

Maria made an eloquent plea for an immediate rescue of the camp. When Reynolds shook his head and said he had no motive power available I really let go. I called attention to the idle Mallet, simmering a hundred yards away. This item enraged everybody. There was a brief uproar. Reynolds got up, now thoroughly angry, and delivered himself as follows:

"Damnit, get back to your schoolhouse and your cockeyed party. This is official business. I'm in charge up here. I know the situation at that camp. Nothing's going to happen there. This helper is going down the west slope in twenty minutes to haul back two work trains. It's also carrying a journal brass for a crippled rotary. That brass has got to get there. We have an important special, the streamliner, and a lot of eastbound trains waiting to head up the Hill in a couple of hours. Nothing's going to delay them. Do you understand?"

As simple as that. Everybody began talking at once. Reynolds listened impassively, tapping his desk with his pencil. Then Lisa tackled him. She went right up to him and talked so low I couldn't hear what she said. All I heard was Reynolds' final remark.

"Nothing doing, Lisa. As usual, you don't know what you're talking about."

Then the phone. It was Carrera again. This time Reynolds answered it. He listened and lied. He lied before all of us. "I haven't got an engine, Carrera. I'm sorry. Put 'em in the cars. We'll be there by seven."

But for the first time I saw the Iron Man waver. So did Lisa.

"What did he say? What did he say?" she demanded. "You don't dare tell us. And you lied to that man."

I was beginning to admire Lisa. And she was getting under Reynolds' skin. He hesitated, just a little. Then he said:

"There was a small slide ten minutes ago. Carried away the pump house. The families are being evacuated to the work cars."

I knew where the pump house was. Not two hundred yards from the company store, which was smack in the center of the camp. I told Lisa that. She turned white with fury. She forgot everybody else. She and Reynolds were the only two people in the universe. And how she told him off.

"You damned liar, you insufferable hypocrite!" she shouted at him. "Everything I've ever said about you now comes true. You enjoy this. You want to see people suffer. You want to see how much they can take. You've done it with me. You're doing it to a hundred people threatened with death and extinction. And for what? Your hollow stinking pride! And the more we try to persuade you to the only human course anyone could follow, the more you bait us and resist. You're no man! You're no railroader! You're a coward, with no real guts at all."

And then she really threw a sixteen-inch shell at Reynolds that struck him.

"I don't know what happened to you. But all your life you've spit upon and covered up everything real. You must have done something terrible once. Something you're so ashamed of you want to make everyone else, the whole world if you could, suffer for it. And that is what you call your life! God, I hate you."

Suddenly Reynolds buckled under the vitriol of that furious girl. He got red and white by turns. His hands began to shake. If all of us hadn't been there I think he might have tried to kill her. Gerson removed his cigar and stared at him, fascinated. Reynolds' right hand shook so that he placed it on the table to steady it.

There wasn't a sound in the room. Lisa saw what she'd done. She looked at him contemptuously for a moment and then joined Maria. Thank Heaven she had sense enough to wait for Reynolds to make the next move.

15

Certainly I, for one, had no idea what Reynolds would do. He was in a rage and cleared the diagram room at once. The bulk of our indignation meeting moved to the gloomy little station waiting room. But I remained where I was while Reynolds stalked out into the sheds without looking at me.

Gerson and I waited. What was he going to do? We heard the Mallet chuff off the siding. Maybe five minutes later Reynolds stuck his head in the door. He said harshly, "Come on, Howie. Climb aboard."

I shook my head. "Go to hell. Leave me out of this."

His voice rose. "Goddamnit, this is an order. Get aboard. We're going to pull those hillbillies out."

I got up slowly, not quite believing him. I glanced out the window at the Mallet and saw a lot of ropes, shovels, and steam hose with jet nozzles being loaded into the cab. So he'd really given in! I didn't say anything. I just climbed aboard the big cab jammed with train-men and half a dozen shovelers, and we started off. We clattered down to Culver City in less than eight minutes with mighty little talk from anyone. Visibility, for the last time that evening, was fair. Great gray peaks against a blue-black sky. A vast white and empty landscape. A gray spectral world. A ghostly, menacing world. Past the cab windows, overtaking us, sped a few flakes of snow driven by a terrific wind at our backs. We stopped at Culver switch and pulled into the long siding, everybody crowding the right side of the cab and looking up at the towering flank of Mount McGregor.

Carrera hadn't been kidding. An enormous bulging nose of snow and ice jutted out from an exposed cliff about fifteen hundred feet directly above the road camp which was being hurriedly evacuated from its lofty site a hundred feet above the rails. Lights flashed as lanterns moved from house to house. Most of the families were already crowding out of a covered stairway leading down to the rails. A few frightened women and children stood huddled against a signal box. Several had climbed into the six work cars but were now being removed and ordered to head up the track. We coupled on in fairly deep snow and I jumped to the ground with others just as Carrera came up to talk over the situation.

Before joining us Reynolds ordered the steam hose and jets fastened to the tender steam hose and the jets used to free as many car wheels as the hose could reach. Then we all stared up at the mountain as Carrera talked. In spite of bitter cold and high wind it was decided to move the families farther up the main rails and away from the possible slide area while the Mallet tried to haul those frozen cars out. If we succeeded we'd load the people on when we hit the main. If we didn't get out, they'd have to walk like D'Alvarez all the way to Summit, a hell of an ordeal in this weather. I think everyone realized the Mallet's double exhaust blasting under that overhang of thousands of tons of snow would provide plenty of vibration to set off a possible slide. The work cars, although partially dug out, had been sitting on that siding for weeks. Wheels were frozen fast to frozen rails; grease and oil waste in journal boxes were iced solidly around the bearing brasses. We'd be lucky if we didn't pull out a few drawbars or tear away the front end of the first car with the power of that Mallet.

The steam jets more or less freed the wheels of the first two cars. That was as far as our steam hose reached. Maintenance men had now herded the thoroughly frightened refugees, stumbling under suitcases, bird cages, and forlorn personal belongings, up the track past the switch stand, where they huddled together against the tearing gusts of wind. Reynolds waved the rest of us up the rails in the same direction. He stood opposite the center of the work train directing the Mallet's engineer, a chap named Wilson, and one of our best. The Mallet started jockeying those work cars, gently at first, then with increasingly violent shoves rocking them back and forth, moving forward slowly to gather up the slack, then backing abruptly with a crashing of coupler knuckles, while Wilson even in that intense cold sweated over the ponderous power reverse.

Those cars were really frozen in. The first two moved a few inches on sliding wheels. The third car budged. The other three might have been part of the mountain. But Reynolds shouted and waved encouragement. After almost ten minutes of this nerve-racking business Reynolds, who had walked back to the last car to observe what was happening, suddenly gave Wilson a violent highball and shouted, "You're free! Take 'em away."

The Mallet sounded two sharp whistle blasts and her exhausts roared. Reynolds grasped the grab iron on the last car. The work train groaned, crunched, and protested, moving out slower than a walk while the last three cars simply slid along on the rails without a wheel turning. Right then Carrera let out a yell and pointed. I looked up and remembered his first phone call to Summit, ". . . half the side of Mount McGregor is ready to let go."

It was going now. No doubt about it. What set it off, whether vibration from the Mallet or great pressure from wind gusts, made no difference. In a slow-moving second we saw the snow nose collapse. Below it a great sectional area of steep snow began to move ponderously down upon the darkened group of company homes, the company store, a tall slender stack, and a single forgotten light still burning in one cabin. We yelled and waved to Wilson, moving slowly towards us in his cab. He looked up and shouted back at Reynolds while his fireman tied down the whistle lever to warn him. At the same time Wilson applied sand to the rails and a rush of steam to the cylinders that made the Mallet leap ahead, drivers slipping and gripping the rails in circles of crimson sparks. Reynolds took one look at that moving mountain tumbling down on him, flung himself off the work car to make better time, and ran as fast as he could towards us in snow and slush. All we could do was to stand there and see if he made it.

This was the second big slide I'd witnessed in less than a month and it was quite different. It wasn't a spectacular avalanche. It was a slow, deliberate, crunching, powerful, ponderous slide that caught up the company camp and with an almost awful deliberation crushed every structure in sight into kindling wood. Then the moving mass gathered more momentum and poured majestically over a rocky ledge on to the right of way—and kept pouring down in a massive irrepressible flood of snow, timber, and rock. Reynolds was like a man trying to outrun a great tidal wave that lapped at his heels and kept on coming. With a final rush the slide picked up the last two cars of the work train, snapped a drawbar, and flung them like discarded toys five hundred feet down the slope below the rails. The air lines weren't hooked up and the rest of the train kept on going. Reynolds was barely visible in a vast cloud of snow dust churned up by the spent slide. But he was apparently safe. Then with no warning at all, in an ironic aftermath, a small slide of ice and boulders we never even noticed leaped off the ledge above him and struck him down.

A lot of us started running for him. We found him lying under three or four feet of rock and snow, out cold, his face bloody and scratched. Wilson had stopped his train not far from us. The rest of that weird rescue and excursion is a blur to me. Laying Reynolds out on the cab floor, pulling the four cars out on the main, piling in panicky refugees, staring up at the savage gash down Mount Mc-Gregor with not a trace of Culver City remaining, while a huge pile of snow and splintered timbers blocked the rails behind us.

We got out of there in a hurry and roared up the Hill as fast as we could, finding just about everybody at Summit waiting for us. CTC, now crippled east of Eldorado, knew what had happened, and every man and machine available was being hauled up the west slope and over the Hill to tackle the mess at Culver City.

Reynolds was conscious but very groggy when he was helped down from the cab. And I witnessed a little tableau. Lisa and Helmholtz stood in the doorway watching the removal of Reynolds from the engine cab. Our usually trim, brusque, and debonair Iron Man was quite a spectacle. His bloodstained mackinaw was ripped to shreds. His face was covered with scratches, all of them bleeding profusely. Wilson, half supporting him, kept wiping the blood from his eyes. Actually, Reynolds looked a whole lot worse off than he really was. He stumbled along between Wilson and a trainman, who took him to the first aid room maintained for just such emergencies. Lisa watched all this for a moment or two and then slipped quietly into the little procession behind Reynolds and disappeared with the rest. Helmholtz didn't change expression but his eyes followed Lisa and never left her while she remained in sight. Behind Helmholtz I saw Gustavson for the first time that memorable evening. His face appeared gaunt and strained. One of his big hands rested on Helmholtz's shoulder.

Alice's party was almost called off then and there. In fact, there was a half hour's debate on the feasibility of going ahead with it. The refugees from Culver City had to be taken care of, at the CTC dormitory, or in nearby homes. And every man on the regular roster or extra board, or however remotely connected with the G.W. in the past, and no matter how many endless hours he'd put in during the storm, was yanked back to work. The Great Western was just about on its back, with a huge slide and torn up track to be removed and re-laid, with a dozen minor disasters to contend with, and both sides of the Hill choked with traffic waiting to roll—the streamliner and Fontaine's special all but forgotten among them.

Topping all this, a little after seven the rest of the guests and the two storm-tired busloads of Truckee visitors managed to get up the mountain in another convoy. The school board finally decided on full steam ahead for the party. A lot of Culver City's refugees were taken over to the school to enjoy some of the box suppers and there was a general feeling that the entertainment and diversion would do a lot to quiet their jangled nerves. And Reynolds, for the first time in his life, and not too accurately, was being hailed as a hero.

Before returning to the school I decided to have a look at Reynolds

187

and get a line on his condition. I had actually forgotten about Lisa and stepped briskly inside the first aid room and stopped short. I didn't have to do or say a thing except to digest that little scene before me. Lisa was sitting on the side of a regulation hospital bed, her face lighted up with an expression of complete rapture as Reynolds smilingly lit a cigarette between her lovely lips. Reynolds was half turned towards me, his battered face a crossword puzzle of bits of Band Aid and painted scratches. He stood firmly and quite relaxed, considering what he had been through. But his expression alone stopped me from going any further into the room. Contrite and humble. Rapt and devoted. This was the Reynolds that Lisa had aroused and I had never seen.

Lisa, too, was illuminated by a flood tide of new-found affection. Struck by her beauty, I studied them for an uncertain moment and then hurriedly retreated. Could Lisa keep her word to me to get on that train with Helmholtz in the morning? I doubted it.

I went up to the road and found Edwards waiting to drive me over to the school again. We skidded into what was left of Route 80 in his jeep. Then he stopped the car a moment, pulled back the weather flap, looked up at Sentinel Peak, and shouted over the wind:

"Hell, Bierce, did you ever see it snow uphill? Take a look."

I looked. The west slope of Eldorado Pass and the whole valley below were blotted out with clouds of new snow sweeping towards us. But to our left the great pinnacle of Sentinel Peak was clearly visible and its relation to other peaks was the cause of an atmospheric phenomenon that perfectly symbolized that mad evening. High above us a hundred-mile-an-hour wind had shifted violently a few points to the west, enough of a change to rip into a huge series of drifts at the foot of the peak, flinging them against the mountain's slopes at about the nine-thousand-foot level. There was no place for this snow to go but up. And up it went, in sheets and inverted cascades, in streamers and whorls, in whirling twisters shooting up to the jagged tip of the peak, a mass of black rock capped with an arrowhead of gleaming ice. A Mad Hatter snowstorm upside down. And the updraft at the top of the peak must have been terrific, for columns of fine snow dust, like rolling clouds of smoke from some arctic volcano, shot high above the mountain and then streamed off to the southeast.

Fresh falling snow abruptly cut off this spectacle. I pulled back into the jeep and said emphatically to Edwards, "Now I've seen everything."

In this hectic atmosphere the party and pageant began with a rush shortly after eight. I was astonished by the number of people who managed to show up in spite of the storm, several of them from nearby ranches arriving on skis and snowshoes, which were stacked in the big main hallway of the handsome new building. Many of the dazed victims of Culver City elected to stay. The kids were greatly excited, both by the slides and the storm, and three teachers had their hands full keeping them under control.

I sat with Captain Edwards, aisle seats, front row to the right, and looked around while Edwards popped in and out keeping up with highway conditions. He was prepared to run us all out and down the Hill at a moment's notice. Almost everyone we expected seemed to be there. The two conspicuous absentees were Lisa and Reynolds, and as Alice began her opening remarks she glanced anxiously down at me. I nodded reassuringly, determined to detach Lisa forcibly from Reynolds if she didn't show up in the next half hour. Her *Mexican Fantasia* was the last item on our program.

Everything went off well. Alice explained the purpose of the party, paid tribute to the energies and initiative of the school board in achieving their goal, helped unveil a bronze plaque in honor of the occasion, and then paid a rousing tribute to Maria and introduced her as the next speaker. Maria looked pale and nervous when she first mounted to the stage. Her eyes roved about the auditorium. Helmholtz and Gustavson were in the very last row, a vacant seat held for Lisa between them, and Gustavson kept looking at his watch with a worried and preoccupied expression. As Maria began the key speech of the evening I went backstage, where I would shortly be needed during the pageant as scene shifter, prompter, and boss-of-all-sorts. Edwards came along to help out. After the more serious part of her speech dealing with the school, Maria paused briefly and then brought down the house with her surprise announcement of the evening—the engagement of Selma and Jack Morris. It was certainly the sensation of the evening. And when Selma, in a clinging cloth-of-gold lamé gown rose beside Jack in his familiar chair, every ridiculous legend about Selma was destroyed for all time. They were a happy couple and their many friends went wild.

I was standing half onstage watching all this, knowing the pageant was next, when I happened to glance towards the back of the hall. I never forgot what I saw. While all eyes were on Selma and Morris, in marched Lisa and Reynolds, arm in arm, proclaiming their mutual joy to the world, and heading all but unnoticed for the front seats which Edwards and I had vacated.

The skin at the back of my neck began to crawl. I glanced at Helmholtz, who had half risen, with Gustavson's hand on his arm. From a pale bitter face his eyes blazed at his beautiful traitor. Gustavson said something. Helmholtz started for Reynolds and Lisa. But Gustavson whirled him about and propelled him into the hallway as if Ted had been some autumn leaf caught in a gust of wind. I ran across the backstage area and opened a hall door just in time to see

Gustavson and Ted disappear through the main entrance. Whew! Why couldn't Lisa and Jim have foregone that insane entrance?

Mechanically I tossed painted backdrops, flats, and props about, as our Donner Pass pageant began, prompting forgetful kids and helping Alice. Every time I looked out over the audience I saw Maria staring up at me, white-faced, full of unspoken questions, a small lace handkerchief twisted in her lap.

Our little pageant was poignantly amateurish but perhaps all the more impressive because of that, and of course the families and friends of the youngsters involved were enthusiastic. Then came Lisa's eloquent music, the rest of the program proceeded smoothly, and finally the curtain came down to uproarious applause. I was talking to Alice, surrounded by shouting youngsters, when Edwards came over with a warning.

"Alice, we're having a swell time, but don't run this past twelve. And have the Truckee kids all ready to go."

Alice laughed. "We'll wind up on the dot. Is it really that bad?"

Edwards snorted. "Are you kidding? We're going to button up the Hill tonight for at least a week. Don't look outside or you'll call this off right now."

Alice was still busy but I took a brief look at the weather. Edwards had every vehicle and bus lined up and ready to go in the parking area. Motors were being turned on and off every few minutes to keep them warm. And again that endless snow poured down in stinging masses on a bitter wind that had already wiped out traffic furrows made less than half an hour ago.

Inside the school, with lights blazing again, the place exploded in an uproar. The solemnities were over. Dancing and eating began —and everybody was in a tearing hurry, knowing that little time remained. I managed a word with Lisa just as Edwards came in looking at his watch.

"Lisa," I said in a low voice, "I've got to know something. Are you going East with us in the morning?"

She turned towards me, her face glowing. "I gave you my word, Howie. Of course I'm going. For as long as Ted needs me. After that . . ."

I thanked her, congratulated her soberly, and moved away. Greatly relieved to know she stood by her decision, I watched Reynolds abruptly leave the room. I crossed over to Edwards.

"Where's Jim going?"

"Back to work," said Edwards. "But he ought to be in bed."

I was worried. "Did you see Gustavson and Ted anywhere?"

"They drove right off. Back to the Gap, I guess." Edwards understood me. "They won't run into each other."

"Rails open?"

"Yes, but it's rough. Fontaine's special and the streamliner are headed up the Hill behind a whole fleet of plows. On time, I hear. But I'm busting this up pretty quick, Howie. You want to go down with me later?"

I agreed. Then Edwards told me a curious item. He said, frowning:

"Funny thing just happened. A rancher named Norton snowed in back of Kingston Flats phoned the sheriff he heard a small plane buzzing around over by Mint Canyon a few minutes ago. Says his wife heard it, too. It sounds screwy to me."

It did to me, too. Flying conditions were as impossible as they could be. A light plane up in that mess wasn't going anywhere. I couldn't figure it out at all. But I managed to get in a dance apiece with Maria and Alice before Edwards broke up the party and loaded everybody into his waiting convoy.

Edwards and one crew remained behind to close up the highway. That would give me another half hour, and after a brief impromptu farewell toast to Alice from a dozen of us still around, I decided to visit the CTC shack, watch the special and the streamliner go through, and find out, above all, if my train East was scheduled to run at all. If it didn't, we were all due for some violent palace revolutions on the Hill.

Edwards ran over in the jeep again and I arrived at the CTC shack just three minutes after midnight. Fontaine's special was due momentarily, practically on time. Eastbound rails were now open to Placer and the westbound were open to Belknap. That meant we still had a single track line intact over the Hill, with the Culver City slide to be cleared by dawn.

Just about all the G.W. brass was gathered in the diagram room. But something surprised me. The atmosphere had cleared. A new and distinct air of confidence could be felt in the room. Someone had placed a small lighted Christmas tree on Gerson's desk and I learned from Fontaine himself that the G.W. was definitely winning a historic battle. He also assured me he was convinced my train would roll into the Gap on time, or nearly so, in the morning. A great weight left me. With Lisa's promise and Ted in charge of Gustavson, I relaxed and listened to tales of woe from other points. The Southern Pacific was being choked to death at Cisco and Donner Summit. One of their Mallets was off the rails at Blue Canyon. The wind indicator at Norden had been carried away in a 115-mile-an-hour blast. And Route 40 had been closed tight for thirty hours. Not a Cascade or Sierra highway pass from Canada to the Tehachapis was open.

But the Great Western's luck was still holding. I breathed easily for the first time that night and went out on the platform to watch our storm parade roll in. Two big rotaries, then flangers and spreaders double-headed by Mallets, everything coated and frosted with snow, moved ponderously like arctic leviathans over the maze of switches onto sidings and passing tracks. Right behind them came Fontaine's final special with its usual two-minute stop, its display of armed guards, and as it whisked off into the cavernous sheds I wondered briefly what the bankers would think if they knew an empty train had just headed for Placer to wait for the streamliner carrying their spoils. I glanced around and saw Fontaine behind me gravely watching the disappearing taillights. His expression was solemn. I didn't wonder.

With clear rails from the west to Summit and the special on its way there was almost a minor celebration in the office as MacIntosh on a company phone ticked off the progress of the streamliner. I believe only four men in that room, Fontaine, MacIntosh, Reynolds, and myself, were aware of Fontaine's switch of that golden cargo to the streamliner. Many officials were openly congratulating Fontaine on the successful passage of his specials and the road's very great victory over the storm. All that power and equipment Fontaine and MacIntosh had marshaled on the Hill had really paid off.

MacIntosh announced the streamliner had passed Warm Springs at twelve-ten and for some reason had lost four minutes below Basco. But it was due very shortly and the brass intended to stay here until the "Fort Knox Scooter," as Gerson derisively designated Fontaine's final special, had recovered its legitimate cargo from the streamliner down at Placer.

To my dying day I'll always remember that last quiet moment at Summit. MacIntosh had relaxed and was grinning across the room at Fontaine, who sat quietly in a corner smoking a long cigar and looking gravely up at the diagram board. The rest of the brass, tired, but triumphant and contented, chatted in low tones or just stood about waiting. I was aware of the thump of an air pump on a Mallet grunting to itself outside the door. Reynolds was sitting on the small of his back in a swivel chair, his eyes red-rimmed with exhaustion, his face stubbled with rough beard and pretty revolting as he picked absently at a loose bit of Band Aid on his chin, while his eyes were riveted on the clock. He was the one man in the room who hadn't relaxed a bit. Gerson had just discarded an inch of cigar butt. He picked a fresh one from a box on the desk and then he leaned forward reaching for his Ronson lighter on the window sill. But Gerson was never to light his fresh cigar that night.

For at precisely twelve-fourteen the dull thunder and reverberation of a heavy and distant explosion rattled coffee cups on the desks, shook windows and chairs, and brought everyone to his feet as rumbling echoes rocketed about from peak to peak, dying slowly away.

My first impression was that a big plane had crashed in our vicinity. It sounded exactly like it and I thought of the plane report to Edwards. But I no sooner reached this almost instant conviction when Gerson's diagram board burst into fireworks and every type of alarm bell in that astounded room went off at once. The one man I was looking at was Fontaine. There was something like panic in his usually quiet eyes.

16

It was Reynolds who leaped to the switchboard with Gerson and began to shove in emergency circuits. A few minutes later Gerson turned to the shaken group.

"I don't know what the hell it is. But it's carried away every damn wire west. Everything's out—somewhere around Black Rock Canyon."

I was still convinced a lost plane in a one-in-a-billion freak accident had crashed on the G.W.'s right of way. I shouted this at Reynolds. But he was wild-eyed, staring up at Gerson's board. The range of expressions on those faces before me was remarkable. Everyone was thinking about the streamliner. Nobody, for a few seconds, dared voice what he was thinking. But Reynolds changed all that. He shouted right in Fontaine's face, his own not two feet away, "Goddamnit, that's no plane. That's 502. Some bastard has blasted that train to hell and gone. I know it! You know it! And we——"

But Reynolds ran into an interruption that numbed everyone. Two more dull but thunderous explosions rumbled through the storm. The last sound waves died away. Not a man in our room uttered a word. And this time the entire diagram board sputtered and went dead, completely dead, like the burned out stick of a spent rocket. It was just as if the Great Western itself had died.

For the first and only time in his adult life, I think, MacIntosh was speechless. He stood in the glare of a desk lamp, like some big dumb animal, his lips working, his mind failing for a few brief moments to function. Outside, trainmen were now running excitedly about. Several of them rushed into the office. It was Fontaine who first recovered himself. I had to admire him. He could take it on the chin, in the worst way, and remain himself. He shoved Reynolds violently down into the nearest chair.

"Shut up!" he snapped at him. Then he faced all of us. "Anyone here without specific duties, get out. No guesswork or rumors. Mac-Intosh—Reynolds—Henderson—Downes—Gerson—you, too, Bierce, if you wish—and all you linemen—get your gear and climb aboard that Mallet."

He turned to the chief signal engineer. "Take your men and follow us down in 5190. Don't crowd us. Give us plenty of room. We don't know what we'll find." He began to fire broadsides of curt crisp orders. He wound up with Gerson. "Notify Placer and all authorities you can reach of a No. 1 emergency. Get state officials alerted on any phones you can. Whatever this is, it's a crisis, and big."

It wasn't so easy to get away from Summit in a hurry. Emergency gear of all kinds, for trackmen, linemen, and signal engineers had to be stowed in the two Mallet cabs and a single caboose. Both engines had to take on water. It was half an hour before we moved out, jammed in the big cab of the first Mallet. What we all dreaded couldn't possibly have happened, we told ourselves. We tried to concentrate on a lost cargo or passenger plane crashing into the streamliner in a freak-of-freaks cataclysm. Or the plane's gas tanks exploding. Or the Diesels blowing up—technically an impossibility with forty octane fuel oil at ten cents a gallon. But that's what we tried to tell ourselves. None of this jibed with those three heavy explosions.

We crept through the sheds, through Cranford Tunnel, and emerged on that wind-blown ledge of granite above Black Rock Canyon. The signals were out. They were simply dead, blank, unseeing eyes that sped by us in the darkness and snow. We pushed around a sharp curve as we approached Thomas' lodge and retaining wall. The tension in the cab was getting unbearable when our chap at the throttle damned near wiped the clock, stopping with such a jerk that several of us piled up against the hot boiler head, cursing. We weren't going any farther. That was definite. It was snowing and snowing hard. But twenty feet ahead of our engine pilot, bridge-high, rose a mass of splintered rock, snow, ice, and raw granite, right across the track, and drifting down into the canyon. A slide and a big one. Man-made, we knew now. We floundered through snow, climbed gingerly over sharp splintered boulders, came to the summit of the slide, started down the other side. I don't think anyone believed what we saw.

Right ahead of us were the three Diesel units of 502, their lights blazing, their engines still idling, and not a soul in sight. Coupled to the Diesels were just two cars, two streamlined mail and express cars. As one man we ran for that shorn train. Engineer and fireman were found trussed and gagged in the first cab. A lone mail clerk, in a similar condition, lay in the first car. Where were the guards? A door of each car, facing Thomas' retaining wall, was wide open.

Lights were on. Fontaine took a look in both cars and just about dropped from shock. I knew what he'd found. Nothing! A shattering lot of nothing. He turned helplessly to MacIntosh and said clearly, "Gone, John. Cleaned out. Gutted. All of it."

We had lost any capacity for further feelings of shock or surprise. Where was the rest of the train? Dimly, I now began to understand something of a pattern. Behind the Diesels and their two gutted cars rose another big rock slide. Beyond that was a red glare half smothered in flying snow. Then we heard shouts. A trainman swinging a lantern appeared on the ridge of the second slide. Over that slide we all scrambled to glimpse an even weirder spectacle. In a drainage ditch burned quite a fire, a distress signal, made from oil waste, seat covers, and benches from the crew's dormitory car. The flames, dying down, threw a macabre glare over the seventeen sleek cars of the streamliner, the last four out of sight around a curve. Trainmen and a few excited passengers were on the ground. Others peered from open vestibule doors. A shout went up when they saw our flashlights coming over that slide.

Two slides. There had been three blasts. Then I got it. I wasn't alone. MacIntosh, Edwards, and Reynolds ran with me towards the hidden end of the train, entered the curve, and confirmed our hunches. The third slide was there, just beyond the observation car. What a fantastic job! The train had been neatly boxed off at the rear by the slide we now confronted, caused by the first explosion. Diesels and express cars had been cut off, run ahead half a mile, two more slides loosed fore and aft to box them in, and their contents gutted and sacked, passengers panicked but unmolested half a mile down the rails, and not a coherent trainman left to explain the impossible.

There's no use stressing too many details of the nightmarish aspects of that incredible Christmas Eve holdup in the midst of a Sierra blizzard just below Eldorado Pass. Everyone who could read or who owned a radio or TV at the time never forgot it and never will. We cleared out the lounge car, organized a temporary investigation committee, lined up the trainmen, while sweating linemen and engineers unreeled wires over the slides and started to set up working circuits patched into the torn-out company wires. We had an emergency phone plugged into the car in ten minutes, another one a few minutes later. Gerson got on the first one and the now famous story of "Fontaine's Folly," that cost Fontaine his job and abruptly ended the careers of ten other Great Western directors and a hatful of lesser officials, poured down the mountain and into the incredulous offices of the G.W., of press associations, radio networks, and all the vast communications machinery of our gadget-strewn civilization.

The first facts uncovered revealed an incredible pattern of events. Engineer E. P. Dutton, rolling the train at about thirty miles an hour, encountered a regulation flare between the rails at Mile 159. He stopped his train and got down to investigate. Seconds later the first blast went off around the curve behind him, out of his vision, bringing down tons of rock on the rails a few hundred yards behind the observation car. Later we realized this slide and the curve that concealed it were vital to the success of the whole fantastic operation. The passengers were thrown into near panic. All of the trainmen, scattered through 502, rushed to the rear end to investigate the blast. But—and this was all-important—so did the two railroad guards and two mail clerks at the head end. Even Dutton and his fireman ran back several car lengths. As Dutton put it:

"Why the hell wouldn't we? The last four cars were out of sight around that bend. Everybody thought the train itself had been blasted. Nobody dreamed of a holdup. We all thought something terrible had happened at the rear end."

Fontaine and all of us were now floored by Dutton's follow-up. First, a single holdup man, wearing a black rubber mask, had crept up behind a single mail clerk standing by his car, slugged him unconscious, and then stuck a gun in Dutton's back, made his fireman uncouple the express cars, toss the mail clerk in one of them, where he was later trussed up, and got this portion of the train rolling uphill before the two armed guards and trainmen, some distance away and barely visible in falling snow, waiting for reports from the rear end, were aware of what had happened. The gunman riding the Diesel cab made Dutton stop at a designated spot just below Thomas' retaining wall. He then fired a single shot, obviously a signal to his confederates, from the cab door. The second two blasts came off at once, neatly boxing in Diesels and express cars between two new slides, which also cut off the rest of the train.

The lone gunman then made Dutton tie up and blindfold his fireman, after which the gunman performed the same service for Dutton. Both engine men swore they heard a platform dolly, a small hoisting truck operated by a gasoline motor, working by the two express cars. They heard voices, a few shouted orders, but not many, a winch hoisting away on top of Thomas' wall, obviously using one of the elevator shafts. It was all over in about twenty minutes.

When Dutton and his fireman finished there was dead silence. Fontaine was aging by the minute.

"But the rest of the mob," he demanded in a queer husky voice, "you didn't see them?"

"Only the first fellow," said Dutton haltingly. "We heard some voices, but not good. Their dolly motor made a lot of noise. And the Diesels were idling."

"How many voices?" insisted Fontaine. Dutton shook his head. "I just couldn't tell, Mr. Fontaine. Maybe two, maybe a dozen." Then he added almost casually, but in a perplexed tone, "Our motors were going, but when it was all over I would swear I heard a plane take off."

Another incredulous silence. I looked at Edwards. He was looking at me.

"In this weather?" asked Fontaine, his voice a kind of croak.

Dutton paused. "It sounded like it, sir, that's all," he said stubbornly.

On went this inquisition. The two guards, already suspected of complicity in the job, were pitiful. Convinced the rear end of the train had been bombed, they simply deserted their cars. So they said. When they tried to get back up the rails to the express cars they were fired at from the top of the wall. Thirty-three million in bullion, bonds, currency, some of it unmarked, negotiable and non-negotiable securities, registered stocks—gone, whisked away, vanished into the limbo of the Sierras under impossible conditions. It made Boston's Brink robbery look like a kindergarten job. A hundred valid reasons why it simply could not have happened the way it did occurred to everyone. Fontaine's face was gray and tragic. He was all through, washed up, and he knew it. And not a Trooper, not a detective, not a law enforcement official could reach us for another hour at least—although a vast army of investigators, press, and radio men from several states were even now swarming for the summit of the Sierras.

The snowy figure of a lineman hurriedly entered the car, conferred briefly with Edwards and Gerson, then headed for Fontaine. Edwards quickly beckoned me and we left the car.

"The signal boys are combing the ridge. I want to get up there and I'd like you along."

It took us over twenty minutes to locate snowshoes back at our Mallet and get on top of the bare wind-swept ridge of rock that led back to the lodge. High winds had also swept clear the entire top of the retaining wall. The big drifts began a hundred feet south. Linemen had rigged a couple of portable floodlights which filtered feebly through the driving snow. But there had been some discoveries. Three insulated blasting wires were found at the edge of the wall. Scratches in the cement and a bit of copper clamp showed where a three-way blasting switch and battery box had rested to set off the blasts. Even through driving snow the spot commanded a fairly clear view of the rails below us all the way to that vital curve.

We could see the first two slides, the Diesels, and dimly in the distance the blurred lights of the streamliner. We saw at once that armed men on this wall could prevent any move to interfere with the methodical unloading of the express cars. The explosives had been carefully spaced, measured to the yard, probably. The man who threw the switches could see everything that happened below him. The whole scene spread out like a child's map. But no child executed this job.

The treasure definitely had been hoisted up the first empty elevator shaft. Splinters, bits of debris, scratches in the concrete, all told the story. Ten or eleven chests, we found later, comprised the shipment. Dim furrows in the snow left that shaft and headed southeast a short distance ending up in heavily drifted snow. But what kind of vehicle could operate beyond the solid ground under us? We pushed forward perhaps five hundred yards, completely baffled, and didn't dare go further and lose the faint glare of the floodlights behind us. We might have been on the trackless reaches of the Siberian steppes. Then I made my first find. Just ahead of me was a lone tamarack tree, bent like a bow before the wind. But something waving from a branch caught my eye. I went over and grabbed it. Clothesline! What the hell was clothesline doing up here? And then I remembered the big clothesline shortage I had encountered a few days ago. Nothing registered, but with a pocketknife I cut off perhaps six or eight feet from a long line that disappeared over a hill, and went back to Edwards, talking with a group of men in the lee of the lodge. I got him off alone and handed him my piece of clothesline.

"What about it?" he asked. All at once I felt foolish. But Edwards was trying to think this one out as calmly as if someone had removed five dollars from a country cash register. He saw me hesitate and added:

"Go ahead, Howie, give. Anything goes in this affair. The sky's the limit. Somebody had a brainstorm. Crazy, cockeyed, fantastic. But he got away with it. *He got away with it.* That we've got to face. No matter what screwy ideas you got, let's have 'em. The linemen broke into the lodge and are searching it now. Hurry up."

So I told him about the big rush for clothesline I'd recently encountered. Edwards frowned hard.

"So what? What the hell good is clothesline up here?"

"If a fellow was on skis he could use it as a guideline," I suggested feebly. "It's mighty crude, but it would work."

"On skis!" retorted Edwards, scornfully. "Where would he go? How much could he carry? Ten thousand dollars? Fifteen? It's no good. Eleven heavy chests have disappeared——" Then he stopped. We looked at each other. Something bit into us simultaneously. Edwards just about yelled at me:

"That goddamn airplane. I know what it was——"

I beat him to it. "That's it. Thomas had a snowmobile. Gustavson told me about it when I first came up here. Clothesline and wire. A guideline over the mountain—but where to, Sam?"

"Never mind that now. That's got to be it. That snowmobile was in the front garage last week when we pulled out the guards."

We both tore downstairs into the cellar, through a furnace room, through another door into a big empty garage. It wasn't there. Edwards and I shook hands. But there was a twenty-foot drift outside the garage door. The snowmobile had been gone for some time. Edwards pulled out a pocket map of the local area. We both studied it in the glare of his flashlight.

"I'm a son of a bitch," he said softly after a long silence. "It's just possible. Just possible. Look at this, Howie. There's clear level ground along this south ridge for three miles. That's a hell of a lot of clothesline or wire for a guide in this weather. But Jesus! Look here. He don't have to go three miles. Just a mile and a half to Bulldog Canyon. There's an old logging trail there, steep as hell, down to Highway 53, snowed in, but passable for this kind of craft. It joins 395 just above Drake's store. If he had a truck near there——"

I shook my head. "This is kid stuff, Sam. With all those chests and thirty-three million? Impossible."

"Hell, suppose he knows what he wants, grabs it, and dumps the rest, here, or out in the snow. He could get away with plenty."

"But where to?" I demanded.

"395 is good enough for anybody's getaway," snapped Edwards. "If he made that, he's in the clear."

An explosion of largely unconscious items I must have been building in my mind for a long time suddenly occurred. And with them lingered the echo of a casual remark made to me by Gustavson a long time ago.

I said abruptly to Edwards, "If it's Thomas, if this cockeyed scheme really worked this way, I know where he is. He's back in Virginia City, and I'll bet a million of his loot he's holed up in the Comstock. He saw me and Gustavson working around the Ophir. I even told him about the mine before that. Once on 395, if he went that way, he could make Virginia City in no time. . . . Did you really search that place?" I demanded again.

"We sure did—but that was five days ago," said Edwards slowly, studying me intently. He said suddenly, "Say all that again."

I did. Edwards hated to take my suggestion seriously but he was beginning to. "We searched Gustavson's lead shaft all the way to the hoist. Put new locks on the shaft and office doors. Had a guard there until two days ago. No soap."

"That's not good enough, Sam," I insisted. Every instinct I possessed was ringing the bell that I had something. "Gustavson once told me the Ophir led into several galleries. One of them an outlet for the old Ophir-Mexican third-line shaft coming out a quarter mile below the office. That means the whole Comstock to hide in— if a man or a mob had to."

"Are you proposing a search of the whole damn Comstock?" asked Edwards soberly.

"Maybe. But I'm telling you this—we know where to begin."

Edwards stood there looking at me, his mind churning. I must have gotten across to him. He struck me suddenly in the chest with the flat of his hand.

"By God, Bierce, I'm going to play your hunch. It's screwy, crazy. But so is everything else about this insane affair. Come on. Back to your damn railroad."

We got down to the rails and the lounge car as fast as possible. We learned a three-car special loaded with FBI, police, press, radio, and TV crews, was headed up the Hill, due in half an hour. But we also learned we had no phone contacts to the east. Edwards thought out loud.

"Can we get an engine?"

"I'll get it."

"Okay. Look, Howie, we're going to play this close to the chest. If we're screwy, I don't want it advertised. Let's get over to Placer, grab an official car, phone Reno for help, and get into Virginia City as fast as we can. If it's a fizzle, no harm done. A lot of people will be at work up here pretty quick and we won't be needed. Let's go."

The group in the lounge car had disintegrated into a mournful, terrible wake. Fontaine looked ninety years old. I got MacIntosh's ear. He wrote out a penciled order for any engine we could find free to run East. We grabbed the order and started uphill along the rails. A lot of things had happened while Edwards and I were plowing about around the lodge. Two work trains had hurried down from Summit. Crews had rigged floodlights in the swirling snow. Under their glare an army of men were clawing through the east slide in order to release the Diesels. More men were swarming over the other two slides. It was planned to haul the streamliner back to Belknap. A lot of people weren't going East tonight.

Edwards and I plowed past the work trains, the Big Hook and wrecking train, past harried officials, and finally grabbed the only engine in a position to move east, a dilapidated ten-wheeler tied to a work train. But it would do. We cut it off, ran around the work train, and rattled uphill towards Summit. There we had a nervous wait of ten minutes while we were cleared into Pioneer Gap and Placer. With CTC not operating yet, a number of orders had to be issued. We got down to Pioneer Gap in seventeen minutes and had to take on water there. While that went on I got down on the ground to stretch. It was quiet, cold, and weirdly serene down here. No snow falling. Just a leaden sky, mountains of white drifts, a few lights here and there marking that portion of the Gap still visible. The G.W. Hotel was about a hundred yards west of the water spout. Edwards yelled to me from the engine. We were ready to go. Then I looked at my watch and got a shock. It was three-four. That meant I wasn't going over to Virginia City and back, no matter what happened, in time to catch any train from the Gap at six-fifty, that morning, whether it ran or not, with Lisa and Helmholtz aboard. I had forgotten time, and my whole schedule was now fouled up.

I yelled at Edwards to hold everything for a few minutes and ran into the G.W. Hotel. The lobby night light was on, with old Dan probably still asleep. The excitement hadn't hit here yet. I grabbed the lobby phone, called the Casa Alta, and got Maria at once. They had just had the news and the place was beginning to jump. Two local reporters had already arrived. I asked for Gustavson. Maria's voice sounded strained.

"Tell me what you want, Howie. They're still asleep. Gustavson left word at the desk that they were not to be disturbed. They are to be called at five-thirty."

"Call them right now," I said. Then I gave her instructions that Gustavson should get Lisa and Helmholtz on the train if it showed up. Maria was to pack up my immediate needs, Pete to take my bag to the train, and I would make every effort to join the train at Placer, or even Benning if I had to drive there. I heard Maria gasp.

"I won't see you before you leave?"

"I'm sorry. Not in this mess. I'm with Edwards. We've got a hot lead."

There was a long silence. "Can you tell me?" asked Maria.

"No time. It's Thomas, though—and we think we know where he is."

"Be careful," she said worriedly after another pause. "I will get your things on the train myself. You think the road will be open?"

"I doubt it," I said truthfully. "If it isn't I'll be back at the Gap by noon. So long."

Twenty-five minutes later we pulled into Placer. Edwards phoned a friend named Carlson, a police lieutenant at Reno, told him what we were up to, and then we grabbed a highway car and sped off. I gathered half of Reno would be roaring into Virginia City right behind us.

We ran through two police road blocks right out of Carson and got to Virginia City a little later. The picturesque old mining town was fast asleep. Like sharp etchings its sagging structures, ancient villas, and the plain brick lines of the old Catholic church rose black and stark against snow-covered roofs and a leaden sky. There had been no new snow here for twenty-four hours.

Edwards drove up to C Street, where we waited awhile, hoping for our Reno reinforcements. But nobody showed. My confidence in my hunch was beginning to ebb. It was bitterly cold, too, though we had the engine and heater on. Edwards looked a little grimly at his watch.

"Let's go down," he said simply. We drove down and parked a short distance from Gustavson's office, cutting off the lights. Edwards got out his flashlight and shifted a gun holster under his left arm.

"Just to be sure," said Edwards, "let's look at Ted's mine first."

We circled cautiously behind the property and came out in the rear shadows of the little office structure. We looked hopefully up towards town, begging to see the lights of a Reno squad car. But there wasn't a sign of life. A clear bitter Washoe wind blew over the hollow where we waited. The creak of old clapboards, a dog barking far away, were the only sounds in that cold predawn darkness.

"Maybe we're lousy dicks. Maybe this is a washout," said Edwards in a low voice. "Let's find out."

We emerged boldly before the mine office and walked towards the shaft and then halted in disappointment. Not a mark, not a furrow of any kind disturbed the few inches of level snow spreading before us right up to the padlocked shaft door.

"All right. That Ophir-Mexican shaft is our last chance," said Edwards.

We threaded down through some vacant lots, past old stone foundations of ancient breakers and ore process plants, past sodden slag piles, eighty years old. Then Edwards grabbed my arm.

"Right ahead of you. Take a look at that."

A rough lane or alley ran through the ruins of old foundations straight before us to a shaft entrance very similar to the gallery operated by Pete and Ted. Fresh tire tracks, a lot of them, had churned up snow and frozen mud. At one place a car had turned around. There'd been a lot of traffic. Edwards pulled out his gun and snapped the safety catch.

Then we both saw it—a small delivery truck parked by a fence near the shaft entrance. Edwards got to it first, a '39 or '40 Ford, thousands like them. Nevada plates. The sides proclaiming in faded flaking paint: Minden Bakery—S. Gottwald," and an illegible phone number. Edwards ran to the radiator and placed his hand on it. I did the same. It was still warm and had recently boiled over. My breathing got a little labored at that point and Edwards must have sensed my reaction.

"Howie, you're hot tonight. No doubt about it. I think Thomas is in there. I'm going to bring him out. But this isn't your chore. You don't have to come along. Just keep out of sight and wait for me."

"Never mind me," I replied in a low voice. "But you're crazy. You can't tackle that crowd alone. Wait for the Reno cops."

"I'll be careful," said Edwards. "But I'm going to look around. I can't wait." He was looking over my shoulder. "Jeez! Isn't that Pete's car?"

I whirled around and my stomach lobbed about like a punching bag. The nose of Gustavson's Hudson was poking out from behind a big pile of weathered crates. Its motor, too, was still warm.

"What the hell do you think now?" asked Edwards, his eyes black with excitement. I couldn't speak. Maria's voice suddenly rang in my ears. I just stared back at him.

"You think Pete had the same hunch or"—Edwards' eyes bored into mine—"could he be in on this?"

"Don't ask me what I think," I said bleakly. "I wouldn't know—not this time. Not any more. But I'm going in with you."

Edwards turned around without another word and trudged off. I followed him with reluctant legs. When we got to the shaft door it stood ajar, an open padlock and chain hanging from a staple. This entrance was two or three hundred feet lower than the Ophir No. 3 and the shaft, illuminated by Edwards' flashlight, led downward at a steep angle, carrying narrow gauge rails for ore cars. The first thing I saw were many fresh footprints in the heavy blue mud under our feet.

I took a deep breath as Edwards plunged in and managed a last look at my watch. It was four twenty-two on the morning of Christmas Day when we entered the blackness of that shaft.

17

I walked behind Edwards for an interminable time, descending the shaft at a steep angle along a heavily cleated section of rotted boardwalk that ran beside the shaft rails. Edwards carried two flashlights, one about the size of a fat fountain pen with a tiny shaft of light which he was using, a second one, a big one, with a five-inch lens, thrust in his belt. I thought then and I think now that it was sheer lunacy for us to walk into that shaft without waiting for more support. But Edwards had his dander up. Nothing could have stopped him.

Every two or three minutes we halted and listened. Nothing but the sound of dripping water, of our own breathing, of distant rivulets here and there. Nothing but blue-black muck under our feet and a small circle of light picking out a bit of rusted rail or wet rock vanishing in shadow.

The shaft leveled off and began to turn. We halted again. Not a sound this time. Not even dripping water here. Edwards whispered:

"We're plenty far down. You still game? What do you think?"

I whispered back. "It's no good, Sam. I vote for reinforcements first."

Edwards was obviously torn. Then his better judgment came to the fore.

"Okay," he said in a low voice. "I guess you're right. If I knew this shaft I'd take a chance. Let's turn around. I——"

Far down the shaft we heard the dull muffled clap of a pistol shot. We couldn't mistake it. Like the sharp slap of one board on another. No other sound followed it. Edwards pulled out his big flashlight and tried to give it to me. He was excited. He said quickly:

"Go back, Bierce. I can't stop now."

I pushed his flashlight away. "Keep going. I can't back up either."

Edwards released the safety catch on his other gun and gave it to me. "Even if you're scared to use it," he said, "it may look like authority at the right moment. Stay ten feet behind me—ready to duck or run."

Walking cautiously, I figure we made another five hundred feet. The shaft opened out into a jumble of old galleries, a junction of ore tracks, fallen rock, a pile of rusted ore buckets, two or three rotted storeroom doors. We didn't know which way to go. Edwards clicked off his light. Far away through one of the shafts, when our eyes got used to the darkness, we saw the faintest reflection of light. The source wasn't visible. Edwards whispered:

"I'm not using the light. We're heading for that."

We made pretty good progress by steadying our left hands along the rock wall of our shaft. Underfoot it was fairly level. As we approached the glow of light it slowly grew. We came to a sharp right-angle turn in the shaft. Edwards got around the corner first. I saw him freeze. Then I turned the angle after him and caught my breath.

About fifty feet ahead of us the bulky shadow of a man holding a flashlight in his left hand, a heavy service revolver in his right, was dimly outlined in a doorway set in solid rock. His flashlight was directed into a chamber concealed from our view. The man stood motionless. His gun covered someone or something. We moved forward slowly, as silently as we could. I barely heard Edwards' order.

"Stay where you are, Howie. I'll handle this."

All at once the sharp beam of his big flashlight shot out and seemed to explode against the figure in the doorway. At the same moment Edwards called out sharply:

"Don't move! You're covered."

The man turned his face briefly, his startled eyes staring into that white blinding shaft of light. Neither his own gun nor light moved at all. But I thought my heart would pop right out of my open mouth. For Pete Gustavson was looking straight at us, but blindly. Edwards yelled at once:

"It's Edwards and Bierce, Pete. Stay just as you are."

Gustavson faced again towards that hidden chamber. I heard him mutter, "Thank God," and then we were with him, looking over his gun barrel into a fairly large rock chamber flooded with light from Pete's torch. It was quite a picture. Four well-dressed men in heavy overcoats, with snap-brim hats pulled low, were up against the far wall, just like a police line-up. One man sat on a box, grimacing with pain, his left hand holding his shattered right wrist, from which blood was dripping. There was a faint smell of cordite in the air.

The chamber had once been an old explosives storeroom, now turned into a hide-out and a good one. There was a charcoal stove.

Crude shelves stacked with enough canned goods for a battalion. Two oil lanterns, lighted, hung from spikes in the rock. Half a dozen bunks, recently used and full of blankets and sacking, filled one side of the chamber. The white faces of the four men were wary and watchful. In the intense light they looked like wax dummies, all except their eyes, blinking at the light, or gazing stolidly at the floor.

"Who the hell are they?" snapped Edwards.

"Thomas' men," said Gustavson. His gun hand began to tremble slightly. So did his voice. "You say Bierce is with you?"

Edwards flashed his light on me briefly. Pete looked.

"I want to talk to him," he said, his voice choking.

"No time now," said Edwards. "I'll take over."

He moved into the doorway, his own gun covering those four frozen, motionless men. He addressed Pete. His voice rose at the puzzles confronting us. "How long've you held 'em like this? Who in hell are you waiting for?"

"I don't know," said Gustavson, expelling his breath suddenly. "I don't know. I had to shoot that fellow. He started to reach for——"

"We heard you," said Edwards. "Frisk 'em all. Right now. Make it fast."

Gustavson, shaking with relief from his long strain, pushed into the chamber and frisked his four captives. He acquired an arsenal —two Smith and Wesson .38s, a fancy .25 automatic, a .32 nondescript, two .22 target automatics with the big front sights, and what I'd never seen before, two wicked-looking 9 millimeter Mausers. Pete brought them all out into the shaft in two trips and dumped them on the ground. Our four gents wilted perceptibly. Then Pete ignored Edwards and turned almost frantically to me.

"Howie," he said thickly, and his words tumbled together. "Ted is here. He's gone after Thomas. Down that gallery to the big chamber, the Comstock. A long time ago he went. I've heard nothing. Nothing!"

My skin began to crawl. "How in hell did you get here?" I blazed at him. "And why are you here? Why? Maria said you were both in bed."

Gustavson blinked. "Then she did not see us go out. We heard the news of the holdup being shouted around. Both Ted and I thought of the mine at once. Thomas had this place spotted, as you know. I thought of the Mexico shaft when I remembered our place was locked. Ted was sure Thomas was here somewhere. We had to find out."

"Good Lord, man—why didn't you bring some police along?"

"Howie, everybody was heading up the Hill. We couldn't even get a phone." I didn't doubt that. Gustavson was looking at me as astonished as I was. "How did you get here?" he asked suddenly.

"Same hunch. You mentioned this once. Remember?"

Gustavson blinked again. He said in a strange voice, "Yah. That's right. I did."

The same hunch. Ted and I.

"I didn't know Ted had the nerve for this. This was foolhardy," I told Gustavson.

"Where are *your* cops?" he rapped out. "But you are right. Ted has more nerve than you think."

Edwards had heard our words. He whipped some of his own over his shoulder. "Cut it. You're wasting time. Hold these guys a bit longer, Pete. We're going after Helmholtz. You're sure Thomas was alone?"

"I think so. I think so," said Gustavson desperately, as if to nail down his guess as a fact. "He was the only one that run out when we stumbled on their hide-out. I did not dare fire because Ted stood in the way. Then Ted ran after him. I told him to let Thomas go. But he would not. And they both have guns."

He moved in to Edwards' place, covering the four men again. He said quickly, "Hurry. No. 7 gallery, the one right here. About a thousand feet, with two turns, to the center of the Comstock."

We hurried off. Edwards used his big light, but aimed it straight at the ground. He had it half covered with his left hand. I couldn't get these developments at all. Gustavson and Helmholtz on top of Thomas' crowd at four in the morning. And Ted, a sick man who hated violence, stalking the redoubtable Thomas with a gun down those black galleries. It was just about unbelievable.

"What the hell goes?" I said aloud.

"Shut up," said Edwards. He sure meant it. We got around the second turn and stopped. At first we heard nothing. Then faint indefinable sounds came to us from some distance ahead. A rythmic creaking or squeaking of timbers that stopped and started up and stopped again. Like two ghosts stalking one another in a black garret. Only they weren't ghosts. Edwards flipped his light briefly along the wall of rock beside us—long enough for us to read a chalked warning: "Stop! Dead End 150 Feet Ahead. No Guard Rail. Take Right Gallery at Rim for Exit."

Edwards began to use the small light again. We went ahead cautiously, then came to a row of rocks, six or eight inches high, laid across the gallery to mark its end. Our thin pencil of light inched carefully over the rocks, hit a blank rim a foot further that dropped off into nothing. I remembered the similar appearance of that quick-ending gallery Helmholtz guided me through for my first glimpse of the Comstock. I had a rough idea of what lay beyond. So did Edwards.

He suddenly shot the beam of his big light dead ahead—and I

caught an awesome glimpse, a different angle from my first view this time, of the massive timbered structures and latticework that rose endlessly in the heart of that wrecked mine. But we weren't prepared at all for what followed. Out of that oppressive silence a voice that shook me, a voice I knew well, the voice of Helmholtz, far above and to the right, shouted down:

"Put out that light! Put it out! That you, Pete?"

Edwards snapped it out. Before he could answer a brief spurt of crimson flame spat at us, far above and farther to the left. A bullet sang off bare rock, just below the gallery rim. Rock splinters tinkled below us.

"Ted!" I yelled. "It's Bierce and Edwards. Pete's okay. Who fired?"

"Howie?" The relief in Ted's voice was like that of a rescued child. He had guts to be where he was, for he was frightened to death. He could hardly speak. He finally called down hoarsely, "That was Thomas. Don't use your lamp. I——"

Edwards interrupted him. "Give us the layout. Quick! Have you got a torch?"

"Yes. So has Thomas," Helmholtz replied. "We're both in a jam. Listen! From where I saw your lamp, Thomas is ahead of you, off to the left a little, but way up, maybe sixty feet. We're both on the same gallery. I don't think he can go up or down. He's got to come back this way. I don't dare use my light. I've been waiting for Gustavson."

"He's been waiting for you," cut in Edwards curtly. "Listen. How good a shot are you?"

"Just fair," said Helmholtz.

"Okay." Edwards raised his voice to a shout. "Thomas! You got one chance to turn yourself in minus a lot of holes. The Reno cops are right behind us. Drop your gun down the shaft. Turn your light on. We'll cover you and take you out. Get moving."

There was a long silence. Then a snarl like the sound of a treed cougar floated down to us. Thomas' voice was almost conversational, remote but menacing.

"Come and get me, you bastards."

Edwards grunted. "Get back against that wall, Howie." He called up to Ted. "Helmholtz! I'm going to pin him with my light. If you see him first—shoot. If we spot him, we'll shoot. You got cover?"

"Yes," Helmholtz called back. "I'm at the right end of the gallery with some uprights around me."

"Lie flat," ordered Edwards. "Here goes."

I was aware Edwards had stooped down. He placed the big electric torch on the ground, carefully propping it at what he figured to be the proper angle on a stone, snapped it on, and jumped back. A wide cone of light was flung high on the Comstock's crisscrossed timbers. Both of us flattened against the rock wall as far from the light as we could get. I looked up, up, up, and saw nothing at first in that forest of timbered galleries and ancient ladders cocked at all angles. Then far above us flashed another spurt of flame, paler now in the light of the torch. A bullet whammed into the gallery, just a few inches from our light. Then we both saw Thomas, or rather just a part of him, looking very small—the top of his head, part of a shoulder, a small target dimly outlined fully seventy feet above us and far back against the opposite wall of that empty mine. He was lying flat behind a big square timber and made a very poor target from where we were. But Helmholtz was right. Thomas was backed up against solid rock, and no ladders up or down. I figured the two men were about a hundred feet apart, with Ted invisible to us in the black shadows to our right.

Edwards drew a careful bead on what he could see of Thomas and fired. We saw no results. But the shot reverberated weirdly for seconds and it certainly got a rise out of Helmholtz. He yelled, "I see him. I see him." Then he fired twice, the flashes appearing way over to our right, farther than I had figured.

Those shots sure registered with Thomas. I'm convinced he was hit. He jumped to a low crouch in the shadows and Edwards fired once more, but this time Thomas wasn't paying us a bit of attention. What followed will live with me to the grave. A savage gun battle blazed out between both men. Helmholtz fired three shots in rapid succession. Thomas fired almost simultaneously at his flashes—one-two-three-four. Thomas suddenly collapsed on the platform. Edwards shouted:

"You got him. You got him. . . . Try it again."

There was a pause. Then Helmholtz fired again, but so did Thomas, twice from his prone position. In a deadly silence that followed we were shocked to see Thomas slowly rise to his feet and pull his gun up to a firing position again. But it was no go. He simply collapsed in a heap. We heard his gun clatter on the platform boards.

"By God, he got him," snapped Edwards excitedly. He jumped to his flashlight, grabbed it up, and swung its cone of light to where we knew Helmholtz must be. At the same time I called out:

"Ted! Ted! You okay?"

There was a little pause. We couldn't see him at first. But all at once he appeared in the full glare of our light, slight and slender far above us, one hand braced on a timber and looking down at us. He seemed all right.

But his voice sounded queer. "I got winged, I guess," he called down.

"Stay where you are," ordered Edwards, running his light up and down the ladders while I spotted the ledge to our right which gave access to them. "We're coming up. We'll get you down. Don't try it alone."

But for once Helmholtz wasn't taking orders. He called out, his voice now stronger, "Focus your light on the ladders. I can make it."

Edwards did so, calling out, "Okay, if you want to try. But take it easy."

I held my breath. Helmholtz looked all right to us. He moved fairly easily and used his arms and legs cautiously but without difficulty. He turned his back on us and our light, then got hold of the first ladder and started down. He was halfway down the second ladder when he stopped. Then he turned his head and looked straight at me, though he couldn't see a thing, facing the glare of that light.

He called uncertainly, "Howie, I can't make it."

I ran to the lip of the gallery. "I'm right here, Ted. Just hang on where you are. Hang on till Edwards gets you."

But like blasted fruit on a vine, his figure seemed to wilt and wither. He managed to turn half around and face us. His expression appalled me. It was so full of desperation and pleading, of finality and farewell. He said clearly, "Howie . . . !" Then he let go and fell. Slowly at first, like a crumpled puppet in our light, then turning over and over and disappearing straight down the great empty shaft of the Comstock. It must have been seconds later when we heard the final crash of his body. We found afterwards that he had two bullets through his chest. He was bleeding to death when he started down those ladders.

I recall sitting down suddenly for a few moments against the wall of rock behind me. When I got up, a small forest of lights was bobbing through the gallery behind us. The Reno people had arrived.

The nightmarish atmosphere of that Christmas morning remains with me to this day. Edwards and I sat outside the shaft in Lieutenant Carlson's car—he had been Edwards' old boss in Reno—while the whole area seemed to explode in news developments as the story broke wide open. First of all, there weren't going to be any eastbound trains on the G.W. for at least twenty-four hours. So I stayed where I was. Chronologically, things went about like this:

At six that Christmas morning Thomas' lodge had just about been pulled apart. Then somebody remembered what Edwards and I should have thought about when we stood outside the lodge in the snow right after the holdup. The wine cellar. An inch-thick steel door was torn down. Inside was the entire bank shipment, the thirty-three million in neatly stacked boxes, untouched, intact. Not a nickel missing. Was that a sensation!

But what was missing was the Great Western's entire shipment, destined for the road's Chicago bankers. There was a cool million in this loot, a lot of it in unregistered coupon-bearing bonds, in a single big iron-strapped strong box. These unregistered bonds were those of the Government and of private corporations. Their coupons could be cashed with little difficulty and without arousing the least suspicion. Just as good as ready cash. Unmarked. Unregistered.

Shortly after this major development, at about 8 A.M. Thomas' snowmobile, bearing a hoisting winch on a sturdy platform, was found in an abandoned barn a mile east of Drake's store on Route 395. Edwards' guesses had been right on the nose.

As the morning wore on the Reno people were frantically combing the Ophir and Mexican galleries, cross-examining the Thomas crowd with no results, when at about ten o'clock Carlson came running out of the shaft announcing the recovery of another golden flood. Under the ancient boards of a small storeroom overlooked in an earlier search, and quite close to the room where Thomas and his men had been discovered, was found some three hundred thousand dollars from the Reno armored car mess. The search was redoubled and an hour later a small pump room disgorged about six hundred thousand in bonds from the Great Western's shipment.

By this time Virginia City was in an uproar and before noon a whole corps of reporters, radio and TV crews were pouring into the old town.

Just before Edwards and I left for the Gap, after a light lunch, he and I with Carlson figured that about two hundred thousand dollars from the Reno robbery and three of Thomas' syndicate members were missing. None of this money, none of the men, ever turned up. We also figured that some four hundred and fifteen thousand dollars of the Great Western's coupon-bearing bonds were definitely missing.

Meanwhile the Thomas crowd, taken to Reno, talked very little. They violently claimed they had nothing to do with the streamliner affair and hadn't even heard of it; that with the road blocks removed on Wednesday, the twenty-third, they were simply planning to make a peaceful break eastward on Christmas morning when Gustavson and Helmholtz walked in and caught them at gun point in their hide-out. A likely story.

As Carlson drove us down through Devil's Gate both Edwards and I were exhausted and badly shaken. I dreaded facing Lisa. For later that afternoon the body of Ted Helmholtz would also return to Pioneer Gap.

18

At eleven o'clock on Monday morning, December 28, a crisp, clear, beautiful morning, with the mountains magnificent and the great snowfall of that month glittering and sparkling in the sunlight, we placed the body of Ted Helmholtz in Maria's family vault in the pleasant little pine-fringed cemetery of Pioneer Gap, half a mile up Tamarack Road, after simple ceremonies at the Presbyterian church in town. The highway patrol had had to plow a way in and dig out the door to the vault, buried in fifteen feet of snow.

A great many people were there, many of whom, I'm sure, had never heard of Ted, never seen him, never knew Ted existed until the dailies of the nation blazoned his name in oceans of black ink across the land. From the moment Ted's broken body had been carried out of the Comstock, from the first news flash of his bizarre stalking and shooting of Thomas under Virginia City, Helmholtz had become a national hero.

Thomas lay in a Reno hospital, still unconscious. He might live. He might not. But the manner of Ted's last adventure and his melodramatic death, the picture of this mild-mannered, quiet, ingrown little pianist, already burdened with a death sentence pronounced by our local doctor, shooting it out with one of the most formidable gamblers in the land within the black recesses of the gutted Comstock, and all this as an incredible topper a few hours after the bizarre events at Eldorado Pass, was just about too much for America's already hyperthyroid press. I visualized thousands of typewriters being pounded to pieces from coast to coast as harried writers poured out millions of words on every minute facet of these fantastic happenings, copy that captured the front pages of the press for five straight days and drove the international crisis back to page 3.

But it was all over now. Helmholtz had won the peace and repose he so richly deserved. He had won it the hard way, and it was a pity to me that he could not view the pyrotechnic press displays and obituaries now showered upon him, an obscure artist in life, a triumphant sensation in death.

When we left the cemetery we drove Gustavson to the station to place him on the Denver Special. He was leaving for Colorado at once, subject to his return as a key witness in the trial of Thomas and his colleagues, scheduled for some time in February.

We stood at the end of the station platform with him, a little group consisting of Lisa and Reynolds, Captain Edwards, Maria and myself, with Gustavson looking gray and drawn. This usually ruddy kindly mining engineer, of whom we really knew almost nothing, was a shaken man who wanted to say so much and knew how to say so little. I think all of us had changed greatly in those last few days. Lisa, though very solemn, looked ten years younger as she stood arm in arm with a very subdued and attentive Reynolds. They were leaving for Oakland in an hour and planned to marry there on Wednesday with Maria present. I profoundly regretted not being able to attend their wedding. But I, too, was leaving as fast as I could, catching 20 east at five-thirty that afternoon. Destination, Betty and New York. The Great Western, after the robbery, had closed down tight for forty-eight hours, but traffic was rolling again and almost on time.

We stood there gazing at the mountains, saying nothing. There seemed to be nothing to say. All of us, I knew, were thinking of Ted. Then I happened to notice that Gustavson, increasingly nervous and now watching Lisa, was on the point of speaking to her. At that moment a Trooper came up to Edwards and said in a low voice:

"Captain, Thomas died in Reno at ten this morning. He never regained consciousness."

After a while the Trooper went away. Edwards commented briefly:

"That saves the State of Nevada a lot of time and money."

Purdy came over and told us No. 48, Pete's train, wouldn't be in for another fifteen minutes. Pete seemed to reach a sudden decision. He beckoned me and Lisa aside. But Maria was close by, within earshot, and watching us intently. I noticed that Pete wet his lips before addressing us.

"Lisa—Howie—I was going to wait, to write you from Denver. But I would like to speak now. I am selling the mine. It is finished. And I have other properties in Colorado." He shook his shaggy head a little. "I am not quite so poor as you think. I must now tell you something, Lisa. I am going to do what Ted would have wanted me to do. You will never give up music, I know that. For your studies, I am going to set up a trust fund for you, in memory of Ted. We had planned to do it anyway. It was all he lived for. I want you to know it will be done. I will write you the details as soon as the papers are drawn up."

Lisa was completely taken aback. So was I. She said quickly: "No, no, Mr. Gustavson. That could never be. I couldn't accept it. That is out of the question now. But I do appreciate your kindness, your generosity. I always have."

Gustavson looked absolutely stunned. "But I wish to do this. Ted would have wished me to do it. It is my greatest wish and pleasure. I have no one. And——"

Lisa's color rose. Her eyes were kind but very bright.

"Don't you see, Mr. Gustavson. I couldn't. I couldn't. Things—everything has changed. It's impossible."

For some reason I was watching Gustavson, not Lisa. I was surprised to see what a really profound shock Lisa's attitude was to him. He appeared completely frustrated. He stammered and stumbled in his speech.

"But—but—everything Ted hoped for, worked for—and I tried to help him—was to be this." He added almost harshly, "It *must* be like this."

Lisa laid a hand on his arm. She was very moved and her eyes filled with tears. Her voice was kind but it was also very firm.

"Can't you understand, Mr. Gustavson, what has happened? Don't you see how ashamed of myself I really am? What Ted's death has done to us all?"

I thought she was going to cry, but she controlled herself and continued. "All my life I have taken what people have given me. And I never returned any of it. I gave nothing to anyone. I've been blind, so terribly blind. And the guilt I feel over Ted's death is an awful thing. I loved Ted. But I used him. I let him make all kinds of sacrifices and always I demanded more—thinking it was for us, for both of us, for our music, our careers—he called it that—his as well as mine. But it was all for me. For me! How could I have been so blind. Now, I could never take a penny—never!—from you, or Ted, or anyone. I'm going to marry Jim. I intend to keep up my music. But for once, I'm going to help Jim, and others, and when that is done, I will help myself."

Then Lisa did begin to cry and Reynolds led her away.

Gustavson looked shattered, bewildered, out of all proportion to the impact of Lisa's refusal. He took me by the arm. He was almost babbling.

"She can't do that. She can't do that," he repeated over and over. "Howie, you must make her change her mind. I have arranged this trust fund. I——"

"Pete," I said, "the way that girl's mind is now, nothing is ever

215

going to change it. Enjoy what you've got. Give some money to the school, if you want to."

Gustavson was looking at me as if I were crazy. I think I returned his expression. His big hand grabbed my arm and tensed.

"We shall see. We shall see," he sputtered. "From Denver, I will mail you your check—I will not forget—a check for ten thousand."

I really thought Pete had gone off his rocker.

"Take it easy. I know what you've been through," I said. "If things turn out okay, send me three thousand—that's all I put in—and take your time about it."

"No!" said Pete angrily, showing color in his face for the first time that morning. "My properties in Colorado are good. I want to do this. I must. Good Gott, Howie, for Ted's sake I have to do it."

"I couldn't touch it, Pete. Three thousand, and no hurry. But not another penny. Now drop it."

Again Gustavson looked completely crushed. His eyes filled with tears. Everyone had been under too much wear and tear. I placed my hand on his arm.

"Get some rest, Pete. And Lisa's going to be beautifully taken care of." I added uneasily, "What did you have in mind as a trust fund, anyway?"

Pete registered just enough to answer me.

"For her studies in Europe, to give her security later on—at least two hundred thousand, more if she needed it. She must have it. She must."

Brother! Talk about delusions of grandeur. Pete sounded to me just like one of those crack-ups who imagines he's a millionaire and lands in an observation ward. I was very thankful as 48's whistle sounded down the valley. Pete got hold of himself. Indeed he just about froze up as we rejoined the others. Maria gave me a tense glance and I nodded my head reassuringly. By the time the train rolled in and we reached Pete's car he couldn't say another word. Not to anyone. I handed up two big suitcases to the porter. The train moved out, Pete standing in the vestibule door with tears rolling down his drawn and rugged cheeks.

Lisa and Reynolds went to her rooms for some last-minute packing. Maria and I walked silently over to the Casa Alta. We went into her office study, where a small fire was burning. There I took off my shoes, arranged some pillows on the divan, leaned back, and placed my feet on Maria's best coffee table. She mixed some brandy and Cointreau for us both. Neither of us had said a word since leaving the station.

For quite a while I sat there, concentrating on a brilliant crimson serape hung over the fireplace. I was trying to add up the score as I saw it. After a time I was aware that Maria was watching me.

"What are you thinking about, Howie?" she asked me in her quiet matter-of-fact voice.

Something tugged at my nerves. I sat up and looked straight into Maria's alert questioning eyes. I said accusingly:

"Maria, you lied to me. Why?"

She was genuinely astonished.

"I lied to you? When?"

"I phoned you from Dan's hotel on the way down from the Eldorado holdup. You told me Gustavson and Ted were asleep. But they must have left the hotel an hour earlier to make that mine ahead of Edwards and me. You were here. Why did you tell me that?"

"I did not see them go out. I found out they had left when I went upstairs later."

"But you never told me that, after other things happened. Why not?"

"You never asked me, Howie."

I studied her closely.

"Was there a lot of shouting in the lobby? When the news of the robbery broke?"

"No. It was very quiet. Mr. Purdy woke me up with the news."

"Pete told me shouting in the lobby woke him up. He and Ted got to Virginia City as fast as they could, with the same hunch I had. But it doesn't click. They got there too early."

Maria looked at me. She said nothing.

I got up. I had struck something. Maria's eyes showed concern. "You are puzzled by something," she remarked.

"Puzzled!" I almost yelled. "Nothing makes sense. It's all crazy. How did they get to that shaft in time to nab Thomas? And how could Thomas, with every cop in five states after him, get up to his lodge and do the job the way he did? Why would he park thirty-three million in his own cellar and leave it there? How could he? *Why* would he do it that way?"

"Thomas didn't do it," said Maria.

Before I could say anything she took a deep breath. She advanced a step closer to me.

"I did lie to you, Howie. Pete and Ted never came here from the party, never slept here at all. Their rooms were just as we'd left them in the afternoon. Miguel told me nobody entered the Casa Alta after ten o'clock."

"Then where did they go?" I asked softly.

"Howie," said Maria firmly, "a few days ago you and Mr. Gustavson brought back a hoisting winch from the mine. Also cables, drums, four boxes of explosives, and many other things. I saw them in the garage. They were gone next day."

"Gone! Who took them? What are you getting at?" I demanded.

217

An idea jarred me. An old idea. "Are you telling me Pete was working with Thomas and brought this stuff up here for Thomas to pull the job?"

"I told you Thomas had nothing to do with it," said Maria.

"Then who took the stuff?"

Maria said in a low voice, "Madre de Dios, do I have to spell things for you? Pete is a mining engineer. He handles explosives. He brought that winch over here. You helped him."

A wall of resistance crashed somewhere in my mind. Setting those blasts was right up Pete's alley. He had also operated snowmobiles in Canada! I even recalled his mention of selling one that remained in our area. The one at Thomas' lodge. It had to be. The clothesline shortage was a cinch. I'd stumbled on it by chance. But the whole fantastic plan—Pete could never dream it up. He hadn't the nerve, the imagination, the daring. He might help execute it—but who created it?

Then I remembered I'd even told Pete, with all the trimmings, about Reynolds' idea of using the streamliner with the special as a pilot train over the Sierras. But I had also told Ted all about it too . . .

I stopped right there. My mind exploded.

"Lord Almighty," I said weakly. Maria nodded almost imperceptibly.

Who created the plan? Maria was trying to tell me. There was only one answer. A dead hero. A night-club pianist. My friend. Theodore Helmholtz.

"Ted and Pete pulled the whole thing?" I almost whispered. "Is that what you think?"

Again an almost noncommittal nod from Maria.

I sat down again, refusing to believe it. If the incredible were true, if Ted had masterminded this colossal job with Pete's aid, who in hell had given them all the information they had to have—train schedules—changes in plans—details of guards and train movements —who had given them all this?

There was only one answer. I had. Howard Bierce, formerly of the Great Western. Ex-Road Foreman of Engines. I'd fed them everything they needed.

"You had better take a drink, Howie. A good one. You look very white."

Maria herself looked frightened at my reaction.

I downed a third of a glass of brandy. Then I thought of Fontaine's croaking queries in the lounge car, to Dutton, the engineer: "Where was the rest of the mob . . . How many voices? . . . Then only one man was seen? Impossible!"

One man. That must have been Gustavson. Helmholtz, up on the retaining wall, could have fired the blasts at Pete's signals. But I knew beyond a doubt that it must have been Pete who had planted the charges, set the flare, wore the mask, held up Dutton, and moved the Diesels while Ted operated the winch and snowmobile at the top of the wall. Ted could also fire down, close range, at any interference with Gustavson. Pete had worked the dolly and unloaded the cars. One man on top. One at trainside. Impossible. Sure. But that's the way it had to be. That's the way it was.

"When did you start thinking like this?" I asked Maria at last.

Maria's face was a mask. "I could not be sure. But I guessed they were up to something, something big, that day Pete told me the mine was all finished up. That day I closed the office door, that 'bad business' you asked me about. Then Ted learned he was to die. A week ago he was desperate, crazy, much more than you realize, Howie. And I loved Ted. I loved him. Even if I had been sure, I might not have tried to stop him."

I was still fighting. "But what would he gain by all this? He'd lost Lisa. He saw it at the party. Reynolds had won. Ted would never pull such a huge stunt just to try and ruin Reynolds."

Maria's eyes were brilliant pin points of black.

"No. Not for that alone," she said evenly. "But think of Ted. You knew him. Think of his situation. So many things worked in him at once. He was not a simple man. And he felt that he had failed—at everything. The mine was no good. His life was almost over. All at once too big a load was added. He lost Lisa to the man he hated most. But you had already told him Mr. Reynolds had suggested moving the money to the streamliner. And don't forget—he and Pete have hated your railroad all their lives, for good reason. I think all the talk about Thomas gave Ted his crazy ideas. Maybe he could still ruin Mr. Reynolds, maybe get Lisa much money, and certainly get even with the railroad—but I think there was something even more important."

"What was that?"

"Ted had to achieve something after so many failures. Everything had gone wrong. The mine kaput. Lisa lost. He was going East to die. He had to do something, just once, something that would mean a great deal to him, no matter how wrong it would be to others. I think Ted was planning a long time to hold up the special, even with all those guards . . ."

"It would have been suicide," I snapped.

"I am not asking for your opinion, Howie," retorted Maria with sudden hostility. "I am trying to tell you how I think this sick man thought. Ted was very desperate. Then, at the very last, you tell them both about the streamliner and the change in plans"—I writhed under that one.—"So look at the fantastic thing Ted did do. And if he could still ruin Reynolds and maybe get back Lisa——"

"Then he was all wrong," I protested. "They won't touch Reynolds. It was Fontaine who accepted his ideas and executed them. It's Fontaine and the board who will take the rap. Fontaine will never mention Reynolds."

"I only tell you Ted would not see that," said Maria with grim patience.

Though I battled this line of thinking, I finally had to accept it. No other solution adequately covered these bizarre events. But so much was missing. And there were so many questions. Why hadn't Gustavson known about Thomas' hide-out in the Mexican-Ophir shaft? Why run into such a mare's nest of disaster? Why didn't Ted and Pete cut down with the snowmobile to Route 395, where their cars were stashed away, and then drive straight to the hotel and divide up the loot in their rooms? I threw these questions at Maria.

"With all the noise about the robbery going on here?" Maria shook her head. "Some things we will never know. Others we can only guess at. But Pete and Ted had not been back to Virginia City since your fight with Thomas. And Pete has always known about that other shaft. He once mentioned it to me. I think they always intended to use it after the robbery. But I don't believe they knew Thomas and his people were in that shaft at all. They just ran right into all that trouble."

Maybe. I thought about my fight over the Boston Bar with Thomas and Fred. That was the shaft where I'd been consigned—with Fred in charge. I was sure of it. I was also sure that Thomas had long been using it as a hide-out for his mob. I went back to Pete and Ted.

"But to hoist all that stuff to the lodge and then leave it there—a hell of a risk, a hell of a lot of work."

"Yes. But that is part of what I just told you. Ted would want to do it that way. Just to show it could be done. To dazzle everybody, puzzle everybody, on the grand scale, as big as possible, bigger than anything Thomas could do. And they succeeded, Howie! That is the crazy part. They got what they wanted. They took what they wanted —and left the rest. They had hoodwinked everybody." Maria looked at me hard. "Everybody but you and me."

Down went more brandy.

"God Almighty, Maria," I managed to say at last, "what's the best way to bring out the truth?"

Maria sat bolt upright and almost screamed at me:

"Are you crazy? What do you mean?"

I yelled back at her. "Look. The Great Western is out over four hundred thousand dollars. A tremendous robbery was committed. The whole Division tied up. I'm an official of the road. You and I know what happened. But how are we going to prove it?"

Maria was purple, but she got her voice down. With a great effort she said almost calmly, "We're not going to prove it. We're not going to do anything about it."

I stayed angry. "The hell we're not. We've got to. If Helmholtz and Gustavson really pulled that job—and they did, they must have —the truth has got to come out."

Maria suddenly blazed at me again. "You are an idiot! Go ahead! Prove it! You said we've been guessing. Sure we have. But let me see you prove it to anyone."

"We've got to try."

Maria got up in majestic wrath and moved almost menacingly towards me.

"Howie! Listen to me. Who talked? Who told our two friends everything? You. You. You." Maria laughed harshly. "You were their accomplice, their ally. And besides, we can't prove anything now. Nothing. Helmholtz is dead and he is a hero. Do you really want to drag out the body of our friend and fling it around in the mud? Maybe he's a false hero, if we are right, but I'm not so sure. To me he was a different kind of man, a brave man. I loved him. But go ahead. You will also ruin two very fine people—Lisa and Mr. Reynolds. And I will deny everything you can say. Also, Gustavson has gone——"

I wilted rapidly under Maria's logic.

"Where's the rest of the money—all those bonds?" I demanded.

Maria said almost demurely:

"I think Mr. Gustavson had them in his suitcases. He came here with only one. And you lifted two of them on to the train. You were very helpful, to the last. Were they heavy?"

I stared stupidly at Maria. I *had* wondered at the weight of those bags. And Maria's arguments were now biting into me. She sensed what I was thinking. She placed one of her hands over mine.

"Believe me, Howie, there are some things once done that should not be meddled with. Look. It is not so bad, really. Lisa and Reynolds have found one another. They have really achieved something together. You are not really guilty of anything—except that you blab too much. You love to talk. As for Ted, he was clever enough to take advantage of all the excitement and worry caused by Thomas. For him it must have been a great achievement. And he paid with his life. Thomas? Such men usually die like that. His men—they will be tried for the Reno robbery and convicted."

"And the missing money?" I demanded again.

Maria's expression softened.

"Do you really think it will bankrupt your railroad?" She made a face. "For a company like yours there are always new bonds. Besides, Mr. Gustavson is a kind man. I think I know why he went back to Colorado so quickly."

"So do I. To get out of the way and hide."

"No. You're not fair to him, Howie. He doesn't want that money. You saw that at the station. I think you will find that some families ruined years ago by the Great Western in Colorado will find things easier from now on. Some old hurts will be healed. And maybe Mr. Gustavson will buy back the family ranch he loved." She raised her eyebrows sardonically. "Maybe the new school up at Summit will be helped, too."

"What makes you think so?"

Maria looked a little smug. "Pete tried to help me, too," she said. "He thought I ought to rest. He wanted to help the hotel and poor Maria in her old age. Nothing much. About twenty-five thousand dollars."

I was speechless for a moment. Then, "You turned him down, too?"

"In a way. I think I said the school needed money more than I did." Her head bobbed emphatically. "Pete will know how to use that money." All at once, Maria's voice hardened and she looked at me sternly. "As for you, Howie, I hope you enjoyed your vacation. Give my love to Betty. But I have a last request to make."

I was through, and I knew it. I said feebly, "What is it?"

"On this whole business, Howie, for my sake, for Lisa, Mr. Reynolds, Mr. Gustavson, and the fine person I knew Ted to be—just this once, please keep your big trap shut. Now mix me another drink."